go FAKE yourself

ELLE MAXWELL

Go Fake Yourself

Cover illustration and design by Elle Maxwell

ISBN 9798361858873

ElleMaxwellBooks.com

This one is for the romance authors.

(Especially the lovely community of indie authors with whom I've had the fortune to connect on this journey.)

01. Weirdest. Interview. Ever.

Audrey

I've always liked to think that if I met a celebrity—or, say, my all-time favorite author—I'd be able to play it cool. In my imaginings, I have enough strength of will to project at least a semblance of nonchalance, no matter how loudly my inner fangirl is screaming.

Well, it was a nice thought anyway. A comforting delusion—one I enjoyed until a few minutes ago, when I walked into this room and came face-to-face with none other than *Victoria Trulette*. In an instant, any hope of "cool" (much less "calm" or "collected") flew straight out the second-story window of this postcard-worthy Beacon Hill brownstone, where the most famous romance author of the century apparently lives. Now I'm seated on a velvet-upholstered chair across from a sleek black desk and the woman whose name has been a permanent fixture on best-seller lists for more years than I've been alive.

Suffice to say, my level of chill is absolutely zero.

"I-it's a pleasure to meet you, Ms. Trulette," I stammer, once I've recovered my faculties of speech.

Plum-colored lips curve upward in a smile that reaches her pale blue eyes. Despite their frosty hue, her gaze is warm behind the turquoise frames of her cat-eye glasses. An overall aura of approachability emanates from her, which helps mitigate the intimidation factor of her presence, at least a bit. Unfortunately, that factor was so high to begin with, I'm still firmly planted in my current state of *totally freaking out*.

"The pleasure is mine, Audrey. Though, please, call me Victoria."

I'm pretty sure this is what people mean when they talk about having an out-of-body experience. *Victoria Trulette just told me to call her Victoria!*

Callie would *die* if she knew about this—not that I can tell her, thanks to the series of scary nondisclosure agreements I had to sign prior to this interview. For the first time in six months, I'm almost glad my best friend moved to Ireland. If we were still living together, I don't know how I'd manage to keep this to myself.

Of course, we both knew there was a chance I'd meet someone famous today, given the nature of the employment agency our friend Jamie works for, which set up this interview. When I caved and let her submit my résumé to their applicant pool, Jamie assured me any placement with her firm's high-profile clientele would pay well enough to make the stringent vetting process worthwhile, as well as the anxiety of dealing with all the cloak-and-dagger tactics. As a junior agent, even Jamie wasn't privy to information about what I'd be walking into today, meaning I showed up to the interview equivalent of a blind date knowing absolutely nothing about either the identity of my prospective employer or the job I'd be interviewing for.

Well, I now have the answer to the former. As for the latter, that remains to be seen.

"Tell me, what brings you here today?" Victoria asks.

Truly, the million-dollar question—because, really, what kind of crazy person even puts themselves in this situation?

A desperate one, that's who. But of course, I can't exactly say that to *Victoria freaking Trulette*. (Nope; not over the starstuck-itus.)

"I recently left my last job…" I trail off, still struggling to calm my racing nerves enough to form full sentences.

"Your position as a personal assistant, for the attorney?" Victoria asks, peering down at a copy of my résumé.

"Um, yes," I reply, trying not to cringe at myself for the lack of eloquence. "I worked for Mr. Simmons for about a year."

I hold my breath, hoping she won't ask why I left. It's not like I'm about to tell her my old boss was an insufferable bully I only worked for because I couldn't find a job in my field after graduation, or that I'm ashamed of myself for staying so long in a position in which I was overqualified, underpaid, and *very* underappreciated. There's definitely no way I'm going into that day a month ago when I quit on the spot, leaving behind my steady salary along with any chance at a positive reference in an uncharacteristic moment of spontaneity. It was the only reckless act of my life, until today.

"Go on," Victoria encourages, those eyes that have yet to leave my face full of patience.

"Well, I've had some trouble finding a new job, so my friend who works at the recruitment agency suggested I submit my résumé. I suppose I thought…why not?"

Way to sound like an intelligent go-getter, Audrey!

A familiar ache rises, shame threatening to pull me under as it does whenever I think about my failures. Unlike my friends, who are thriving in careers they love and settling into long-term relationships, I'm no further along as a successful adult than when we graduated from college a little over a year ago.

With a mental slap, I yank my mind back to the present. I cannot afford to get lost in my head right now; I *need* this job. The failure I'm failing is nothing compared to what will happen if I mess up this interview. Moving back to Florida to live with my mother would be the equivalent of sounding the death knell for my independence. My spine straightens at the reminder, resolve shooting through me.

My answers to Victoria's subsequent queries are far more poised, and I finally start to settle into the interview with a bit of confidence. Until she veers away from the safe topic of my time at Boston University in a turn so drastic it has me choking on air.

"Pardon me, ma'am, would you repeat the question?"

Surely I misheard her—because there's no way she just asked me about my dating history! *Right?*

"I want to know about *you,* not just what I can learn from this." The piece of paper holding my résumé makes a flapping sound as she waves it in the air. "So, let's talk about relationships. I want to hear everything: dating, formal partners, casual sexual encounters, et cetera."

Lord help me. Victoria Trulette, the woman dubbed the "Queen of Spice" by her fans, actually wants to hear my romantic résumé! I'm uncomfortable discussing such matters even with my friends, so this conversation would be awkward no matter what—but with *her?* I vividly recall the first time I snuck one of her books home from the library, how equally titillated and scandalized I was as I devoured it by flashlight late at night after my mom was asleep. (Let's just say Victoria Trulette books do *not* fade to black after a sweet kiss!) In fact, I recognize that very title on the bookshelves which take up an entire wall of the room. Remembering the parts that so shocked me at fourteen, I feel my cheeks, which were already growing warm, blaze into what I'm sure is an unflattering red.

Victoria literally *claps* with glee, exclaiming, "Oh, she *blushes*! That's wonderful. Readers really eat that up in a protagonist."

What in the what? Weirdest. Interview. Ever.

I somehow manage to survive the next several minutes as Victoria prompts me through a recitation of my first crush, first date, first kiss, and so on—blushing like crazy the entire time. My gaze keeps drifting to the side, where the rows of paperbacks bearing Victoria's name seem to taunt me with reminders of the explicit contents within their pages. Am I really sitting here telling the woman who wrote such erotic scenes that the entirety of my sexual history can be counted on a single finger? I've never been so mortified.

Where's a hungry black hole when a girl needs one?

When we're finished with that line of questioning (thank goodness), Victoria remains silent for a long moment, eyeing me as though deep in thought.

I try to maintain eye contact but fail, shifting my focus to her hair. The dark red bob falls to a couple of inches below her chin, where it tapers to an angle so crisp I wonder if she had it cut this morning. It is classy with an artistic flair, just like the rest of her appearance. Regardless of the three-plus decades she has on me in age, there's no question that this woman is cooler than I could ever hope to be. I mean, if asked, I wouldn't think the combination of maroon hair, plum lipstick, pale blue eyes, and turquoise glasses would work together, especially paired with floral-patterned kimono-style top and wide-legged slacks, yet Victoria pulls them off to perfection.

By comparison, I feel downright frumpy with the bun I wrestled my unruly hair into this morning and the outfit of skirt and blazer I'd thought was stylish when I charged it to my poor overburdened credit card for this interview.

"All right, then. Now that we've gotten to know each other a bit…" *A bit?* She knows more about my sex life than my BFF! "Let's get down to business."

Finally! I sit up straighter, eager to hear about this mysterious job opening. For curiosity's sake, at least—because, let's face it, my chances aren't looking good. My romantic background is even less impressive than my work history.

5

"Where else are you applying in your search for employment?" Victoria asks, all but confirming my suspicions—while, I note with disappointment, *still* not shedding light on the job.

I shrug, not wanting to admit that the last month drained my meager savings and I'm willing to do just about anything at this point if it will save me from having to return to Florida.

"All kinds."

"What would you pursue if you could do absolutely anything with your future? What are your dreams, Audrey Mitchell?"

I swallow, mouth suddenly dry. Victoria's eyes on me are bright, eagerly awaiting my answer. Now would be a great time to say something impressive, even if I have to lie, but my mind is completely blank of anything but the dismal truth.

"I...actually have no idea."

Dear black hole, please hurry up.

"Hmm," Victoria murmurs. Instead of the disappointment I'd expected to see on her face, she's looking at me as though I'm a puzzle that needs solving. "Well, we can't have you simply sit around all day. Readers want a multidimensional protagonist with a full life and an interesting character arc. Though I suppose your plight might be relatable to some in the demographic."

Is she talking to me, or herself? Unfortunately, her next words provide no illumination.

"Are you aware I write romance novels?"

I nod my affirmation, feeling more confused by the minute—not to mention a bit woozy from the conversational whiplash.

"Do you know how difficult it is to devise a truly fresh fake-relationship scenario?" Fortunately, she doesn't wait for my answer, as I don't have one. "It's nearly impossible! The trope is immensely popular, meaning it's all been done already. In some cases, not simply done, but arguably *over*done. Now, I'm not casting judgment. I, too, find myself hard-pressed to innovate on the theme, beyond the standard scenarios." She holds up a hand and begins counting them out on her fingers.

"The prince of a kingdom in need of a queen, or vice versa... The heir or heiress to a fortune, whose trust or inheritance includes a marriage stipulation... An athlete or celebrity who needs to be seen with a nice, wholesome partner to heal his or her soiled public image... I've even seen a variation where the athlete wants a fake girlfriend to ward off fangirls so he can focus on his sport.

"Let's see... We have the hired escort or faux wedding date—a timeless classic. There's the *My Fair Lady* coaching slash makeover scenario. In modern adaptations, that often presents as the popular boy raising a girl's social profile for the benefit of another whom she desires, or vice versa... The bodyguard who needs to stay close but keep their role incognito publicly... The charade to appease pushy parents... Custody battles... 'Marriage of convenience' is a trope in and of itself... Undercover agents... And immigration scenarios, such as unions created so one character can earn citizenship, of course."

"Of course," I echo, as she seems to expect a response now that she's run out of fingers.

I've read books with quite of few of those general plotlines, so at least what she's saying isn't entirely out of my frame of reference. Still, I have no idea why she's telling me all this.

"So you see, it's terribly difficult to come up with something readers haven't seen before. Yet there's a singular satisfaction to being the first to explore new territory—a product of ego, perhaps, but true, nonetheless. And I do so enjoy a challenge."

When she pauses, I finally ask the question that's been on the tip of my tongue since I arrived.

"Ms. Trulette..."

"Victoria."

"Victoria… May I ask, what exactly *is* the job we're talking about?"

She beams, appearing delighted with herself. "I find myself in a fortunate financial situation—gratuitous, even—and I've had some difficulty coming up with a compelling idea for my next release. So, I thought, why not make use of that prosperity to contrive my very own fake relationship scenario, then gain inspiration from real life as I watch it play out?"

"And the job…?"

"Well, isn't it obvious?"

She pins me with eyes that are intent and expectant, waiting for me to connect the dots. Seconds pass, but no "aha" moment occurs. From where I sit, there is nothing obvious about any of this. Victoria eventually sighs, as though by needing it spelled out for me I've spoiled some of her fun.

"Audrey, darling, I'm going to pay you twenty thousand dollars to be in a fake relationship for the next two months. And then I'm going to write a book about it."

02. Color Me Skeptical

Walker

She's got to be shitting me.

The words almost pop out of my mouth, but this is still a job interview, so I manage to censor myself.

"You're kidding, right?"

Victoria's crystal-blue eyes are all kinds of mischievous. She's kind of a fox, honestly. I've never been into older women—especially ones with big-ass diamonds on their fingers—but there's no denying the woman has presence.

"Oh, I assure you I am very serious."

"Two months, twenty grand?"

"That's correct."

Damn. Foxy or not, this lady might be certifiable.

My old high school buddy Craig did say the gig was weird when he mentioned an opportunity for fast cash had come across his desk. Craig's some kind of hotshot executive at a recruitment agency nowadays, and a few weeks back, I met him downtown with the shirts he ordered for his company's intramural softball team. After losing his shit over my kickass designs, he asked why I'm not doing my screen-printing thing full time. Which led to me explaining I didn't have the funds…and here we are.

Wonder if that nondisclosure I signed means I can't tell him "weird" was a major understatement?

But... *twenty thousand dollars.* I know guys who have done a lot weirder things for a lot less of a payout.

"So, you want me to be some girl's 'pretend boyfriend.' What does that mean, exactly?"

"It's quite simple. For a duration of sixty days, you and Audrey—your female counterpart—will need to convince the rest of the world, including your family and closest friends, that you are in a genuine, committed relationship. I have a series of tasks and challenges for you to complete while playing that role, while I observe and gather your impressions on the experience. All of which I will fictionalize and, with luck, turn into the next sensational best-seller."

I shove a hand into my hair and tug, before remembering about the shit I put in it to make myself presentable for this interview. As I remove my fingers, I can already feel the strands resuming their usual MO of haphazard flopping, though stiff from the gel. I probably look like a psycho porcupine. Whatever. Nothing I can do about it now.

Okay, time to get my head in the game... Yeah, this whole thing is next-level nuts, but if playing along with Victoria's little experiment is what it will take to finally quit working at my dad's auto shop and make a go of my business for real, fulfill my lifelong dream of earning a living with my art? I guess I can chill in the weird lane for a couple of months.

"And of course, for the duration, you'll need to move in to the condo I've arranged for you two."

Hold up. Wait one fucking minute.

In my mind, a cartoon roadrunner screeches to a halt so fast he burrows four feet into the ground.

"You want us to *live together*?"

Victoria's nod is serene, as if this little tidbit she's just thrown out isn't a pretty hard nonstarter. "Oh yes, cohabitation is essential. Forced proximity brings things to a head more quickly and creates tension that readers find particularly enticing."

I'm halfway out of my seat, ready to hightail my ass out of here, away from this crazy job and whatever "*bringing things to a head*" means. I exhale hard and sit back down—after all, I've got twenty thousand reasons to stay put. Picturing how pissed Dad will be when I succeed because of my art—a waste of time, he's always said—lends some extra sticking power to keep my ass glued to this chair.

"What's your endgame here?" I ask Victoria. It feels like I'm missing something. "What are you expecting to happen?"

She smiles again. *So glad I amuse you, lady.*

"I have been blessed with success in my life and have the money to spare, so I decided to put it to use injecting a little reality into the fake-relationship concept. I want to write a book inspired and informed by real life and see how it differs from fixed expectations based on fiction. As for what I want from *you*..." She's not winking at me, but she might as well be with that glint in her eyes. "Well, of course it would be ideal for you and Audrey to fall in love. Readers do enjoy their happily ever afters."

My left brow, the one I can move independent of the other—yeah, it's badass AF—quirks at her.

Color me skeptical.

"That isn't to say," Victoria goes on, "that I *expect* you to fall in love, nor do I want you to fake it. I consider it my job to cultivate the environment and provide opportunities, and all I want you to do is be yourself. You will only be required to pretend while in public, where, as I mentioned, it is imperative to convince the people in your life that you and Audrey are truly dating."

If I were a better man, now is probably the time I'd speak up and clue Victoria in to the fact that if she's looking for a love match, I am not her guy. I've had one serious girlfriend, and I fucked that up without even trying, ruining a long-standing friendship in the process. Since then, I've dated, sure, but never cared enough to take things beyond the casual. And honestly, it doesn't feel like I'm missing anything. Relationships are a whole lot of stress and responsibility I don't need or have time for. I've got plenty of that shit in my life already, and my family takes priority. Short story? If Victoria wants me to "fall in love," there's a one hundred percent chance she'll be disappointed.

But I'm not *that* good of a guy. I'm also no stranger to disappointing people…just ask my dad.

"I sense that you're a young man who values direct communication, so I will be frank with you. I went through a difficult period a few years back, and the book I managed to produce during that time was not well received by readers or critics. While, as previously mentioned, I've had the fortune to enjoy a long, fruitful career, public favor is a fickle beast. One failure is all it took for speculation to arise that I've lost my touch and elicit calls for me to step aside and allow the next generation to take it from here. The faceless masses do so revel in watching public figures fall from grace."

Victoria leans forward, elbows perched on her classy black desk. I bend forward too, drawn in by the magnetic force of her energy.

"To be blunt, my next release needs to be a wild, unequivocal success. I may be getting up there in age, but I'm far from ready to be put out to pasture. I plan to prove it."

I admire the fire in her eyes. Perhaps more than most, I relate to the need to prove yourself, to face the haters, to refuse to go down without a fight. I've known Victoria less than an hour, but damn if I'm not already rooting for her to give them hell.

Compelling as her war cry may be, I need to keep my head and remember why I'm here.

"Back to this job. What's the catch?" She's right; blunt is my style. "Are you gonna be living there with us? Will there be cameras, mics? This won't actually turn out to be one of those reality TV shows?"

Victoria's looking at me like she's kind of impressed. Yeah, I may be a big guy who works on cars, but I've got a brain too. I even got into college; I just chose not to go. (*Chose* being a generous fucking word for that situation, but I try to avoid moseying down that particular pothole-ridden memory lane.)

"I can assure you, it is not a TV show. There must be some level of monitoring in place so I can observe, but I promise to respect your privacy as much as possible. My lawyer and I have drawn up a full contract detailing everything, which she is finalizing as we speak. I am open to negotiation if there's anything in that document that makes you uncomfortable."

"Can we nix the living together thing?" I ask immediately.

"No." Her response is no-nonsense, but she's smiling at me like I'm an amusing little boy. To her, I guess I am. "Now, before you ask any further questions, I need you to answer one of mine. Will you accept the job?"

"You haven't offered it to me yet," I say, surprised. "I figured there were other candidates."

"Consider this my official extension of an offer. There *were* other candidates," she admits, voice dropping conspiratorially. "But I'm quite taken with you. That roguish smile, the quick humor…not to mention you've got the rugged mountain-of-a-man look down to a tee—what are you, six foot three? I'll need all of those stats. We do so love a rough-around-the-edges hero with an artist's soul."

"Aw shucks, Vickie. You don't gotta flatter me. The money'll do just fine." I bust out some of the North Shore accent I usually tone down. (That's "Nawth Shaw," by the way.)

"Is that a yes, then?"

Fuck it. How hard could it be?

13

"I think I'd be an idiot to say no, for this kind of payday. Don't think I won't read through that contract, though. I'm gonna make sure there's no funny stuff hidden in there. But if it's what you say it is, then yeah, I can be your guy."

03. This is Really Happening

Audrey

This agreement made between Ms. Victoria Trulette (hereinafter referred to as **"V. Trulette"**), Mr. Walker Garrison (hereinafter referred to as **"MALE MC"**), and Ms. Audrey Mitchell (hereinafter referred to as "**you**" or **"FEMALE MC"**). Mr. Garrison and Ms. Mitchell are also referenced collectively as **"the MCs"** ("MC" here used as an abbreviation for "main character") or **"the Protagonists."**

The parties hereto mutually agree as follows:

1. Description of Employment

You agree to enter into a state of employment with **V. Trulette** in the capacity of **FEMALE MC**, playing counterpart to **MALE MC** in a fake relationship of a romantic nature for the duration of 60 (sixty) days.

The primary objective of this role is to convince all outside parties (here defined as all persons other than **MALE MC, FEMALE MC, V. Trulette**, and such others explicitly identified by **V. Trulette**) of the legitimacy of this relationship.

2. Conditions of Employment

Additional conditions and expectations of this role include, but are not limited to:

a. For the project's duration (60 days) you will relocate your residence to the condominium secured by **V. Trulette** for this purpose, where you will cohabitate with **MALE MC**.

b. You are responsible for participating in this project 7 days a week with a general understanding that you may pursue other employment between the hours of 9am and 5pm Monday through Friday. Outside of these standard business hours, you will make all reasonable effort to have open availability for participation in any activities, events, or trips as instructed by **V. Trulette**.

3. Compensation

The Protagonists shall be paid $5,000 at the outset and $5,000 at the end of 30 days, with the final payment of $10,000 to be made at the project's conclusion, to total an amount of **$20,000.**

4. Surveillance Release

Protagonists agree to cooperate with various monitoring measures as deemed necessary by **V. Trulette,** which may include but is not limited to video monitoring, sound recording, interviews with **V. Trulette** and/or professional specialists, psychological assessment, etc. Such data will remain confidential and accessible only to **V. Trulette**, her associates, and professionals bound by commensurate terms of non-disclosure. In addition, you will be required to keep a daily journal documenting your experience of this project, to be recorded in a confidential online document accessible by **V. Trulette** et al.

4. Sexual Activity

For the duration of the project, you will not engage in any outside romantic liaisons, which include but are not limited to: dating, kissing, sexual intercourse, cunnilingus/fellatio, flirting (through electronic means or face to face), and phone sex. All the these are allowable, and even encouraged, in a consensual capacity between **Protagonists.**

Umm…Is it hot in here?

I'm suddenly boiling up as I read through the world's strangest employment contract. I sneak a glance at the boy—correction: *man*—seated beside me, but his focus is glued to his own copy of the contract. One foot is propped atop his opposite thigh, the packet of paper resting on his bent knee. The pose emphasizes the size and strength of those legs.

It takes effort to tear my gaze away and return to reading.

5. Confidentiality and Nondisclosure

If either of **the Protagonists** is found to have disclosed to outside parties, including all family and acquaintances, the details of this agreement OR the actual nature of the relationship is ascertained by an outside party through their own powers of observation, the binding nature of both **Protagonists'** contracts will be rendered forfeit. In such a circumstance, the reinstatement of any or all the the conditions of this contract, including but not limited to remittance of payment, amount of payment, and termination of the project, will be at the sole discretion of V. Trulette.

You also agree not to share any personal details about **V. TRULETTE**, including her home address and contact information. Violation of these terms may result in legal action against you.

Signed this _____ day of _____

Once finished, I stare at the document in my lap so intently the words become an illegible blur.

You need this job, I remind myself as my pulse races and the urge to flee the room floods me.

From my side, I hear shuffling papers and the thud of a large boot hitting the floor. Then long limbs enter my peripheral vision as my soon-to-be fake boyfriend (!!!) stretches them out in front of him. I look over, trying to be discreet about it. *Walker*. Victoria introduced us when we arrived, but so far, we've only interacted for a quick exchange of "hellos" before getting to business. (Well, I said hello. He kind of grunted, which I choose to translate as a greeting.)

Walker is big. Tall and thick in a way that hints he is one solid mass of man underneath the faded T-shirt and ripped

17

jeans. He's tanner than I am, suggesting he spends time outdoors frequently. There's a vaguely hipster look to him, though I'd bet money he'd be offended by the description. He doesn't strike me as one of those guys who'll pay for designer clothes manufactured to look grungy, or expensive haircuts designed to be artfully messy. Walker's medium brown hair is *actually* messy, a little long on top, sticking out in a haphazard manner that shows he doesn't spend hours in front of the mirror styling it (perhaps not even minutes). It's hard to tell if his facial hair is an intentional beard or just a thick layer of accumulated scruff from failing to shave. Either way, it adds to the overall sense that he's not trying to impress anyone with his grooming.

He's...hot. Intimidating. Completely out of my league—like our leagues aren't in the same universe.

He reminds me of the guys Callie and I sometimes ogle on Instagram and TikTok for fun—the kind of man I'd never actually approach outside of my phone screen. In fact, in any other situation, I'd take one look at the man beside me and walk right in the other direction. Not that I'd expect *him* to even notice *me*, but I'd keep my distance anyway. When I see a guy that attractive, my self-preservation instincts kick in and immediately recognize the potential for harm, as one might assess an array of blades and determine which will cut the deepest.

When it comes to potential boyfriends, I stick to butter knives. Walker? He's a freaking machete.

Gray eyes with a hint of green meet mine. Of course—of freaking *course*—instead of playing it cool, like I *haven't* been staring at him for an unknown amount of time, I flinch (a generous euphemism for my painfully conspicuous full-body jerk). Seriously, I might as well hold up a neon sign flashing the words, YES! I WAS JUST CHECKING YOU OUT!

My new roommate, *with whom I'll be sharing a bed*, barely reacts, his head not even turning fully in my direction. I watch

18

the muscles along the side of his mouth quirk in an almost-smile, and the eyebrow closest to me lifts. Then he simply moves that slightly angled chin back so he's facing forward.

I breathe out, the exhale so heavy as to be audible to everyone in the room. My face warms with embarrassment, especially when I find that Victoria is watching us closely, no doubt studying the interaction that just occurred and taking mental notes so she can write about it later. Ugh!

"I'm gonna need some more time to read this thing again before I sign it," Walker says.

And here I was, ready to sign right now. Wow, I'm truly awful at this adulting thing.

Victoria nods. "Of course. Are there any questions I can answer at this time?"

Walker leans forward, and I try hard not to fixate on the movement of his strong shoulders beneath the T-shirt as he plants both elbows on his knees.

"The nondisclosure stuff. Help a guy out with the lawyer gibberish. Does this mean if we tell anyone or someone guesses, you could fire us or dock our pay?"

"Exactly. Maintaining the perceived authenticity of your relationship is crucial."

"Ms. Trulette, can you explain the, um…" I feel my cheeks flame. I keep my face resolutely forward and try to pretend Walker isn't sitting right next to me (impossible, by the way). "Fourth section?"

Yes, that last bit comes out so squeaky I sound like a little mouse, but come on… The section is titled "Sexual Activity". A word hasn't been invented yet to describe this level of awkward.

"Of course—and again, call me Victoria," she replies, utterly unfazed by the section of the contract we're all looking at that *encourages* Walker and me to engage in *cunnilingus* and *fellatio*! "What is your question about it?"

If my face gets any hotter, I am liable to melt into a puddle right here—which, now that I think about it, might be a blessing. There's no way I could experience this much mortification in liquid form, right?

"Um…" *Don't look at Walker.* Do not *look at him; just say it…* "You're not, like, paying us to have sex, are you?"

"Yeah," Walker surprises me by chiming in. "This shit makes it sound like you're expecting us to perform, like breeding zoo animals."

"No, certainly not," Victoria responds, not even reacting to Walker's language, while I'm over here wincing at the disrespect. "No intimacy is required of you, short of some casual affection while you are in public playing the role of a couple in love."

I'm not sure what's more palpable in the room—relief at her confirmation this *isn't* a subversive sex-for-money situation, or the resounding echo of the word "love" as it lands between us with the subtlety of a five-ton weight.

"We included this section to ensure that during this experiment, you do not engage in any extracurricular romantic relations. That would be quite counterintuitive to our objective of convincing the world you are deeply committed to each other, don't you agree?"

I nod. Walker is silent, presumably doing the same, although I still can't bring myself to look over there to find out.

"As for the bit about particular intimate behaviors—which I assume is the source of your discomfort, Audrey" —*uh, yeah, she would assume right*— "lawyers do love specificity, and we wanted to cover all our bases, as it were. The purpose is to have complete clarity on all actions that are prohibited outside the framework of this experiment. Any such acts perpetrated *within* the experiment, well…" Her smile is the definition of lascivious. "You are two young, attractive, single adults, and you'll be spending a lot of time together for the next two months. What you do—or don't do—on your own time within the walls of the condo, is utterly your decision."

Then she actually *winks*.

I was almost chilled by the AC when I first entered this room, but now it feels like I'm sitting in a sauna.

What are you doing, Audrey? Get out now while you still can!

Funny, that cautionary voice in my head sounds a lot like my mother. She would love nothing more than to have me back under her roof, which is the fate that awaits me if I don't take this job. Since I can't afford to pay my rent on the first of the month, which is only a few days away, I already have a subletter lined up to temporarily take over the lease on my apartment. I am out of options. It's this job and moving in to the condo with Walker, or maxing out another credit card on a flight to Florida.

I refuse to choose door number two, because if Mom has anything to say about it, there will be no return flight in my future. Yes, rationally, I know that I'm a twenty-three-year-old grown woman—no longer a trapped teenager—and my mother can't *make* me stay in Florida. However, it would be foolish to underestimate her—or, honestly, to *over*estimate myself. - Despite the bravery I somehow manifested when I moved away for college against her wishes, I'm under no illusions about my own fortitude, or how much influence my mom still has over me. Shameful as it is to admit, I can't say with any degree of certainty that the independence and sense of identity I've claimed over these last five years would survive being back there, immersed in the environment that created the sheltered eighteen-year-old who arrived in Boston afraid of her own shadow. I fear any progress I've made since was largely constructed out of strength borrowed from Callie and glued together with the false security of distance, sure to melt upon first contact with the humidity outside the Orlando airport.

"Audrey?"

The sound of my name in Walker's deep voice is a defibrillator shocking me back to the here and now. It hits so hard I'd be unsurprised to find burn marks from the paddles on my skin later.

"Yeah?"

"You're real quiet over there. Anything you wanna add?" His lips twitch, as though he's amused to have caught me spacing out.

"Um…" I scan the contract again, determined to say *something* to partially redeem myself so I don't look like a compliant airhead as well as a squeaky blusher with a staring problem.

"I know we have to tell people that we're dating, but what about the living together thing? My mom is already going to be surprised when I announce I suddenly have a serious boyfriend." Understatement. "If she finds out I moved in with him, she'll probably fly up here and try to convince the police that I've been kidnapped and sold into a trafficking ring or something."

They laugh. I decide to let them believe I'm joking.

"I'll give you leeway to address that detail—or not—as you see fit," Victoria concedes.

"Thank you." There. I proved I can speak (somewhat) coherently, *and* I have one less thing to worry about.

"Anything else? Walker?"

Victoria eyes him with blatant admiration. I suppose there's no reason to hide that you're looking when you're paying for the view.

He nods. "Yeah. Level with me about this surveillance shit, Vickie."

I cringe again at his use of profanity—and the overly familiar nickname. Is he always this flippant and crude?

"Vickie" appears unfazed. "What would you like to know?"

22

"This language is pretty fu–*freakin'* vague. I sign this, it's like giving you a blank check. Talk to me—us—" he includes me with a head tip and another flash of gray eyes "—about what we're really walking into. Is the whole apartment bugged? Where are the cameras?"

They're questions I had as well but wasn't sure how to bring up politely. Obviously, Walker has no such hang-ups. He did just censor himself from using the f-word, though, which means there are *some* limits to his disregard for Victoria's position of authority.

"I'll have your first-person accounts via the daily journals, and we'll speak in person at our check-in meetings, but I *must* also have a way to conduct some more objective observation. For outings or events where you are 'in character'—scenes, if you will—I have acquired portable recording devices I'll ask you to wear. As for the condo, perhaps just video and sound recording in the kitchen and living room?"

"Video, but no sound," counters the man who has seemingly designated himself our joint advocate.

"This isn't *The Bachelor*," Victoria counters, amusement evident in her voice. "I don't need muted B-roll footage to use as background for voice-overs and commentary."

"I thought you wanted this shit to be real. You think we're gonna be acting natural if we know everything we do is on tape?"

"A fair point, and one I shall keep in mind. However, we cannot forgo surveillance in the condo entirely."

Once again, Walker surprises me by turning and asking me, "What do you think?"

After a moment's hesitation, I shrug. "I'm pretty uncomfortable with all of it. But I'm going to do this, so I figure I'll just get used to it."

A wrinkle forms between his eyebrows. "You're cool with cameras in our place?"

His wording smacks me in the face with reality. *Our* place. As in, the place we're going to live in together. Where we'll be *sleeping in the same bed.*

You will NOT blush, Audrey Mitchell. You are a freaking adult, and you can handle this like one.

"Are cameras really that much worse than microphones?"

"What if I want to walk around naked?"

At that, I choke on air and have to cough a couple of times before I'm able to speak. (And yes, I am definitely blushing.)

"Do you *do* that?" I ask at a pitch three times higher than normal.

"I might."

I'm hit by another coughing fit. Water leaks from my eyes as I hack, clearing my airways. When the tears subside, I see Walker smirking. The jerk is enjoying this! He said that just to mess with me, and unfortunately, he's succeeded. Because now it's impossible not to wonder what he looks like naked.

Ugh. *Stop being pervy, Audrey!*

Focusing on annoyance helps me clear my flustered mind and regain some balance. Now, to prove I have more of a backbone than I've demonstrated thus far today.

"I think you can survive shelving the nudist tendencies for two months. Though I'm sure Victoria wouldn't mind." (I probably wouldn't either, but I would never admit it.)

"All right, back to business," Victoria says, although her eyes are glinting with amusement. "There will be plenty of time for banter and foreplay later."

Now it's Walker's turn to cough at the word "foreplay." I'd find the turnabout satisfying, except my cheeks are burning. Again.

"Now, as to the contract," Victoria goes on smoothly. "I am amenable to forgoing the cameras. What do you say to sound recording only, in the common spaces?"

Lips pursed in thought, Walker rubs a hand along the edge of his jaw. His palms must be callused, because even from two feet away I can hear the scrape of his skin against the long stubble. The sound is surprisingly alluring.

Finally, he dips his chin in agreement. They both look to me, and I nod as well, ready to be done with this meeting.

"Very well. I'll have my lawyer make those amendments, and then email you the updated contract to sign."

"When does this thing start?" Walker asks.

"The condo is ready, and I'm eager to begin. How does Friday sound?"

Friday? As in *three days* from now?

Massive shoulders lift as my new fake boyfriend shrugs. "Okay by me, if it works for Audrey."

As terrified as I suddenly feel, there's no justifiable reason to delay, so I say, "Yep. That works." If my voice cracks a little bit, there's nothing I can do about it.

Holy cow. This is really happening.

[CONFIDENTIAL PROJECT RECORDS]
DAY 0

NOTE FROM VICTORIA

(Left on the kitchen counter prior to move-in)

Hello my darling protagonists,

Welcome to your home for the next two months! I am so glad you've both decided to partake in this endeavor, and I look forward to navigating the coming adventure together.

This initial week is all about preparation! Today, your only task is to relax and get to know each other using the set of icebreaker questions I have sent to you both via email. Tomorrow will be your first team-building outing (details to come later).

My assistant Matilda stocked the kitchen so you can settle in without delay. She also emailed you instructions for accessing the online documents where you will record your daily journals.

I'll be in touch soon, and we will, of course, see each other Wednesday at our first check-in meeting. In the meantime, I eagerly anticipate reading your journal entries!

Sincerely,

Victoria Trulette

Hey guys—

Your portable mics are in the box on the counter. Victoria got top-of-the-line models that are nice and discreet (and waterproof!). They're made to look like Fitbit wristbands, but instead of tracking your physical activity, they record sound when powered on. As you know, Victoria wants you to wear them whenever you're leaving the condo together. You don't have to do anything with the audio files; they'll automatically sync to the cloud via Wi-Fi. Just be sure to recharge the wristbands in between wears!

My number is in my email signature. Feel free to text me if you have any questions.

Have fun!

Matilda

(Victoria's assistant)

04. Awkward Maserati

Walker

Before I've even had a chance to wrap my head around this whole thing, it's Friday. Game time.

The condo is killer, not that I'd expect anything less with Victoria footing the bill. It's painful to even think about how much that bill must be, but since I'm not paying it, you'd better believe I'm going to enjoy the perks while I can. Smack-dab in fancy-ass Beacon Hill, the primo location is only a couple of blocks away from both the Boston Common and the boss lady's house.

My home for the next two months is pretty small, just one bedroom and one bath, with an open plan living room and kitchen—the minimal square footage no doubt having more to do with Victoria's little matchmaking scheme than a lack of funds. (Wouldn't want us to have too many opportunities to get privacy and space from each other, right?)

Every inch of this condo screams "expensive as hell." If I had to describe the aesthetic in one word, it would be...*white*. White cabinets, speckled white granite countertops, whitewashed hardwood floors, a wall color that probably has a fancy name but is basically *white*... I'm afraid to touch anything, sure I'll dirty it up. Even the couch acting like a boundary between the two "rooms" is off-white. Who gets a *white* couch?! (But then I see the huge-ass mounted flat-screen and figure I'll get over my hang-ups fast.)

I drop my beat-up duffel bag onto the gleaming hardwood floor. The once black fabric, long since faded to gray, looks as out of place here as I'm sure I do.

Should I have left my boots out in the hallway? My favorite steel-toed Carhartts are as old as the bag, so it's doubtful anyone in a building like this would try to take them—unless it was to chuck them in the garbage chute. Which would suck. *Right, scratch that idea.*

"Hello?" I call out, kind of hoping my new "girlfriend" isn't here yet. But no dice; she emerges from a door on my left, which must lead to the bedroom.

"Hey."

Audrey gives me a little wave, elbow tucked tight to her body so only her hand and forearm move. It's awkward as fuck. Awkward seems to be this girl's default setting, based on that hour we spent together in Vickie's office. She was timid and stiff during the whole meeting, and painfully polite—not even speaking up about that crazy contact until I nudged her. (Prissy, too. I didn't miss her scrunched-up nose every time I cursed.)

On first impressions, I've got Audrey pegged as an uptight, sheltered little princess. She's probably used to nice, nerdy guys who wear ties to work and sit at a desk all day surrounded by their framed diplomas. No wonder she kept sneaking looks at me that alternated between fascination and fear, like I'm some wild animal she's never seen up close before.

Although, there *was* that moment toward the end of the meeting, when she surprised me by showing some feistiness after I made that crack about hanging out naked. (Is it something I do, in my own room? Sure. But I wasn't raised by wolves. I know how to keep my pants on, and when.) The confidence looked good on her. Let's just hope she relaxes around me and gets back to that sooner rather than later, or this is going to be a wicked long two months.

"How's it going?"

"Okay," she says, doing this nervous shifting thing that makes her look like a kid who has to piss. *Guess we're still a while away from chill.*

A glimpse of something bright has my gaze falling to her feet, which are clad in fuzzy yellow socks. They're ridiculous. I bite back a smile.

Besides the socks, she's wearing a pair of leggings that show off a little of the shape she was hiding under that long, hippie-style dress she had on when we first met. She's got great legs, right in the sweet spot between toned and curvy. Her top is a baggie tank that's so long it hides the upper half of her thighs. No way I'm getting a glimpse of either ass or tits while she's wearing that—which, I won't lie, is disappointing.

When the silence gets uncomfortable, I search for something to say. Polite chitchat is not my specialty.

"So, uh, how long have you been here?"

Right when I've started wondering if *I'm* going to have to be the talkative one in this "couple," Audrey switches from awkward silence to awkward rambling like a Maserati goes from zero to sixty.

"Maybe an hour? I know I left my place at ten, but I'm not sure how long it took to get here and unload and everything. I started unpacking, but then I stopped, because I wasn't sure how much closet space you'll need, and there's only one dresser. I didn't want to just use up all of it, because that would be rude, right? So, I figured I'd wait until you got here. I don't want to get off to a bad start with this, you know…with our, uh, *roommate* situation."

There's that blush again. It's cute. If I saw it under other circumstances, I might even say *real* fucking cute.

"Nah, it's cool. I don't mind living out of a bag for the next sixty days."

Her eyes—brown, a medium shade I can't properly make out from here—bug out wide in horror. "Oh no! I couldn't let you do that. I'm happy to share."

I chuckle at how big of a deal she's making over this. Fidgeting, she messes with her hair before releasing it from whatever had been keeping it piled on top of her head. Her hair was up the other day too, so I'm a little mesmerized by the locks that tumble down past her shoulders. Unfortunately, I only get to enjoy the view for a second before she expertly twists it back into a bun, hidden away again.

Now, I'm eyeing that bun, its contents a hell of a lot more interesting than they were a minute ago. I don't know what to call the color of her hair. It's not brown or blond, but somewhere in between. Dirty blond, I think they call it? I snicker to myself, the term "dirty blonde" bringing to mind something entirely different. Something that does *not* fit with my first impressions of this girl at all.

"Are you going to come in?" she asks me.

Damn, but she's right; I'm still planted in this same spot right inside the door like a dumbass. Hefting my duffel onto my shoulder and toeing off my boots, I head over to the bedroom.

Audrey shuffles backward so I can enter the room, sliding along the hardwood floor in those crazy socks. I'm about to comment on them, but the sight of her luggage steals my attention. It's spread across the bedroom floor, and there's a *ton* of it.

"Pack light, much?" I count two full-sized suitcases, a couple of bags the size of mine, and a taped-up cardboard box. *Who needs that much stuff for two months?!*

"I know, it's a lot," she says, feet shuffling again as she ducks her head in embarrassment. "But I was able to find a subletter for my place for the next two months, so I needed to clear pretty much everything out of there. I won't clutter up the bedroom forever, I promise. There's a closet in the hallway where I figure I can stash most of it."

Well, now I feel like a dick. If I didn't share a place with my brother, I'd probably have tried to do the same thing. "Smart. No point paying for somewhere you're not going to use for two whole months."

That earns me a small smile, sans blush. *Score.*

"You know what, why don't you take the whole closet?" I say, hoping to keep my winning streak going. "I just need two or three of those dresser drawers, and I'll be good."

Her eyes dart to my duffel, as though visually weighing its contents, before agreeing.

There. A halfway-decent start to this lucrative sham of a relationship.

Only 59.5 days to go.

[CONFIDENTIAL PROJECT RECORDS]
DAY 1

Transcript Excerpts: Condo Recording

Truncated and Annotated by Matilda

A = Audrey Mitchell, W = Walker Garrison

12:30 PM

A: "Should we get started on Victoria's questions now?"

W: "Let me guess. You were one of those nerds who did your homework right away instead of waiting until the night before it was due. Right?"

[silence… A probably blushing]

W: "Fine. Can we at least eat before being good students?"

A: "Okay."

12:40 PM

W: "Bacon, nice! You want a BLT? You have to tell me how you like your bacon, though, because otherwise, you're getting it nice and crispy."

A: "Oh, no bacon for me, thank you."

W: "You don't eat bacon?!?!"

A: "I'm a vegetarian."

W: "Of course you are."

A: "And what does that mean?"

W: "Nothing. It just figures."

1:00 PM

W: "You don't eat bacon at all?"

A: "Do you need me to read you a definition of vegetarianism? I could even pull up some lovely animal slaughter videos if you'd like to educate yourself."

W: "Nah, I'm good."

2:00 PM

W: "Right, here we go. First question: 'Why did you take this job?'"

A: "Um, I'm in between jobs, and I have a friend at the recruitment agency who helped me get an interview… I honestly didn't have a lot of other options… Well, none, really. And, well, it's a lot of money, you know? When do you find a chance to make this much so fast without doing something, like, illegal? Plus, I'm a fan of Victoria Trulette, so it's kind of cool. The concept is sort of interesting, right? It's a unique opportunity, if you think about it. So…yeah. Your turn."

W: "Good money for something easy. It's a no-brainer. You overthink shit too much."

3:00 PM

A: "Discuss your education history." Well, I lived in Florida through high school, then I went to Boston University and graduated with my bachelor's degree in communications a little over a year ago. Communications is kind of a public relations slash digital marketing hybrid that has some business classes too."

W: "I know what communications is, but thanks for dumbing it down for me with CliffsNotes. Anyway, I went to Lowell public, graduated high school there. That's the story […] Not everybody has the dough and the luxury to put off making a living for four years, you know. […] Whatever. I saw your face…"

4:00 PM

W: "Next one: 'Does your name have a story or particular significance?'"

A: "Nothing too complicated. My mom has always loved Audrey Hepburn. Strong resemblance, huh?" [sarcastic delivery, perhaps bitter?]

[rustling]

A: "What are you doing?"

W: "Looking this chick up."

A: "It's not important…"

W: "Nah, now I'm curious. Huh."

A: "Yeah, I know, she's beautiful. Anyway…"

W: "I mean, she's okay, but she's way too thin. And she pulls off the short hair thing, but yours is way better. You've got a cuter nose too."

A: "That's…so nice, Walker. Thank you."

W: "Don't thank me. I just call it like I see it."

A: "Thanks anyway."

W: "Whatever, next question."

Audrey's Journal

Hello!

(Is it okay if I address this directly to you, as a sort of "Dear Diary" letter, or should it be a third-person account of events? I should have asked before.)

As you know, Walker and I moved in to the condo today. It is lovely! Thank you so much for providing such beautiful accommodations for us. My favorite part is the little balcony/porch off the bedroom.

I suppose you'll want our first impressions of each other, not just the living space. It seems unnecessary to share any details about Walker's physical attributes, as you obviously know how handsome he is. His communication style is very forthright and colorful, and he is a bit of a jokester, which will take some getting used to.

We made it through quite a few icebreaker questions today. They were an efficient way to begin getting to know each other, and I've already learned a lot. Then Walker ordered us pizza for dinner, which was very nice of him. I would have offered to cook, but I'm glad I didn't have to, as moving is quite tiring.

I hope this is sufficient for now. I'm sure I'll have more to say tomorrow!

Thank you again for this opportunity!
Sincerely,

Audrey

Comment added by Victoria Trulette: Whatever format you prefer to write your entries in is fine with me, my dear.

* * *

Walker's Journal

Hey Vickie,

First time getting to read my inner thoughts. How pumped are you right now? Don't lie, you've been looking forward to this.

Well, we moved in today. Obviously. I won't talk about the apartment, because you're paying for it. You know what it looks like. It's the nicest place I've ever stayed, I'll tell you that.

I bet you twenty bucks Audrey is over there writing what she thinks you want to hear, but I won't bullshit you, Vickie. Today has been awkward as hell. We're tiptoeing around each other like total strangers (because, you know, we are). Audrey's still nervous around me, and I don't know how to be the smooth, charming guy who puts her at ease. You probably should have hired someone with a little more skill in the schmoozing department. (Too late now...no takebacks!)

No point repeating the stuff we talked about. We stayed in the kitchen and living room, so you have the whole thing on tape. Have fun listening to that... It's riveting shit. Bring popcorn.

Walker

PS: You set me up with a vegetarian? Really, Vickie? How am I supposed to pretend I love a woman who doesn't eat bacon?

05. Queen-Sized Elephant

Audrey

"Hey. I'm gonna jump in the shower now, unless you want to get in there first?"

I stare at Walker. *"Get in there?"* Does he mean the shower, or is he asking if I need the bathroom for...*other things?* I cringe.

Wait. He's going to be in there showering *naked.*

Oh Lord—later tonight *I'm* going to be naked in that shower, with him right in the next room!

At some point, I might even have to *poop* while he's in the apartment!

My heart is beating so fast I'm certain he can hear it, and my cheeks are hot. *Ugh, more blushing.* It's been happening all day, everything Walker says or does tripping the switch on my facial thermometer.

"Earth to Audrey? You wanna shower first?"

"No, thanks." And there I go, squeaking again. "You go ahead."

He eyes me like I've got some screws loose, and I can't even blame him. Once he disappears into the bathroom, I drop one blazing cheek onto the island in front of me, willing the cool of the granite to seep into my skin. Only after I hear the shower turn on do I allow myself an audible groan—then immediately regret it, as I remember about the microphones.

I kept my journal entry as upbeat as possible, not wanting Victoria to regret hiring me despite the collection of awkwardness those microphones captured from today. Honestly, though, chances are she's already reevaluating whatever madness led her to pair Walker and me together in the first place. We couldn't be more different—a mismatch all the more evident after the icebreaker questions we went through earlier.

Well, if Walker and I are going to burn down in flames as a fake couple, at least we'll be doing it in a beautiful condo.

I feel a bit like Dorothy dropped on the other side of the rainbow. All this pristine luxury is certainly worlds away from the cheap particle-board furniture I left behind at my old apartment, a windowless, basement-level studio that seems gloomier than ever by comparison to this condo. Uncertain as I am about this experiment I've signed on for, I wasn't the least bit sad about saying goodbye to that studio for a while. I've always hated the place, but it was all I could afford on my own since I opted not to find a new roommate for our two-bedroom apartment when Callie moved out. Callie and I met when we were randomly paired together in the freshman dorms at BU, and we've lived together ever since. Or at least, we *did*, until her boyfriend asked her to move to Ireland with him at the end of the year-long exchange program that had brought him to Boston.

Ironic, how I was willing to move in to The Cave rather than let some girl I didn't know take over Callie's room, only to find myself living with a strange *boy* in a condo with a single bedroom and only one bed—where I will be *sleeping with him*.

While, yes, Victoria made it clear we aren't required to do anything *but* sleep. However, the language in that section of our contract entitled "Sexual Activity" left the door for *more* uncomfortably wide open. Under normal circumstances, I wouldn't worry about a guy like Walker being interested in *me* that way, but our situation is far from normal.

After all, Walker is a man, with, you know…*needs,* and our contract prevents him from having those needs met outside of this condo for the next two months. (Which is probably a long time for him. For me? Not so much.)

What if he's expecting to do so *inside* the condo…with *me*?

Okay, sure, I find Walker attractive (I'm not *dead*) but I am so not ready to go there with him. In my experience, the hotter a guy is, the more likely he is to be full of himself. Why expend energy being sweet and sensitive when there are easier options throwing themselves at you left and right? If my ex—who was by no means a Casanova—found me lacking as a sexual partner, Walker would definitely chew me up and spit me out faster than you can say "goodbye, twenty grand." Because if we hooked up only for him to reject me, how could I possibly keep living with him and playing his fake girlfriend after that humiliation?

Before I arrived this morning, I had decided to handle the situation like a mature adult. I intended to negate some of the awkwardness by simply acknowledging the elephant in this condo—the one shaped like a queen-sized bed. But then Walker showed up, looking even better than I remembered and a million times more intimidating, and I chickened out. Now the day is almost over and my chances to point out that elephant before we have to climb under its pale gray coverlet are dwindling.

Instead of woman-ing up when Walker emerges from the bathroom—thankfully, clothed in pajamas, despite his threats of nudity—I flee to the bedroom like the coward I am to grab stuff for my own shower. I take my time, shaving and washing my hair, enjoying the luxury of multiple showerheads. (Okay, I'm totally stalling.)

After braiding my wet hair, I put on my sleepwear selection for the night: the baggiest shirt and sweatpants I own. (Unnecessary shapeless boy-repellant sleep outfit? *Check.*)

Now, to deal with that freaking pachyderm.

"Um, hey."

At my timid greeting, Walker looks up from his one-handed phone scrolling. "Hey."

He's lounging on a mountain of pillows propped against the white headboard. The ceiling lights are off, but he's switched on both nightstand lamps. I note—with no small amount of consternation—that the man is just as gorgeous in their warm glow as he was in the sun-drenched living room this afternoon.

Self-conscious with his eyes on me, I manage to stumble over my own feet during the short trip to the empty side of the bed. Thankfully, Walker refrains from commenting, but I don't miss the twitch of his mouth or the amusement crinkling the sides of his eyes. *Well, this is off to a great start.*

Rather than joining him under the covers, I perch on the edge of the bed and summon every ounce of the courage I don't possess.

"I thought we should maybe, um, talk."

"Sure. What's up?"

To his credit, he doesn't point out that we've spent most of the day talking, answering Victoria's questions, though an upward tick of his eyebrows betrays his bemusement.

"So, this is super awkward, right?" I blurt out. His lips twitch again, but he doesn't speak. "I know we have to share the bed, but, uh…"

Geez, this is even harder than I'd imagined! My blush is hotter than it's been all day—truly, no small feat.

"I mean, there was all that…*stuff*…in the contract, but I'm not looking for a real relationship right now, you know? I just

41

don't think we should, um…" I lamely wave my hand at the empty expanse of bed between us.

Walker's snort is amused. "Trust me, I'm not looking for a relationship either. I'm good keeping things professional."

When he sees I'm still tense and making no move to get into the bed, he sighs and adds with more than a hint of impatience, "Don't worry, princess. You're not my type."

Then he returns to tapping at his phone as though I'm not even here.

Well, then.

That wasn't embarrassing or anything!

I crawl under the covers and curl up with my back to him, hugging my side of the bed so closely, the tops of my knees are hanging over the edge. Squeezing my eyes shut, I wish for the oblivion of sleep to save me from what a fool I just made of myself.

Because apparently…that elephant? The invisible tension? It was all in my own head

06. What Are Pretend Boyfriends For?

NEW MESSAGE IN GROUP TEXT

VICTORIA: Please be out front at 8 AM to meet the transportation I've arranged for your first teambuilding outing. Wear a bathing suit and attire appropriate for an outdoor activity. Further details will be provided later.

Audrey

Last night, I lay awake for hours, body held hostage from the much-needed respite of slumber by my restless mind. Hyperawareness of Walker's presence amplified everything, so the smallest sound—the hum of the air conditioning kicking in, the whoosh of a car passing outside, the mournful wail of distant sirens—sent me jerking to full alert, obliterating any progress I'd managed in the direction of dreamland.

When my alarm rips me into consciousness, it feels like I've only been asleep for twenty minutes. Eyes still closed, I fumble for my phone to silence the offensive noise, muttered invectives streaming from my lips about the inhumanity of scheduling plans this early. I'm not what you'd call a morning person, even under the best of circumstances. After last night? The struggle is so very, very real.

Sounds from the kitchen indicate the man responsible for my exhaustion had no such problems getting up. Not that I can truly place the blame on Walker, much as I'd like to. He was the perfect platonic bedmate—he didn't snore, never strayed from his side of the bed, didn't kick me or steal the covers.

Nope, this one's all on me. Twenty-three years old, and I'm lying here a sleep deprived mess because sharing a bed with a man is so foreign.

I mean, I *have* slept with a boy before… *A* boy. As in *one*. And we only spent the night together a couple of times, well over a year ago. That fact has never seemed so pathetic as in this moment, as I suffer the consequences of my inexperience.

I've yet to so much as lift my head from the pillow when Walker pokes his face into the room. Darker than usual brown hair suggests he's recently showered, as does the whiff of fresh, clean male permeating the air. He's already fully dressed, in a pair of olive-green board shorts and a white T-shirt just tight enough to hint at impressive pecs and biceps. The smile on his face is wider than I've yet to see, engaging both sides of his mouth.

"Good, you're up. Didn't want you to sleep through whatever fun Vickie has planned for us."

Oh no. He's one of *those* people. The ones who wake up with the sun like freaking roosters, all loud and smiley about it.

This relationship is officially doomed.

"Cheerful in the mornings, huh?" I shoot him my darkest glare, but he has the nerve to laugh. "Come on, day's a-wastin'."

"In a minute," I mumble.

A put-upon sigh escapes his lips, but his demeanor is still unnaturally good-natured—more evidence that he's an extraterrestrial swamp creature who thrives in the dawn hours.

"I guess I could bring you coffee, if that will get you moving."

My eyes open fully for the first time, the promise of caffeine lending me energy to move my head in a vigorous nod.

Moments later, he returns with a large white mug from which a thin trail of steam rises. I all but grab it from his hands, humming with happiness as I swallow the sweet nectar of life. I thank him without removing my lips from the rim.

"Sure. What are pretend boyfriends for?"

I'm too busy gulping down my coffee to tell him that I actually have no idea what pretend boyfriends are for. But if coffee delivery in bed is on that list, I think I'm going to enjoy this arrangement a lot more than I'd expected.

* * *

By 8:00 AM, I've managed to shower and get dressed, thanks to the two cups of coffee in my system. After the elevator ride down from the fourth floor, I follow Walker out the front doors of the building, where a black SUV is parked at the curb. Freddy, an older white man with an impressive gray mustache, introduces himself as our driver.

This car puts my older-model compact SUV to shame; the luxurious back seat Walker and I climb into is a far cry from my stain-riddled fabric seats and rusted hubcaps. A plexiglass privacy window separates the back seat from the front, making it feel more like a limo.

"Oh! I forgot to turn on my mic," I realize as Freddy starts to drive.

I press the power button on the side of my wristband's rectangular watch face, thankful I at least remembered to put it on in my near-zombie state. I check and see Walker is wearing

45

his as well, though the band around his wrist is black versus the pretty rose gold color of mine. They look exactly like fitness trackers. No one would ever know they're actually recording devices.

"This is some Grade A James Bond shit," Walker echoes my thoughts.

For the next few minutes, Walker attempts to pry our destination out of Freddy.

"I don't get the point of the secrecy," Walker complains when he is unsuccessful.

"It's for dramatic effect. Victoria's loving playing Tyra Banks."

"Who?"

"Never mind." Of course he hasn't watched *America's Next Top Model*.

As the SUV barrels down the highway, I drop my head back against the seat, the temporary revitalization from those cups of coffee fading. I rub my eyes, which feel like they're full of sand, then succumb to a jaw-cracking yawn.

"Bad night?" Walker asks.

"Couldn't sleep. You know, new place." Cough. *One with a new bed that comes with you in it.* Cough.

I only realize I've begun to drift off when I'm startled awake by Walker's knuckles rapping on the privacy glass.

"How can I help you?" Freddy asks after sliding the partition open.

"Can you pull over the next time you see a Dunkin' or Starbucks? I'm sure Vickie's got us on a schedule, but my girl needs coffee."

"My girl?" I mouth at him once the window closes.

"Gotta practice this boyfriend shit. What?" he asks, when I keep staring.

"Walker—" My chest feels all warm and squishy with gratitude at his surprising thoughtfulness. Plus, no one's ever called me *their* girl before. I can't deny enjoying it even though it was fake.

Then he has to go and ruin the moment by opening his mouth.

"You're prickly when you're tired. I figure, if we have to spend the whole day together, I'd better save myself some pain and feed the beast."

Ahh, *there's* the Walker I'm coming to know and... Well, just know.

07. Rain Check on the Groping

Walker

Thank fuck for Starbucks. After downing that frilly iced coffee in record time, Audrey no longer seems on the verge of passing out or stabbing me with the nearest pointy object if I look at her the wrong way.

Things I never wondered, but now know after my first twenty-four hours as Audrey's "boyfriend": she can be a feisty little thing when tired. Having Freddy stop for coffee was a stroke of genius, one I'll be remembering. The combination of exhaustion and caffeine puts her in a nice middle ground where she lets go of the nerves and shows some personality, minus the stabbiness.

Now, if I can only figure out how to keep her in this state for the next fifty-eight days...

"'Are you a dog person or a cat person?'" I read the millionth question of the weekend off my phone. (And there's still fifteen billion to go; lucky us.)

"I've never had any pets, though I like both dogs and cats. But if I could, I think I would get a dog. I volunteered at an animal rescue with Callie, my BFF, while we were in college. It was *so* tempting to take a puppy home, but they weren't allowed in our apartment."

Something else I've learned? Girl is incapable of answering a question with a single word—or, say, less than a hundred.

"What about you? I'm betting you're a dog person."

"Bingo." I wink.

My solid gold joke flies right over her head, but I'm not about to sing the stupid song. Whatever. I give myself a mental fist bump anyway for the one-word answer. My brother Luke might have the market cornered as the "silent and broody Garrison brother" these days, but all this talking is taking it out of me.

Freddy slides open the privacy window a crack to give us a five-minute warning. (So damn weird—seriously, do rich people think they're too good to breathe the same air as someone who drives their asses for a living, or do they just get off on pretending anyone gives a shit about their conversations?)

Our phones ding with an incoming message from Victoria, as if on cue. (Perhaps literally. I wouldn't put it past her to have the car bugged.)

> VICTORIA: All right, I know you're dying of suspense, especially you, Walker…

Forget romance; the woman should've been a comedian. She knows damn well I'm here for the paycheck and give zero fucks about the details.

> VICTORIA: It's a beautiful day to go kayaking! I've called ahead and reserved you a tandem kayak. Simply give your names at the welcome desk. Have fun!

I'll admit it; I'm curious to see Audrey in a bathing suit. I've still only got the vaguest idea of her body, because she's always so damn covered up. She wore a big-ass tee and sweats to bed last night, and even now, she's in leggings and a long, loose tank.

49

(Now, look. This is a practical need. I'm supposed to play the infatuated boyfriend here. Is wanting a little visual inspiration so much to ask? It's basically for science!)

Fingers snap directly in front of my nose, pulling my attention up to Audrey's scowling face.

Was I staring at her chest? To steal a phrase from my old Magic 8 Ball, *"Signs point to yes."*

"Sorry, did you say something?" I grin at her shamelessly.

"I was *saying*..." Damn, she's sliding back into Bitch Mode. We might need another coffee run. "That I've never kayaked before, and I asked if you have."

"Yup."

"Is it hard?"

With anyone else, I'd go for the obvious joke, no question. But I'd rather not risk pissing her off when we're about to be stuck on a boat together.

"It's easy. And Vickie got us a tandem, so I can do most of the work."

For some reason, this annoys her.

"I can pull my own weight," she snaps.

"Suit yourself."

"Um." Just as fast as the feistiness arrived, it's replaced by worry. "Aren't kayaks the ones where your legs are strapped in, so if you flip, you can get stuck underwater?"

"Nah, it won't be that kind. Rivers around here are calm, so we'll have the easy in and out seats. Don't worry, Big Bird."

"Big Bird?"

"Don't think I missed those yellow socks the other day."

I've been saving this one, but it was worth busting out now. She scrunches her nose, showing her dislike of the nickname, anxiety about kayaking forgotten.

In the parking lot, I hop out, eager to stretch my legs after what felt like far longer than an hour in that car. Audrey's sitting in the open back seat with her legs hanging over the side, rummaging around in that giant bag she nearly bit my head off for teasing her about earlier. Producing a tube of sunscreen, she holds it up in offer. After whipping off my shirt and tucking it into the waistband of my shorts, I grab a handful and start rubbing it on my face.

When I look up a minute or so later, I find Audrey still fully dressed, having made no move to start applying her own sun protection. She's just sitting there frozen, staring at me. Her gaze is so intent on my bare chest, I dip my chin to check for a spider or something—but nope, just skin. I do note with some satisfaction that I'm looking good, my muscles more defined than they've ever been after all the upper body work I've been doing, tagging along to Luke's workouts (one of the only ways I can spend time with the broody fuck lately).

Huh, when did my abs turn into a six pack? *Hot damn, I am one sexy motherfucker.*

Audrey is *still* fixated on my body. Amused as hell, I gesture back and forth between her and my chest. "Uh, you two need a minute alone?"

Her head jerks like I've broken her from some kind of trance, and she whispers, "I've never seen them in real life before."

When I start laughing my ass off, she seems to fully shake out of her daze. Awareness quickly morphs to embarrassment that has her face turning an impressive shade of tomato red.

"I can't believe I just said that!" she moans through the fingers now covering her face.

That makes me lose it all over again. Tears are actually leaking from my eyes, I'm laughing so hard. Once I'm finally under control, I wipe under them with a fingertip, careful not to blind myself with sunscreen.

Audrey is still hiding behind her hands like that monkey emoji. I sigh.

"Hey, it's fine. That was priceless." When she doesn't emerge from hiding, I try a different tack. "Don't think I wouldn't be checking you out too, if you weren't hiding under all those clothes."

The hands drop, along with her jaw, like I've shocked her.

"Do we need to do exposure therapy or something? Go ahead, touch them." I motion at my abs in a *"have at it"* gesture.

I don't know what's funnier—the second's pause where I'd swear some part of her is considering my offer, or how quickly she comes to her senses and shakes her head, face still looking like she's already roasted in the sun for a full day, sans the sunscreen now sitting forgotten beside her.

No way can I help myself from messing with her just a bit more.

"How's this… I'll give you a rain check on the groping."

She hustles away to the dressing rooms to the soundtrack of my chuckles.

Well, *that* was good for my ego—if, you know, it had suffered any kind of damage last night when Audrey refused to get into bed without making sure I'd keep my unworthy hands off her. Which, of course, it didn't.

* * *

Audrey isn't winning any awards for upper body strength or endurance, but she'd medal in stubbornness, for sure.

We've been at it for about an hour, and Audrey's visibly worn out from all the paddling. The tandem kayak is well-balanced and would be easy enough for me to propel alone, but no matter how many times I've mentioned this to her, she refuses to pull up her oars and rest. I don't get it; I can *see* her arms shaking barely a foot in front of me, and over the last fifteen minutes, her strokes have been getting progressively slower and sloppier. Gotta respect how determined she is to stick it out, but someone needs to stop her before she legitimately hurts herself.

I tap her on the shoulder. "Hey, let's hang out here for a minute."

"Oh. Are you okay?"

It's cute how concerned she sounds. *I'm* not the one whose arms look like they're about to fall off.

"Just time for a break. Figured we could multitask, knock out a couple more of these questions." To illustrate, I retrieve the plastic baggie with my phone from my pocket and dangle it in her face.

She does a shitty job of masking her relief as she pulls in her oars and rests them on her lap.

Before pulling out my phone, I wipe my hand dry on the back of her shirt. Audrey squeals and whips her head around to scowl at me, and I can see my shit-eating grin mirrored in her sunglass lenses.

Audrey spends a couple of minutes agonizing over which type of Asian cuisine is her favorite takeout food. (Apparently, she loves them all.) I don't even need a second to name mine as Brooklyn Bros Pizza, the place in Everett my brother and I order from all the time.

"I've never heard of it," Audrey says.

"It's the best. I'll have to take you sometime." The words slide off my tongue without thought. It's something I might say on a real first date. Which this is not. I move on quickly.

"One more and then we'll start paddling back?"

"Better make it a good one," she teases.

It sounds like she's smiling, though I can't see it. Everything about her body posture and demeanor is relaxed, happy. It's a good look on her.

"Right. Next question says we have to talk about our first kisses. You go first."

"Isaac Bernstein, freshman year of college."

"You had your first kiss in *college*?" I can't keep the incredulity from my voice because...*really?* Sure, she seems innocent and comes off a lot younger than twenty-three, but *damn*. That means she was, what, eighteen or nineteen? I wonder how old she was when she lost her virginity? If she even has...

"Yes." Yeah, I earned the defensive tone. But how could I *not* react to that?

"Was it any good?" I ask, moving us forward.

"It was fine."

"So terrible, then."

She laughs instead of answering (because we both know I'm right).

"And you? Let me guess, you were six?" she asks.

"Eleven, actually. Jeanie Mancuso, under the bleachers."

"Could you be more of a cliché?"

"What can I say? Bleacher make-outs are a cliché for a reason. They've been the wingman for many a horny adolescent boy."

"Classy."

Not a word anyone would ever use for me—a good thing for both of us to remember.

We paddle back at a relaxed but steady pace. When the docking place and the parking lot are in sight, I slow my strokes and reach forward to tap Audrey's shoulder again. She peeks back at me with eyebrows lifted quizzically.

"We kept the kayak upright the whole time. Maybe you have beginner's luck?" She looks so pleased, I have to bite back a smile. I *tsk* and shake my head, feigning seriousness. "Sorry, but I can't let us turn this thing back in without giving you the full experience."

"Wha—" She cuts off in a high-pitched screech as I throw my full weight to one side of the kayak and flip it over, sending us into the frigid water.

Audrey is still pissed at me as we trudge up the narrow strip of beach, carrying the kayak back to the rental window. Dripping wet and vibrating with irritation, she reminds me of a hissing cat that's been tricked into a bath. I can't help snickering. Since we're both being crazy mature right now, it's only fitting that she responds by sticking her tongue out at me.

Once we return the kayak, the little prank backfires on me— or pays off big time, depending on how you look at it. Bemoaning her soaked clothes, Audrey grabs the hem of her shirt and starts wringing it out. Then, without warning, she pulls it up and over her head.

My entire field of vision is suddenly filled with creamy skin. *So much skin.* Unnoticed by Audrey, whose entire focus is on her anger over the wet shirt, I devour every inch of her exposed torso with my eyes—the sprinkling of freckles on the tops of her shoulders, the soft curve where her hip meets her waist...and *tits.* Full and round and perky, and far more generous than I'd expected, her breasts swell beyond the edges of her bikini top, despite the fairly conservative style doing its best to contain them. Her nipples are hard from our plunge into the water, perfect round pebbles clearly visible where they're poking through the dark blue fabric. Then she begins to wring the T-shirt with both hands, vigorous in her agitation—totally unaware how each movement causes her tits to bounce and flex.

Jesus Christ. I bite back a groan and tug on my shorts to do some necessary readjusting as my groin gets tight.

When she lifts her head, I just barely manage to redirect my gaze in time to avoid being caught. She glares at me, utterly oblivious to the fact that I've just spent the past few minutes ogling her.

"This is going to take forever to dry, and I didn't bring another shirt!" she accuses.

I shrug, never one for apologies—especially when I'm not at all sorry. That shit was hilarious.

Wait... She's going to be shirtless the whole ride back?

Although a part of me is totally on board for that scenario, I find myself offering her my shirt. She takes a moment to decide, conflict written all over her intriguingly transparent face. I watch her weigh the merits of being clothed herself versus spending an hour subjected to my ab-tastic gloriousness, before finally accepting the shirt.

I'm both disappointed and grateful when she emerges from the bathroom in a skirt she apparently had in that giant bag, which spares me from adding a visual of her ass to the bikini-clad tits now burned into the backs of my retinas.

On the plus side? I don't have to worry about my fake girlfriend's sex appeal any longer.

08. My Buddy Jack

Audrey

I'm in the middle of a giggling fit. You know the kind—when the amusement stops having anything to do with whatever you initially found funny, spiraling out of control until the laughter becomes its own entity, a self-fueling monster you have no choice but to let run its course.

Although I can't see him through my watering eyes, I can hear the deep rumble of Walker chuckling over on his end of the couch.

Maybe that's the manly equivalent of giggling. The thought strikes me as so hilarious that I nearly tumble off the couch onto the floor, barely managing to right myself at the very last moment. Walker is so amused by my near miss with catastrophe that his man-giggling turns into a full belly laugh.

We're drunk.

Well, *I'm* drunk. "Tipsy" may be a more accurate term for Walker's current state of inebriation. Totally unfair since this is all his fault. Him, and the bottle of Jack Daniel's he bought on our way home after convincing Freddy to stop at a liquor store.

The coffee table boasts an impressive array of empty takeout boxes that previously contained Italian food from the restaurant where Freddy took us after kayaking. No doubt, when Victoria made those reservations, she envisioned us seated at a table for two, enjoying a romantic, late afternoon meal. But given Walker's childish antics with the kayak and our subsequent shirt shortage, we opted to take our orders to-go instead.

Propriety and health regulations aside, I personally think a good percentage of the restaurant's patrons would have thanked us for providing them the entertainment of a shirtless Walker. His body is…ridiculous. The man is plenty attractive clothed, but who knew he was hiding Marvel casting-call-worthy abs? I've never seen anyone this toned who wasn't on a screen (as I mortifyingly told him earlier). Our entire ride home was a torturous battle of willpower, trying to keep my eyes off the shirtless man beside me, when all my baser instincts wanted to do was stare. Predictably, my attempts at subtlety failed—meaning Walker knew exactly what was going on. The gorgeous jerk didn't even try to hide how hilarious he found it.

Alas, he's wearing a shirt now since we took turns showering off the lake water and changed into comfy clothes before eating.

For the last few hours, we've been answering icebreaker questions and doing shots. Walker's so-called drinking game has no discernible rules as far as I can tell, something I stopped caring about a while ago.

"You read the next question. But first, drink," Walker commands, handing over the whiskey. Although we started out using glasses like civilized people, at this point, we're just drinking straight from the bottle. I'm no longer weirded out by putting my mouth where his has been, and I've stopped coughing every time the liquor burns down my throat—both sure signs that I'm drunk.

I appreciate the extra sip of alcohol in my system when I read the next question, which is about our relationship with our parents. Not a topic I'm ever eager to talk about, though I admit to some curiosity about the cloud that comes over Walker's features whenever he mentions his dad.

Yep, *that* cloud. The one currently darkening his face and pulling down his brows, the muscles around his mouth tight.

Walker's answer is succinct and communicates as little as possible, leaving me even more certain there's some kind of strain between him and his dad. When he grabs the bottle and takes a long swallow, I try (and fail) not to stare at the strong column of his throat and his bobbing Adam's apple.

Who knew *throats* could be sexy? (Everyone, probably. Sometimes I still feel hopelessly behind, like I'll never quite catch up from all I missed during the sheltered first eighteen years of my life.)

"Your turn." Walker's voice is scratchy, like the liquor scraped his vocal cords on its way down—and why do I suddenly find *that* sexy too?

Stop drooling and focus! Drinking can lead to loose lips, and I don't want to accidentally overshare. If Walker can be sparing with details, then so can I.

"I grew up with just my mom and I'm an only child, so we're close. Mom did everything for me. Revolved her whole world around me. I'm lucky to have her."

"I sense a *but.*"

Seems my tone gave away more than the contents of my carefully chosen words. *Dang it, Jack! Work with me here.*

"She's…overprotective." *Hello, understatement, my old friend.* "It can be a bit much. That's one reason why I moved away for college." *The* reason, but that's more than Walker needs to know.

"What about your dad?"

"My dad…" I'm twenty-three; I should have this spiel mastered by now, but there are some things that just never get easier to talk about. "He left us when I was four."

There. Succinct yet comprehensive.

"Does he visit you? Stay in touch?" Walker asks.

I shake my head in the negative; I don't trust myself to use words in my inebriated state, when he's just landed on the deepest, rawest place in my soul. Not that his question was invasive. The assumption is a natural one—because plenty of people leave their spouses, but what kind of parent walks out and never spares his child another thought?

Oh, that's right. Mine.

I'm oddly touched by Walker's ornery grunt, like he's angry at my father on my behalf.

Fortunately, he drops that topic. *Un*fortunately, our next question isn't much of a reprieve.

"What was your longest relationship?" I read.

"One year," he says. His answer surprises the heck out of me. "We were friends in high school, became something more just before graduation, didn't work out."

I wait for him to continue. When he doesn't, I start doing an obnoxious slow clap. "Wow. I think you're on track to usurp Victoria as the best-sellingest romance author ever. The way you spun that tale, I feel like I was there! I mean, the intrigue! The *detail*!"

"Shut up." But he's smiling as he playfully shoves me in the shoulder—then steadies me when I almost fall over.

"So…? What was her name? Why did you break up?"

"Suri. And I don't know." He shrugs. "Like I said, we didn't work out."

I roll my eyes, then stop when it makes me dizzy. Okay, no more eye-rolling; it does *not* pair well with drunkenness. It's also childish and doesn't look attractive on anyone.

Not that I want to look attractive to Walker or anything.

I don't!

Wait, what are we talking about?

"Who broke it off?" I ask, finding the thread of our conversation again.

"Technically, she dumped me, but it was my fault. She basically threw down an ultimatum, saying it was either move in together or break up. I said we weren't moving in, so…"

"After a year? That's fast. And you were only, what, nineteen?"

He grunts, which I think indicates agreement, though I'm still not fluent enough in Man Noises to say for sure.

"She took it all real serious, real fast. Looking back, I think maybe she had a thing for me for longer than she copped to. If I'd known she already had us halfway down the aisle in her head, I wouldn't have gone there with her."

She definitely made a tactical error with that ultimatum, but I can't help sympathizing with this girl I've never met. Here she was, thinking she'd reached the "happily ever after" in her friends-to-lovers story, only to learn Walker wasn't reading the same book.

"Whatever. Your turn. Longest relationship?"

Oh, right. For a minute there, I got so caught up in learning about Walker, and having fun teasing him, I'd totally forgotten that I need to answer the question too.

I try to figure out what I can say without confessing too much. Dating wasn't an option when I was growing up, so I was completely inexperienced when I went to college. When Ethan and I started dating, I'd only had a few awkward kisses. I might actually die from shame if Walker knew that I delayed for six months before finally giving Ethan my virginity, only to have him break up with me a week later.

"My ex-boyfriend Ethan. We met in class and dated during my senior year of college." *There. Nice and simple.*

"Well, come on. You've gotta give me more than that after making me spill. How long did you date?"

"Six months."

"Really? Huh." He sounds as surprised as I am that he's had the longest relationship between the two of us. "I figured you were a monogamous long-term boyfriend kind of girl."

"That would require finding boys who want to date me monogamously for long periods of time."

Walker groans. "No. Don't do that thing where you put yourself down and I'm supposed to compliment you or whatever. I hate that shit, and I suck at it, even with people I've known more than a couple of days."

"I was *not* fishing for compliments!"

"You were throwing a pity party."

"I'm just stating the truth. You might not understand this, because you and your superhero muscles are probably a magnet for the entire vagina-having and/or penis-liking population, but I am not exactly the kind of girl who has guys lining up to date her."

He stares at me blankly for a moment before the corner of his mouth twitches.

"Okay, there's no way I can just pass over *'vagina-having, penis-liking population.'*"

He cracks up, while my face burns hotter than the whiskey in my system. This isn't like earlier. Now he's laughing *at* me.

"I can't remember the last time I heard someone say *penis* or *vagina*, much less in the same sentence."

"I don't like the other words!" I sound prudish even to myself, but I *don't*

"You're kind of a stick-in-the-mud. Anyone ever tell you that?"

Yes. "No."

After a minute, he says, "Okay, fine, I'll play Go Fish. But don't say I didn't warn you I'm shit at this."

Uh-oh. I think I'd rather *not* hear whatever he's about to say, but I don't have a chance to stop him before he continues.

"What *'kind of girl'* you are's got nothing to do with anything. All you need to do is chill out—and maybe work on the blushing... And make sure you're not hungry or tired around anyone you're hot for—just, you know, be *you,* and there will be guys in that line."

I blink. All the alcohol in my brain is slowing my ability to process his words, but...I think he just gave me a compliment? Kind of? A compliment wrapped in an insult and delivered in blunt Walker-speak, but still.

Ugh, I can't even with this boy!

Whatever. My buddy Jack and I are in no state to even begin deciphering the two-hundred-pound conundrum that is Walker Garrison. We'll leave that one for Sober Audrey to deal with later.

[CONFIDENTIAL PROJECT RECORDS]
DAY 2

Transcript Excerpts: Condo Recording

Truncated and Annotated by Matilda

A = Audrey Mitchell, W = Walker Garrison

10:00 PM

W: "This says we have to come up with our 'meet-cute.' The fuck is a meet-cute?"

A: "It means we need to decide what story we're going to tell people when they ask how we met."

W: "Okay then, let's do this thing."

[extended silence]

W: "I say we keep it simple, because you're a shitty liar."

A: "Hey!"

W: "It's not a bad thing…usually. But not exactly helpful for this gig."

A: "I can be a convincing actress when I need to be! … I can!"

W: "Whatever you say, babe."

A: "Ugh. 'Babe' is so generic! It reminds me of those obnoxious, cocky guys who don't care enough to learn a girl's name, so when they walk up to her at a bar or whatever and get all in her space with their overapplied cologne, they just say, 'Hey babe,' in this way that you just know they think they're God's gift to humankind and the girl should be honored she's getting hit on."

W: "You have some very specific feelings about that nickname."

[Silence]

W: "Fine, checking 'Babe' off the potential nickname list…"

A: "Can we get back to the assignment? What should our story be?"

W: "Well, obviously, we met, and you immediately had the hots for me. Maybe you chased me around a little until I agreed to take you out."

A: "Har. Har. You're hilarious."

W: "How about we say you brought your car into the shop?"

A: "And I suppose this is the point when I fell for you on sight?"

W: "Fine, Miss Snark. We'll say it was mutual."

A: "Fine. So I brought my car in and…?"

W: "We got chatting, and I asked you out for drinks."

A: "Just drinks? Why not dinner?"

W: "Are you seriously bitching at me about the details of our fake first date right now?"

A: "It matters! You take someone to dinner if you're serious about them. Coffee is more casual. So are drinks, but they can also just be a formality before going to bed together."

W: "Okay, princess. Let's say I took you to dinner, so people don't think I was trying to get in your pants."

A: "Just."

W: "Huh?"

A: "So they don't think you were just trying to get in my pants. To be convincing, we need people to think we're attracted to each other."

W: "It'll be a stretch, but I'll see what I can do…"

Audrey's Journal

Dear Victoria,

I enjoyed kayaking far more than expected. Eeven though Walker tipped our kayak at the very end, the scoundrel.)

I'm not sure what else to say. I'm in the bathroom right now trying to get this done because I don't know if I'll remember to do it later, but my mind is a little fuzzy.

I have to confess that Walker and I are drinking on the job. Kind of a lot. It's all his fault!

By the way, have you seen Walker's abs? I know that makes me sound like a shallow gossip, but since you're a romance writer, I feel it's imperative you see them for yourself, so you can provide accurate descriptions for your readers. Actually, you should take a picture of them to use on the cover of the book! It would sell a bazillion copies.

Sincerely,

Audrey

Comment added by Victoria Trulette: Drinking is certainly not prohibited on this job! So don't worry about that at all. As for your suggestion RE: Walker's abs, I very much appreciate the tip, and I have made note of it.

* * *

Walker's Journal

Hey Vicks,

Thumbs up on the kayaking and the Italian food.

Thumbs down on the questions.

W

Comment added by Victoria Trulette: This isn't a Yelp review, Walker.

Comment added by Victoria Trulette: Also, that nickname is horrid. I am not a topical vaporous cold remedy.

09. Point in the "Walker's Not a Dick" Column

Walker

Audrey is still conked out on the couch when I wake up, and she doesn't stir once while I make coffee and get ready for my run. I go over to check for signs of life after she sleeps through me dropping a full water bottle on my bare foot and cursing up a storm.

She looks like a fluffy burrito, wrapped in that blanket. Albeit, a hot mess of a burrito, with her hair sticking up everywhere. I'll say it; she's a cute hot mess. (And yes, she is breathing.)

New item for the list of shit I now know about Audrey: girl cannot handle her liquor. She's the dangerous kind of lightweight too, because she really had me thinking she could hang for a while there. By the time I realized she was trashed, it was too late to do anything but make her drink water. Not long after, she passed out right there on the living room couch.

I tried waking her up so she could move to the bed, but she just mumbled grumpy nonsense and swatted at me like I was an annoying fly. So, I left her there.

Listen, I've spent one weekend with the girl. While I now know her birthday—July twenty-sixth—and how she likes her coffee—eighty percent sugar—we're nowhere close to familiar enough for me to be carrying her to bed honeymoon-style. Is there even a way to do that without touching her ass? I'll tell you who has two thumbs and wasn't gonna find out.

So, yeah, she slept on the couch. Before I went to bed, I pulled a trash bin over, which I figured pretty much covered my responsibilities as her "boyfriend" of three days.

On my run, brown eyes filled with pain keep popping into my mind uninvited. When Audrey talked about her dad last night, it was obvious that loser's actions eat at her. Ironic, how the absence of her father and the presence of mine could fuck us up equally.

When I get back to the condo, Audrey's still on the couch in the exact same spot as when I left, except now she's sitting upright and her hair is wet from a shower. When she looks over at me with a tentative smile, I see something else has changed; she's wearing glasses. They're brown, that thick plastic hipster style. I've gotta admit, she works the librarian look.

"Nice glasses."

She fiddles with them, looking self-conscious. Why can't I ever say the right thing with this girl? I make her uncomfortable even when I'm trying to give a legit compliment.

"Oh. Thanks. I usually wear contacts, but since I fell asleep in them last night, my eyes needed a break."

"Right. You feeling okay?"

"Yes, thank you. I'm sorry about last night. I don't drink much."

"I noticed." Her nose scrunches at my teasing—I can't help it; she's so fun to rile up. "No worries, we'll just take it easy on the whiskey next time."

Her skeptical face suggests she's not interested in a "next time," but that shit's happening if I have anything to say about it. She's fun when she's drunk.

Note to self—alcohol is a good substitute for relaxing Audrey, if exhaustion plus caffeine is unavailable. PS: Buy more Jack Daniel's.

"I made a casserole. You're welcome to help yourself," Audrey says.

"Cool, thanks."

She doesn't need to tell me twice. I pop it in the microwave and add ketchup at her suggestion. A minute later, I'm in heaven.

"What is this?" I ask, remembering to swallow before talking—the kind of polite stuff I don't have to worry about at home with my brother.

She rattles off a bunch of ingredients that we apparently had in the fridge.

"It's fucking delicious."

"Are you sure? It's vegetarian," she teases.

"Hey, food is food. I'm not giving up my wings and burgers, but if all the shit you make tastes like this, I'll eat your cooking any time."

She beams. Well, lookie there. One point in the Walker's Not a Dick column. *Huzzah.*

I'm working through my second plate of casserole when I notice the TV. Are those...puppies?

"What are you watching?"

"It's called *Santa Buddies.*"

"And why are you watching this? In August? With the sound off?"

"There's a whole series of Buddies movies about a bunch of golden retriever puppies—Halloween, superheroes, even space. I don't care about the plots, but I like looking at the puppies."

I don't know if she slipped some Crazy Sauce into that casserole, but her explanation sounds totally reasonable to me.

"Puppies in space, huh? I may need to see that one."

We're smiling at each other, like two normal people who could even be friends. Huh.

10. Whoomp, There It Is

NEW MESSAGE IN GROUP TEXT

VICTORIA: Hello! I hope your first weekend together was enjoyable. While I know other endeavors will require your attention on weekdays, please start thinking about informing friends and family about your relationship—a task I'd suggest is best done sooner rather than later.

Walker

Mondays are usually busy at the shop, and today is no exception. There's a car in every bay, and most of the guys are already at work as I hustle to my spot and step into my navy-blue "Garrison Auto" coveralls. I built in extra time to get here because I knew traffic getting out of Boston would be brutal, but I still end up late and agitated from the bitch of a commute.

Tommy Fontanelli comes over from the next bay and claps a hand on my shoulder in greeting—only wiping it down with a rag *afterward,* no doubt leaving a nice five-finger print of black grease on my back. Not that it matters. These coveralls have seen far worse.

I give Tommy a shove for being an asshole anyway, though there's no force behind it. This asshole is basically a second brother. Growing up, Luke and I spent as much time at the Fontanelli house as our own.

"Hey, I thought you had some gig going in Boston."

"Yeah, but it's mostly nights and weekends."

Tommy nods, making the black hair he keeps in a perpetual state of "almost long enough for a ponytail" flop into his eyes. Seems like a pain in the ass if you ask me, but according to Tommy, girls go crazy for it. He produces a ball cap from his back pocket, shaping the bill before slipping it on backward to keep the dark strands out of his face.

Even though we've all got work to do, Tommy abandons the minivan he has on a lift and leans against the concrete pillar between our bays, settling in to shoot the shit like he's got all the time in the world.

"What is this gig anyway?"

Good thing Audrey and I got our stories figured out this weekend.

"House-sitting. This loaded old lady's paying me a shit-ton of money to live in her apartment in Beacon Hill for two months."

"How'd you score that deal?" Pete, the shameless eavesdropper, calls out from my other side.

"I have a buddy whose company was listing the job and happened to mention it." And hey, that's even true.

"This lady have any more houses that need watching?" Pete asks.

"Dunno. I mean, you know I'd hook you up, but seeing as she likes me, I don't think she'd be into your scrawny ass."

Pete throws a dirty rag at me. It falls short, flopping to the floor after traveling barely a yard. He shoots Tommy and me the middle finger when we laugh at him.

73

When we're done fucking around and Pete's back to minding his own business, Tommy says, "I bet Luke's glad your ass is gone and he gets the house to himself for a while."

"Yeah, probably."

We share a look. Tommy is the only one outside of immediate family who knows how rough things got for a while there after Luke's accident. It's nice to have someone who gets it—no words are needed in this brief moment of mutual acknowledgment of how different my brother is now, or the lingering worry at how closed-off he's become.

Then the moment's over.

"This gig mean you're moving forward with your screen printing?" Tommy is also one of the only people who knows I have plans to build my business into a full-time thing.

"That's the idea."

"Good for you. It's about time."

He doesn't know how good it feels to have that easy support. My dad's reaction to the same news would be a hell of a lot different... *Will* be, which is why I'm not telling him until absolutely necessary.

I change the subject, deciding to go for broke. "And it works out, 'cause my girl lives in Boston."

"Your girl, huh?" Tommy's smile widens. I swear this guy is the worst gossip I've ever met, including my mom, who works at the grocery store and prides herself on being "in the know" about everything in the community. Telling Tommy is a strategic move that ensures I'll only need to have this conversation once; by the end of the day, every guy in this garage will know I have a girlfriend.

"Yeah, I, uh—" The lie gets stuck in my throat, and I have to clear it. "I actually met her here when she brought in her car. RAV4, eight years old, but in good condition."

He nods. When you work in our business, a person's car says a lot about them. A compact SUV like the Toyota RAV4 is reliable, practical, not flashy. And that is actually what Audrey drives, so it's one less lie to keep straight.

At the far end of the garage, my dad comes through the glass-paned door that leads to the office and waiting room. Like the little busybody he is, Tommy immediately calls out, "Hey, John! You know your boy's got a girl down in Boston?"

"Only one?" Dad quips just as loudly. All the guys snicker like a bunch of preteens, assuming the comment is just more of the harmless shit-talk we throw around on the regular. They don't hear the underlying bite, but I sure as hell feel it taking a chunk out of me.

"Yep, just the one," I say through a forced smile, keeping my expression carefully neutral despite all my muscles stringing taut in a fight response. I know better than to let Dad get to me. But unfortunately, after close to twenty-five years of trying, I've yet to develop an immunity to his shit.

This particular dig isn't even original. My father is forever determined to paint me as an irresponsible player, just one of the many reasons I'm a waste of space. I mean, sure, I was a little rowdy when I was younger. Dad did catch me in the back of his truck making out with a girl that one time. Okay, twice. And yeah, it was two different girls. But that was high school, almost a decade ago.

Fuck, I've been so busy lately, I haven't gotten laid in months.

Just let it go. Focus on work. I pick up the clipboard someone's helpfully left at my station and scan the work order for the cherry red CR-V in my bay.

Since God has better things to do than answer my silent supplication for Dad to pass me by, my old man stops at the CR-V's front bumper. He takes the clipboard from me and spends a minute telling me how to diagnose the problem—like he hasn't been putting me to work here since I could hold a wrench. It pisses me off, but I bite my tongue and wait for the other shoe to drop.

"You about done screwing around down in Boston yet?"

Whoomp, there it is.

"It's only been a couple of days," I grit out. "The job's two months, like I already told you."

Dad scoffs. "Yeah, '*the job.*'"

His mocking use of air quotes takes me from pissed off to *really* fucking pissed off. I exhale through it. *I will not get into it with my dad today. I* will not *get into it with my dad today.*

"Whatever, Dad. Gotta get going on this. Busy day." I turn my back on him and riffle through my toolbox. The tension in my shoulders only starts to release when I hear his receding footsteps.

Only my father could make me this tense after a five-minute interaction.

The CR-V is an easy fix, the part replacement a task I've done a thousand times, leaving me way too much headspace to stew over that shit with Dad.

Usually, I'm a pro at letting my father's disappointment roll right off me—as I should, considering I've had a lifetime of practice. But for once, I can't seem to brush it off. Bitterness clings to my gut, festering.

Dad's put-downs were one thing back when I was a teenager hell-bent on acting out, having decided with adolescent logic that if he was going to be disappointed in me anyway, I might as well live down to his expectations. But the man has some balls to treat me like a lazy good-for-nothing now. No acknowledgment of everything I gave up, working here full time since the day I graduated high school, instead of pursuing a career of my own. There's no chance Dad's unaware that I've been running myself ragged for years, taking on extra hustles—all those late-night Uber shifts driving drunk idiots— just to make my rent because of how often he dips into my paycheck. (Yeah, being the owner's son is not as cushy as you might expect.)

I doubt he's even given a second thought to how I gave up a partial scholarship and my chance to attend art school because the shop was in trouble and my family needed me here. Then again, the things I want have never mattered to my father. All that's ever mattered is his messed-up obsession with using his sons to vicariously live out his dreams of army glory that got derailed when our grandfather died and he had to take over the shop.

No, to Dad, I will always be the fuckup. The disappointment, the son who refused to be a good little soldier and fall in line with his plans. Because of that, nothing I do will never be enough for him—we both know it, but damn if my refusal to try hasn't always made him real sore. Unfortunately for him, I've never been one for the pointless masochism of exercises in futility.

At least he had one perfect son in Luke, who always seemed happy enough to play that part—the high school football star headed to a decorated army career via West Point.

Problem is, the old man's oh for two these days, because even Luke isn't *that* Luke anymore.

11. Selective Truths

Audrey

I'm holding my phone, which is shaking... No, wait, that's my hand. My current task has me so anxious I feel physically ill. My heart is pounding, I'm sweating, and there's a pit of nausea swirling low in my stomach.

All because I'm about to call my mom and tell her about my new "boyfriend."

Correction: I'm about to *lie* to Mom about my new boyfriend.

Conversations with my mother are already like tiptoeing through a minefield, even when we're only talking about the mostly boring details of my day-to-day life. Five years and over a thousand miles have done little to curb her urge to micromanage, so I've learned the hard way that when it comes to sharing information, less is more. However, necessary lies of omission are one thing; outright lying about being in a relationship with Walker is a different animal entirely.

Thus, the flu-like symptoms.

Time is up to avoid this talk, though; our first check-in meeting with Victoria is tomorrow, and I don't want to disappoint her when she asks if we've told our parents. Although, I suppose I could call Mom in the morning instead...

Chickenshit! Callie's voice taunts.

Shut up! You're imaginary and in Ireland.

Great, I'm fighting with the voices in my head. That's got to be on a checklist somewhere to determine whether you're losing it. (If so… *Check.*)

I squeeze my eyes shut and tap Mom's number on my screen. She picks up on the first ring.

"Audrey! Where have you been?"

Drama right from the get-go. She's acting like I dropped off the face of the earth, not missed a few phone calls. I inhale deeply, trying not to absorb her anxiety.

"Hi, Mom. I'm sorry I haven't called you back. Like I said in my texts, I've been busy with work." *Technically true.*

"Are text messages all I warrant these days? You can't spare a few minutes to call your mother?"

"I'm sorry, Mom."

"I worry about you working so much. Your boss should hire a second assistant if he's so busy."

Okay, so some of my lies of omission are beefier than others—like letting Mom think I still work for Mr. Simmons. It just seems best to wait and inform her of this life change once I have a new job lined up (a real one I can actually tell her about).

"Are you at least home from work now?"

"Yes." Of course, she also doesn't know that "home" means something different than it did last week. Maybe I'm more practiced at this lying thing than I realized.

"Good. That man works you too hard."

She has no idea. As far as Mom knows, Mr. Simmons was a benevolent boss who treated me with respect…and she *still* gripes that I'm "working too hard." Which I take as proof that I made the right decision to keep my work stories upbeat and tame.

"I'm fine, I promise. How are you? What's new?"

As I knew it would, the question buys me a lengthy reprieve while she talks my ear off about her job at the bank and the latest charity project her bible study group is working on. It's always a relief to hear my mom is happy and keeping busy. Leaving her for college was the hardest thing I've ever done. Mom was devastated by my decision to go to a school out of state, and I worried about her being lonely. She didn't exactly have a thriving social calendar when I was growing up—and she certainly didn't allow me to have one. Now, with the circle of friends she's met through her church, Mom has a more active social life than I do. Which makes me feel like the most pathetic twentysomething alive but definitely eases my guilt.

"That's great, Mom. I'm glad you're having fun."

"How about you? What's new with you?" she asks.

Our conversations are always a bit of a tightrope walk, especially when it comes to my social life. On the one hand, now that Callie's in Ireland, Mom frets incessantly about me being "alone," but nothing sets her off on a worry-filled lecture faster than hearing that I'm meeting new people and spending time out in a "dangerous city." I swear the woman has an alert on her phone for gruesome crime in the Greater Boston area. She loves spouting those statistics, while remaining stubbornly deaf and blind to similar crime in Orlando.

My standard strategy is deflection—keep her talking about herself or stick to safe subjects like reality television shows. Unfortunately, that isn't an option today.

"Actually, I'm kind of seeing someone."

Dead silence meets my statement. A quick check confirms the call hasn't dropped; I've just rendered my mother speechless for one of the few times I can remember in my life. My heart rate picks up.

Calm down. Remember the plan. Right. I've planned out a series of selective truths that will be easier for me to pull off than flat-out lies.

"His name is Walker. We met a little while ago," Basically true—it *has* been almost a whole week. "But I didn't want to mention it to you until I was sure about him."

"And you're sure now?" Her voice is heavily laced with skepticism; she's really asking whether my judgment can be trusted. Although I didn't actually pick Walker, I hate that I deserve her doubt, because I *did* choose Ethan. Mom doesn't know all those details, but I couldn't hide what a mess I was after the breakup, which gave her more than enough ammunition. I have no doubt she will wield it in perpetuity.

"Yes, I'm sure." This one's a straight lie. It sits heavy in my stomach like a chunk of cement.

Before she can comment, I barrel forward with my carefully crafted statements.

"This thing with him, it's different. We don't have a ton in common, but we have a connection." *Truth.* "Connection" is basically a synonym for being legally bound together, right?

"I can see myself with him for a while." *Truth.* Sixty days, to be exact.

"We're hanging out a lot." *Truth.* If you count living together as "hanging out."

Finding an opening, Mom jumps in with a rapid-fire barrage of questions. "Where did you meet him? Does he have a job? Is he close with his mother? Does he go to church?"

I answer as concisely as possible, forcibly keeping my voice steady and my breathing even.

We met via a mutual acquaintance I know through work. A stretch, but technically true. (And better than the story Walker and I concocted; even hinting at car trouble would send Mom into a tizzy.)

Yes, he's a mechanic and an entrepreneur. Mom respects a strong work ethic, so I can tell this detail earns some grudging approval.

Yes, he's close to his mom. Not in the way my mother would define it, but they're close enough.

I gloss over the church thing. (Kind of like Mom chooses to pretend she didn't hear me when I told her I don't attend weekly services… And I don't remind her that when I was growing up, *she* only went to church on holidays.)

Mom goes off on one of her diatribes about taking irresponsible risks, reiterating the dangers of trusting men and citing examples from true crime shows I'm certain she only watches to glean material for this purpose. Normally, her lecture would be far more extensive and she'd likely be in hysterics by now, but she has to leave soon for her weekly bible study group meeting. (In further news of my candidacy for Daughter of the Year…yes, I know her schedule and timed this call accordingly.)

"You know I only want you to be happy, honey."

"I know," I reply, even though we're both aware of the unspoken caveat—she wants me to be happy *in Florida with her.*

"I don't know what I'd do if something happened to you." The break in her voice is unrehearsed, and my heart aches. For all her faults, she truly does love me.

I just wish her love didn't come with strings whose ties I can only slip from with a thirteen-hundred-mile buffer between us.

12. Weird FaceTime Double Date

Audrey

"Oh my God! You're alive!"

I roll my eyes at Callie's melodrama. "It hasn't been *that* long. We texted the other day."

"Barely. And we haven't had a real call in forever. I've missed your face!"

Hearing that my best friend misses me as much as I miss her fills me with warmth. It's reassurance I couldn't have fathomed ever needing before she was bedazzled by an Irishman and whisked away to his homeland across the sea. Okay, it's not fair of me to villainize Patrick; I really do like the guy, and not only because he makes Callie so happy. (Yep, a redheaded Irish guy named Patrick... My bestie's soul mate couldn't have been just a *little* more original?)

I've put on a brave face for her when we talk, because I don't want her to feel guilty about following her heart, but ever since Callie left, I've been floundering. The truth is that I don't really know how to do this "life" thing without her. It's unlikely I'd have even gotten through that first year at BU without running home to my mom if not for Callie. From my first day in Boston—when I arrived at the dorms wide-eyed, sheltered, and utterly unprepared for the realities of the world, as clueless about normal socializing as dating—Callie has been my human touchstone. My safe place, my one-woman cheering squad and chosen family. My *person*.

It's now been six months since we ugly cried through our goodbyes outside Logan Airport. Although I feel her absence every day like a piece of myself is missing, so far, our friendship has withstood the distance and the five-hour time difference.

Instead of rehashing any of this, I gasp in mock outrage and try my best to emulate her theatrics. "You miss my face? Does that mean you *didn't* put out that framed picture I gave you? I expected to be front and center where you'd have to look at it and remember me every day."

"I *did*. It's in the living room!"

I have to close my eyes when she moves, turning my screen into a nauseating blur. When the camera stabilizes again, she comes into view holding the framed photo I gave her as a going away present. (Mostly as a joke... I don't usually go around framing photos of just me. *Weird*.) She gazes at it lovingly, petting the glass.

"Cut it out, you weirdo." I laugh, feeling happier and more relaxed than I have all week.

"I will not. I love this photo. But it doesn't move!"

"So, you're telling me if you had a Harry Potter-style photograph of me, that moved and talked or whatever, you'd never need to actually speak to me again?"

"No, I'd still want to talk to you. But that would be awesome! I would carry it around with me everywhere, show it the sights around Ireland, have long conversations with it, maybe bring it to bed with me at night..."

"So creepy!" I start cracking up all over again.

"I just love you. And I miss you. What's up? I feel like you're avoiding me."

Guilt assails me, because I *have* been avoiding her. Lying to my mom was bad enough, but this is Callie, the person who knows me better than anyone else in the world. Thank goodness we're on a video call, because there's zero chance I could pull it off in person.

"I figured I'd at least hear from you after the mysterious job interview last week."

Here goes nothing. "I did get the job, actually. But it's part time and temporary, so the hunt continues."

"It's still a job, so yay! Who are you working for? Or are you not allowed to tell me?"

"I had to sign a nondisclosure agreement."

Who knew I'd ever be grateful for that NDA? It helps that Callie is familiar with the employment agency because of stories about recruiting for the rich and famous that our friend Jamie has told us (without using names, of course), so the secrecy isn't totally unexpected.

"Boo," Callie pouts, the expression one most grown women couldn't pull off, but she manages to look adorable. "But you like it? You're happy?"

"It's…okay." Walker is downstairs at the gym so I'm alone, but I still glance over my shoulder to confirm the bedroom door is closed.

"Hmm. Ominously vague. It's nothing like The Asshole, though?"

"It's not. I promise."

Callie is the only person I've told what really happened with Mr. Simmons that last day, how he crossed the line from criticism and bullying to sexual harassment. She was so furious, I thought she would actually hop on a plane to Boston just to kick some lawyer butt.

Then she tried to convince me to press charges, but he's a *lawyer*. Even if I had the money to sue him, he'd just drag

85

things out and bury me in paperwork and other legal nonsense until I went totally broke, as I saw him do to other people many times while under his employ.

"Good."

My petite best friend may look like a fun-sized pixie with her big, expressive eyes, heart-shaped face, and short, dark hair—strangers often compare her to Snow White—but she's feisty as all get-out and is fierce when it comes to protecting the people she loves.

"But…" Here goes.

She sits up straighter, BFF Spidey senses catching on to my serious tone even from another continent.

"Just spill. You'll feel better after you do."

Doubtful.

"I-met-someone," I rush out, before I lose my nerve.

Callie's reaction is so high-pitched, it threatens to overwhelm the range of my phone's speakers.

"*EEK!* Tell me everything."

If only. What I wouldn't give to talk about all of this with her *for real…*

"I don't know. It's different from anything I've experienced before." *So true.*

"Ohmygod!" Callie claps, eerily reminding me of Victoria. "Okay, I totally forgive you for ditching me since you've been busy with the beginnings of a torrid love affair."

Nothing I've told her merits the description "torrid," but she does love her hyperbole.

"I need more! *Details*, woman. What's his name? What does he look like? No—just send me a picture."

"His name is Walker, and I don't have a picture."

"Take one. I expect it to be in my messages when I wake up tomorrow."

I sigh, hoping Walker is game for a quick selfie later. Knowing Callie, she will hound me until she gets that photo.

"There's something else."

She gasps and drops her voice to a whisper, bringing the phone way too close to her face so her eyes, nose, and mouth take up my entire screen. "Have you slept with him?"

"No!" The denial comes out too fast, but I figure that's okay because it would be very unlike me to jump into bed with someone this early...or, you know, *ever*. (Lord, Callie would be *so* disappointed in me if she knew I snuck out to sleep in the living room again last night.)

"Well, what is it?"

You can do this, Audrey. I have my story all planned out. I even practiced in front of the mirror. (After Walker left for his workout, obviously. I could never recover from the humiliation if he overheard me.)

"Since this job is only part time and I've been worried about money, I found someone to sublet my place for a few months. So, I'm kind of...staying with Walker."

"You're living together?!"

Once again, her pitch assaults my eardrums, making me wince.

"Just *staying* with him," I repeat, convincing no one.

"Wow. This is *big*. So are you—"

She's cut off mid-sentence by the bedroom door opening behind me. I didn't even hear Walker return, but he's clearly been back long enough to shower, as he's striding into the room wearing nothing but a towel around his waist.

NOTHING.

BUT.

A.

TOWEL.

Walker's eyes go wide, as surprised to find me in here as I am that he's back. Mine widen in return—half in shock, half in awe at his body, and half in silent warning that I'm on a video call with Callie.

Okay, so clearly the sight of Walker shirtless annihilates my ability to do basic math. It's *that* droolworthy.

"O-M-G, is that him?" With the way my phone is propped on the pillows, Callie has a clear view of the door, meaning there's no chance I can play this off like he *didn't* just walk in looking *like that*.

To his immense credit, Walker rallies more quickly than I do. He makes his way over, all casual, appearing completely unconcerned about only wearing a towel. (A towel, I might add, that is barely big enough to cover him up…)

"Sorry to interrupt, babe. Can I say hi?"

"*Yes!*" Callie shouts, adding, "Aim the camera at him more."

Resigned, I do, repositioning my phone so Walker is now fully in the frame. My entire body is acutely aware of him standing behind me, so close I can feel the heat of his bare chest against my back.

"Hey, Callie. I'm Walker. Good to meet you. I've heard so much about you from my girl."

I want to glare at him for the "my girl." He's laying it on a little thick there. She knows we met less than two weeks ago!

"Well, *our* girl only just told me about you, but I can see why she'd want to keep you all to herself."

"*Callie!*" I whisper-hiss. Is she *flirting* with him?

Walker just laughs, displaying his carefree, cocky, *"Oh hey, I'm sex on a stick and I know it"* smile. "She's not the only one. I've been hogging as much of her time as I can."

Then he kisses the top of my head. I can barely feel it, but a stupid dreamy sigh escapes me before I can stop myself. Callie looks similarly swoony.

"I won't crash any more important BFF time," Walker says, oblivious to the shock wave he's just sent through my ovaries. "I'm gonna grab some clothes and then I'll be out of your hair. Talk to ya soon, Callie."

"You take good care of her!" Callie calls as he walks out of the camera's range, but she's obviously too charmed to put any real threat behind the words.

With a series of frantic hand gestures and eyebrow waggling, I silently beseech Callie to contain her reaction until Walker leaves the room. She either misses the message, or ignores it.

"Oh. My. God. *AUDREY!"*

"I know," I whisper, acknowledging her awe at a mere fraction of her volume. Walker hears me anyway—his husky chuckle sends a wave of goosebumps over my skin.

A head covered in unruly ginger hair pops up behind Callie.

"Everythin' good?" Patrick asks. "I ignored the first few screams but thought I'd check in just in case." In his Irish accent, "thought" comes out as "taught."

"Audrey has a boyfriend," Callie exclaims.

My cheeks flush hotter, knowing Walker can hear every word. No doubt he's eavesdropping shamelessly—he's certainly taking his sweet time getting clothes!

"Oh?" Patrick appears fully on the screen at Callie's side. "Hey, Audrey. Cheers."

"Hey, Patrick. And, uh, thanks."

"Do I need ta have a talk with him about treatin' ya well?"

Callie and I both burst out laughing. Patrick is the sweetest, least intimidating man I've ever met, so the idea of him having a *"talk"* with Walker is hysterical. His fair skin reddens, and I watch his lips move as he mumbles something that gets swallowed by our giggling.

"Thanks, though, Patrick. That's sweet," I finally say when we have a hold of ourselves.

"Babe!" Callie turns to her boyfriend, eyes alight like she's sharing the juiciest gossip of the year. "They're *living* together. And he's *hot*. He just walked into the room in a towel, and I think I counted a six pack!"

Patrick and I both frown at her. "He can hear you," I hiss. Behind me, Walker is no longer trying to hide his laughter.

"You know, maybe FaceTime isn't the best way to talk to Audrey," Patrick says. "Voice calls are good enough, yeah?"

His little possessive moment is so cute, Callie gives him a peck on the cheek before patting it with her hand. "I love it when you get jealous, babe, but you're being silly. You know my heart belongs to your handsome ginger self."

Walker comes back over, ditching any pretense that he's not listening.

"Hi, I'm Walker."

"Heya. Patrick," the Irishman responds, polite and friendly as ever, even while ruffled by Callie swooning over Walker's body.

"Hey man, I didn't know Audrey was in here on a call. I won't make a habit of shirtless FaceTime appearances."

Patrick nods while Callie sticks out her bottom lip in disappointment. I roll my eyes at all three of them.

How did this best friend video chat turn into a weird double-date situation?

"I'm going to steal my girlfriend back now," Patrick declares. "Good to see you, Audrey. Walker. Nice to meet ya."

Patrick does that male head nod thing which Walker returns—apparently that move translates internationally.

"Call me soon!" Callie commands, bugged-out eyes screaming that we have a *lot* more to discuss. Then Walker and I are alone staring at a dark screen.

90

I glare up at him.

"It was an accident, really," he insists. But the cocky jerk is grinning, clearly pleased with himself. "That seemed like it went well, though, right?"

I blow out a breath and nod, dropping my phone onto the bed so I can run both hands over my face. "Yeah, I guess."

"See? Nothing to worry about." He gives me a friendly pat on the shoulder—the complete antithesis of that tender kiss to my head from a moment ago—before leaving the bedroom to, one can only hope, get dressed.

EMAIL FROM VICTORIA

From: Victoria Trulette
To: Audrey Mitchell, Walker Garrison
Subject The Intangibility of Intimacy

My dearest protagonists,

Now that you have familiarized yourselves with the pertinent details of each other's lives, we must turn our attentions to familiarity of a more physical nature.

As important as it will be to keep your stories straight and demonstrate knowledge of each other in conversation, it is the *unspoken* that will truly cement your believability as a couple, especially in front of friends and family. We want no underlying sense of discomfort to give away that you were strangers mere days ago! Further, lovers give off an intangible "vibe" born of intimacy, and the people who know you best are the most likely to look beyond surface-level displays and take notice if such a connection is absent.

Becoming comfortable with casual touch in private will make any displays of affection you show in public appear more natural and lend authenticity to your charade. As they say, practice makes perfect!

We'll start small. Today, your assignment is to hold hands for half an hour.

Sincerely,
Victoria

13. The New Cooties

Audrey

The second Walker gets home from work, he proclaims, "I say we do this thing now, just get it over with." His back is turned to me as he peers into the fridge, but I think I hear a muttered *"holding fucking hands…"*

Knowing I am something Walker wants to "get over with" shouldn't fill me with hurt. I'm not exactly thrilled or looking forward to this homework assignment either, but my stupid heart can't help taking his disgruntlement personally. Does he really find me so repulsive?

Beer in hand, Walker plops onto the couch and starts flipping through channels. I follow on leaden feet, mentally cataloging labels of who this man is. (Clearly, I'm in need of the reality check.) I visualize each one as a brick fortifying my protective mental walls.

Coworker. Roommate.

As soon as I sit down, The Beatles "I Want to Hold Your Hand" starts playing from Walker's phone. I can't help my giggle, at which he smirks, proud of himself.

Jokester. Clown.

"Ready?" he asks, cutting off the music.

No. "Sure."

I suspect he's aiming for a smile, but the twist of his lips comes off as a grimace.

We get off to an inauspicious start… Okay, it's disastrously awkward. We fumble, hands flipping back and forth, always somehow out of sync. It takes multiple tries before we finally manage to thread our clumsy fingers together in a comfortable position.

I blow out an unsteady breath, releasing the air I'd been holding during that seemingly interminable fiasco.

Suddenly, we're laughing. I couldn't say which of us starts it because the other follows so quickly it feels simultaneous. Our laughter is more about releasing tension than true amusement, but I do feel a bit better afterward.

"Well, I'd say we flunked that part," Walker observes in his usual blunt manner. "Good thing this is just for participation points, huh?"

I roll my eyes at him. *Jerkface.*

"Seriously, that was awful. I think your awkward thing is starting to rub off on me."

Make that *jerkface with the emotional intelligence of an infant.*

"What can I say? It's the new cooties."

Walker bursts out laughing—for real, this time—my strategic use of humor successfully masking my bruised feelings.

Seems he's not the only one picking up new habits from our association.

Over the next few minutes, we relax, until holding Walker's hand feels comfortable. Our hands almost feel…*natural* together.

I do a mental scan through my memories, trying to recall whether Ethan ever held my hand and coming up blank. I'd certainly remember if it had felt like *this*, right?

"So, when's the last time you held a girl's hand?" I ask to distract myself from more unsettling realizations.

"Damn, I don't even know. Years, probably."

I suppose hand-holding isn't exactly a priority when he's picking up girls in bars. I force down the surge of envy.

Player. Lothario.

"I bet *you* hold hands with all the guys you date."

"Are you calling me a hand-holding slut?" I gasp, channeling Callie's dramatics.

"Maybe. Am I right?"

"Wouldn't you like to know." My bravado is false, of course. I've hardly dated anyone, *ever,* and none in recent memory. But I'm enjoying this playful little exchange. It almost feels like we're flirting for real.

Not. Mine.

Speaking of stupid thoughts...

No matter how hard I try, my focus refuses to stay on the TV. I mean, this is a good episode of *How I Met Your Mother*, but it can't compete when I'm touching Walker Garrison.

Walker's hand is rough, covered in calluses that reflect the kind of man he is: active, capable, powerful, his skills varied but all of a tactile nature. Working on cars, creating artwork using various media, screen printing his shirts... He influences the world around him in a physical manner, and these calluses are the manifestation of that, which makes them kind of beautiful. I don't even mind the abrasive texture against my skin. I actually kind of enjoy it, as well as the comforting warmth of his hand surrounding mine.

Given his height and overall solid frame, it's unsurprising that his hands are so large—there's that thing people say about big hands, and my mind drifts to wondering whether there's really a size correlation...

OH MY GOD, AUDREY, STOP THINKING ABOUT THE SIZE OF WALKER'S PENIS!

He's sitting right next to me, holding my hand, for goodness' sake! *Keep your mind above his waist, you perv.*

Fortunately, his attention is on the show, so he misses the heat that floods my face. *Un*fortunately, stopping my thoughts from straying to inappropriate places is easier said than done, given we're sitting closer than usual for the sake of our assignment. *Much* closer. The heat coming off his body is a tangible presence at my side. I look down at the leg only a breath away from mine; his thighs are so muscular his well-worn jeans have to stretch to accommodate them while sitting. I might even use the word *bulging*, which could also apply to a part of his anatomy a few inches higher that I am decidedly *not* thinking about...

"You okay over there?"

"Oh! Yep." I try to adopt a neutral expression that hopefully says, "I am completely innocent and was *not* just thinking about your penis or squeezing your thigh to see if it's as firm as it looks."

The final twenty minutes pass in the blink of an eye. We both jump a bit at the dreadful squawking when his phone timer goes off. After shaking his newly freed hand dramatically, Walker makes a show of stretching out both arms, as though he's just performed a strenuous activity. I roll my eyes at his antics.

When he changes the channel to watch sports, I use the excuse to escape to the bedroom, needing some alone time to put my head back on straight.

Okay. So, I lost my mind for a bit there. It happens. I don't know where all those thoughts came from, but everyone gets possessed by a sex-starved monster with a big thigh fetish every once in a while, right?

RIGHT?!

That's the explanation I'm going with, because this is *not me*—I don't get crazy, lusty impulses about guys who are out of my league, and certainly not ones I've only known for a couple of days.

It's humiliating, really. We've barely begun this little social experiment, and here I am, already sliding into the role of witless test subject, falling right into the trap Victoria's laid for us.

For his part, Walker seems entirely impervious to our boss's matchmaking machinations. Which makes it all the more crucial that I do *not* let myself get attached. I need to curb these little sprouting feelings, pull the unwelcome things out by their nascent roots before they intrude any further into my heart. And *stat*.

Because, lest we forget... *I. Am. Not. His. Type.*

Time to find some metaphorical gardening shears. If this is my reaction to just holding his hand, I might not survive whatever Victoria throws at us next.

14. This Domestic Shit is Weird

Walker

I took today off from the shop—what's Dad gonna do, fire me?—to move my screen-printing stuff into the new warehouse space I've rented. Though nothing fancy, it's a major upgrade from the corner of our basement where I've been doing my shirt stuff until now, squeezed between the laundry machines and boxes of the landlord's crap. Now I'll be able to take on larger orders and even do multiple at once, especially when all the new equipment I ordered with my first paycheck from Victoria comes in.

After hours of cleaning and hauling boxes, I'm wrecked when I get back to the condo. My skin is sticky from layers of dried sweat, thanks to the warehouse's lack of AC and the mid-September day that apparently decided to dress up as July when it woke up this morning. All I want is a shower and to eat the entire contents of the fridge.

I find Audrey on the couch in the spot I'm coming to think of as "hers," once again with her hair tied into a bun and laptop open in front of her. When she twists in my direction, I see she's also wearing those glasses I like a little too much.

"Hey. How was the move?"

"Fine. All done."

"You like the new space?"

"Yeah. Uh… Did you have a good day?" I force myself to ask. This domestic shit is weird. At home, Luke and I never bother with the *"Hi, honey. How was your day?"* rigamarole— hell, most days, I'm lucky if my brother comes out of his room long enough for me to see him at all.

I try to pay attention while Audrey chatters on about job applications, but now that the shower is mere feet away, it's starting to call my name urgently.

"I've also been looking at your shirts."

What? She went through my clothes? I mean, we're sharing a dresser, so it's not like she doesn't have access, but…that's weird, right?

"They're really amazing, Walker."

She seems to have missed the *"Oh shit, is my fake girlfriend a major whack job with a clothing fetish?"* look on my face, because she's smiling at me brightly.

Oh, my *shirts*. As in my screen-printing business. *Right.*

Damn, I need food. And about a gallon of H2O, since my dumb ass forgot to bring a water bottle with me today.

"I've been scrolling through your Facebook page for like an hour now. I'm really impressed. I had no idea you could do *this*."

I shuffle my feet, not knowing how to respond. From the way she's waving at her computer, I think she might even be on my page right now, which makes me feel weirdly vulnerable. My artwork feels kind of personal. I mean, something can't be *that* personal if you're putting it on shirts people will walk around wearing, but still.

Audrey hasn't stopped talking, her eyes lit up with excitement.

"Is it only custom orders, or do you have some generic designs you sell? I couldn't find a website, but I remember you saying you're working on that? The engagement on your

Facebook page is impressive. Do you use Instagram? What about Etsy?"

My head is spinning more and more by the second. When she pauses for breath, I try to recall what all she's just asked me.

"Uh…yeah, it's just custom orders. And no, I don't do girly shit like Instagram and Etsy." My lip curls at the thought.

Her frown is disapproving. "It's not '*girly*' to put your product in front of more potential customers, which is what using those platforms would do for you."

I've been standing at the edge of the living room, ready to make my getaway. Seeing that she doesn't look anywhere near done with this conversation, I drag my weary ass over to the couch and sit, staying near the edge so my grimy clothes make as little contact with the expensive furniture as possible.

"How do you get orders now?" Audrey asks, her perkiness the exact opposite of my dead-on-my-feet exhaustion.

"Mostly referrals, friends of friends, that kind of thing. Sometimes through Facebook messages."

"It's really impressive how well you've done with such limited infrastructure."

I bristle, hackles immediately rising at any hint of condescension. "It's just a side gig. I haven't had real time or money to put into it."

She shrinks away from my biting tone. "I know. It was a compliment. You're going to be a huge success once you have that time and money."

Well, that appeases the snarling, prideful beast in me a little, though all of this is really rattling that fucker's cage.

"I do think you should at least look into Etsy and Shopify. It's a cheap way to spread your reach without investing in SEO."

"I don't know," I say when she keeps staring at me expectantly, as if I'm going to make an Etsy account right here and now. "I like the art, coming up with the designs, working with the people to figure out what they need. I'm good at that—and the actual printing. All this other stuff…social media, marketing, whatever, seems like a waste of time."

"I understand why it may seem that way, but it's really crucial to growing a small business in today's market. Oh! Have you ever looked into print-on-demand sites like Zazzle or Society6? They wouldn't bring in a lot of revenue but might be a nice passive income stream."

She scoots closer and angles her computer screen toward me. It's cool to see her all fired up like this—or it would be, if I had any clue what the fuck she's talking about.

"See? With one click, you can list your design on a shirt, pillow, phone case, and laptop skin. We can do a little market research and choose a few designs to try. You could even print some inventory to sell directly through your site once you have one. Speaking of which, Callie is a web designer. I'll see if she can fit you into her schedule this month…"

"Whoa, whoa. Hold up."

Audrey's talking so fast, spitting out all these ideas, clicking through websites and pointing at stuff like I should be following what she's doing, and that dizzy sensation just keeps getting worse. My chest is tight, my struggling lungs as overwhelmed as the rest of me. I feel like my business just got an overhaul in the last two minutes, and it's suddenly transformed into something I don't understand and have no control over.

"I didn't agree to any of this shit. It's my business. I make the decisions."

"Of course. I'm only trying to help."

"Yeah, well, I didn't ask for help." *Fuck. Give a guy a minute!*

"Okay. I'm sorry." She's not meeting my eyes anymore, and she's lost the animated demeanor. She sounds like she might even be on the verge of tears.

Goddammit. I didn't mean to make her cry. There's a headache brewing behind my temples, a mixture of physical exhaustion and the nagging tension of impending guilt.

Unable to deal, I stalk into the bathroom without another word.

Audrey's Journal

Dear Victoria,

I suppose you already know what happened earlier from the recordings. I'm sorry. I doubt your goals for this project include having to listen to me embarrass myself over and over.

Honestly, I feel so stupid right now.

When Walker got home, I was just *so* excited to tell him how amazing I think his work is. Instead, everything in my head came out in one big rush of nerdy babbling. I basically word-vomited all over him.

I don't blame him for not wanting my opinions. Who am *I* to give *him* business advice? I'm just some girl with a communications degree who wasn't even good enough at it to get a job in the field.

I really was just trying to help. Instead, I overstepped and made him mad, and in the process, I let my stupid feelings get hurt.

(He didn't have to be such a jerk about it, though.)

Audrey

* * *

Walker's Journal

Chicks, man. Can't live with them… Nope, that's it.

They're just so…crazy. Like, you start getting comfortable and thinking they're maybe kind of cool, and then they get these ideas and try to take over. Out of nowhere, they get all up in your face, talking a mile a minute, throwing all this shit at you that makes perfect sense to them but really needs to come with a decoder ring or something.

And they do it at the worst times, like when you've just come back from a long-ass day of moving, so you're not in the best mindset to, you know, overhaul your entire business *right that second*. Especially when you've only understood maybe half of the shit they said.

Then when you shut them down, they look crushed, like you just told them Santa Claus isn't real or that leggings are going out of style. And yeah, maybe that comes out harsher than it should because of the dehydration, and having that much stuff fly at you all at once short-circuits your ability to tone down your inner asshole.

So now, I'm the bad guy, when all I wanted was to take a frickin' shower!

15. Axes. And...*Alcohol?*

NEW MESSAGE IN GROUP TEXT

VICTORIA: Time to take your relationship ruse public! Tonight shall be a soft debut, an opportunity to practice among strangers before you face the scrutiny of your loved ones. Walker, I want you to plan this date night. I look forward to seeing what you come up with. Audrey, you'll have your chance another time. Don't forget to wear your microphones!

Walker

I'm ninety percent sure this little assignment is Victoria's way of punishing me for being a jerk to Audrey.

Do I deserve it? Yeah, probably.

By the time I went to bed last night, I'd cooled off enough to acknowledge (at least to myself) I'd fucked up. I was way too harsh with Audrey, who's sensitive about shit to begin with. It's not her fault the whole thing hit on a particularly sore spot of mine—feeling ignorant, less-than, unqualified. So, I did what I always do, and I lashed out.

All the same, apologizing has never been a strength of mine. I decided to just give her some space and hope she'd get over it by morning. (Yeah, it was a faulty strategy.)

At least I know her sneaking out of bed to sleep on the couch had nothing to do with me being a dick yesterday since she's done the same thing every night this week. (And what the hell is up with that? Is sharing a bed with me really so terrible?)

Now, we're supposed to go on our first date when my "girlfriend" has been avoiding me all day. Audrey's barely even looked at me, and the few times we have interacted, she's been so goddamn polite it's almost robotic.

Her behavior could read as pissed off, but my gut says it's far worse—she's *hurt*.

It's official: Robo Audrey is worse than Shy Audrey or Stabby Audrey. Where's Hand Walker His Ass Audrey? I'd prefer that to the freeze-out.

Acting like a dick isn't new to me, and Audrey is definitely not the first person whose feelings I've hurt. The thing is, I can't remember it ever bothering me this much before. Guilt's riding me hard; the urge to fix things has my insides twisted up worse than bad seafood.

Now I have a few hours to come up with a kickass date that will earn me some brownie points and get me back in good with both Victoria and Audrey.

Who knew a fake girlfriend could be as much work as a real one?

* * *

I always feel weird sitting in Freddy's back seat like some kind of privileged prick, but I'm not about to turn down free transportation—especially since the part of Somerville we're headed to isn't a cakewalk to get to via the T.

106

The vibe between Audrey and me on the drive is still a little stiff, but we're slowly inching back to our normal bantering thing.

"You won't tell me where we're going?" she asks me again.

"Nope. It's a surprise."

"Careful, you're starting to sound like Victoria."

"I consider that a compliment."

Audrey can accuse me of pulling Victoria-style dramatics all she likes, but the truth is that I'm not sure how she's going to react to what I've planned, so I figure the best strategy is to wait until we're almost there to tell her. That way, she won't have time to overthink it. If she just keeps an open mind and gives it a chance, I think she'll enjoy herself. I know I'm sure as hell going to.

Traffic's a pain as always, but our slow progress has me way twitchier than usual—something to do with being stuck in this back seat alone with a girl I am trying really hard to keep my eyes off.

Audrey *showed up* for our date tonight. She looks hot and it's confusing the hell out of me. Which I suspect was her goal—that this is some kind of diabolical female retribution thing, and she got ready tonight with the specific intention of punishing me for being an asshole.

As a torture tactic, it's fucked up, but effective. Especially when you can look but can't touch. (At least in private, as Miss Priss made very clear that first night.) She's shoving my face in what I'm missing. Like, *"Check out how bangable I am, you big, dumb brute."*

And damn, but she sure does look bangable. First off, she's wearing jeans. While I've seen her in leggings and it's a good view, everyone knows denim can do magical things for a woman's ass—and let's just say Audrey's ass plus those jeans equals some crazy sexy hocus-pocus.

Her shirt is simple, but unlike most of the tops I've seen her in so far, it hugs her form. Dark green, with long sleeves, it dips in a subtle V neck with a slit and buttons down the middle. Maybe I'm more sexually deprived than I'd realized, because those little buttons are driving me crazy. I can't decide what I want more: to button up that top one for my own sanity, or to pop open the second and find out how much more skin would be revealed.

Yeah, I'm totally losing it. Fantasizing about a glimpse of cleavage? When the guys and I go out, we're usually surrounded by women who'd make what Audrey is wearing right now look like a nun's habit.

Audrey doesn't usually wear much in the way of makeup, and although tonight she's clearly got a bit more on than usual, it's still classy. Just enough to emphasize her sweet features and make her pink lips glisten. Lips which I've never specifically noticed before but are now warring for my attention along with that *goddamn button*.

Worst (best?) of all, she's wearing her hair down for the first time since we met. Thick, wavy locks fall past her shoulders, a mixture of light brown and dark gold. It's the kind of hair that gives a guy ideas. My fingers tingle in anticipation of how it would feel to grab a fistful and wrap it around my hand, use that grip to pull her head toward mine so I could take her mouth, or direct it somewhere lower...

Fuck me. See what I'm saying? This is evil female magic, right here.

"Walker?"

Audrey's voice grabs my attention. Shit. How long have I been staring at her in silence with my mind drifting into Inappropriateville (Population: Me)?

"Yeah?"

She's looking at me like I've lost my marbles, no hint of the female satisfaction I'd expect, given I've fallen right into her trap. Making me wonder if it even was a trap in the first place.

The girl does realize she's smoking hot, right?

"Freddy said we're getting close. Are you going to tell me what we're doing now?"

When I do, her reaction is hilarious.

"Axes. And...*alcohol*?" She sounds appalled.

"It is an ax throwing place, and yes, they have a bar."

"Ax. Throwing," she repeats, like she can't wrap her mind around what she just heard and is looking for me to correct her. I don't.

"Throwing. *Axes?*" It's cute that she thinks switching the word order will change anything.

"Yes. They have these coaches who teach you what to do, and then you get to aim for targets. It's kind of like darts, but way more awesome." When she continues gaping at me in horror, I add, "It's legit, I swear. It's a chain. They have locations all over the country."

"No one in their right mind would let me throw an ax. Especially with alcohol around."

"You'll be fine."

"Is this your sneaky way of trying to kill me and make it look like an accident?"

That has me laughing even harder.

"That's not a *no*."

"It's not a no, because that's so crazy I decided I wouldn't even respond to it."

A few minutes later, we're signing liability waivers and getting our hands stamped for entry.

The place is hipster as fuck, but I don't hate it. The building is a renovated mechanic's shop that's still mostly cement inside.

One long wall is covered in lanes where the ax throwing happens. Walls made of reclaimed pallets delineate them, with a ledge at the head of each lane separating the people waiting their turn from those who are throwing foot-long hatchets at targets crafted from more unfinished wood. On the opposite side is the "bar," an open area with picnic tables where people sit drinking trendy craft beers and canned cocktails off the chalkboard menu.

I get the cheapest beer option, which is still criminal—no $2 Bud Light here; damn I miss Murphy's, my usual haunt. Audrey spends forever deliberating before choosing a fruit-flavored alcoholic seltzer. (Like I said, this place is so fucking hipster it's ridiculous.)

Conversation is basically impossible, between the music and the dull chatter of people in the bar and waiting at the lanes, not to mention the constant thwacking of blades meeting wood and the shouting of enthusiastic employees MCing the action while making sure no one fucks up and hacks off a finger. Audrey's eyes are huge as she takes it all in, and not in excitement. But hey, she's not actively giving me the cold shoulder at the moment.

It's not long before we're called up and told we'll be sharing a lane with three other couples—also walk-ins, apparently on their own date nights.

I throw an arm around Audrey's shoulder, pulling her in even closer when she stiffens, and say in her ear, "We're in public, which means it's showtime. You ready to convince all these people you love me?"

Her hair smells good—coconut, maybe? I let myself linger an extra moment with my nose buried in the strands, breathing it in.

Dammit. I *really* need to get laid. If I weren't so hard up, I wouldn't be struggling to keep my dick from getting hard—or up—because of some shampoo. Too bad the contract I signed means the girl beside me is my only chance of getting some any time soon, and she made it all too clear that will not be happening. Even though I *know* she's attracted to me. I haven't forgotten the incident with my abs at the kayaking place... And yes, maybe I've taken to walking around the condo shirtless more than necessary, just to enjoy her reaction.

As an experiment, I casually brush Audrey's hair to the side, letting my hand graze her skin once her neck is bared. My smile is dark with satisfaction when she shivers. *That's what I thought.*

She shoots me a warning glare before returning her attention to the plaid-wearing staff member who is giving instructions. My arm stays around Audrey, and I even let myself run my fingers through her hair a bit—Victoria would expect us to put on a good show for our first official outing, right? Never mind that none of the real couples are getting their PDA on.

I pull Audrey more tightly to me so I can rest my chin on top of her head. We're close enough that I feel it when her heartbeat speeds up.

When our coach slash cheerleader divides us into two smaller groups to start practicing throwing, Audrey takes advantage and pulls away from me. I'm not sure what's flustered her more, the PDA or having to throw an ax.

As it turns out, Audrey's not half bad at throwing, even though she looks terrified and she does this flinching thing after the ax leaves her hands. Every. Single. Time. It's kind of hilarious and hella entertaining.

"I know you're nervous, but it's not gonna bite you!" our coach yells, unaware he's embarrassing Audrey even more by drawing attention to her.

"It's not a boomerang," I chime in after her next throw followed by full-body recoil. "It won't fly back at you."

She rolls her eyes at me where I'm leaning on the barrier wall, waiting my turn to throw. "I know!"

"Then why are you doing that?"

"I don't *know*," she whines. It's childish but kind of adorable. "I'm not *trying* to. I can't help it."

"What do you think is gonna happen?" our group cheerleader asks.

"It's just a reflex or something." It's seriously amusing watching Audrey restrain the urge to roll her eyes again, far too polite to sass or whine at a stranger, like she did with me.

"That target can take it, honey. Now, go again."

[DAY 9]

16. "You're a Douchebag, Walker."

Walker

"I can't believe I beat you!"

Audrey skips through the crosswalk as we leave the ax throwing place. It's hard to hold on to my sore pride over losing the final tournament when she's so damn proud of herself. She really did smoke me, making it to the last round before losing to some bearded guy in flannel who looked like he throws real axes on the regular…in the woods. At bears.

Honestly, tonight was a lot of fun. I surprised even myself when I suggested we grab one more drink across the street before Freddy picks us up. Equally surprising, Audrey agreed—a win I'm claiming, even if those three fruity seltzers had a hand in it. I'm just glad that ice wall she put up earlier is finally gone.

She's in a good tipsy place right now, but I am going to make sure it's *only* one more drink. I haven't forgotten how she drank herself into oblivion trying to keep up with me last weekend. So damn stubborn and strong-willed, such a surprising combination with her awkwardness and innate innocence, yet somehow it all adds up to…Audrey. A girl I'm beginning to think is not at all who I'd expected her to be.

We're able to find seats in the back room of the bar. I tamp down a grimace at the price of Audrey's cocktail, ordering myself a draft beer. We push our stools closer and lean in so we can hear each other over the music. The scent of her hair hits me again, and the low lighting does nothing to dim the brightness of her eyes.

True story: happiness is a good look on Audrey Mitchell.

If this were any other date, and she were any other girl, I'd lean in those extra couple of inches and kiss her right now.

The fuck? Yeah, I'm going to pretend that thought didn't just cross my mind. Shit is complicated enough as it is.

"So, you done being mad at me?" I ask. No better way to kill an unwanted mood than to remind a girl you're a prick.

"I'm not mad at you," she says. I lift a brow, calling bullshit. *"I'm not!"*

I guess I shouldn't be surprised she's gonna make this difficult. I scoot just a bit closer.

"Listen, I get it. I was a dick. I probably deserved the freeze-out today. I'm just asking if we're good now."

"I wasn't...*pissed.*" She's so damn cute, stumbling over that word like it's something a hell of a lot dirtier. "I was embarrassed." She mumbles the last word against the rim of her glass, almost like she hopes I won't hear her.

No two ways about it—there's nothing cute about making a girl look as despondent as she does right now. *Damn, I am a Grade A douchebag.*

"Hey." The word comes out a little rough, but it gets her eyes back up to mine.

I swallow and remind myself this girl's too soft for the crude way I usually blunder through communication. That's the bottom line with us, isn't it? She's a polished stone that has no business rubbing up against my raw edges. Too bad she's stuck with me.

114

"You've got no reason to be embarrassed. It was solid of you to speak up with ideas that could help me, especially stuff I wouldn't know because you learned it in a class. Not your fault I wasn't in a good place to hear it. Don't take that on, yeah?"

She still looks uncertain, a hell of a lot less confident than a few minutes ago when she was crowing over her victory, so I try to get her back to that happy place by asking about her job search. But the new subject only seems to deflate her more. If I couldn't tell by her body language that she's forcing enthusiasm for the personal assistant interviews she's got scheduled, all I'd have to do is ask the poor lime in her drink, which she's now pulverized with her straw.

"Why aren't you applying for marketing jobs, like what you studied?"

Then Audrey starts talking about how she's not good enough for the jobs she actually wants. I find myself getting more pissed off by the second, watching the vibrant woman I saw earlier slipping further and further away. Finally, I can't take listening to any more.

"Fuck that." I think we're both a little stunned by the intensity of my reaction. "You love that shit, and you're good at it. Even I know that, just from hearing you talk about it for five minutes." She came up with all those ideas for my business in less than a day!

She looks unconvinced. I wonder how much of that insecurity is thanks to my behavior last night, and I kind of want to kick my own damn ass.

"I mean it. Stop selling yourself short or saying you're not good enough. Anyone who makes you feel that way, just tell them to go fuck themselves."

The sound she makes is somewhere between a cough, a laugh, and a snort. I'm pleased to see the sassy sparkle in her eyes as she silently challenges me to recognize my own hypocrisy.

"You need to stand up for yourself. Even to me. I'm serious—you should have told me off last night. Just said, '*Shut the fuck up, Walker. You're being a douchebag.*'"

Her quiet giggle and slow smile make that fist in my chest that's been there this whole day finally ease completely.

"Go ahead, say it," I goad, wanting more of that smile. "'*You're a douchebag, Walker.*'"

Her laughter sounds like victory.

"Okay. Now talk to me about Instagram. But use small words."

17. The Pillow Wall

Audrey

I lie awake staring at the ceiling, acutely aware of every rustle of the sheets and slight movement in my periphery as Walker's chest rises and falls. As the minutes crawl on, my mind, helpful as always, conjures up the tick-tick-tick sound of a clock's second hand. The mental soundtrack grates on my already tender nerves.

After all these days, shouldn't I be past this foolishness? Apparently not, because I haven't managed to sleep beside Walker all week. Since the surprisingly restful night I spent on the couch after our whiskey confessional, the promise of easy sleep has drawn me back to the living room. Each night I try to stick it out, but it looks like I'm going to lose that battle once again.

Pillow in hand, my toes have just touched the floor when I'm stopped short by Walker—who I thought was fast asleep. *Dang.*

"Where are you going?"

"Bathroom," I whisper, clutching my pillow tighter to my chest in hopes he won't notice it.

"Bullshit."

I squint against the sudden flood of light from the lamp on his nightstand. Although he's fuzzy without the aid of my contacts or glasses, I can tell he's sitting up, facing me. In the halo cast from the lamp, I can make out the silhouette of his hair sticking up in all directions.

"You're gonna go sleep on the couch again."

My jaw drops open. I thought I was being so stealthy!

"You really didn't think I'd notice you've been sneaking out of bed all week?" I can almost *hear* his raised eyebrow.

Oh man. I am so freaking *busted.* I slide back into the bed and sit against the headboard with my knees pulled up to my chest, feeling like a child caught misbehaving.

"Do I snore or something?" Walker asks.

"No, nothing like that. I've just been having trouble sleeping."

"With me."

"Well, yes. But, no. I mean, it's not *you.* I'm just used to sleeping alone, so this is weird for me. I can't seem to relax."

"It's weird for me, too."

"Really? I guess I figured you'd have a lot more experience with, you know...co-ed sleepovers." Even the allusion to sex has me stumbling over my words.

"There you go assuming stuff about me again, princess."

Oh no, he's busted out the "p" word. I must have struck a nerve.

"No, I wasn't... I mean..." How do I explain without fully baring my insecurities by admitting that *anyone* would have more experience than me?

"I mean, you're probably right about me having logged more miles than you in the sheets, but I wouldn't say there's been a whole lot of *sleeping.* If you catch my drift."

I bite back the retort on the tip of my tongue, that his drift was so obvious even the people down the street caught it.

118

"It seems like you've been sleeping just fine," I say, opting for the high road.

"I've always been an easy sleeper. Doesn't mean this won't take some getting used to, for both of us. If you'd actually give us the *chance* to get used to it."

I hope the lamplight is too low for him to see my shame-scorched cheeks.

"Especially because our contract mentions sharing the bed, so if Victoria finds out, it could mean a cut to our paychecks."

I gasp. "I didn't even think about that!"

"She hasn't brought it up and I'm sure she would if she knew, so I figure we're good. But let's not risk it anymore, yeah?"

"Yes, of course. I'm *so* sorry."

I'm so disappointed in myself for not considering the implications of my actions.

"Now, we've gotta fix this. How do we make you comfortable? What can I do?"

Well, there goes my breath. Walker's dedication to his "funny tough guy" persona is impressive; he's a pro at pushing people away with crude jokes and constantly testing boundaries, like he's daring anyone and everyone to write him off. But then he has these little lapses, moments when I get a glimpse beneath that prickly surface, of a good man with a kind heart, who is fun but also attentive and supportive, as he was on our date tonight. *That* man is more dangerous to me by far, because I like him a little too much for my own good—or his.

Truly, for both of our sakes, it would be better if Walker keeps *that* guy buried for the next fifty-some days. It will be much easier to remember this thing is fake if he sticks to being crude and antagonistic.

"You don't need to do anything. I'll get over it." *Somehow.*

He startles me by jumping up and leaving the room, returning a moment later with his arms full of what I recognize as the extra linens from the hall closet.

Dumping them on the bed, he proceeds to build a wall down the center using pillows and blankets. Since he seems to have a plan, I deem it most helpful to stay out of his way, so I just sit back and watch. The glow from the lamp highlights parts of his face, while casting others in even deeper shadow, making him into a Picasso painting of angles and blocks of colors paired with my nearsightedness.

"There. Now you can sleep without worrying about me coming over there and taking advantage of you."

"I wasn't worried about *that*," I cry, horrified that he thinks I've been sleeping on the couch because I'm scared of him.

"Jesus, I'm teasing. You've gotta lighten up, Mitchie."

"Veto." The ridiculous nickname routine is so familiar by now, the denial pops out automatically, though for once, my usual annoyance is nowhere to be found.

"Thank you, Walker." I'm almost teary-eyed over his touching gesture.

"It's just a pillow wall," he grumbles. Goodness knows we wouldn't want anyone to acknowledge him being sweet!

Once the lamp clicks off and we're settled on our respective sides of the impressive wall Walker built, I whisper into the darkness, "Hey, Walker… You're not *always* a douchebag."

His half-amused, half-annoyed grunt makes me smile.

Just for tonight, I'll allow myself to take comfort in this side of him. Tomorrow, I will shore my defenses back up with all of the very valid reasons I have *not* to fall for Walker Garrison.

Despite being mostly symbolic, Walker's pillow wall actually allows me to relax. I close my eyes and, for the first time since we started this adventure, I sleep a full night in our bed.

DIRECT MESSAGE THREAD: VICTORIA AND SIOBHAN

V = Victoria Trulette

S = Siobhan McMahon, fellow romance author and dear friend

S: How was week one of your experiment?

V: For the most part, I stepped back and observed how things developed between them naturally, with only a few assignments as a nudge to get to know each other.

V: I confess, I'd hoped for more progress by now. In the books, forced proximity spurs intimacy quite quickly! Alas, there were no fireworks—except for a few interpersonal conflicts that pushed them apart rather than together.

S: Well, part of the goal is to test reality against fiction! Romance characters tend to jump into bed faster than most of the real people I know.

V: A fair point. Fiction certainly skewed my expectations regarding the power of "only one bed."

S: What about the faking?

V: They went on their first public date last night. Faking their relationship in front of strangers is hardly a challenge, but you know as well as I that the act of faking is less important to the novel than the situations created by usage of the trope as a plot device. Last night, I believe the shared experience bonded them, and it was beneficial to spend time together outside of their daily routine. In the end, what I truly want is for them to fall in love.

S: Yes, but we also know forcing them to feign feelings can spark genuine ones, especially when the performance requires physical demonstration.

V: What we really need are some scenes where they meet with friends and family.

S: As for the intimacy, you gave them a week, and proximity alone hasn't done the job. It's time to start pushing. They're not being paid to live rent-free in a nice downtown flat.

V: Indeed. The next phase begins now.

[CONFIDENTIAL PROJECT RECORDS]
DAY 10

EMAIL FROM VICTORIA

From: Victoria Trulette

To: Audrey Mitchell, Walker Garrison

Subject: A Date with Dr. Smith

Hello, my dears!

Please come to my house at 4:00 PM tomorrow, as I have arranged an appointment for you with Dr. Jenny Smith. Dr. Smith is an old friend of mine whose specialty is counseling couples, and she has agreed to lend her expertise to the social experiment I am conducting as research for my next novel.

I told her no details about our experiment save the pertinent lines of your contract which consent to recording your sessions. She does NOT know your relationship is fake. Your challenge is to ensure she remains none the wiser on that front.

Love,

Victoria

PS: For the sake of credibility, I informed her that you have been together for six months.

18. Couple's Therapy?!

Audrey

Arriving at Victoria's house for our appointment with Walker by my side is a relief, his bulk a tangible reminder that I won't be facing this alone. Funny how I find his presence comforting, when there have been so many times over the last ten days when it was anything but.

Something shifted between us on our date the other night, for the better. Definitely not an outcome I could have expected when I started that day so embarrassed I could barely look at him. However, at some point between popping open my second can of spiked seltzer at the ax throwing place and when I fell asleep on my side of Walker's pillow wall, we settled into a comfortable truce, one that could almost be called a tentative beginning to friendship.

Yesterday, we even sat down and talked about his business. Our meeting was surprisingly productive, and we've already made plans to continue collaborating. All without drama.

So, at least for today, my fake boyfriend and I breach the brownstone's front door as allies.

Victoria isn't home, so her assistant Matilda greets us at the door and tells us Dr. Smith is already waiting for us upstairs in the office.

(I feel nothing that bears the slightest resemblance to jealousy when Walker flashes Matilda a flirtatious grin I've never seen before, one he apparently saves for pretty girls who attract his attention without a contractual obligation or monetary incentive. I'm also unaffected, hovering off to the side with nothing to contribute while they banter about football and the Patriots. Nope, completely fine over here.)

It's jarring to see an unfamiliar woman seated at Victoria's desk. Dr. Smith and Victoria appear to be around the same age, but that's where their similarities end. Unlike Victoria's dark red bob, Dr. Smith's hair is shoulder-length and blond. And where Victoria's fashion aesthetic might be called "chic artist with a bohemian flair," Dr. Smith's is "tailored successful businesswoman" from head to toe.

As Walker and I take our usual seats in front of the desk, Dr. Smith introduces herself—encouraging us to call her Dr. Jenny or Jenny, unaware Walker would have taken that liberty regardless of the invitation—then tells us a bit about her background, how since receiving her doctorate in psychology, she's focused on working with couples.

"I can't believe Vickie sent us to fucking *marriage counseling*," Walker mutters, not quite low enough for our new therapist to miss.

"I gather your primary reason for being here is Victoria's experiment?"

"Victoria is the *only* reason I'm here," Walker says.

I wince, but the woman across from us looks neither surprised nor offended. Apparently, she also possesses whatever makes Victoria immune to Walker's antagonism... If only I could bottle some of that up for myself!

"What?" Walker asks me, catching my look of disapproval. "It's true. We're here because Vickie sent us. Should I have made up some big problem with our relationship?"

Perhaps we should have strategized before this appointment. As it is, we'll have to improvise, meaning I have little choice but to follow Walker's lead. (Lord help me.)

"No, the truth is good." *Oh, the irony!* "You could be more polite about it, though."

"Sorry, babe."

"That was a great example of healthy communication," Jenny praises—clearly not realizing Walker's apology was seventy percent sarcastic, and thirty percent opportunistic, as he's now trapped me into playing along with the nickname he knows I hate.

"While I know you're not here by choice, you may thank Victoria for this someday. Counseling is most effective *before* a relationship is in crisis, although, unfortunately, most of my clients don't come to me until they've reached that point."

I can only hope my expression conveys less skepticism than Walker's.

"I understand you've recently moved in together?" Jenny asks next. "How is that going?"

We discuss some of the ups and downs of cohabitation. (I was an only child with a single parent; sharing a bathroom with a man is an adjustment, to say the least.)

Once she's lulled us into a false sense of security, Jenny announces, "Now I'd like to try a communication exercise I use with many of my clients. This is a form of role-play."

"Oh, so you're one of those kinky sex docs, huh? I gotta warn you, that's not really Audrey's thing," Walker quips…because *of course he does.*

I don't even try to suppress my glare.

"This exercise is actually about *empathy*." Jenny's tone is even, but there's a subtle reprimand beneath her words. Walker looks legitimately chastened. She just put him in his place so effortlessly! That's it; the woman is my new hero. "It's about putting yourself in each other's shoes. I'm going to ask questions, and I want you to respond as your partner. Please turn and face each other."

Jenny gestures to me, once we've repositioned our chairs. "How are you today, *Walker*?"

I pitch my voice as low as I can manage. "I don't want to be here."

Walker snorts at my attempted "man voice" (and perhaps my accurate statement).

"That's understandable," Jenny replies to *Walker*. "So, how are you feeling?"

"I'm, uh, uncomfortable."

She nods and turns to the real Walker. "*Audrey,* how are *you* feeling today?"

"Hi," Walker says, his faux-female voice a hundred times more horrible than my male one. *"I'm Audrey."*

"I do *not* sound like that!" I cry. Admittedly, my voice comes out far shriller than usual, undermining my righteous indignation.

"How about moving forward, you use your own voices and focus on saying the *words* as your partner?" our therapist suggests calmly.

Walker's agreement is accompanied by a petulant pout.

"Let's try that again. *Audrey*, how are you today?"

Deprived of his comedic diversion, Walker is uncharacteristically lost for words.

"*Walker* says he doesn't want to be here and feels uncomfortable. What about you?" Jenny prompts.

"Yeah, I'm uncomfortable and don't want to be here either. But I'm too polite to say that and I don't like disappointing people, so I'll smile and only say things I think you want to hear."

Dr. Jenny's lips twitch in repressed amusement.

"Would Audrey actually say those words?"

"Whoops, thought we were mind reading. If you just want what she'd *say*, then it would be something like, '*I think this will be an interesting opportunity.*'"

Walker slips back into his terrible falsetto at the end. I don't know if Jenny is delivering one of her quelling glances, because I'm too busy gaping at him to protest. Where did that insightful answer come from? Because he is right on the first point, and the latter is *totally* something I would say.

I feel *seen*. It's not necessarily a pleasant sensation.

"Excellent. Let's continue…"

Walker's Journal

V —

I've got to say, I'm disappointed in you. I'd have figured your lady balls were big enough that you'd at least stick around to watch the carnage after throwing us to the wolves. If you were a dude, and not the person behind my paychecks, I might even call it a dick move.

We killed it, though, don't worry. No way the doc thought we were anything but a normal, low-key dysfunctional couple. Lucky dysfunction comes naturally to us, huh?

Just between you and me—is Jenny a *real* therapist, or is this like the movie where that one chick has her friend pretend she's a shrink? I remember watching it with my ex and feeling bad for Matthew McConaughey. But after all of this, I think that guy and I could swap notes over a beer. Maybe he's based on some poor real-life sucker who was hard up for cash too.

W

Comment added by Victoria Trulette: Dr. Smith is very much a "real" therapist. I'm sure she would be more than happy to provide you with her credentials at your next appointment if you ask. However, I am impressed by the *How to Lose a Guy in Ten* Days reference. An excellent example from the modern romantic comedy film canon.

Reply by Walker Garrison: I'll take your word for it. (Please don't tell Jenny I asked.)

Reply by Walker Garrison: As for the movie, I'll just say that at 19 I was willing to put UP with a lot, when the result involved a girl putting OUT.

Reply by Victoria Trulette: Surely since the age of nineteen you've matured greatly and could claim no such thing at present.

Reply by Walker Garrison: This is the exact kind of situation those old white dudes were thinking about when they came up with the Fifth Amendment.

19. Inner Cuddleslut

NEW MESSAGE IN GROUP TEXT

VICTORIA: Today's assignment is to cuddle for thirty minutes to further build on your physical comfort with each other.

WALKER: Can you define "cuddling," Vickie? I might need an instruction manual. Or you could draw us a diagram!

VICTORIA: I am confident you'll figure out it.

Walker

In my experience, when it comes to cuddling, there are two kinds of girls.

First, you've got the naturals. These chicks are like puppies; when it's comfy time, they crawl right on up and curl themselves around you without a second thought, getting their snuggle on—and yeah, that shit can be nice.

On the flip side are the ones who have ultimately turned me off cuddling entirely. There's no way of telling which kind a girl will be ahead of time; she may be sexy as hell and know exactly how to use her body with finesse when it comes to getting sweaty and getting off, but as soon as the fucking is over and it's cuddle time, that same two-legged, two-armed coital goddess transforms into a clumsy multitentacled squid creature. Suddenly, there are limbs flailing everywhere—arms flopping, legs kicking, fingers grasping and poking—dozens of knees and elbows materialize to assault your softest spots, including those manly bits she was just treating so well. Something as simple as spooning in bed or hunkering down on the couch for a movie becomes a feat of endurance and survival.

Like I said, it's real hard to peg which girls are which just by looking at them, but at the risk of sounding like a dick—you know, more than usual—I've got a gut feeling Audrey is going to fall into the squid camp. Let's be real; the girl could make breathing awkward. It's hard to imagine she's about to bust out some smooth moves she's been reserving for snuggles.

You can hardly blame me for being a little on edge all day, knowing what's on tonight's agenda. Now it's "go time," and I'm trying not to openly cringe as I anticipate the next thirty minutes. I click blindly through streaming movie options, psyching myself up as if for battle.

Suffice to say, I'm thrown for a serious loop when Audrey crawls onto the sofa and tucks herself right up under my arm, like this is something we've done hundreds of times. Her head goes on my chest and one arm curls around my middle, and it feels…simple. Comfortable. Natural. Decidedly more puppy than squid. *Huh.*

"Is this okay?" Audrey whispers against my pec. (Which can't be the most comfortable pillow—I've been keeping up my reps so I don't fall too behind for the next time I lift with Luke, and these bad boys are rock hard.) "Walker?"

Shit, now *I've* made it weird. She sounds cautious and unsure, clearly worried my silence means she's doing something wrong, when the exact opposite is true.

"Yeah, pumpkin, this is good. We're way better at this than hand-holding, huh?"

She snort-laughs and vetoes the nickname (as expected), but with her pressed up against me like this, I can feel the tension easing from her muscles. *Fuckup neutralized.*

Opening credits scroll across the screen as we hit play on our movie. Audrey relaxes more of her weight into me, but I'm still holding myself carefully, my guard up, not trusting how well this is going. She starts to shift position, and I instantly brace, sure this is it, when the flailing and eye-gouging and ball-crushing commence. But...nothing happens. A minute passes, and then another, and Audrey shows no sign of imminently endangering either one of us. I peek down at the girl sprawled across me. Confirmed: just the two arms and two legs.

Crazier still, this feels...*good.* At the very least, I'd have expected it to be weird in a normal, non-tentacle squid creature way.

Yet right now on this couch, Little Miss Audrey is cuddling the ever-loving shit out of me, and I am *into it.*

Sure, since splitting with my ex, Suri, I've occasionally been known to indulge in and even enjoy some pre- and post-coital snugs—before I got smart and decided it wasn't worth risking testicle injury by tentacle anyway. But this right here is a genuine first.

Who would have thought that of all the Audreys I've met so far—Blushing Audrey, Babbling Audrey, Drunk Audrey, Robo Audrey, Hangry Audrey, Tired Audrey, Bitchy Audrey (kinda redundant, since this is usually just hangry/tired)—my favorite would turn out to be Get All Up in My Space for Cuddletimes Audrey?

I sink back into the couch, finally letting myself relax and savor the feel of soft, warm woman. Like it's got a mind of its own, my arm, which she wriggled under like a motherfucking snuggle pro, pulls her in a bit closer. I try *not* to think about the tits I can feel pressed up against my chest (unlikely).

Finally tuning in to the movie, I find part of my attention still split by Audrey's hair, which I seem to be developing a low-key obsession with. I swear this girl's hair is its own living creature and the beast refuses to be tamed, which is why it's always busting out to do whatever the hell it wants, despite her best attempts to cage it into a civilized style. (Huh, I actually have a lot more in common with Audrey's hair than the girl herself.)

This cuddling business means I'm up real close and personal with her crazy bun, which is currently the size of a small planet and making a bid to climb up the side of my face. If I mentioned it to Audrey, she'd get all embarrassed and apologetic and try to fix it. I probably should, since it's damn near obscuring my view of the movie, but I keep my mouth shut. I kind of don't mind it…and I am not mad at all about the proximity to whatever sweet-scented hair shit she uses that I'm always getting whiffs of.

Real talk—I may have some kind of latent shampoo fetish because I am all about sitting here huffing this vanilla and coconut shit.

Twenty minutes into our Victoria-mandated half hour cuddlefest, I glance down and see Audrey's eyes are closed, her breaths slow and even. It takes a hell of a lot of trust to fall asleep on another person like this. When I think about that, and how less than a week ago she was nervous enough around me that I needed to build a pillow wall, I get a funny feeling in my chest—this pressure made up of part warmth and part pain, unfamiliar but not exactly unpleasant. In fact, I feel kind of fuzzy around the edges, like I'm half asleep too, even though I'm definitely wide awake.

The numbers counting down on my phone remind me the alarm will go off in ten minutes and disturb the sleeping girl in my arms. Without another second's thought, I tap on the screen to turn off the timer.

Whatever. This movie's good, and I'd probably stay out here to finish it anyway. No reason I shouldn't let Audrey sleep for a while. The justification is at odds with the little smile on my lips as I shuffle even deeper into the comfy couch, settling in for the long haul.

This fake relationship job has its downsides for sure, but looking ahead at the next forty-whatever days, I do not hate the thought of more opportunities to embrace my (previously undiscovered) inner cuddleslut with Audrey.

I'm not sure how the movie ends, because at some point I drift off as well, contentment lulling me to sleep with my arms full of soft, sweet-smelling woman.

* * *

Audrey

I wake up warm, deliriously comfortable, and cocooned in a spectacular male scent. I've never had the gift of a specific palate (seriously, drop me in one of those wine tastings, and while everyone else is going, "Ah, yes, I detect cinnamon and cedar and a hint of bergamot"—what even *is* bergamot?—"and the rind of an orange from central Florida picked on the eighth of June," I'll be over here like, "Umm, it's…red?"), so I can't quite describe it, except that it's sexy… Something I never knew a smell could be. No suffocating chemicals, like that aroma is mostly *him* with the subtle addition of body wash.

But his scent is just the cherry on top of the delicious experience of being *surrounded* by Walker. His hard yet surprisingly comfortable body beneath me, his heavy arms wrapped around me, and what I suspect is his chin resting on top of my head.

It's pretty much heaven. I'd be happy to stay here indefinitely.

Unfortunately, I have to pee.

I try explaining to my bladder that I'm in the middle of something important, making a compelling argument to wait. Stubborn thing that she is, my bladder refuses—not caring in the slightest that, for once, every other member of Team Audrey's Body is in full accord. *We do not want to move* from our current position for the foreseeable future.

When I can't hold off any longer, I carefully begin to extract myself from Walker's hold. Gently, so gently, I shift the massive arm that's holding on to me like a koala with its favorite teddy bear. Maybe, if I don't wake him, I'll be able to slip away, do my business, then return to cuddling, with him none the wiser.

I gasp as Walker wakes up with a jerk, setting me aside as easily as if I actually were a teddy bear and popping off the couch so fast it all seems to happen in a split second.

"Sorry," I whisper, cringing. "Just...need to use the bathroom."

"Right."

His sleep-roughened rasp is as textured and uneven as his unshaven jaw, which cracks open on a yawn. It's weird to sit here while Walker's on his feet right in front of me, but just as I'm about to stand, he reaches up to stretch his arms, and the view freezes me in place. I stare, entranced, as his shirt lifts to reveal a hint of golden skin, ridged abdominal muscles, and a strip of hair that starts just beneath his belly button and disappears into the low-slung sweatpants that look old enough that the elastic in the waistband seems liable to give up any second...

"Uh, bathroom?" Walker's voice rips me from my trance, his lips quirked with amusement as he reminds me why we're both awake.

My bladder seizes the moment, waving her hands in the air with an annoyed, *"Uh, helllloooo?"* With warm cheeks, I shuffle to the bathroom to appease the demands of the little dictator.

When I'm finished, I find the living room empty. Walker is in bed, already fast asleep again over on his side of the pillow wall. I sigh. *So much for resuming the snugglefest.*

EMAIL FROM VICTORIA

From: Victoria Trulette
To: Audrey Mitchell, Walker Garrison
Subject: The Art of PDA

Hello my darlings,

It was a joy getting to see your lovely faces yesterday at our check-in meeting! Now, as promised, I present your next assignment.

As an element of standard dating behavior, public displays of affection are extremely variable. The meaning and practice of PDA differ drastically from one relationship to the next, due to any number of factors (personal, environmental/societal, etc.). Some partners have no qualms about intimate touch and kissing in public, while others avoid contact entirely except in private. While I urge you against the latter strategy—subtlety does us no favors in our current endeavor—how and to what extent you incorporate PDA into your portrayal of a couple is a decision that can only be made by the two of you.

That being said, I always find it best to prepare for all eventualities. After all, we cannot rule out the possibility that a time will come when you are required to kiss in order to maintain your cover. Doing so for the first time under strenuous conditions is hardly a recipe for success.

I am sure you've already anticipated what comes next: *Practice!* While I shall not define a specific duration for this assignment, I do believe in this case there is no such thing as *too much* practice. *wink emoji*

Sincerely Yours,
Victoria

20. Kissing: Check!

Audrey

I've been attracted to Walker since the moment we met—and, unfortunately, that attraction has only grown over the last two weeks. Walker's particular brand of "hot" isn't something that can simply be forgotten or ignored. Like the man himself, his attractiveness is not a passive quality content to linger in the background. It is aggressive, lunging out and punching me in the face every time I lay eyes on him. I keep waiting for the force of that impact to lessen over time, but so far, each glimpse is as intense as the first.

Living in such close proximity with the man was dangerous *before* I had firsthand experience of how delicious it feels to wake up ensconced in his arms. It doesn't even matter that he put the pillow wall back in between us at the first opportunity and was already gone when I woke up this morning—my inner defenses against Walker Garrison are one hundred percent less stable than they were twenty-four hours ago.

And now, thanks to Victoria's assignment, by the end of the night, I will have actually *kissed him*.

I'm not freaking out, you're freaking out!

Obviously, I struggle to focus all day and make zero progress with my job search. I'm so worked up by the time Walker gets home from the auto shop, the instant I hear the jangle of his keys, I jump off the couch and run to meet him at the door.

Walker steps into the condo, takes one look at me hovering in the middle of the room wringing my hands like a human-shaped ball of tension, and bursts out laughing.

"Hold on, tiger. We'll do the thing right away, so you can stop thinking about it. Figured you'd want me to clean up before putting these paws on you."

He holds out his hands, displaying dark streaks of what I assume is car grease.

"There was an older lady pulled over with a smoking engine on my way home, so I stopped and checked it out for her."

I have never been compelled to literally *jump* a man in my life, but the urge rushes through my veins with a force that shocks me silent. The only thing in my mind is how much I want him to put those sexy, old-lady-helping hands on me immediately, grease and all.

He scoffs. "Yeah, that's what I thought." Before I can say a word, he stalks off to the bathroom, shutting the door behind him. Within seconds, the shower turns on.

All of five minutes later, he's joining me on the couch smelling like body wash and clean man. I scan his face for signs of irritation about what happened before but find only a crooked smile. As much as I want to explain what he'd misinterpreted as me being a snob, it seems silly to bring it back up if he's already moved on, especially when the explanation is so embarrassing.

"Should we do this? I know how you like to do your homework right away."

At the reminder of our assignment, a horde of manic butterflies takes flight inside my chest cavity.

"I'm nervous," I blurt out.

He smirks. "Yeah. I got that, loud and clear."

Seriously? He couldn't be a gentleman, just once, and *not* point out my awkwardness?

"By the way, I didn't hear you shoot down *tiger*. Does that mean we've finally found your official nickname?"

I roll my eyes. He wants to play this game *now*?

"No to tiger."

"Are you sure? It's kinda badass."

"Yes, I'm sure."

With a grin, he mimes crossing something off on an invisible clipboard. I sigh, reluctantly amused by his theatrics.

Then the man goes and once again proves his penchant for doing the unexpected.

"Okay, kiss me."

"Just like that?" I wheeze, airway suddenly tight.

"Just gotta break the seal. It'll be easy after that. We're practicing what we'd do in front of an audience, so we can keep it pretty PG... Unless you want to be the kind of couple that gets freaky in public." His eyebrows waggle in a ridiculous dance, then he pretends to wait for my answer. (As if I'd ever agree to *that*!) "Right. Show me how you'd kiss me if we're around people."

He makes it sound so simple, my hours-long anxiety spiral seems ridiculous. So what if I've never initiated a kiss before? Even *I* can handle PG, right?

Clutching close every spare molecule of confidence within me, I lean in and press my lips against his.

There. What was I worried about? I barely even felt that! (With my lips, anyway—my heart is racing like crazy.)

"Well?" I prompt him, feeling pretty dang proud of myself.

"Yeah, that works—" my heart soars "—if our goal is to convince people I'm your brother." I can almost hear the *whoosh* as it plummets back to earth.

142

Irritated, and a bit hurt, the words fly out before I can think better of them. "Show me how *you'd* do it, then."

I know better than to bait a man like Walker Garrison, but by the time I realize the challenge I've thrown down, it's too late; his mouth is already on me.

In the space of two seconds, Walker obliterates anything I thought I knew about kissing.

First, he shows me what a quick kiss *should* be between lovers: a closed-mouthed caress that I unquestionably feel with my lips (and many other parts, besides). He even lingers slightly before pulling away, the perfect performance of a boyfriend reluctant to part.

For a second, I think that's it, that the lesson is done, but in the next, he's back and kissing me again. I press in closer, eager for further instruction. He delivers, and it's nothing short of enlightening.

Walker makes it clear that first round was merely a brief introduction, as he proceeds to thoroughly acquaint our mouths. Slowly, he brushes his lips back and forth over mine in a light whisper, leaving them tingling and sensitive. When he suddenly increases the pressure, making full contact, the rush of sensation echoes throughout my whole body. So simple, almost innocent, yet he has me utterly captivated and desperate for more.

His pressing tongue seeks entrance, which I grant immediately. The kiss takes on an edge of hunger with the introduction of our tongues—progressing beyond first greetings and on to something less polite. Walker has lifted his hands to either side of my face, lightly holding me in place where he wants me. Those long, slightly rough fingers tighten their grip minutely just as his tongue begins to move faster, plunging deeper, sweeping my mouth like he's impatient to taste every inch. Emboldened by the small signs that he's affected too, I reach up and caress his stubble-covered jaw, reveling in the prickle as the short hairs scrape my palms.

Walker makes a noise deep in his chest, then his mouth is prying mine open wider and the fingers on my chin are tilting it, adjusting the angle at which he's devouring me, claiming me with his tongue and lips with a skill that trips my tingling nerve endings into a frenzy.

Now this, *this* is kissing.

I'm dizzy, overwhelmed by the pleasure of it all, and by the craving that fills me for more—more of this, more of him, just...*more*. I want those hands touching me, not just my face, but all the newly needy places his kisses have lit up. I want to climb on top of him, to rub my aching breasts against his hard body and find some friction to appease the throb of desire in my sex.

Realizing I'm well and truly turned on—something that's never happened so quickly and never with such intensity—shocks me back to reality. I pull away, gulping in air. I don't know at what point in all of that I closed my eyes, but when I open them now, I find myself staring into gray irises that I'd swear shine with a mirror image of my own desire. Those eyes are darker than usual, the color reminding me of storm clouds, and I have the fleeting, nonsensical notion that they must be the source of the lightning I just felt zinging through me. Walker and I stare at each other, an intensity vibrating between us that's as foreign to me as the frantic throbbing between my legs that's keeping time with my heartbeats.

This man just aroused me more with a single kiss than my ex-boyfriend did in six months of dating. My mind whirls, torn between panic and the urge to close the slight distance between us, press my lips to Walker's, and fall back into the maelstrom. Discover what further epiphanies might await in doing *more* than kissing him...

"Walker, I—" Unsure why I began speaking in the first place, I break off abruptly, at a loss for words.

How do I tell Walker without *telling him* that the last time—the *only* time—I got physical with a man, he shattered the fragile confidence I'd fought so hard to build, and that I'm still working on the repairs? How do I express the depth of my fear of disappointing him? Or am I brave enough to forge onward without those confessions, to simply let go and explore what he's awakened within me?

Abrupt as a flipped switch, the storm I thought I saw in Walker's eyes disappears, the transformation so fast I immediately begin to wonder if it was ever there at all. As he shifts away to settle on his usual side of the couch, his face is completely neutral. He nods.

"That'll do."

"What?" I feel dazed, his seesawing mood only sending me further off-balance.

"See? Not so hard. Kissing: check!" With a carefree smile, he once again pantomimes crossing an item off a list.

Then, with a pat on my head like I'm a dog or his little sister, he declares he's going to work out. I'm still frozen in place on the couch when he leaves for the gym a few minutes later.

As soon as he's gone, I groan loudly, not even caring if the microphones pick it up.

What in the ever-loving heck just happened?

I've always believed I'm not a very sexual person. I dragged my feet for *six months* before finally sleeping with Ethan—and even then, I gave in more out of guilt than any actual desire to do the deed. In the year and a half since he dumped me (when the challenge was gone, I apparently wasn't good enough in bed to keep around), no part of me has mourned the absence of sex from my life.

Then I met Walker and discovered I've been wrong all along. I'd just never met a guy until now who "does it for me," as Callie would say. And isn't it the cruelest cosmic joke that I finally find the one who *does*, and that guy is *Walker*?

Because whatever I thought I felt or saw, it's clear from Walker's actions that kiss had zero effect on him. The singularly most passionate experience of my life was a *joke* to him.

I bury my face into a pillow, wondering what will suffocate me first, the fabric or my humiliation?

21. Massholes & Mindfucks

Walker

There are things about living downtown that don't suck; the traffic isn't one of them. Our Beacon Hill condo is only four miles farther away from the shop than my house, distance-wise, but slogging through Boston congestion adds forty-five minutes to my morning commute.

Fun times.

It takes me twenty minutes to reach I-93 North, when I could've walked it in ten. Once I'm no longer dodging cars, bikes, and pedestrians who all think they have the right of way (the designation "Masshole" is a real thing, and it doesn't apply only to drivers), I cut the music and tell the AI chick in my phone to call my brother. It's been too long since I checked in—plus, being alone with my thoughts right now is dangerous. These last few days, they keep circling back to that mindfuck of a kiss without my permission.

I drum my fingers along the top of the steering wheel, their rhythm faster than the tinny ringing that fills the cab of my truck. It rings for so long I've resigned myself to leaving a voicemail when Luke finally answers.

"'Sup."

"Hey. On my way to the shop. Got a while of highway ahead, figured you could entertain me."

"That's what the radio is for, asshole." Luke sounds amused, though, just a little bit, which I'm taking as a win. He's a tough nut to crack nowadays.

"Yeah, yeah. So, what's new?"

"I'm *fine*, Walker. I'm a fucking adult. You don't need to check on me." No amusement now. The hostility is more familiar these days anyway.

"Jesus. Can't a guy just call to shoot the shit with his brother?"

"Fine. Shoot," he gripes. At least he didn't hang up on me. It wouldn't be a first.

"My gig in Boston is going okay, thanks for asking." He grunts. It's pretty much the same response I got when I told him I had to move out for a couple of months, not caring as long as I'd still pay my share of the rent. "The place is sweet. There's even a cleaning service that comes once a week."

It's also bugged for sound twenty-four seven. Oh, and it comes with a girl I have to pretend I'm dating, who I definitely-not-pretend kissed a few days ago. Kissed the hell out of, if I'm being real, when no way did I expect to get carried away like that. She goddamn lit up for me too, but afterward, there was this look on her face like she was trying to figure out how to pull an "It's not you, it's me."

The girl one hundred percent wants *me. She just doesn't want...me. Her prerogative; I don't need the complication anyway. Except, I can't seem to stop thinking about it. And I'm just so fucking confused.*

If I were having this conversation with the old Luke, I'd probably say that last bit aloud. Some of it, anyway. We've never sat around talking about our feelings—that's not how Garrison men roll, especially with John "rub some dirt in it" Garrison as our paternal role model—but growing up, I always knew I could tell my brother anything. No matter how different we are, we had each other's backs without question.

Things are complicated now, though, for more reasons than that NDA I signed.

"They feed you too?"

Wow. Lucas Garrison, initiating more conversation? Maybe he does miss me.

"The kitchen came fully stocked, and whoever did it wasn't messing around. Also had some killer Italian food a couple of weeks ago."

"Nice."

"Yeah. Hey, you need anything while I'm on your side of the river?"

Wrong thing to say.

"No, *Mom.*"

Just like that, he's back to grumpy and belligerent. You'd think I insulted him, not offered to swing by with a few groceries. Though, in his mind, they're probably the same thing.

"Okay, okay. If you change your mind…"

"I won't."

He hangs up without saying goodbye.

"Yeah, nice talking to you too, asshole," I say into the dead air.

Next time we talk, I'll have to bite the bullet and feed him the story about my new "girlfriend." Probably should have gotten it over with just now, but whatever. There are a lot of days left in this thing.

22. Monet For Sure

Walker

TOMMY: Yo! Drinks @ Murphy's tonight
DECLAN: Fuck yeah
XAVIER: I'm there
PETE: Garrison, you in?
TOMMY: We better see your ass there

I wince at how loud my phone's vibrate setting is, sneaking a peek at Tommy's latest message. I'll reply later—once I'm out of here, far, *far* away from Victoria, who, for all I know, can scent the chance of a "public socializing" scene like a frickin' bloodhound. The woman is extra thirsty for juicy material at the moment, too, since Audrey and I just finished disappointing her with the "lack of detail" in our descriptions of practicing PDA. (Hey, *I'm* no romance author.)

After shoving my buzzing phone into my pocket, I look up to find myself pinned by an ice-blue gaze. Plenty of people have told me I'm hard to read—aka every woman I've ever dated—but Victoria's laser-sharp stare gives off the uncanny sense that she can see right through me.

My attempt to look innocent is ruined by another loud buzz sounding from my pants. Why didn't I leave the damn thing at home? (Note to self—Turn phone off before next check-in meeting. Also, find new friends.)

"Anything you'd like to share?" Victoria asks. I'd swear the woman *knows* I'm trying to hide something. I wouldn't be surprised if she somehow even knows *what.*

Beneath Victoria's intense scrutiny, my talent for coming up with solid lies on the spot fails me.

"Just some guys from the shop talking about meeting up for drinks tonight. I'll tell them no." I don't even know why I bother with this last bit, but a guy has to try.

"Oh no, this is perfect. You *must* go and introduce Audrey to your friends."

"Murphy's is not a nice place you bring a date," I warn. "It's a dive bar—just this shitty hole-in-the-wall around the corner from the shop." Much as I try, I cannot picture Audrey in our townie hangout.

"Nonsense. If you generally spend time there, it is exactly where you should bring Audrey, to further integrate her into your life."

I grit my teeth. For the most part, I've come to terms with this pretend boyfriend thing, but "*integrating her into my life*" sounds way too real.

"Go on and respond to your friends," she urges.

I open my mouth to protest more before snapping it shut. By now, I've learned when Victoria has that look in her eyes, resistance is futile.

Fuck my life.

WALKER: I'm in. Bringing my girl

* * *

The bases are loaded, and the Red Sox need one good hit to smoke the Cubs on their own turf. On the TV, the talking heads are discussing what a win would mean for the Sox's season, which I'd usually give a damn about. Today, I can barely keep my attention on the screen, too distracted by the closed door to the bathroom, where Audrey has been getting ready for-fucking-ever.

What the hell is she doing in there? Audrey's usually quick with the girly shit, but *of course*, she'd pull this the one time I'm crawling out of my skin dying to hit the road and get tonight over with. My leg is bouncing hard enough to create a loud jangling from the keys in my pocket, the sound only putting me more on edge.

Finally, the door clicks open. When Audrey walks into the living room and finds me staring her down, she ducks her head shyly. Her hair is in a tidy braid, which falls to drape over her shoulder at her movement. The shirt is covered in colorful flowers with some type of frills along the collar and tucked into jeans (way less sexy ones than she wore on our date last week) with a bright pink ribbon tied through the belt loops.

All I can do is picture her walking into Murphy's beside me, wearing this outfit—it's as good as strolling in with a big ole sign announcing, *"She doesn't belong here! She's too good for him! This relationship is obviously fake!"*

"Walker? Is this okay?"

Audrey's shuffling her feet nervously under my blatant inspection (feet which are in exact miniaturized replicas of my old high school math teacher's loafers).

I dig deep, trying to dredge up some patience.

"Have you got anything less…" *Fuck, how would a nice guy say this?* "sorority bake sale?"

She deflates, then wordlessly turns and scurries off to the bedroom. Another girl would probably slam that door behind her, but Audrey's too damn classy for that. (Or *me*, which is the whole problem.)

Bogaerts hits an epic homer, and the flat-screen fills with a high-def replay of the Sox running the bases while the Cubs players watch with their thumbs up their asses. It's a killer play, but even the Sox can't lift my current mood. Shutting off the TV, I direct my full attention to the bedroom door. I swear, I'm ready to break the damn thing down and drag Audrey out here if she doesn't emerge in the next five minutes.

Lucky for both of us, it swings open four minutes and thirty-five seconds later.

But then I see her and wish she were back behind the closed door. I squeeze my eyes shut, blocking off the image for a moment in hopes that will help me get a handle on my shit. Unfortunately, when I blink them back open, the sight is no less affecting than before.

It's hard to believe there was a time—not too long ago—when I looked at Audrey and questioned her sex appeal. Now, I'm wondering if I was really looking at all back then, because clothing alone couldn't create the total smokeshow in front of me.

It sure helps, though.

Her new outfit is as different from the shapeless dress she was hiding in when we first met as the sun is from the moon. Honest to God, if I saw the girl standing before me in a bar, I would try to pick her up, no question. (A realization I seriously don't need to deal with when I already have that damn kiss repeatedly sneaking its way into my spank bank.) Skintight jeans and black boots with heels I already know will make her ass look like a piece of fucking art. Her hair is loose; my eyes follow the tantalizing golden-brown waves down to the shadow of her cleavage. Yes, cleavage—nothing excessive, but the V neck of the sleeveless dark purple number she's changed into is deep enough that thinking about her wearing it in Murphy's, where my boys and every random motherfucker there can see her, has my blood boiling.

And, okay, maybe a decent percentage of that blood is migrating south—the region that shares an area code with my pants zipper, to be specific. Which only pisses me off more, because I know my shameless friends' thoughts will be a thousand times filthier.

"*What?*" Audrey demands at my silence. I can't tell if that break in her voice means she's on the verge of bursting into tears or slapping me.

"Look…" I dig the heels of both hands into my eye sockets and breathe out slowly. This ragey reaction is irrational to the extreme, and I need to get a lid on it. "This is super casual, okay? Most of the guys will be coming right from the shop, probably wearing shit with grease on it. Just…throw on a T-shirt or something? *Please?*"

Personally, I think I do a pretty damn good job of sounding like I'm *not* going out of my mind imagining Tommy's eyes on Audrey's tits. No gold star for restraint from my fake girlfriend, though. She simply turns on her heel and stomps back into the bedroom without another word. (And, yeah, those boots, her ass… Monet-level masterpiece, for sure.)

Not two minutes later, she's back in a plain gray long-sleeved T-shirt. The jeans are the same, but this shirt falls farther past the waistband, and her flat, ballerina-style shoes at least don't draw extra attention to her ass. I miss the sex goddess hair, but the bun is better for my blood pressure.

The knotted tension in my sternum loosens with relief. *Now* she looks like herself, the girl I first met and wouldn't have given a second thought or look under normal circumstances. (Or so I'm going to keep telling myself. Maybe with repetition, my brain and eyes will even believe it.)

"Happy now?" Audrey huffs.

"Perfect. Thank you."

* * *

We take my truck, because I don't know how I'd explain it if any of the guys saw us being dropped off by Victoria's hired car.

Neither of us talks on the drive. I know Audrey's nervous, but for once between the two of us, I think I take the cake in the anxiety category. Tonight is different from all the other shit we've done so far. I've known most of these guys for years, and I grew up with Tommy. So yeah, I'm sweating about lying to their faces—not to mention that I'm wearing a fucking wire like some kind of narc. They're all solid, so it's not like Victoria's going to be hearing anything illegal, but still. It's an invasion of privacy that *they're* not being paid a mint to deal with.

Fuck it. I'm paying for drinks tonight. That will soothe at least some of the guilt clawing at my chest right now.

We're pulling into the microscopic parking lot before I'm ready. The guys and I always just walk here from the shop, so it feels weird shoving my truck between painted lines so old and faded they're more suggestions than guides at this point.

"You sure you want to do this?" Audrey asks.

"Nope." I don't have to turn my head to know she wilts in her seat at my blunt response. She was looking for reassurance, and I'm being a dick. I sigh. "Yeah. Let's do it."

I try to see the place through Audrey's eyes. Purportedly an Irish pub, the only Irish things about Murphy's are the faded shamrock on the sign out front above the chipped letters spelling "I SH P B," and a decades-old framed Jameson poster on one wall. The owner Chaz, whose last name isn't even Murphy, lifts a hand in greeting from behind the bar, wearing a checkered flannel shirt that looks like it was already old when I was in elementary school—which is also likely around the time it stopped fitting his beer gut. The bar takes up an entire wall of the space, lined by mismatched stools. Tall pub tables are crowded along the other wall. The narrow room is dark, and despite how Chaz tries to keep it clean, it perpetually smells faintly of stale spilled beer. Objectively, the scent isn't roses, yet it triggers a flood of fond memories that finally ease some of the tension in my body. There's even a comfort in the familiar sight of Old Russ nursing a beer in the far corner, where he's been a nightly fixture as far back as my memory goes.

"The boys are in the back room," Chaz tells us, yelling to be heard over the music blasting through the overhead speakers. No jukebox in this place; Chaz is in charge of the music, which is an eclectic mix of, as he puts it, *whatever the fuck he wants*— and any man who dares to question him is liable to have his ass thrown out.

"Thanks, Chaz. Can I get a pitcher of draft?"

He pours beer into a plastic pitcher and hands it over with a stack of cups before turning those bushy eyebrows, more gray than black these days, to Audrey. "And what can I get you, darlin?"

"You got any fruity cocktail mixers back there?" I ask. "My girl isn't really a beer drinker."

Audrey jabs me in the side (*ow*, the girl's got bony elbows... I was trying to be helpful!) and pastes on a sweet smile for Chaz.

"Oh no, I'm fine. I'm happy with whatever you've got in there." She nods at the pitcher of beer in my hand, which I know for a fact she's going to hate. *Suit yourself, princess.*

Tucking the cups under one arm, I free up a hand that I offer to Audrey, pleased that she takes it in hers eagerly. I see her shoulders rise in a nervous breath as I feel myself do the same, and then we walk hand in hand into our first real test as a fake couple.

The back room is small, a couple of rickety high tops and a well-loved (read: old as the hills) pool table that Declan and Pete are currently hovering over.

Tommy sees us first, inciting a cheer that the other guys instantly join.

"Jesus," I snort. "I haven't been gone that long."

"We're cheering for the beer, asshole." Tommy chugs the contents of his glass then wastes no time helping himself to the pitcher in my hand and refilling it.

Then he directs his most charming smile over my shoulder. "Oh hey, beautiful, didn't see ya there."

I turn and realize Audrey is stopped a few steps behind me, hesitating at the doorway. I lift an eyebrow, calling her out for hiding, then grab her hand and tug her into the room.

Xavier, a new guy at the shop whose reputation as a ladies' man is well-known, steps right up. He does a corny little bow before grabbing Audrey's free hand and kissing it like some kind of fucking fairytale prince. Her entire face goes pink.

"Welcome, pretty girl. I'm Xavier. I'm sorry you're here with this beast, but whenever you're ready to be free of him, just say the word."

Audrey giggles and flushes even more when he winks, causing my vision to go as red as her face.

"All right, all right." I give a swift kick to one of his feet, sending him stumbling out of his ridiculous pose, and pull Audrey closer to my side. Holding her there, I send a warning look to the rest of the guys in the room, discouraging any more hand kissing nonsense. A few others come up and introduce themselves, but I'm glad that most drift back to their own conversations and we're no longer the center of attention.

I peek down at Audrey. She still seems a bit nervous, but she did pretty well with all of the introductions, her natural shyness actually working in our favor, as it makes any awkwardness related to our faking less noticeable. As for me, my own nerves evaporated the second I saw Xavier put his lips on Audrey's skin. (Not because I was jealous or anything. Just pissed off that he would be so disrespectful when he thinks she's my girl.)

For the moment, it's just the two of us and Tommy, who is as big of a flirt as Xavier but at least has the decency to dial it down when I'm *right the fuck here.* Then Danny and his girl Talia join our little circle, and the presence of another female seems to put Audrey a bit more at ease.

The pitcher is already empty, so Tommy suggests we go out to the bar for another one. I glance at Audrey again, seeing she and Talia have gotten to talking. Talia's one of the chillest girls I know, and Danny's good people. Audrey will be fine with them for a minute.

"You good?" I ask Audrey as Tommy and I are about to leave. Her eyes are wide when she tips her chin up to look at me, but she nods.

Aware we have an audience (and with the stakes feeling raised standing in front of a real couple), I lean down and kiss Audrey on the forehead. I can't say it's something I've done much in the past, but the move feels surprisingly natural.

At the bar, Tommy and I shoot the shit with Chaz while he fills two pitchers with beer (since the first one went so fast). We've got years of history between us, so it's easy to get caught up talking, but I don't realize how much time we've spent out here until I catch the Sam Adams clock mounted behind Chaz's head.

Shit. I hadn't meant to leave Audrey for this long.

"Hey, let's get this beer to the guys, and I should get back to my girl."

We say goodbye to Chaz and head toward the back room.

"So, what do you think about Audrey?" I find myself asking Tommy, not sure why even as the words are coming out of my mouth. Sure, it will make Victoria happy, but no one's ever accused me of being a teacher's pet.

"I like her. She's...real."

Of all the words he could have used… Damn, if that isn't a kick in the nuts.

"Genuine, you know?" He's not wrong; Audrey is as real as it gets, even if this thing between us is nothing but fake. "I'm happy for you, Walk."

I'm a little shook, to tell the truth. "Thanks, Tommy."

Never one to stay serious for too long, Tommy pops a grin that warns of trouble. "And damn, that ass…"

I shove him. Hard. "Get the fuck outta here about my girl's ass." Even knowing he's screwing with me, there's nothing fake about the warning edge in my voice.

When we step into the back room and I lay eyes on Audrey, that edge turns into a feral sound I've never heard come out of my throat before. She's over at the pool table holding a cue stick, and fucking Xavier is standing way closer than necessary with his hands on her, "adjusting her positioning."

Oh, *fuck* no.

23. Walker's Girl

Audrey

"You good?" Walker asks, his voice soft in that way I have no defense against.

I nod. It's not as if I can be honest, like, "Actually, I would prefer it if you stayed glued to my side the whole time we're here, 'kay thanks."

Then, that forehead kiss—which dissolves me into a swoony, human-shaped pile of mush. (Curse the man for being about to make me swoon when I'm still mad at him from earlier!)

He and Tommy leave, and I try not to spend too long looking at Walker's butt. Tommy's is nice too, and they're both wearing the heck out of their jeans, but my eyes are stuck to Walker.

I realize my "don't stare so long it's obvious" mission has failed when Talia, whom I've just met, snorts. "Oh, girl, you've got it *bad.*"

My face flames at being caught ogling Walker. Talia just grins at me and snuggles into Danny, sipping her drink. Whatever she ordered has a lemon and a straw—it looks like something I'd enjoy far more than the lukewarm beer I'm planning to nurse all night.

"No worries, I still check out Danny's ass every chance I get—even after five years together and pushing his giant spawn out of my hoo-ha."

I'm glad I didn't have any liquid in my mouth, because I totally would have just done a spit-take. Danny just stands there grinning proudly—about the compliment to his behind, his ability to create a large baby, or both, I couldn't say.

"It's so nice to have another girl around," Talia says. "Hopefully seeing you with Walker will inspire these other animals to find their own women to settle down with."

Shame hits me hard. Here I am lying right to these nice people's faces, and they think Walker and I are "settling down"!

"Oh, no—we're really new."

"Pshh, Danny says you're shacking up. That's big for Walker, so it must be serious."

Oh lord. "*Shacking up*" sounds so...sordid.

"Don't listen to her," Danny tells me. "She just wants some babies to play with, and she's pretending we're not having any more."

"Grow yourself a vagina, Daniel Mendez, so *you* can get ripped in two pushing a watermelon out of it, and then we'll have as many as you want!"

I giggle. They're adorable together, and I enjoy Talia's flavor of outrageous. She reminds me a little bit of my friend Jamie.

For a few minutes, we talk about their almost-two-year-old, Charlie. Talia whips out her phone, rapidly swiping through photos of a cute baby who looks just like Danny. Then they decide it's time for them to go relieve Charlie's *abuela* of babysitting duty. Before they leave, Talia insists on swapping contact info, which makes me feel even guiltier about my deception.

Once Danny and Talia are gone, I peek at my phone to check the time. I watched the bartender fill up that pitcher earlier, so I can personally attest to the fact that it takes less than thirty seconds and it's not like the place is crowded, so Walker and Tommy haven't been gone this long because they're stuck waiting in line—which leads to the undeniable conclusion that Walker is avoiding me, probably embarrassed about claiming me in front of his friends. My heart sinks.

Keeping up with the man's mood swings is like being on a roller coaster blindfolded. I can't even *think* about tonight's outfit fiasco without wanting to burst into tears. Even so, I wish he were here right now. Mad at him or not, I can't deny that I feel safer and more comfortable when he's by my side.

Obviously, he doesn't feel the same—which shouldn't hurt as much as it does.

Most of the remaining group is hanging out by the pool table, so I drift over in that direction, trying to fade into the background. I'd rather avoid having to make conversation with anyone, especially because I've already forgotten most of their names.

My hopes of sliding under the radar are squashed when I'm approached almost immediately. Now this one, I *do* remember—it's Xavier, the first guy I met today. I start blushing, just as I did earlier when he kissed my hand.

"I'm Audrey," I manage after he reintroduces himself.

"I know." I flush even hotter. Xavier's cocky smirk suggests he knows exactly how attractive he is and gets a kick out of making girls flustered.

He *is* seriously good-looking—not as hot as Walker, but that's a steep bar—so of course, his presence scrambles my brain. Artistically rendered tattoos cover the majority of the light-brown skin visible in his tight T-shirt, trailing up his neck and around lean but defined arm muscles. I swallow. The man would be at home on any of the bad-boy thirst trap accounts Callie and I follow on Instagram and TikTok.

Xavier's hand lands on my back; the heat of it seems to sear right through my cotton shirt. A glance over my shoulder at the doorway fails to conjure Walker's reappearance, so I let Xavier steer me closer to the green-felt-covered table.

"You like pool, pretty girl?"

When I admit I've never played, Xavier insists on teaching me. I try to demur, but some of the other guys catch on and start crowding around with enthusiastic offers of assistance, leaving me no choice but to go along with it.

As my self-appointed personal tutor, Xavier apparently favors an extremely tactile teaching methodology. Although he never touches me inappropriately, the man makes an art of working appropriate touching into his instruction. After just a few minutes of him adjusting my stance and hold on the stick, my upper body feels like a map of scorched earth from all the lingering trails of heat left by his hands (a sensation which, admittedly, is not altogether unpleasant).

A little crowd of guys has now congregated around the pool table, calling out encouragement and (often conflicting) advice as I proceed to prove myself the worst pool player in the history of bar games. Being so flustered by all of the attention on top of Xavier's constant proximity does nothing to help my already dismal hand-eye coordination. You'd think I'd be in a catatonic state from embarrassment by now, but somehow, after my first few failed attempts at hitting a cue ball, I find myself laughing along with everyone else.

"What's going on?"

I'd know that voice anywhere—Walker. He's just inside the doorway beside Tommy, both of them holding full pitchers of beer. Despite myself, my whole body seems to sigh and relax at the sight of him, though that relief falters a bit at his frown. Walker's intense focus is aimed in my direction, but not quite at me; his eyes are locked on to Xavier's hand on my arm. I shrug the hand off and scoot to the side, only for Xavier to throw an arm around my shoulders and pull me back into him. A vertical crease forms between Walker's brows.

"Your girl's never played before, so we're teaching her," Xavier says.

"She can't play for shit!" Pete adds, to a chorus of male chuckling.

Looking decidedly unamused, Walker sets down his pitcher with an audible thud and stalks over—and truly, "*stalk*" is the only word for it. Everything about Walker's movements and the intensity of his expression screams of a predator with its prey in sight.

This time, Xavier lets me duck out from under his arm and put distance between us. But his toothy white grin is unapologetic and his voice more than a little suggestive when he says to Walker, who has reached us in record time, "You've been missing out, Walk. This is a great opportunity for some *hands-on assistance.* Don't worry, I kept your girl company."

Even as Walker's face darkens, Xavier's flippant attitude doesn't waver. I don't know if he's failed to notice the waves of violent energy coming off Walker right now, or if Xavier is one of those insane people who enjoys courting retributive claws and teeth by poking dangerous animals. I take another step away—I actually *do* have survival instincts, and they're blaring at me with warnings of danger.

In one smooth motion, Walker reaches out and pulls me against his body.

"Hey, baby. You okay?"

I nod; actual words are impossible with Walker's front pressed along the entire length of my back, that voice of gravel mixed with gentleness spoken so very close to my ear, and the sheer quantity of testosterone currently flying around.

At my affirmative, Walker's entire body stiffens behind me, and he pivots so that he's partially shielding me from Xavier. On his next words, that hint of softness in his voice hardens to something unyielding and borderline feral.

"You keep your *hands off*, or *you're* gonna need *assistance.* Get me?"

Low enough to be inaudible beyond the three of us, the threat is so clear that even Xavier's wayward survival instincts finally kick in. He takes a couple steps backward, perhaps realizing just how close he's come to this particular beast's teeth.

That's all I see of Xavier's reaction, because in the next instant Walker is kissing me, and everything else ceases to exist. All that predatory energy refocuses on me, and my body responds to his aggression with an instinctual submission that has nothing to do with fear. My lips part instantly at his demand for entry, and then it's all I can do to hold on and try not to drown in the onslaught of sensations as he claims my mouth with his lips and tongue and teeth.

When Walker breaks the kiss, I blink open my eyes as though emerging from a deep sleep. I'm clinging to him so tightly I've probably left fingernail imprints in his biceps, but I can't seem to let go. In fact, I seem to have forgotten how to control my body at all. If not for the grip of his hands at my waist, I'd probably crumple onto the floor right here.

My senses slowly come back online, and I hide my face in Walker's chest when the rushing in my ears fades and I register the clapping and catcalls coming from behind us—because we're still at the bar with his friends, in freaking public!

"Okay, okay. *Your* woman. I get you."

My head pops up, the sound of a voice from so close startling me. *Oh my goodness, how did I forget about Xavier?* Xavier's hands are raised in a pose of surrender and he's backing away slowly, but I still have serious concerns about his sense of self-preservation, because he's smirking. Then, apparently unable to resist poking Walker one last time, Xavier winks and says, "I don't blame you for wanting to keep her all to yourself. I would too."

Walker's growl is so quiet I doubt even Xavier—who is now swaggering away in the direction of the beer—heard it. A fact that seems downright impossible, given that the vibration of the sound leaving Walker's chest transfers into me, reverberating all the way down to my toes with the force and devastation of a category 10 earthquake.

"You really okay?" There's no suppressing my shiver when Walker murmurs into my ear, mouth so close I can feel the warmth of his breath and the faint scrape of his stubble against my skin.

"Yeah." I hope my voice doesn't sound as tremulous to him as it does in my own ears.

Then I'm forced to shake it off and plant myself back in reality, socializing with Walker's friends as if I haven't just had one of the most intense moments of my life.

Maybe Xavier does have some sense beneath that careless façade, because he keeps his distance from us for the rest of the night. Even so, as we hang out with his friends for another hour, Walker holds me to him the entire time, his hands never once leaving my body.

If Xavier's hands on me were hot with an edge of danger, like venturing too close to a flame, Walker's are a full-body submersion in a Jacuzzi. Which only sends my mind drifting to comparisons between a loofah and the texture of Walker's calluses, how they'd both feel dragging over various areas of my body...

STOP THINKING ABOUT WALKER AND BATHTUBS!

I don't participate much in the conversation; it's taking all my mental power to keep my face neutral and pleasant while my body and emotions are in an uproar.

He's not really *being possessive and tender. He's just putting on a show to make it look real for his friends,* I try to tell my subconscious and my body. (They ignore me, too busy throwing a party to which they invite all of my hormones and girly parts.)

It would be so very easy to read more into that show of territorialism, to see it as a sign that Walker actually feels

166

something for me, but I know better. Here I am, judging Xavier for a lack of self-preservation, when my own once-formidable protective instincts seem to dissipate as soon as Walker touches me.

As my mind clears and I think it over, I reach the conclusion that Walker's confrontation with Xavier ultimately had little to do with me. That was about *his* ego, *his* male pride and sense of ownership being threatened.

I know in romance novels, it's considered swoon-worthy to have a man "claim" and "own" you, but I just feel…objectified, literally. Treated like an *object* caught in a tug-of-war between two little boys. Am I really supposed to have hearts in my eyes because Walker essentially peed all over me in front of some other males?

It's *pee*, for goodness' sake. What is romantic about that?

I decide to mention this to Victoria so she can pass the insight on to her fellow romance authors.

On the plus side, thinking about being urinated on, like a wooden fence post marked by a dog to show he's tough, works wonders toward cooling any fluttery feelings that might be lingering after that kiss.

Text Message Thread: Victoria and Walker

VICTORIA: Walker, it behooves me to inform you that it is never acceptable for a man to dictate what a woman does or does not wear on her body, regardless of relationship status.

WALKER: I hear you, Vickie. I know I came off as a dick there, but what she was wearing first would have outed us as fake for sure. And you should have seen the second outfit—it was basically a ticket for a nonstop flight that would have landed me behind bars the first time some horny asshole laid eyes on her.

VICTORIA: All sentiments you might have verbalized in a manner lacking the dictatorial misogynist delivery. Sentiments you should have verbalized, period, since your failure to provide any form of explanation for your behavior made it very much a "dick move."

WALKER: Loud and clear. I'll do better.

VICTORIA: I am not the person to whom you should address that declaration.

WALKER: Geez, Vick. Can't you ever just say shit normal, like, "Tell Audrey, not me."

VICTORIA: Tell Audrey, not me.

24. The Donkey Show

Audrey

"Mine."

Walker growls the word into my ear. At the feel of his warm breath and the scrape of his stubble on my neck, I gasp and squeeze the rock hard biceps beneath my fingers tighter. Then he's kissing me again, making love to my mouth with that oh-so-skilled tongue of his. My legs are spread open as I sit on the edge of the pool table with Walker standing between them. He's hard behind the zipper of his jeans, which he presses against my sex with just enough pressure to make me desperate for more.

A hand on my chest guides me to lean back slowly, until I'm lying all the way flat on the green felt. Walker leans over me, his body looming so large he takes up the entirety of my vision, like he's the only thing in the whole world. Huge, callused hands run along my legs, starting at my knees and traveling all the way up my thighs to rest on either side of my pulsing core.

"Yes," I whisper. I'm squirming, aching, and he's so close to where I need him.

His fingers start to move inward...

Never in my life have I felt such hatred for the obnoxious electronic chime of my phone alarm. I chose this particular sound because it is too awful to sleep through, and it's certainly accomplished its goal today, ripping me from the most amazing dream with the worst timing ever. (Thanks a *lot,* Past Audrey, you responsible little sadist.)

Walker's side of the bed is empty—not a surprise, as he often runs or goes to the gym first thing in the morning. Which is for the better, because I'm certain my face and chest are flushed with arousal, and there's no way I could hide how hard my nipples are, seeing as they're currently trying to burrow straight through my shirt.

Freaking Walker. This is all his fault, him and his little performance at the bar last night. What my sex-starved subconscious seems to have conveniently forgotten while trying its hand at producing soft-core dreamland porn is that its chosen leading man has no interest in playing out such scenes with me in real life.

Sure, the man will kiss the living daylights out of me for "instructional purposes" or to prove a point in front of his friends, but while I'm here waking from a restless night of sheet-twisting erotic dreams, overheated and throbbing with unfulfilled desire, Walker seems to have forgotten those kisses completely, or else considers them too inconsequential to even mention.

Ugh. All of these…these…*feelings*…are complete insanity. I mean, I'm not even sure I *like* Walker half of the time!

Of course, the problem is the *other* half of the time, when I like him a little too much.

And as far as *wanting* him? I'm afraid I'm going to need to retract all of my inquiries and applications, because it's looking like that's about to be my full-time job.

* * *

VICTORIA: I believe another date night is in order. Audrey, it is your turn to make the plans.

GO FAKE YOURSELF

My grumpy mood persists all morning. By the time I get Victoria's text message, I've replayed the events of last night over in my head so many times my irritation has turned into full-blown anger.

I mean, what *was* that? The humiliating interlude about my clothing, abandoning me with strangers for twenty minutes, the sudden overprotective tactile boyfriend act...and *that freaking kiss*.

If that kiss was Walker pretending, he needs to dial it down. We're not gunning for an Oscar here!

Yes, as a couple, we're fake, but I'm still a real person. There's nothing fake about my feelings, which he treats so carelessly.

I'm...well, I'm just really, really *pissed off.* I am sick and tired of getting my feelings hurt due to Walker's nauseating mood swings and how he always seems to be the one with the upper hand.

For once, I have all the power in my hands, thanks to Victoria's assignment. The timing is too good not to take advantage of this rare opportunity to dole out a bit of well-earned payback.

Let's see how Walker likes it when *he's* the one being thrown out of his comfort zone.

Now, to find the perfect plan...

* * *

"You're really not gonna tell me where we're going?"

I give him a Look. It translates approximately to: *Oh, you mean the exact thing you did to me?*

But then I have to turn and look out the window to hide the grin I can't suppress, the same one that's been on my face ever since I stumbled across an event listing for *The Donkey Show* last night.

171

Freddy drops us off outside the Oberon theater in Cambridge. Walker eyes the location, and I see him take note of the show's name on the marquee outside, but he makes no comment. He grumbles when I retrieve the bounty from my afternoon visit to the party store and insist that he wear the plastic peace sign necklace I bought him.

"There's a seventies theme," I explain. No longer able to bite back my grin, I give in to amusement at his growing confusion, downright giddy as I anticipate his reaction to what's in store for him tonight.

Bedecked in my own seventies accessories, a slightly smaller peace sign necklace and a multicolored tie-dye headband, I declare us ready to venture inside. We visit the bar first, where Walker insists on paying for his own beer (even though he gripes the entire time about the price). Once in the theater, I pull him into the open space in front of the stage, knowing from the pictures I saw online that this spot will give us the *full* experience.

"What have you gotten me into?" Walker asks, eyeing the large group that just arrived dressed to the nines in bright seventies costumes.

"You'll see," I singsong.

We continue people watching as the room fills around us. It's quite the varied mix. While there seem to be a number of groups embracing the seventies theme with their attire, most people are in casual clothing or clubwear, suggesting this is only the beginning of their Friday night. I count eight different bachelorette parties, easily spotted due to the requisite white or hot-pink pageant-style sash worn by the brides (or, in one case, groom).

"Here we go!" I clap as the lights change and music begins to play.

"Here we go," Walker echoes with far less enthusiasm.

The Donkey Show—named after the infamous donkey from Shakespeare's *A Midsummer Night's Dream*—is loosely based on the play. Characters from the story act out some of the basic scenes through a medley of seventies music. It's Shakespeare...disco-style.

There's dancing. There's singing. There are acrobatics and aerial tricks. Above our heads, we watch the entrance of a scantily clad Titania, a leggy white woman in shiny black thigh-high boots with sky-high platform heels, tiny metallic-purple shorts, and a glittery pink cape, her torso bare except for two butterflies attached to her nipples. She flies perched in a suspended hoop from all the way in the back of the theater to the stage in front.

The whole thing is cheesy and so OTT it's ridiculous. It's *amazing*. I'm dying to tell Callie about it; she would *love* this.

The performers—whose costumes range from skin-baring ensembles like Titania's to afros and bell bottoms, with bright colors and shiny fabrics galore—utilize every available inch of the space, their antics spilling from the stage into the center area. Meaning we're standing right in the midst of the action. Just as I intended.

My favorite among the cast are the fairies—a handful of very fit men, bulging muscles on full display since they wear only tiny metallic shorts and their wings...plus a ton of body glitter. When not performing, doing acrobatics on the various platforms set around the floor or carrying Titania on their shoulders while she poses dramatically, the fairies interact with the audience, often dragging members in to dance with them.

As if a higher power deigned to grant my wish, no sooner have I thought about trying to draw the fairies' attention to Walker, than one approaches us. (More plausibly, he's gravitating toward Walker's Super Grump face or his general hotness.) Although Walker grabs my shoulders and tries to use me as a human shield, the fairy—a very tall, very muscular, *very* shirtless Black man covered in body glitter—has zeroed in on Walker as his chosen target. Walker silently beseeches me to save him, but I simply step aside, clearing their path out to the center of the floor. Even his betrayed glare can't wipe the guilt-free smile off my face.

You know what they say about turnabout... That was Shakespeare too, right? Smart, smart man.

* * *

When we exit the theater, Freddy is waiting at the curb. Upon catching sight of Walker, he has us wait while he retrieves a blanket from the trunk that he drapes along the back seat, mustache twitching all the while.

A wise move, seeing as Walker is *covered* in glitter. Although he's tried to shake it off, you know how glitter is...stubborn and clingy, especially in his hair, though I also spy a few sparkly specks clinging to his face. I giggle, not for the first, second, or even third time tonight.

"Laugh it up," he mutters, brushing a hand through his hair in another ineffectual attempt to rid it of glitter.

His side of the bed is going to be *soooo* pretty tomorrow.

More laughter bubbles out of me.

"Yeah, yeah, you got me."

I did. I *so* did!

We can thank Walker's new fairy friends for his current state (grumpy and sparkly). After that first fairy pulled him onto the floor, my fake boyfriend became a favorite of the fairies. At one point, there were *five* of them dancing around Walker—and occasionally *on* him, explaining the sheer quantity of transferred glitter. I think they enjoyed his broody vibe, or at the very least, they were undaunted by it.

I took pictures. So. Many. Pictures.

Tonight was everything I could have hoped for and more.

Maybe the best part is that they targeted him all on their own—it's not like I called ahead of time to arrange it (though I totally should have). I can't help thinking it was karma.

They say she's a bitch, but what they don't mention? She's a *glittery* bitch.

As Freddy drives us back across the river, Walker finally gives up his efforts to de-glitter himself and turns to me.

"Hell of a way to tell me I'm a dick, when a couple of words would have done it."

I laugh the entire drive home.

[CONFIDENTIAL PROJECT RECORDS]
DAY 22

Walker's Journal

V—

Don't be fooled by Audrey's shy, innocent, blushing act—underneath is a vengeful little minx.

DISCO. SHAKESPEARE.

Yeah, I looked it up afterward, and that's what they call it.

I'd bitch about the singing and dancing except I'm still covered in glitter, so that's all I can focus on right now. (Why "still?" Because I've already showered TWICE.)

Glitter. On. My. Face. I also found it in some places that… Yeah, I can't even begin to guess how it got there. Those fairies must have been working some kind of sparkle voodoo shit.

I'll telling you, Vickie, the girl is evil.

Off to shower. AGAIN.

W

* * *

Audrey's Journal

Dear Victoria,

I know I should apologize, but honestly? I'm not sorry.

I am attaching pictures. I think once you see the visual evidence, you'll understand why it was worth it.

— Audrey

Comment added by Victoria Trulette: No need to apologize on my account. Far be it from me to interfere in what you deem appropriate retributive action; that is entirely your prerogative. However, I do appreciate the photographic evidence. (Matilda asked that I convey her thanks as well.)

25. Vino Sans Veritas

VOICEMAIL ON WALKER'S PHONE

"Hello, Walker. This is your mother. The woman whose bladder you sat on for nine months? Maybe remember that the next time you decide to send me to voicemail. I know that phone is glued to you at all times, so don't think I'm unaware you ignored my call.

"Your father wants to pull out the grill before the cold weather hits, so we're having a family dinner tomorrow night. I expect to see you there, with this new girlfriend you apparently have. Bringing her is the least you can do, seeing as *Tommy Fontanelli* got to meet her before you so much as mentioned her existence to your mother."

Audrey

Sunday afternoon on our way to Walker's parents' house an hour north of Boston, we stop at a grocery store to buy vegetarian patties I can eat in lieu of burgers. (Or in Walker's words, "Gotta grab some of your veggie shit to throw on the grill.") On top of the bottle of wine I'm bringing for his mother, at the last minute I decide to grab a bouquet from a display near the front. I pointedly ignore Walker's childish muttered taunt of "*brownnoser.*"

If only I could harness some of that man's effortless blasé! Anxiety kept me awake most of the night, and the extra cups of coffee I drank this morning to compensate only made me jittery on top of my nerves.

Even setting aside how badly we need to pull this off for the sake of our contract with Victoria—only thousands of dollars on the line here, no pressure—I've never done the "meet the parents" thing before. My ex-boyfriend certainly made no attempt to introduce me to his mom and dad.

Do I even *know* how to behave around a real family? Mine was far from a model two-parent household. Blurry snippets from the first few years of my life are the only memories I have left of my father, and while I'm sure some single moms manage to provide their kids with a nice functional upbringing, my mother's compulsive need to protect me by holding me close didn't make for the healthiest of familial dynamics.

Then there's the other reason—one I barely want to admit to myself—why I am, as Walker would say, losing my shit.

In spite of myself—and even in spite of Walker, who continues to provide plentiful reminders of his flaws—I care. I *care* about Walker and, in turn, about making a good impression with his family. It's embarrassing, how badly I want them to like me. No matter how many times I remind myself it doesn't matter if they approve of me as long as they believe we're real, I'm sick to my stomach from the intensity of my desire for it. I doubt I'll even be able to choke down any of the veggie burgers we just bought.

Yes, I fully plan to engage in a healthy dose of mental self-flagellation later for this plummet off the Feel Nothing for Walker wagon. For now, I might as well put my weakness to good use, tapping into my genuine fondness for Walker to aid my portrayal of "convincing girlfriend" in front of his parents and brother.

Admittedly, doing so won't be difficult—I need only picture Walker surrounded by adoring bare-chested fairies,

179

grumpy but resigned to his glittery fate. No part of him enjoyed being made a spectacle of, but he stood there anyway. A lesser man would have walked right out of that theater rather than set aside their hetero male ego. My intended revenge backfired, because I left the show not only less angry, but liking Walker even more than I did when we arrived.

The man in question navigates us off the highway and through a residential neighborhood lined with mature trees and modest homes whose well-lived New England character I far prefer to the bland cookie cutter aesthetic of my mom's new construction development.

Our final destination is a one-story beige house with dark brown shutters. A long driveway runs along the side of the house and disappears around the back, but instead of pulling into it, Walker parks his truck on the street. Preparing for a quick getaway?

My heart is pounding so fiercely, I fear I'll pass out before we even make it to the front door. Then Walker grabs my hand and gives it a squeeze.

"Come on, girlfriend. Time to meet my folks."

Just like that, my nerves calm; the deafening roar of anxiety inside me fades to a whimper. He's telling me that we're in this together, and that reassurance somehow makes this seem less insurmountable. I try not to cling too tightly to the stabilizing comfort of his hand as Walker leads me up the shrub-lined walkway. Instead of knocking, he uses his own key to let us in the front door, then hollers, "Hey, Ma! We're here!"

Before I can scold him for his poor manners, a woman yells back, "In the kitchen!"

Well, I suppose that's just how things are done in the Garrison household. It's…refreshing.

To our left, a man turns the corner, propelling himself into the foyer in a wheelchair.

"Luke," Walker says, though I can't tell if it's for my benefit or a greeting.

What should happen next: I paste on my politest "New Person" smile, introduce myself to Walker's brother, and offer my hand to shake, all while keeping my eyes on his face and away from the chair he's in. I should be friendly, perhaps say that I'm happy to meet him.

What *actually* happens next: I stare, stunned, my brain utterly stalling out as I try to process this new information.

Yes, the wheelchair is entirely unexpected, but had that been the only surprise, I could have rallied. What sends me over the edge into speechlessness is the double whammy of the chair and Luke's face...because it's one I recognize.

The medium-brown locks are longer, the beard fuller, but not even his facial hair's efforts to take over his face can hide the familiar features beneath. There's no mistaking that elegantly contoured jaw, the stupidly perfect nose, or the masculine browbone and forehead over which strands of unruly hair have fallen. His eyes are colder and harder than the ones I've memorized but have the exact same shape and hue of his irises, a unique mixture of muted green speckled with blues and browns that appears gray in all but the brightest lighting.

Oh. My. God. Luke isn't Walker's brother—he's Walker's *twin*.

And he's in a wheelchair? How has Walker not mentioned *either* of these not-so-little details? The omission is so unthinkable that I find myself scanning back through my mental files, all of our hours talking through those icebreaker questions, though I already know I won't find anything. This is *not* the type of information I would have forgotten. If anything, the few stories I can recall Walker sharing about his brother involved football and the antics of two active, able-bodied boys.

A nudge to my back, delivered by Walker's elbow, breaks me from my daze and brings my attention to my prolonged silence.

181

Oh no, how long have I been zoned out? I've definitely passed the point of awkward into socially inappropriate, but have I surpassed even *that*, all the way to creepy territory, or worse, insulting?

FOR GOODNESS' SAKE, SAY SOMETHING, AUDREY. ANYTHING!

"Hi, I'm Audrey."

I reach out to shake his hand, my smile as unnaturally bright as my voice, stretching the edges of my mouth in my desperation to compensate for my misstep. That smile wavers as the seconds drag on and Luke does nothing but glower at me, pointedly ignoring my proffered hand and *not* lifting either of his from the rims of his chair's wheels. Luke remains silent and utterly still, but there's tension radiating from every inch of his body, from his stiff shoulders to the bulky arms held so taut his considerable muscles seem to be straining to overpower the constraints of his skin.

I drop my hand, my heart aching. It's clear that to Luke, (whose opinion is the only one that matters), my behavior was absolutely insulting. I swallow down sorrow and regret and force myself to meet his disdainful gaze, the eerie familiarity of those gray eyes making the cold hardness aimed at me all the more painful.

He must think me unforgivably rude, if not some kind of bigot, prejudiced against people who have disabilities. When, really, I was simply caught off guard and reacted in the most awkward way possible. Shame fills me. I have never wanted a redo so badly as I do for the last five minutes.

(Come on, universe, help a girl out with a one-time CTRL+Z? No?)

"I-it's wonderful to meet you, Luke. Walker has told me so much about you." *Though apparently, he left out some extremely crucial details.*

"That's funny. He hasn't mentioned you at all," Luke deadpans.

"Nice, bro," Walker growls.

Well, look who finally decided to participate! Through narrowed eyes, I silently promise Walker that he and I will be having *words* about this later.

"Luke, I—" My mind races, searching for words, anything I can say to fix this mess.

Luke doesn't wait for me to come up with something. Pivoting without another word or glance, he heads out of the room. Rather than diverting his path around me, he barrels straight ahead so I'm forced to jump out of the way to avoid his wheels running over my feet.

I deserve his cold treatment and more, after how I just completely ruined that. Tears of self-recrimination and disappointment prickle behind my eyes, but I blink them away. In their wake, fury rises hot and fast, overtaking me as I turn in near slow motion to the remaining Garrison twin in the room.

"Why didn't you tell me?" The hissed accusation is far from what I'd like to do, which involves screaming right in that face he never told me has a living carbon copy. But with Walker's family so close, I have to settle for trying to liquefy his brain with my glare.

I take full responsibility for how badly I handled that, and I'll be kicking myself over it for a long time to come—but that ruinous meeting would never have happened if Walker had *warned me*, rather than setting me up to be blindsided.

"I was gonna tell you," Walker mumbles, refusing to look at me. He does seem to feel guilty—which is great, but doesn't do anyone much good *now*, does it? Especially Luke.

"When?" I'm still whisper-shouting.

Walker opens his mouth, but his mother's voice saves him from delivering whatever insufficient excuse was about to leave his tongue.

"*Walker!* Get back here!"

Walker grabs my hand and leads me to the back of the house, where we find his mother in the kitchen, mixing something in a large bowl. I relax somewhat at Laura Garrison's casual appearance. She's dressed for comfort, in a pair of light jeans and a "Lowell High Football" T-shirt, her straight blond hair pulled back in a simple ponytail, and when she turns around to greet us, I note the gray eyes she passed to both of her sons. When she tugs Walker to her for a hug, it's hard not to gawk at their size discrepancy; she stands well over a foot shorter than her son, his massive arms completely swallowing her up. Who would have guessed his mother was pint-sized?

Mrs. Garrison quickly proves that what she lacks in physical stature, she makes up for in personality. As swiftly as his mother reached for him, she pushes Walker away (something I note he allows without protest). Then she swats him on the cheek—and none too gently, based on the sound when her hand makes contact.

"I don't see you for months, and then I have to find out you have a girlfriend from Tommy Fontanelli?"

I duck my head to hide my amusement at witnessing this tiny woman scold Walker, who actually looks chastened.

"Ma, this is Audrey. Audrey, Ma."

Before I can even say hello, Walker's mother is hugging me. I also have multiple inches on her in height as well as a couple (dozen) pounds, but the woman grips me to her with arms that are surprisingly strong. I only barely manage to save the bouquet in my hands from becoming a casualty of her aggressive embrace.

She gushes over the flowers (but even more so the wine), hugging me again while saying to an amusingly shamefaced Walker, "When's the last time *you* got me flowers, huh?"

With a holler (that definitely appears to be the norm in this house), Mrs. Garrison summons Luke to the kitchen.

Luke dutifully allows his mother to pile covered platters of seasoned meat and veggies onto his lap, while doing a thorough job of pretending I don't exist. I hold the back door open for them as Luke rolls down an aluminum ramp (if only I'd seen *that* little hint earlier!) followed by Walker, whose arms are similarly laden with food for the grill.

Just before the door slams shut behind them, Walker turns to wink at me. It takes effort to push down my anger and remember I still need to play the devoted girlfriend. *Think of the fairies. Glitter!*

Instead of handing me something to carry as well, Mrs. Garrison asks me to stay and assist her in the kitchen. Except when we're alone, she leans back against the counter in a relaxed pose.

"Um, did you need my help with something?" I ask hopefully.

Her lips curve with mischief. "Oh no, everything's done in here. I just wanted some girl time alone with you. Let the boys grill meat and grunt at one another for a bit."

I laugh before realizing what "girl time" means—I'm about to face my first parental interrogation. On the plus side, it can't possibly go worse than my introduction with Luke—but given I'd categorize that as "catastrophic," the thought provides little comfort.

"So, I hear you're living with my son," Mrs. Garrison says with little inflection, gesturing for me to hand over the bottle of wine.

"Oh. Well," I stammer, trying not to wilt beneath her open appraisal (or drop the bottle). "It's, um, temporary. But yes, ma'am."

"You're a sweetheart, so polite. But it's Laura, not ma'am. We don't do formal in this house."

Laura pulls out two wineglasses and fills them nearly to the top. One is pushed into my hands even as I try to decline. (If

I'm going to survive today, it seems like I should hold on to all of my mental faculties.)

"Honey, I've lived with Garrison men for almost thirty years. You and I both know you've earned this."

On *that* note, I have no choice but to clink my wineglass with hers and follow suit as she takes a drink. The wine is surprisingly tasty—but it's the shared smile of commiseration and feminine camaraderie that spreads warmth through my body.

It's official: I *really* like Walker's mother.

"Now, tell me more about you and Walker. How did you meet? How did living together come about? Is he treating you well?"

This time, I tip my glass back all the way and pour the wine right down my throat, not arguing when Laura grabs the bottle and tops off both of our glasses.

Let's just hope this *vino* doesn't bring out any *veritas*, or this fake relationship is going to be over far sooner than planned.

26. I Am SO Telling Jenny

Audrey

After dinner, Laura banishes me from the kitchen after refusing my offer to help with the dishes, conscripting Walker for the task instead.

My quest for childhood photos of Walker leads me into the living room, where I suddenly find myself alone with Luke. Walker's twin doesn't look up, although he must have heard me come in. His body language screams "*leave me alone*" loud and clear, but I step farther into the room instead of heeding the message. I *have* to try apologizing to him. This may be my only opportunity.

"Hey."

Only turning halfway in my direction, Luke makes a sound that could either be a greeting or an introduction for me to "eff off." I choose to interpret it as the former.

"Luke, I'm sorry about earlier. Truly, so very sorry."

"Don't worry about it." With his flat tone and continued refusal to look at me, the words are far from reassuring.

"No, really. I mean it. Please let me apologize."

Finally, he looks at me. His face is absent of emotion, the blank mask similar to the one Walker adopts when he's shutting me out, except Luke has a hardness to him Walker can't match even at his coldest. I wonder if someone who hadn't made such a careful study of his brother would notice the darkness dwelling in the depths of Luke's eyes, even shuttered as they are now.

Trying to cancel out his blankness, I let all of my sincerity and remorse show. "I *am* sorry. Walker never mentioned anything when he's talked about you, so I was surprised, and then I just froze up, and..."

"Seriously, babe, don't worry about it. My feelings ain't hurt."

There's no missing the sardonic bite beneath his careful insouciance. Something about that cynicism gives me the impression Luke expects nothing more from anyone—which, for some reason, bothers me immensely. I've been dismissed, but I find I can't let this go. I want to stomp my foot like a petulant child at his nonchalant dismissal of my awkward but heartfelt apology, to *make* him listen until he actually believes me.

"Please, Luke. I *hate* that we got off to such a bad start. I know I haven't earned it, but I hope you'll give me a do-over. I don't want you to think I'm a big jerk. At least without getting to know me. I mean, once you get to know me, you might still think I'm a jerk, and that's okay, I guess. But I *need* you to believe me when I say I'm not *this* kind of a jerk. I honestly just wasn't expecting the..."

"Wheelchair," Luke fills in, at the same time I say, "Twin thing."

Embarrassment heats my cheeks as I admit, "Well, uh, yes. That too."

His expression shifts the slightest bit. It's not a smile or anywhere close, but he's no longer outright scowling at me. Luke proceeds to stare me down while I force myself to hold his gaze. If he's trying to intimidate me, it's working, but I can't give up. This is too important.

Maybe I passed some kind of test, because the intensity suddenly fades, the tension around his mouth loosening further.

"So, you're gonna prove to me that you're a jerk?"

Encouraged by the faint note of teasing in his words, I leap into the opening he's provided and start talking. Okay, *rambling.*

"Well, *I* don't think I'm a jerk. I'm, you know, usually pretty nice, for the most part. I have a couple of friends, and they seem to think so. But Walker says I get bitchy when I'm tired or hungry…definitely when I'm both. I'll try to be fed and rested whenever I'm going to see you—we'll just need to avoid early mornings, because unlike your brother, I am *not* a morning person—but I can't one hundred percent promise that you'll never be on the other end of my hangry bitchiness."

Now his beard twitches, a distant cousin of a smile. "Hangry?"

"You know, when you get cranky because you're hungry?"

"I know what hangry means."

"Oh, right. Sure. Of course."

"You talk a lot, huh?"

"I guess so. When I'm uncomfortable, I either get really quiet or I talk too much. I'm sorry for word-vomiting all over you."

Luke looks down at his chest, then each of his shoulders, before deadpanning, "Nope. Vomit free."

Humor ripples over the hardness in his eyes, and within that unruly beard, his mouth curves into a bona fide smirk. Which is basically a smile!

Before I can embarrass myself by busting out in a little happy dance at the victory, Luke surprises me by directing his next statement somewhere over my shoulder.

"You think it's cool to call your woman a bitch, bro?"

My jaw drops. *Did he really just…?*

"The fuck?" Growled words resonate through my whole body as a solid wall of heat presses up against my back. The voice is nearly identical to that of the man in front of me, yet I would know the difference anywhere. When did Walker get here?

How much did he hear?

"I didn't say that!" I hiss at Luke.

I twist and crane my neck, trying to angle my face up to look at Walker, but with him standing so close, I have to settle for speaking to his stubble-covered frown.

"I didn't say that!" I repeat, my pitch higher now with a touch of desperation.

"Bitchy isn't much better." Luke's retort has me spinning back in his direction, adding my own glare to the one Walker is undoubtedly giving his brother from above my head.

"Seriously?" Walker asks. "I leave you two alone for half a second, and you're already ganging up against me?"

"Yeah, pretty much." Luke shrugs.

Any further protest dies at my lips when Luke suddenly grins. My first glimpse of a real smile on him, teeth and everything, renders me literally speechless. Sure, it's snarky and somewhat taunting, but even so, Luke Garrison's smile is gorgeous. That smile turns him from attractive in a grizzly, broody, somewhat scary, and definitely untouchable way, to a man every woman who's ever lusted over lumberjack photos online would sign up for *Bachelor*-style. I am helpless to suppress the answering curve of my own lips.

At my back, Walker grumbles and plants his hands on my hips in an obvious claiming gesture. My brain remembers that I'm furious with him, but my body is fully on board with our current circumstances, especially when Walker pulls me even closer against him by tugging on my belt loops…a tug I feel resonating somewhere far more intimate.

Holy. Cow.

Then Luke cocks his head to the side and asks Walker, "Is that *glitter* in your hair?"

To which I giggle so hard, I'm almost crying.

* * *

We're back at the Garrisons' dining room table, on which Laura has just set a tray of cookies and brownies. Walker and Luke waste no time digging in and piling sweets onto their plates. The enticing aroma of chocolate and fresh-baked sugar makes it tempting to follow suit, but I restrain myself to a brownie for now.

"Milk?" a deep voice asks from my right.

I hand my glass to Walker's father with a murmur of thanks and a smile I'm not quite brave enough to pair with full eye contact. As broad as his sons and nearly as fit, with the same shade of brown hair, although speckled with gray and worn in a buzz cut, John Garrison makes for an intimidating presence. The Garrison patriarch hasn't spoken much (his reticence second only to Luke's) and though he's been welcoming, there's a sternness to the man that unnerves me—perhaps a result of his time in the army, where Walker has mentioned he served. All I know is that I breathe a bit more easily when he goes to take his seat at the head of the table.

With an ease born of much practice, Laura slides back into the role of conversational facilitator that she's taken on all evening.

"What do you do for work, Audrey?"

Usually a safe topic, the question is decidedly uncomfortable at the moment. I can't exactly say that what I'm currently doing for work is shacking up with her son and pretending to be his girlfriend in exchange for an exorbitant sum of money.

"Um, I've been picking up some shifts through a temp agency while I look for something more long-term. Actually, I'm also working with Walker on his screen-printing business, consulting on some marketing stuff and online merchandising strategies I learned in school that I think will help with his expansion plans."

"That's very nice of you," Mr. Garrison says, both his words and his tone oddly stiff.

"I'm really not doing much. Just setting him up on a few sites to increase his visibility. His designs are so amazing, the product sells itself."

I consciously keep my back turned to Walker. He's so weird about compliments and would never brag about himself, but *someone* has to. His family should know about his accomplishments.

"We tried some social media ads last week, and Walker's already gotten a bunch of inquiries about potential orders! The response rate was impressive, way better than any of the start-ups I worked with during my college internship. I'm confident he'll have enough business soon to move forward with this as his full-time career."

Loaded silence follows my statement. The atmosphere at the table is heavy with tension, particularly coming from Mr. Garrison.

I get the distinct feeling that I've inadvertently hit a minefield, one everyone else at this table knew about except for me. Yet another way Walker failed to prepare me for this dinner. (I am *so* telling Jenny about this at our next therapy session.)

"Oh! I forgot the ice cream," Laura says, breaking into the quiet.

She begins to rise from her chair, but her husband stops her. "You sit, I'll get it. Walker will come help carry spoons and bowls." He doesn't phrase it as a request.

The men disappear into the kitchen, both sets of broad shoulders visibly tense.

"I'm sorry," I say once the door clicks shut behind them, not knowing what exactly I'm apologizing for.

"Oh, don't worry about it, honey," Laura reassures me. "They just—"

The door of the old house is thick enough to muffle the words but not to block out the rumbling of male voices on its other side—which is enough to recognize their contentious tone.

Luke, Laura, and I sit at the table in awkward silence, no one touching their food. The talk happening in the kitchen is clearly meant to be private between Walker and his dad, but the men's steadily rising volume makes overhearing unavoidable unless we leave the room.

"Always fighting, my boys." Laura's attempt at lightening the mood falls flat, perhaps because her words ring with truth.

Suddenly, the intensity and volume of the argument escalates. Walker's deep timbre is so similar to his father's that I can't tell who starts yelling first, only that they are soon both shouting. Although the words are still indiscernible, the anger between them is palpable.

Laura stands in an abrupt motion, her chair screeching as it scrapes against the floor. "I'll be right back."

Now alone in the dining room, Luke and I don't have to wonder about what happens next, because within seconds, Mrs. Garrison's feminine cadence joins the fray, carrying over the other two so loudly we can actually make out her words.

"IF YOU TWO CAN'T MAKE IT THROUGH ONE FRICKIN' DINNER WITHOUT GETTING INTO IT, AT LEAST LOWER YOUR VOICES! THE WHOLE NEIGHBORHOOD CAN HEAR YOU!"

"That's one way to do it," Luke mutters.

A moment later, Walker storms out of the kitchen—"storm" an apropos word since his face is thunderous—and with a short "We're leaving," keeps on going right down the hall toward the front door.

I have no choice but to jump up and follow, barely managing to call out my thanks and apologies to his mother over my shoulder before rushing after him.

I don't think Walker would drive off without me, but in this state of mind, I can't say for sure. And he's not about to get away from me that easily. We have unfinished business to discuss.

Walker's black mood follows us into his truck, rendering the atmosphere inside the cab far darker than the night that's fallen outside it.

"Walker—"

"Don't."

As growls go—a subject on which I'm quickly becoming an expert—it's a formidable one. Last month, that growl would have sent me running for the hills. Even yesterday, it would have been enough to make me back down from this conversation. But not today. Today, I am *livid,* and I am not in the mood to play the lamb to Walker's Big Bad Wolf.

"Do not *growl* at me, Walker Garrison! We need to talk."

"Can we just...*not* right now?"

Hearing Walker's uncharacteristically defeated tone, I hesitate. I peek over at him, only able to see brief glimpses of his face as we pass beneath streetlights. The deep shadows cast along his features by the intermittent flood of light only accentuate the lines of tension inscribed there from the confrontation with his dad. Compassion threatens to overtake me, but I force myself to stay strong. I imagine titanium armor clicking into place around my heart.

"Why didn't you tell me about Luke?" I repeat my words from earlier, letting my hurt and frustration bleed through.

"I just never got around to it."

Seriously? "You didn't have enough opportunities during the five *thousand* hours we spent talking through those icebreaker questions?"

We're at a stoplight; I watch him bend over and knock his temple against the steering wheel—once, then twice, and a third time, his profile bathed in a muted red glow.

When he speaks next, his voice is hard, warning he's nearing his limit and won't tolerate much more. "My brother isn't a topic I talk about, and I'm not gonna start now just because you've met him. End of. Nothing more to discuss."

"Walker—"

Limit reached. The clouds hovering throughout the cab break; Walker's raised voice booms like thunder at close range.

"Jesus, Audrey, drop it! I know you tend to forget, but we're on mic, and I, for one, don't want every single fucking detail of my life—and especially my brother's life—to be fair game for some goddamn romance novel!"

End of, indeed. We finish the drive in silence.

27. Big Dick Energy

Audrey

I've yet to decide whether it's unfortunate or lucky timing that we have our second therapy appointment with Dr. Jenny the day after dinner with the Garrisons. I'm leaning toward the latter.

"I understand you had dinner with Walker's family last night." Jenny dives right in, obviously prepped by Victoria. "How did that go?"

"It was fine," Walker answers.

Oh no, he doesn't. I am not playing along today. I've just come from a temp assignment where I collated and stapled documents for hours on end, leaving my mind free to fixate on the events of yesterday. By now, I'm nearly as worked up as I was then. He is not ducking out of this conversation again.

"His family was great, but there was drama," I tell Jenny. "We left before dessert."

Walker glares at me. "We would've stayed for dessert except *someone* opened their mouth and shot off about my business, and much as I like my mom's baking, I wasn't real thrilled to stick around and get chewed out by my dad some more."

Hmm. So *that's* what the fight in the kitchen was about?

"Well, I wouldn't have if you'd given me a heads-up not to mention your business. We could have avoided a lot of uncomfortable moments if you'd told me *anything* ahead of time, like a warning that you and your dad don't get along or, I don't know, that your brother is not only in a wheelchair but that he's your *TWIN*."

"Jesus, I don't know why you're so hung up on that."

"HE HAS YOUR FACE!"

"All right," Jenny chimes in. Apparently, her therapist playbook states that once someone starts shrieking, it's time to intervene. (The shrieking was me, if that was in question.)

"We're off to a good start—" Well, that's one way to put it, as Luke might say. "But let's take a step back for a minute. You've never met Walker's brother before?" she asks me.

I don't look at Walker, but I can feel his accusing glare burning into the side of my face. Yeah, I guess I should have thought this through a little more instead of letting my anger take the wheel. Will Jenny find it suspicious that we've supposedly been dating for six months and I only just met Luke?

"Luke isn't very social," Walker says, doing damage control. "And he hates coming into the city."

"Hmm. And Luke is your twin?" Jenny asks.

His attempt at a shrug is stunted, his muscles too tense to pull off nonchalance; he *really* does not want to talk about this. "Yeah. Used to get mistaken for each other all the time, before…"

"The wheelchair?" she prompts.

Walker nods.

"And how would you describe your relationship with your father?" Jenny throws out the sneaky subject change.

Walker doesn't take the bait. Instead, he pastes on a smirk and aims a thumb in my direction, saying conversationally, "Hey, Jen Jen, what do you think about Feisty Miss Audrey

197

over here? I think they call it Big Dick Energy. It's a good look on her, huh?"

For some reason, *that* is *my* limit.

"Is *everything* a joke to you?" I'm almost shouting. "Do you think it's *funny* to create uncomfortable situations for me? Do you not realize I wasn't the only one affected this time? I screwed up and embarrassed not only myself but also Luke, because you thought setting me up to be blindsided was hilarious!"

"I wouldn't use my brother's situation as part of some kind of joke."

"So, you just *couldn't be bothered* to tell me you have a *twin*, and oh by the way, *he's in a wheelchair*?!"

"I told you. I don't talk about my brother, not with anyone."

"I understand that, Walker. I really do. But I'm not just *anyone*. I'm your...girlfriend." I catch myself, remembering the role we're supposed to be playing just in time. Yikes, I need to be more careful. Difficult when I'm this upset.

He groans, a hint of true remorse bleeding into the sound, though his words are pure frustration. "What do you fuckin' want from me? It's not like I can go back and do it different. How many times do I have to say I'm sorry?"

A moment ago, my voice was raised, but now I can barely make it audible with such thick emotion clogging my throat. "Well, since that's the first time you've said it..."

Soft delivery notwithstanding, my words pierce Walker with the sharpness of a needle; he deflates right in front of my eyes.

Face shifting into an expression that is utterly unfamiliar, Walker renders me helpless to do anything but hold his stare as intense emotion pours out of him. For a moment, we are alone in this room—no Jenny, no recording device capturing every second for Victoria, no experiment or contract or thousands of dollars at stake—just the two of us.

So when he says, with those eyes full of sincerity boring into me and a voice that for once holds no hint of humor, "I *am* sorry," I believe him.

* * *

A few hours later, Walker finds me on the tiny balcony off our bedroom.

I hear him slip out through the French doors, but I keep my attention focused outward on the sparse nighttime activity of Beacon Hill on a Monday. It's cooled down considerably since the sun set, but I've stubbornly delayed going inside, wanting to grasp on to the façade of solitude for as long as possible.

Our therapy session ended on a far better note than it began, but I'm still feeling a bit raw. Too much has happened in too short a time, and I haven't had a single moment alone to process it.

Walker clears his throat. "Uh, I found that hipster seltzer shit you like at the store."

I turn and see he's holding a can of the same spiked seltzer I ordered at the ax throwing place.

"We're good, Walker. You don't have to—"

"It's not apology seltzer." He runs his other hand through his hair, making the already messy look even more chaotic. "Okay, it's kind of apology seltzer. Or, like, 'I know I've been a dick recently and you didn't deserve it and I'm going to try to do better' seltzer."

I give him a small smile, touched by the gesture but not quite ready to declare everything fine and forgotten. I'm starting to realize I've done that too often in my life, subverted my own feelings and needs to smooth things over for other people and keep the peace.

A particularly aggressive gust of wind makes me shiver. "Come inside, will you? I'll sleep on the couch if you want to get away from me. You don't have to freeze your ass off out here."

Another inner wound begins to scab over. I let him give me a hand out of the low deck chair, and we step into the warmth of the condo, trapping the tenacious wind on the other side of the glass doors.

"You don't have to sleep on the couch," I tell him.

"Cool. You can choose the TV show tonight," he replies

Walker's Journal

Vickie,

I bet you're just loving all this shit going down lately. You're welcome for the drama. I guess it's the least we can do for all that cash you're throwing at us. My dad's a real Prince Charming, huh? Did you have fun listening to him rip me a new one for daring to even consider quitting the family business? Wouldn't want him to have to hire someone else he'd actually need to pay consistently versus whenever he feels like it.

All jokes aside, and I mean I'm serious as a heart attack here, V, my brother is off-limits. Use me however the fuck you want for your book, I don't care. But *he's* not getting paid to play lab rat for you, and I swear to God, you'd better not exploit his situation for some book sales.

I know there's not a whole lot I can do to stop you, and I don't want to go all "I'll ruin you on Author Yelp" or whatever, so just…please. I get how it might be tempting for you to turn him into some Hallmark movie sobfest, but I'm asking you not to. He's not a part of this. You feel the need to chop a few grand off my paychecks for that, do it.

Deal?

Walker

28. No Shit

Walker

I dragged Luke out of the house today to help set up my new screen-printing equipment. My brother can't draw for shit, but he'll decode those instruction manuals a hundred times faster than I could.

One point for this warehouse building—the freight elevator makes it accessible for Luke. As I watch my brother roll himself into my studio, emotion slams into me hard and fast. I quickly turn my back so Luke doesn't misinterpret my expression as pity. It's not; it's rage. Even after two years, I still have these random moments of overwhelming anger at the sheer injustice of it all. Luke did everything right his whole life: worked his ass off to get into West Point, dedicated himself to serving his country, only to be felled by one stupid civilian kid texting at the wheel. A lifetime of effort and nonstop dedication to achieving his dreams, erased in the handful of seconds it takes to run a red light at fifty miles per hour.

Fate is a sick, twisted motherfucker; don't let anyone tell you otherwise. Only a sadist with a thirst for cruel irony would deal someone so undeserving such a shitty hand.

After a quick confab about the various boxes I've set beside the folding table that came from our basement, Luke dives right in. I leave him to it and go back to working on the tables that will be replacing the old plastic one Luke is using. When I asked the building manager about the wooden shipping pallets I spied in the loading dock, he was more than happy to let me take them off his hands, so I now have two stacks as tall as my shoulders waiting to be broken down and repurposed into large worktables and shelving installations.

It feels incredible to see the studio space I've been planning and dreaming of for years actually come to life before my eyes. The fact that I'm getting the tables and shelving for basically nothing is a stroke of luck. I smile, thinking how excited Audrey will be when I tell her the money I'd budgeted for furniture can now be used for web and marketing spend. She's really fucking good at this stuff, and working together has been surprisingly easy.

"So, what's up with Audrey?" Luke asks, like he knows I'm thinking about her.

"What do you mean?"

"I mean, what's the deal with you two?"

"What deal?" I ask slowly, hoping he's not going where I *think* he's going with this.

He gives me that superior big brother look. (He's forty-five minutes older, a fact he'll hold over my head for eternity.) It screams *"you're an idiot."*

"She's not your type, for one. And I can tell you're not fucking her."

Thank fuck I'm not wearing my mic right now, since it's a workday and Audrey isn't here.

At what must be my look of shock mixed with a tiny bit of panic from that millisecond before I remembered my wrist is bare, Luke scoffs.

"I've known you your entire life, dipshit. You think I can't tell when something's off with you?"

"You want a beer?" I abandon my tools for the mini fridge and the six-pack we just put in there. The cans aren't quite cold yet, but I don't care—any beer is better than no beer for this conversation.

"Uh, sure." He's looking at me like I've lost it—just wait until he hears what I'm doing for money.

(Give me a break; he's my fucking twin. Lying to him is impossible. Anyway, there's no mics, so Victoria never has to know—and fuck, I could use someone to talk to about all this.)

Once I pop open my beer and take a long drink, Luke says, "Okay, start talking. What the fuck is going on?"

"It's not what you think. I mean, I'm not sure *what* you're thinking, but I guarantee it's not this." Damn, I'm rambling like Audrey. "Okay. I signed an NDA, so you have to keep a lid on this. But, that lady I said was paying me to house-sit? Well, she's a romance author, and she's paying me and Audrey each twenty grand to fake date for two months."

"No shit?"

"No shit."

It's dark out and we've annihilated the six-pack by the time I've finished answering all of Luke's questions.

"Fuck, man." He blows out a breath, scratching his bushy beard.

"Yeah."

"You *really* haven't had sex with her?"

I laugh far harder and longer than the moment warrants. It's not the beer—I barely feel three beers spread over a few hours. Maybe my brother's onto something, looking at me like I've got screws loose. I can feel something inside me that's been wound tight for weeks starting to release now that I've gotten that shit off my chest.

And for some reason, in my state of borderline delirium (maybe I'm high on relief?), I find it hilarious that of everything I've told him, *this* is what Luke is hung up on.

"You were the one who called it. How, I don't even wanna know."

He shrugs. "You think I don't know what you look like when you're getting laid?"

"Bro, disturbing."

"Shut up." He gives me a shove that nearly sends me tumbling sideways between his ripped arms and my near-delirious state. "I mean you're less of a moody prick when you're getting some, not your come face for Christ's sake."

I make a show of reaching out to cuff him by the ear, but it's halfhearted.

"But you're sharing a bed, and nothing? She's hot."

I'm surprised by how much it bothers me to hear him call Audrey hot.

"You making eyes at my girl?"

"She's not really your girl, though, is she?"

Technically, he's not wrong, though things feel a hell of a lot more complicated at this point. But even with my brother, I'm not about to dive into what a confusing mindfuck it all is. I'm definitely not discussing how I've started losing track of what's for show when we're out in public, or how it's getting more and more difficult to keep my hands off her when we're alone. Or the kiss—scratch that, kiss*es*—we're pretending didn't happen, but that I've replayed in my head a million and one times. (Mostly in the shower, with my fist around my dick, let's just be honest.)

Nope, not going there.

Instead, I say, "You don't know that, remember? I need you to fake it until the sixty days are up, so you don't screw me out of this money."

"Yeah, yeah. I got it." Then he breaks out into a shit-eating grin. "So, after next month, Audrey's fair game."

Is Luke being serious or fucking with me? I'm eighty percent sure it's Option B, since he hasn't gone out with anyone since the accident, but that other twenty percent makes me feel a little violent. If I let on that he's gotten to me, though, it will just egg him on. So, I let it go.

"Let's get out of here. I'm starved, want to grab a pizza for dinner?"

We get Brooklyn Bros and eat it back at our place over some video games, and it feels like old times. Like...*old*, old times. For these past few hours, it's like I really had my brother back.

I'll have to remember talking about my shit makes Luke forget about his. Maybe I'll even suck it up and let him tease me about making a move on Audrey.

Maybe. I'm not a goddamned saint.

29. Overstuffed Sausage

Audrey

JAMIE: Oliver PROPOSED!

My friend attaches a photo of her left hand, which sports a brand-new, very sparkly—and *very* large—diamond ring.

Go ahead and click "submit" on my nomination for Worst Friend Ever, because upon learning that one of my best friends just got engaged, my initial reaction isn't happiness for her. Nope, my self-centered brain jumps immediately to panic. My first thought is that I am losing her, that I'm being left behind. Again.

Oh my God, Jamie's getting *married*. Meanwhile, I'm over here aimless and unemployed, and the closest thing I've had to a relationship in years is with a guy who's being paid to pretend he likes me.

With a mental slap to the face, I force myself out of my self-pity spiral. *This is not about* you, *Audrey.*

AUDREY: OMG, congratulations!! I'm so happy for you!!!!

There. Maybe I went a bit far overcompensating with all the exclamation points, but I am satisfied I've now done my duty as a good friend. Jamie replies with another photo, this one a selfie of her with her boyfriend—I mean, *fiancé,* so weird

They're both beaming with pure joy as she holds up her ring-adorned hand.

I feel ashamed all over again. I *am* glad for her; Jamie's a good person who deserves this happiness. If her joy happens to double as a giant mirror shining light on the emptiness in my own life…well, that's a *me* problem.

The following day, she messages me again.

JAMIE: My moms got a last-minute flight, so we're having the engagement party this weekend.

Jamie grew up in Ohio, but her parents come and visit her regularly, so I've met them a few times. (If only my mother could be half as cool as either of hers!)

JAMIE: You HAVE to be there!

Oh, hi there, generous side portion of guilt. You can go right next to the entrée-sized plate still littering my emotional table from last night. Despite Jamie's multiple attempts to connect and make plans, I've been avoiding her ever since this experiment started. Besides Callie, and possibly my mother, Jamie will be the hardest person to convince that Walker and I are a real couple.

JAMIE: And bring your boyfriend (!!!) plus an explanation why I didn't know about him until Callie told me in our DMs.

Looks like my time for stalling just ran out. There's no such thing as *good* timing when it comes to introducing your fake boyfriend to your closest friend on this side of the Atlantic, but it still feels too soon.

Big girl panties on, Audrey. If Jamie doesn't believe we're a real couple, she'll tell Callie, and this house of cards Walker and I have been living in will collapse right on top of our heads.

* * *

At the cocktail lounge downtown, we are directed to a cordoned-off stairway. A sign reads "Reserved for Private Party."

Walker whistles. "They rented out the whole upstairs?"

"Her fiancé's family is really wealthy. Jamie also makes a lot of money. She actually works for the employment agency—that's how I got this job." At Walker's eyebrow quirk, I clarify, "Jamie isn't assigned to Victoria's account, so she doesn't know about our contract."

Oh, how I wish she *did*, so I had someone to talk to about all this!

I was so nervous about tonight, I sought fashion advice from Matilda, not anticipating she would offer to lend me an outfit from her own closet. Both the dress and heels are stunning and, no doubt, look gorgeous on her. On me? I don't think they've invented a word yet for what a massive error in judgment it was to leave the house like this.

On the designer heels that are higher than I've ever worn before, ascending the single flight of stairs feels more like walking a treacherous tightrope. If not for the wooden banister I'm currently clutching for dear life, there's every chance the velvet rope blocking the staircase for the party would find itself imminently traded out for yellow crime scene tape, denoting where I fell and met my demise at the hands of unwise vanity.

As for the dress, which Matilda insisted would be perfect on me...I don't even know where to start. It's black, tight, and *very* short, the hem landing at a place above my knees heretofore untouched by public air. Even with the sheer black tights I added underneath, the exposure is uncomfortable. Here I was, hoping to boost my confidence by looking fabulous—instead, my current aesthetic is less "sleek seductress" than "overstuffed sausage."

Typically, Walker isn't helping matters by looking infuriatingly gorgeous, sporting facial hair grown out long enough to be called a beard and wearing a pair of newish jeans with a button-up shirt that lands somewhere between businessman and flannel lumberjack. The buttons at his wrists only lasted about ten minutes before he rolled up the sleeves, which only made him hotter. (Curse the man for proving there's truth in that sexy forearm thing romance authors are always going on about!)

Granted, chances are high I'd be drooling regardless of his grooming or attire. Despite all of my brain's coaching, my body refuses to accept that Walker is off the menu—all he needs to do is enter a room and BAM. My cells instantly start humming at a frequency of horny point five hertz.

I survive the perilous journey upstairs (with help from Walker, who offers a steadying arm about halfway up), and we finally make it to the party. The downtown restaurant is one of Jamie's favorites. Its upscale industrial vibe with a hint of rustic charm makes for a perfect party atmosphere—classy without being pretentious, much like my friend. The room is filled with people but not too crowded, the lights dim but not too dark, and the music is loud enough to set the mood while still allowing conversation—which is all great, except, for once in my life, I'd prefer a suffocating crowd into which Walker and I could slip under the radar.

There's a complimentary coat check, so we hand over our jackets. Walker tries to get me to give the attendant my cardigan too, but I refuse, holding it closer to me and hunching protectively. He backs away, palms raised in surrender, but his lips are curled into his customary infuriating (and far too sexy) smirk.

Even knowing it's overkill, I button up the cardigan just a bit higher. This piece of clothing is the only thing standing between my "girls" and an untimely public debut. (Funny story: Matilda is smaller than me in most ways, but I'd expected boobage to be the exception. Nope, the girl must just wear killer bras. In other words, my breasts are basically busting out of this deep V neck.)

"Let's go find Jamie," I say to Walker's collar, willing him not to comment on all the leg I'm showing in this dress. I think something in me might snap if I have to endure a single word of teasing or mocking look from him tonight. I'm self-conscious enough, and Walker has a proven record of making me feel two inches tall.

Never hard to spot in a crowd with her vibrant hair acting as a beacon, I head straight toward Jamie. Tonight, she stands out more brightly than usual, not only because she looks gorgeous in her white lace minidress (*she* doesn't look like a bloated bratwurst) but because she is glowing with happiness. As soon as Jamie sees me, she rushes over and throws her arms around me at full speed. The momentum would have sent us tumbling to the floor if it weren't for Walker's bulk at my back.

Faced with my friend's huge smile, her commercial-perfect white teeth on full display, my responding smile is effortless, all anxiety forgotten for a moment. Her eyes are a bit glassy, which I know from experience means she's already downed a few glasses of her favorite champagne cocktail, and also explains why she refuses to release her hold on me—Jamie is what I call a "cuddly drunk"—until her future husband joins us, having walked over at a more sedate pace.

All selfishness is gone now that I'm standing a foot from their palpable bliss, and when I offer my congratulations to Jamie and Oliver (whom I've known for a few years now), the sentiment is entirely sincere.

My stomach twists into nervous knots when conversation turns to my "boyfriend"—who has now wrapped me in his arms from behind, playing his part to perfection—but the introductions go over more smoothly than I could have hoped. It helps that Jamie is firmly ensconced in her champagne-colored love bubble; plus, we are constantly interrupted by well-wishers wanting the happy couple's attention.

It's not long until they're called away, but before they go, Jamie pulls me into another hug, squeezing me as she squeals into my ear that she's so happy for me and singing Walker's praises. This smile, I have to force. She means well; I'm aware Jamie thinks she's complimenting me by commenting on Walker's hotness. She couldn't know that her reminder of his physical appeal is a salty sting in the open wound of my unrequited feelings.

After Jamie and Oliver leave, we spend some time with her moms, Catalina and Katya, who are also enamored with Walker. Seems his charm is universal… Go figure.

Walker and I then proceed to track down every waiter walking around with appetizer-laden trays, on a mission to leave no appetizer untasted—he eats the non-vegetarian treats for both of us, a burden he bears with great enthusiasm. We stop a few times to chat with people I know from college, but most of the faces in this room are unfamiliar, Jamie being an incurable social butterfly with a much larger social circle than mine. Fortunately, as it saves me from too much obligatory socializing…or playing the perfect girlfriend to Walker's eerily convincing adoring boyfriend act.

I'm on my tiptoes, about to suggest to Walker that we find Jamie and say our goodbyes so we can head home, when the sound of my name in an all-too-familiar voice brings both my feet and my stomach plummeting back to earth. That sound triggers a mental time machine, and I suddenly feel as vulnerable as the heartbroken twenty-one-year-old who last heard it.

The force of Walker's inquiring gaze feels like it's boring into the side of my face, but I can't answer his silent question, can't even look at him, because it takes everything in me to make myself turn around and face my past.

30. Tit Mirage

Walker

I've spent most of tonight—when I wasn't scarfing down heavenly (but miniature) appetizers—trying *not* to think about how much it cost Audrey's friends to reserve this entire floor. Dropping this kind of dough for just a few hours, on top of the apps and free-flowing open bar, shows they're not just rich, they're *filthy* rich. Not that I couldn't have come to the same conclusion just by looking at the giant rock Jamie has on her finger. Everyone Audrey and I have encountered so far who wasn't staff fairly reeks of money.

At least Jamie doesn't seem snobby, as I might expect. The bubbly redheaded bride-to-be is sweet, and she appears to think Audrey's the shit, which, above all, sells me on her. When they came over to chat with us, the fiancé wasn't too talkative, but he didn't give off any douchebag vibes, despite the suit that likely cost more than my monthly rent.

So, that has occupied about fifty percent of my headspace since we got here. The other fifty percent (or, let's be honest, probably more) is focused on keeping the situation in my pants from becoming a public one. And this one is all on Audrey. Her and that fucking dress.

She looks incredible. I've been having a hell of a time keeping my eyes off her legs and ass, which this dress is doing some serious justice. Ever since she walked out of the bedroom earlier, my rogue lizard brain has barely stopped imagining flipping the hem of that dress up to get an even better view.

Is she wearing any panties under those tights? Inquiring minds want to know.

I didn't get much of a look at the top half of the dress before she covered up with a sweater, and curiosity has been dogging me ever since. Because, the brief peek I *did* get? *Mouthwatering*. Now, I'm dying for her to ditch that sweater so I can confirm—was that glimpse really as hot as I'm remembering, or is this my horny mind conjuring up a luscious tit mirage?

But, like I said, even with the grandma sweater, I've been semi-hard all night, because the lower half and overall impact of her is just that good. (Yes, her hair is down, and yes, I am all about getting my hands on that, too.) Thus, the wrestling match with the guy behind my zipper.

"I don't think we've tried that one yet," Audrey says, pointing as a waiter exits the kitchen. I focus on the new prey, thankful for the distraction.

When did I become the guy hoping there's *not* any meat in whatever is on that tray? Oh, right, sometime over the last thirty days when I apparently handed over my balls to a five-foot-six vegetarian with hair that deserves its own zoo exhibit.

Fucked. I am so incredibly fucked.

Appetizer acquired and consumed (it was some kind of tiny toast with goat cheese and fancy herbs on it—delicious *and* veggie friendly), I savor the momentary reprieve from socializing, sipping my third beer and eyeing Audrey's glass in case she needs another cocktail.

"Audrey."

The voice is male, and one Audrey clearly recognizes, based on the way she immediately tenses and her face drains of color—which is all it takes for me to hate this guy before ever setting eyes on him.

When I take Audrey's hand as we turn to face the unknown enemy, I feel it shaking. Seriously, who the fuck *is* he? A first glance shows nothing remarkable. Just another head of perfect blond hair and set of expensive threads among many in this room. *He's* got Audrey shrinking into herself?

"Ethan." Audrey's voice is meek, smaller than I've ever heard it. For that alone, I'm primed to give this kid's plastic surgeon a whole lot of business.

Wait… *Ethan,* the guy she dated in college for six months? Oh yeah, that surgeon's billables just shot through the roof in my fantasies.

"Hey, I'm Ethan. And you are?" Oh, fuck no, he's not trying to talk to me—*or* Audrey—in that condescending tone.

"Walker. The boyfriend." As he's already proven himself unworthy of any effort at civility, I stare him down and ignore the hand he's offered to shake.

Never have I been so grateful for Luke's grueling workout regimen. It's damn satisfying, watching the cockiness slowly fade off his face as Audrey's ex takes me in. *That's right, pretty boy. I could end you without breaking a sweat.*

Just waiting for him to give me that first reason to step in, I stand sentry at Audrey's shoulder while they do the obligatory small talk thing—mostly the dude talks about himself, typical narcissistic prick. Finally, he slithers away to go do some other fuckboy shit elsewhere.

"You want to tell me what that was about?" I ask the instant he's out of earshot.

"Not really."

As if I weren't pissed enough, her shaky voice and trembling hands send my agitation to the next level. I hate how she's curled into herself right now, clutching the sides of her sweater together like she's cold, when this room is damn near tropical.

215

An orange blur rushes toward us—Jamie's speed downright impressive in those tall-ass heels and her painted-on dress. Every eye in the room follows her progress as she bullets straight to Audrey from the section of the room where the blond pissant has his arm around some brunette chick. Subtle, the girl is not.

"Ohmygod, I'm so sorry! I had *no idea* Ethan would be here! You know I'd never do that to you. I invited Tilly—can you believe she's dating him?! I didn't know, I swear."

Looking panicked, Jamie examines Audrey head to toe, as if checking for injury. "Are you okay? What do you need? What can I do?"

Jesus. First Audrey, now the redhead. Based on all the dramatics over his presence, whatever went down between this guy and my girl must have been major.

Not really your *girl, dipshit.*

Maybe not, but she *is* my responsibility. At least for the next thirty days.

I stand guard at Audrey's back as she and Jamie have a hushed, rapid-fire conversation. My face is fixed on the "I'll Fuck You Right Up" setting—a warning that if anyone messes with her, they'll be answering to me.

Yeah, I'm talking to you, Micro Dick Junior the Fifth.

The girls are talking in circles, Jamie apologizing repeatedly, with Audrey reassuring her. I'd be pissed that this chick is making Audrey's drama about herself, but her distress seems to be genuine, based on care for Audrey, which works in her favor.

"Do you want me to make them leave?" Jamie asks, cementing my approval.

Hell yes.

"What?" Audrey asks. "How would you even do that?"

"I don't know. I could just ask them to go, I guess."

I'd be more than happy to offer my services in escorting them out. In fact, it would be my motherfucking pleasure. But of course, Audrey's too nice.

"You're the sweetest, but I'd never ask you to do that. It's fine. I'm fine," Audrey declares with faux confidence that convinces literally no one.

Jamie lingers for a few more minutes, fluttering around Audrey like a concerned orange butterfly. Inevitably, she's called away again—the bride, or whatever you call a newly engaged female, is in high demand at her own party—but not before the girls hug again and Jamie gives me a Look that silently orders me to look out for Audrey.

I dare anyone to try and stop me.

"Do you want to leave?" I ask Audrey when we're alone.

"No."

There she is. Under all that sweet and quiet, this girl is a fighter.

"You know what? Fuck that guy. You're winning this," I decide aloud.

"What do you mean?"

"We're going to make sure that turd not only knows you're over him, but that he goes home and cries himself to sleep thinking about the best thing he'll never have again and didn't deserve in the first place."

"How?" She sounds unsure, but it's good to see that stubborn little spark of fire back in her eyes.

"Come with me."

I lead her by the hand away from the main cluster of people and down the hallway toward the coat check and restrooms. There's a bit of an alcove in between them, and I steer Audrey into it, her back against the wall so my body will block her from the view of anyone who walks by. Arms braced on the wall by her head, I lean down to bring our faces level.

217

It's brighter here than out in the bar, and the light is hitting Audrey in a way that makes it look like she's glowing. For a moment, I'm transfixed by her delicate features, my eyes brushing over her cheeks and lips, lingering on the freckles on her nose. Another freckle calls my attention right along her jawline. If we were alone, I can't promise I could resist the urge to taste it.

Focus on the mission. She needs this win.

"All right. First, I gotta know what we're dealing with here. Did he break your heart?"

"I guess so."

"Were you in love with him?" *Why the hell did I ask that?*

"No, I wasn't in love with him."

The relief is swift and powerful, and not something I'm going to think about right now.

"Did he hurt you?"

"No," Audrey assures me. Her eyes slide to my hands, which are curled into fists. "Not, you know, physically."

Aw, shit. She sounds small again, defeated. When she ducks her chin like she's trying to hide, I don't even think before my fingers are on her soft skin, and I'm tipping her face back up until I can see her eyes. They're swimming with a sadness I feel echoing through an ache in my own gut.

"Tell me." I try to gentle my voice, not wanting to scare her by revealing the violence churning beneath my surface at the thought of her being hurt in any way.

"He didn't actually *do* anything. He just stopped being…interested in me. He made me feel like I wasn't good enough, and I guess seeing him tonight brought those feelings back." She takes a breath that hitches partway through. "It's stupid. I'm making too big a deal of it."

"Nah, Freckles." The name just pops out. No intention, all instinct—similar to the way my fingertips are tracing the line

218

of her jaw, when I hadn't even realized I was still touching her face. "Hurt is hurt. He made you feel less than, and that ain't all right. But you and me, we're gonna show him what's what. I promise, you're gonna walk out of here tonight as the fuckin' winner. Just follow my lead. You with me?"

My roots are coming out, my words slipping into patterns that don't belong at this fancy party, but Audrey's looking at me like a goddamn prince, all of my previous fuckups forgotten in this one moment where I've gotten it right. Every light brown and golden hue in her eyes is visible in this light, and when she nods, those starbursts are full of a trust we both know I don't deserve—but fully plan to keep anyway. My chest is so full of some warm, unnamable sensation it feels like it just might combust.

I step back before I do something that will keep her from getting the win she needs so badly.

"Now give me that sweater, and let's get back out there."

"It's a cardigan," she mutters. I grin and hold out my hand, wiggling my fingers.

Audrey angles herself slightly away from me as she slips out of the "cardigan." I suddenly see her self-consciousness through a new filter. Was that rancid cum-wad the one who gave her these insecurities? Is he the reason she shrinks away from attention and questions her own appeal?

I've never wanted to introduce my knuckles to someone's nasal cartilage so badly. Unfortunately, that's not on the immediate agenda.

A couple seconds later, Audrey turns back around, and I can't even spell the word "*agenda*."

No lie, I am instantly closer to sporting full-on wood in public than I've been since I was a fourteen-year-old walking erection. The blood rushes to my groin so fast I have to breathe through a wave of light-headedness, but my eyes stay open and on Audrey. I couldn't look away if I tried.

Holy *fuck,* she looks… I don't have the words. What even *are* words? My eyes hungrily trace every line and contour of Audrey's body—not only her newly revealed cleavage (absolute oasis; confirmed) but how her ass and legs look even *better* now that my view of her curves is uninterrupted by the cardigan, (which I am totally burning when we get home).

I find myself contemplating crazy things, like dragging her into a public bathroom and getting my hands on her. Plunging my fingers into the deep V of her neckline, exploring those full breasts that she's clearly been hiding from me. Pushing up the hem of that dress and finally getting my answers about what she is (or isn't) wearing underneath. And while I was down there, I'd get a good squeeze of that ass that looks like it would fit perfectly in my hands. With dizzying speed, my mind fills with all the things I'd do if we were alone in a room behind a locked door, free to give in to something I've only right this minute decided to stop denying I want.

What does it say that it took a knockout dress to force me to straight up admit I want to fuck my fake girlfriend?

Yeah, I said it. I want her.

I. Want. Audrey.

Holy. Shit.

"Walker?"

Shit. I've been standing here trapped in neutral from my visceral reaction to the sight of her in that dress, stalled out by the gut punch of looking and really letting myself *see* her for the first time. And since I'm being honest with myself, that dress couldn't have been my tipping point if I weren't already on that edge…pushed there over thirty days with a woman who entices me in a way mere clothing could never accomplish.

But all Audrey knows is that I've been staring at her without speaking. My silence has put uncertainty on her face that I do not like at all. She looks like she's a heartbeat away from putting the sweater back on, so I snatch it from her hands.

Now, time to set things straight. In this exact moment in time, my only mission is to make sure this woman is one hundred percent certain that she's beautiful.

I tilt her chin up to look at me again. Those gold-flecked brown eyes reflect a healthy dose of trepidation, but mixed in there is that spark of faith I don't deserve but am too selfish not to keep.

"You look fuckin' gorgeous tonight. You do know that, right?"

This blush, I like a whole lot—her cheeks flushed pink in pleasure a damn sight better than being stained by embarrassment. But the shyness has a vein of insecurity running underneath it that I'm only just now recognizing.

My mouth drops to her ear, like if I place the words directly inside her, she won't be able to doubt them.

"You are beautiful and sexy as hell."

I let myself linger, breathing in the sweet sunshine scent of her hair. When I nudge some of it aside with my nose, exposing her pretty neck, she shivers. I smile. Now that I'm done lying to myself, I have no problem playing a little dirty to get Audrey on my wavelength.

"Is he looking?" she asks a bit shakily.

"Nope."

I get way too much satisfaction from her sharp little inhale at my honesty. My canary-smug grin isn't easy to push down, and it's even more difficult to step back from her, but there's still a plan to execute and an assclown to put in his place before I can get her alone.

"Time to get back out there. Go find someone you know, and let's talk to them."

With more confidence in her step than before, Audrey walks into the main room and approaches a couple standing at a centrally located area of the bar. *Perfect.* After making our introductions, the three of them start talking about some class they had together in college. I tune them out with a plastered-on expression of, "I'm listening and low-key interested, but don't try to engage me." I step in closer until Audrey's back is pressed to my front, then put my hands on her hips, silently coaxing her to relax back against me. When she does, muscles loosening bit by bit until every inch of her body is molded to mine, a shout of victory resounds through me.

Captain Limp Dick's obnoxiously bright tie flashes in my periphery. With my face buried in Audrey's hair, I sneak a peek at him. His girlfriend is trying to get his attention, but he's ignoring her and gaping at Audrey. Exactly as I'd planned; yet my inner caveman wants to drag her out of this room, away from his unworthy eyes.

Refusing to spare that waste of carbon any more time or energy, I redirect those things to the far worthier pursuit of tracing Audrey's hemline with my fingertips—not giving in to the urge to venture beneath the dress, just trailing a slow path across her thighs. When she doesn't push my hand away, the victory tastes sweeter than anything we've eaten tonight.

We're both aware that my ministrations are hidden by the bar top where her ex has no chance of seeing, and she's letting me do it anyway. This position gives me the ideal vantage point to watch the goosebumps spreading across her skin at my touch, and those feel like mine too.

After a while, Audrey's friends make their excuses and leave, needing to get home to their dog (or kid—again, I wasn't listening), leaving us alone in the crowded room. Feeling drunk on her, I start running my palms along her body, feeling her curves through this nearly nonexistent dress, though I only let myself stray a few inches up or down from her waist. I smile to myself when I feel her shifting against me, trying to get even closer.

After a quick check to confirm that her ex is still looking (he damn well is), I drop my mouth to her ear.

"Still with me?"

"Mmhmm." She sounds a little drunk—I hope on me, at least as much as the cocktails she's had tonight.

"Feel like a winner yet?"

"Mmhmm," she repeats.

Sounds like a green light to me. And my patience has run out.

I spin her around, leaning down at the same time as her face is lifting. Our mouths meet in the middle, the connection so natural you'd think we've done this a million times before. Along with the instant spike of arousal, I'm filled by a deep sense of relief. It's like I've been slowly dying of thirst but didn't realize it until now, and Audrey's mouth is the only thing that can quench me.

We don't take it slow, mouths open and tongues engaged, a hint of desperation to the kiss like we're trying to devour each other. I wish to God we were anywhere but here in the middle of a room filled with people, someplace where I could press her against a wall and claim that sweet mouth the way my body is screaming at me to do, or better yet, a bed…

Whoa, there. You're still in public. I ease away, even though it's the last thing I want to do, especially when her eyes open slowly and I see them glazed with lust, pupils dilated, silently begging me to keep kissing her. Pleases the fuck out of me that Audrey is so into this she's forgotten where we are, but I know she'll be embarrassed later.

I push her hair over one shoulder, just for an excuse to touch it, to keep touching her. "You're so fucking sexy right now, and everyone in this room knows it, including your dickface ex."

Her face shutters and she starts to pull away, but I hold her close. With a quick, reassuring kiss, I tell her, in a voice so low no mic could possibly pick it up, "Whatever you're thinking, stop. Not a single fucking thing about that kiss was fake, you hear me? Making your ex regret hurting you is a bonus, but don't think for a second that I haven't been dying to get my hands on you all night, even *before* you took off the cardigan."

I do the useless hair tucking thing again just for a reason to touch her. I almost don't catch it when she speaks, her voice is so faint.

"He said I wasn't worth it."

"What?" I lean in closer, and this time, I hear her nice and clear.

"Ethan. He was my, um, *first*. We dated for six months before I, you know… But he broke up with me a week later. He said I wasn't worth all that waiting."

My entire vision goes blood red.

"He said *what* to you?"

There's a soon-to-be dead man in this bar, and I'm fixing to be his Grim fucking Reaper.

31. "Oh."

Audrey

There's outright murder in Walker's eyes as he pulls away and begins scanning the room for Ethan.

"I'm going to fucking bury him."

Mayday! Mayday!

"Walker!" I grab on to his shirt with both hands. "We're not *actually* in one of Victoria's books. You can't just go around punching people. In real life, that's how you end up in jail!"

"Might be worth it," he mutters.

Okay, while I've enjoyed my fair share of romance novels with possessive alpha-type heroes, I never thought that would be something I'd find appealing in real life. But Walker basically declaring I'm worth going to jail over? My desire for him rockets to stratospheric levels (and I was already pretty far gone).

"Let's just go home."

Whatever Walker reads on my face wipes the violence right off his features, replaced by enough heat to melt butter...or panties.

"Yeah?"

With the intensity in his eyes right now, I get the sense he's asking me a lot more than a simple confirmation that I'm ready to leave this party.

And I still say, "Yeah."

Walker and I hustle out of the bar at record speed. In unspoken agreement, we get a cab rather than calling Freddy. The short drive home and four flight trip up the elevator both pass in silence. About now is when I could give in to the nerves and start panicking—and I probably would, if not for the steadying reassurance of Walker's hold on my hand, which hasn't let go this entire time.

At our door, Walker crowds me from behind. The heat of his body and the sheer force of his presence cause me to fumble twice before I manage to get my key in the lock. Then he pushes my hair to the side and starts kissing his way from my shoulder up to my neck, and I almost lose track of what I'm doing (or where I am... Recalling my name might even be a challenge). With a sensual chuckle right against my skin that instantly erupts into goosebumps, Walker reaches around and covers my still hand with his, guiding me to finish unlocking and opening the door.

Almost forcing me to run to keep up, Walker pulls me into the bedroom. We power off our wristband mics, then Walker takes mine and tosses them both across the room. I'm about to reprimand him for the careless handling of the undoubtedly expensive technology, when he once again steals all thoughts from my mind, (not to mention the air from my lungs) by dropping his hands to my waist and propelling me backward until my back hits the wall. Hands press on either side of my head, and I find myself once again caged in by corded arms and the bulk of a powerful body. Unlike when we stood in a similar position at the bar, the heat I noted in his eyes then is now ablaze and suffused with intent.

I swallow. His eyes watch the movement then slide from my throat down my whole body in a slow perusal that is so carnal, by the time he makes his way back up to my face, my heart is pounding and arousal tingles through every extremity. I press my thighs tighter together in an attempt to ease the ache between them. Walker's gaze catches that too, and his nostrils flare like he knows exactly what it means. He is a primal creature in this moment, and the knowledge that I'm his prey breaks through the daze of lust, my brain piping in with a warning not to let myself be caught too easily.

(The lady protests, after making out with him in the middle of a bar and running straight home to the bedroom with him... Yes, I'm rolling my eyes at myself, too.)

"We're alone," I point out, eyeing the closed bedroom door and the dresser where my rose gold wristband landed at an angle atop his black one. "There are no microphones. No audience to perform for. No assignment from Victoria."

Comprehension dawns in his eyes. I am unprepared for the soft smile, even more so the sweet kiss he presses to my forehead—the act such a contradiction to his predatory stance. How am I supposed to safeguard all the pieces of myself from this man if he's going to wage a full-scale assault on my defenses by hitting all sides at once?

"And what does that tell you?"

When I don't answer, he says, "What it means, Freckles, is that when I kiss you this time, it's for no reason except that I want to."

My heart is pounding so wildly it's louder than my shaky whisper. "You keep calling me Freckles."

"You keep letting me."

Defenses fractured and all but decimated, I can't help bringing up the words I've replayed all too often over the last month.

"I thought I wasn't your type?"

His fingers caress my cheek with a gentleness so at odds with the rough strength of the man they belong to.

227

"You should know by now I have asshole moments and not to take it personally. I don't mean half the shit that comes out of my mouth."

"You didn't mean it?" The crack in my voice reveals more than I'd like about how much his response matters to me.

"It seems I've got a new type these days."

"That was a good answer." Dang, I hadn't meant to say that out loud, much less in an airy whisper that does nothing to hide how affected I am by him.

"What about you? I thought you wanted to keep things professional?"

His tone is teasing, but I sober at the reminder of the risk I'll be taking if I let myself get swept away by his charisma.

"My reasons for saying that haven't really changed," I admit. "We only have a few weeks left, and I really want to make it to day sixty without any wounds I'll have to work on healing after this is over."

"That's a pretty glass half empty way to look at things. Why not think of it as making the next few weeks as fun and enjoyable as possible? And, Freckles? I promise we'll have a lot of fun, and I will make sure you enjoy yourself as hard and as often as you'll let me."

Oh boy. The sensuality blazing out of Walker right now is as intoxicating as liquor. It seeps into my very soul, suffusing my insides with warmth more encompassing than any whiskey. I can feel my limbs loosening under its potency.

"Fuck me...that dress on you." Lord, that low, gravelly murmur paired with that heavy-lidded gaze sweeping over my body is lethal. "Killed, having to make nice all night when I could barely keep enough blood in my head to form words."

"Blood in your...? Oh."

"*'Oh,' she says*... I swear I'm gonna fucking kill that guy if I ever see him again."

I blink, disoriented at his sudden anger. "What? Who?"

"That loser ex of yours."

At the reference to Ethan, I try to avert my eyes, but Walker nudges my face back to his.

"The way you said 'oh,' looking so goddamn surprised...like you have no idea I've been struggling to keep my cock down all fucking night... It *wrecks* me that he made you doubt yourself, fucked with your head so much that you have no idea how hot you are. Makes me wish I'd told you every time I've been hard over you, because then, no way would you say *'oh'* like that."

My breathing is so ragged I'm nearly panting, those words as effective at turning me on as any romance novel I've ever read. More, because it's *him* standing there talking about *me*.

"Every time...?" If this were one of Victoria's books, she would call my words "breathy," and she wouldn't be wrong.

"Baby, you've been the face in my head while I'm jerking it for weeks now."

"That's really crude and I should find it disgusting, but...instead, I think it's sweet." To tell the truth, certain parts of me think it's *more* than sweet. "What have you done to me?"

"Not nearly as much as I'm gonna do to you as soon as we're through with the talking portion of tonight."

I laugh, overwhelmed by all that is him, his words, the fact that this is really happening. The hint of boyishness bleeding into his cocky smile serves the fatal blow to my lingering willpower.

"Now, can I please take that dress off you like I've been dying to for the last million hours?"

"I've only been wearing it for, like, four hours."

"Come here, smartass."

Walker doesn't wait for me to comply. He closes the final distance between us and takes my mouth in a scorching kiss.

* * *

Walker

When has kissing ever been like this? In high school, maybe, back before sex was a given and life was all about sneaking kisses during the school day and making out for hours in the bed of my truck. Maybe not even then.

All I know is that kissing Audrey is a next-level experience, one a guy could seriously get addicted to.

Sure, you could say I'm just horny after not getting laid in so long, but this raging hard-on, this all-consuming need, is about a lot more than mere sexual deprivation. It's *her*. It's *us*. We're fire together.

At the risk of sounding cheesy AF…sign me up for the burn.

All the built-up tension from the night (fuck, from the last thirty days) has finally combusted, and we're eating each other's mouths like it's going out of style. I've got Audrey pinned to the bedroom wall, with her dress pushed up to her waist and her legs wrapped around me, my bulging zipper pressed between her thighs. When she starts shifting her hips, seeking friction, I grab her ass in my hands and squeeze, encouraging her to grind against my erection.

When she does, a noise rips from my throat. I can feel the heat of her pussy even through my jeans and her tights. It's pure instinct that has my hips thrusting, shoving my cock into that heat. Audrey makes this little sound I swear I could eat for three meals a day—so I do it again. And again.

But it's still not enough. I want to devour this girl. Consume her. Inject myself into her bloodstream like she's slipped into mine.

I love having her up against the wall like this, but I need more. I want her spread out beneath me on the bed with my hands free to touch her all over. I turn and carry her the couple steps over to the bed, laying her down as gently as possible.

After clicking on the lamp and shoving aside the pillow wall, I join Audrey on the bed, noting tension in her body that wasn't there a moment ago.

"What is it?" I ask, caressing her hair. She's so beautiful; at this moment, she looks like a sensual angel with her delicate features flushed and lips swollen from kissing. But I hate the tentativeness that's overtaken the lust in her eyes. "We don't have to do anything else. It's your call."

Audrey bites her lip—a nervous action, not one of seduction, but my cock still pulses inside my jeans.

"I'm sorry. I guess I got nervous all of a sudden."

"Don't be sorry. We don't have to do anything else. We can press pause and just go to sleep if you want."

My inner horny bastard revolts at the thought, but apparently my drive to care for this girl is even stronger than the urge to fuck her.

"No, I don't want to press pause."

Thank fuck.

"Me neither. Now, what do you say about taking off these tights?"

That smile. It's the prettiest thing I've ever seen, and it's all mine.

32. High Maintenance

Walker

My jeans are on the floor, having joined Audrey's tights there at some point, along with my shirt and her dress. As it turns out, she was wearing a pair of pink panties beneath those tights… Panties over which I'm currently rubbing her as she strokes my cock through my boxer briefs. The feeling of her lace-covered breasts brushing against my chest is a delicious kind of torture.

I couldn't say how long we've been making out in bed, but I don't think I've been this hard in my entire life. I. Am. *Dying*. (But you can tell the folks at my funeral it was worth it.)

When her fingers slip beneath my waistband, the sensation of her smooth hand wrapped around my cock is so damn good, I almost come right then and there.

"Is this okay?" Audrey asks, peering up at me with adorable shyness.

"Yeah, it's good." Understatement of the millennium. "Is *this* okay?" I trace along the edge of her panties, fingertips flirting with the skin just beneath the waistband, dying for her to say yes.

She nods, and I swear I get a taste of what it's like to win a Super Bowl championship.

Feeling her is a turn-on all by itself. Deep in the most primitive parts of me, my inner male roars with satisfaction when my questing fingers travel lower and find her slick with arousal. I drag some of that wetness back up her slit slowly, searching, until I land on that sensitive little spot that makes her breath hitch and her hips surge upward, seeking more contact.

Well, hello there, Audrey's clit. We're gonna be good friends, you and me.

And still, we're kissing, my tongue thrusting in earnest now. I almost lose it when she matches my rhythm, her hand now pumping me in sync with my tongue fucking her mouth.

My hips buck upward on instinct, pushing my erection harder into her soft, warm hand. She squeezes my sensitive tip; it feels so fucking good I increase the speed of my tongue in her mouth, and—*oh, fuck*—she keeps pace without missing a beat.

Shit, I'm close. I need to do something quick, or I'm going to be the one bringing an early end to this party.

"Tell me how to get you there," I pant. "What do you need?"

Her steady tempo falters. "What?"

"I'm close, baby. I need to get you off. Tell me what to do."

"Don't worry about it," she says. "Just let me make you feel good."

Yeah, not happening. I'm an asshole, but I'm not *that* kind of asshole.

"I don't come if you don't come."

"It's kind of difficult. I'm, um, a little high maintenance."

Her hand starts jacking me again. The head between my legs is all for giving in to the obvious distraction tactic, but my upper brain is still functional enough to see the glaring red flags popping up everywhere.

With a show of willpower no one I've ever met would believe me capable of, I call a time-out. It's gratifying to see the reluctant disappointment on Audrey's face as I remove my hand from her panties and guide hers off my dick, but however much I *want* to keep going, I *need* to know exactly what the fuck she means.

"What do you mean, you're 'high maintenance'? Did that scumbag asshole—whose name we are not bringing into our bed—put that idea in your head?"

"Well, it's true," she says.

"Can't say I'm surprised he never got you there." The flicker over her features confirms my guess. *Typical.*

"But it's my fault." The worst part of that statement? I'm pretty sure she actually believes it.

Definitely should have broken his nose.

All right. Enough of that worthless piece of shit. This isn't about him; it's about Audrey.

"Can you make yourself come?" I ask.

A giant pile of contradictions, this girl. She can jerk me off like a champ, but bring up orgasms or masturbation and she flushes all the way to her hairline with embarrassment. (Damn, she's cute.)

"Sometimes?" She doesn't sound entirely sure. "But even, um, *alone*, it's not easy and takes a while."

I hate how insecure she looks right now, how ashamed.

Before I can figure out what to say, she rushes out in an artificially bright voice, "I'm okay, really! I don't need it. This has been amazing, and I don't want you not to enjoy it just because you think it's your responsibility or something to make sure I finish."

"I don't come if you don't come," I repeat. There's not enough time in the world to address all the problems in what she just said.

"*No!*" She sounds like she's in pain. "See? That's so much pressure. If you're waiting for me, I'll just be worrying about that."

Okay. She needs to get out of her head, and I can see that's going to be challenging.

I never could turn down a good challenge.

"You got other plans?"

"No…"

"Good. Me neither."

I reach out to play with her hair, which is huge from my hands being in it. It's never looked more like a lion's mane. If she saw herself in a mirror right now, she'd be totally horrified.

I love it.

"So what if it takes a while? I'm in no rush. Are you? Because personally, there's nowhere else I need or want to be for the rest of the night."

Truer fucking words…

She flushes with shock and what I hope is pleasure, then droops again. "But I'll hate if you're uncomfortable the whole time you're waiting for me to…*you know.*"

Hmm.

"Will it make you feel better if I go first?"

She likes that suggestion. (I'm not exactly complaining about it either.)

Damn, it's been way too long since I got laid. Almost embarrassingly fast, Audrey has me right back on the verge, hips pushing up into her hand almost of their own volition. When she squeezes my ruddy cock head then drags her thumb along the top where my slit is slick with precum, I go from *almost there* to *coming like a goddamn fire hose* in a second flat.

After I take a moment to recover and wipe away the evidence of how hard I just came, I turn my attention to Audrey. She was into what we just did, but now that it's her turn, she's practically vibrating with anxiety.

"What are you afraid of?" I ask as gently as I can manage, when gentle's not something I've ever really had in me.

"Disappointing you."

Fuck, if that confession, said in the tiniest voice possible, doesn't break something in me. *She's* worried about disappointing *me*?

"Impossible." I kiss her, because I can't *not*. Still, she appears unconvinced. "This isn't a pass-fail exam, Freckles."

"Isn't it, though?"

An automatic denial is right there on the tip of my tongue, but I swallow it back and take a minute to really think about it.

I guess, from a certain angle, you could see sex as a game with only one successful result; if you make the other person come, you win, and if you don't, you lose. Losing *should* make a person want to get better, work harder, so they can win next time, but I've known plenty of assholes whose egos won't let them ever accept blame for a loss. It pisses me off to the extreme, thinking of Audrey's ex pinning *his* failures on *her*, making her think she's broken or something.

Here's something I didn't know when I had my first fumbling sexual encounter at fifteen, but that grown-ass men like Audrey's ex should have learned by now: like anything worth winning, making a woman come is as much a mental game as a physical one.

I admit I was feeling cocky earlier, looking forward to introducing Audrey to true pleasure, as if my success were a foregone conclusion. But I'm realizing I need to shelve that ego, stat. It won't matter what kind of A game I bring or how many women I've left satisfied in the past, not if Audrey's head is tied up in stress and doubt. Even the best athletes can psych themselves out if they let the nerves take over.

Maybe we just need to take that pressure off.

"How's this—you agree to relax and let me make you feel good, and instead of pass-fail, we're going to grade my efforts by how *close* I can get you to coming."

(I have zero intention of stopping until Audrey has the best orgasm of her life. I can do this all night—I'm scheduled at the shop tomorrow, but I'll happily call out and keep going through the day if that's what it takes. That's not what she needs to hear right now, though.)

"Yeah, I guess we can do that."

Her tentative smile makes me feel like a superhero.

"All right, let's say…a 'C' means you at least feel it on the horizon, and a 'B' means you get somewhere close."

"And an A?"

Fuck yes, she's playing along.

"Hmm…" I pretend to think about it. "Give me an A if I get you closer than anyone has before." (I know damn well Audrey's only been with the Fratty Fucker, but I refuse to bring his presence into this moment.)

"Okay."

Real talk? I've never been this nervous before, not even the first time I fingered a girl or when I lost my virginity. But I push that away because my head needs to be one hundred percent in this game.

Not that *head!* I scold my reawakening dick. *You had your turn.*

After kissing the living shit out of her until we're both panting for breath, I turn my attention to the pretty pink nipples poking through her bra. I close my teeth around one and bite lightly right through the lace—then I do it again, because I have to hear another one of those little gasps she just made. In

237

ELLE MAXWELL

minutes, the fabric is so saturated it's transparent, and Audrey is squirming and gasping, rushing to help me when I go for the clasp. We both groan once I finally have my hands on her bare breasts, which are everything I'd imagined, lush enough to fill my hands and then some. I dive in like a starved man, sucking and kneading and licking her until she's so worked up, when I pull her onto my lap, she needs no encouragement to straddle me. Arousal soaks through her panties as she rubs herself on my cock—which is rock hard again, because that's what this girl does to me.

I swear, I could come again just from the sight of her using me for her pleasure.

Then I'm peeling off her panties, and Audrey is finally naked, laid out on the bed like all my dreams come true. I proceed to live out a particular fantasy of mine, kissing my way down her body on a mission to taste every single freckle. By the time I reach her pussy, she's flushed all over and already looks well-fucked. I spread her with my fingers to expose her swollen little nub, which I begin circling with my thumb. Alternately kissing her nipples and her mouth, I slowly work one finger inside her. Shit, she's so hot and tight, we both need a deep breath.

Slowly fucking her with my finger, I direct my tongue to her clit. Pure satisfaction sizzles through me at her gasp. Carefully noting her every sound and reaction, I begin spelling out the alphabet over her clit, tongue tracing one letter at a time. (I would never admit this to a living soul, but I stole this move from one of Victoria's books. Yes, I read one…or three. What? If you were me, you'd be curious too.)

Audrey wasn't lying; even as worked up as she is, it takes a good while—and a few strategic distraction tactics when I notice she's getting into her head, thinking too much about what is (or isn't) happening—before I get to taste the sweet, sweet victory of her orgasm.

And damn, if it isn't worth every minute.

Lost to anything but chasing her release, she's grinding herself against my face, grabbing my hair with both fists while I suck her clit and pump two fingers in and out of her tight pussy. It's hot as hell. I'm so fucking turned on, when she makes this little keening sound I feel right in my balls and her inner muscles start rhythmically squeezing my fingers, there's no way I can hold back from slipping my free hand between my legs where my cock is solid steel and leaking precum. I pump myself with fast strokes as I work Audrey through her orgasm, drawing it out as long as possible. She calls out my name on a breathy gasp, and just like that, I'm coming too, even longer and harder than before.

After a moment in which we do nothing but try to catch our breath, she asks, sounding incredulous, "Did you just...? *Again*?"

"Fuck yes, I did. That was so damn hot." I grab her for a long, deep kiss, twirling my tongue around hers to make sure she can taste herself.

But I'm drained (literally), and neither of us has the energy for another round just now. I fall back against the bed, feeling more than a little come-drunk.

"So that's what an orgasm is supposed to be like," Audrey breathes out with a note of wonder. She sounds a bit intoxicated as well. "The big O. I think I've only managed *little* o's before."

I smile, wondering how it's possible for one person to be so damn sweet. Feeling like the handful of inches between us is a handful too many, I tug her so she's draped over my body, not caring that we're both sweaty. And then, because I can, I plant a kiss right on top of her slightly damp hair.

"So, do I get an A?" I tease.

Her eyes are sparkling when she tilts her head up to look at me, and it's a damn fine sight. "Is Walker Garrison fishing for compliments? Fine, you earned it. That was an A plus *plus*."

If I puff my chest a bit and fall asleep shortly after feeling all kinds of cocky and pleased with myself, well…you would be too.

33. It's a Biological Thing

Audrey

It's déjà vu of the most beautiful kind, waking up to the warmth and all-encompassing comfort of Walker's arms. Only this time, there's morning sun filtering in through the curtains over the French doors, we're in bed, not on the couch, and instead of having a muscular chest as my pillow, Walker is spooning me from behind. Speaking of *behinds*…there's something hard and quite large pressed against mine through the pajama pants I put on before we went to sleep.

My face burns, thinking about that *something*, remembering everything we did last night in vivid detail.

Hands down, that was the best make-out session of my life. The best make-out session of *anyone's* life—and I'd attest to that fact under oath.

Now, I'm here being spooned to my heart's content, for once awake before Mr. Morning Person. Not wanting to disturb him, I extract myself from his embrace with care and tiptoe to the bathroom. I do my business and brush my teeth, then return on even softer steps, hoping I'll be able to slip back into bed and resume my place as the little spoon to his big one.

Plan in motion and nearing successful execution, I yelp with surprise as the man I thought was still unconscious grabs me by the hips and drags me the rest of the way onto the bed. He settles me against him and wraps me up in his arms with a sleepy rumble of contentment, like I'm his favorite teddy bear—a role for which I will volunteer anytime.

"Thought I scared you away with the woody," he mumbles sleepily into my neck.

So typical of Walker, to come right out and address the erection in the room. (Which I can once again feel asserting its presence against my backside.)

"No, um, I…"

For goodness' sake, Audrey, less than twelve hours ago, the man's fingers were inside you and his face was between your legs, doing otherworldly things to you with his tongue. You can discuss his erect penis like a freaking adult!

"I know that's a…biological thing in the mornings." *Lord, I'm a dork.*

Voice deeper and raspier than usual, Walker says against my neck, "Oh no. There's morning wood, and then there's 'waking up with your hair in my face and your ass against my crotch' wood. Trust me, Freckles, no biology could get me *this* hard. That's all you."

"Oh," I say, doing the breathy romance novel heroine thing again.

In a move so fast I barely know it's happening, he rolls us, and I find myself on my back with Walker hovering over me, now fully awake. His stare is dark and predatory.

"I thought we talked about the 'oh.' "

"I'm sorry?"

His eyes narrow, and in an impressive feat of strength that garners the notice of every one of my feminine parts, he drops into a partial push-up that brings our faces closer together while still holding his body weight off me. *Serious swoon material!*

"Don't apologize. Just means I have more work to do. Didn't fully get my point across last night."

"Your point?"

"That you're sexy as fuck, and it should never come as a surprise you make my dick hard."

"And how will you do that?" I don't know where that flirty question came from.

Based on Walker's grin, he likes it. A lot.

I'm starting to think he might even like *me* a lot...but I can't let myself go there. Next thing you know, my inner deep-seated romantic will be painting pictures of us happily coupled up on days sixty-one, sixty-two—maybe even one hundred and sixty-two—and I can't forget that no such declarations have been made. His exact proposition was to "have fun." No mention of feelings or anything beyond the experiment.

Last night, I made a decision to let myself have this, have *him,* without overthinking and ruining it. I'm in crazy lust for the first time in my life, and by some unbelievable cosmic stroke of luck, he wants me back. So, I'm going to turn off my higher level brain processing and give in to the demands of my body, which wants Walker, Walker, and a little more Walker, just for good measure.

Maybe I'll regret this in a month. For now, I'm just eager to let Walker fulfill his promise to make sure I "enjoy myself as hard and as often as I'll let him." (Which, based on last night, he is more than capable of doing.)

"Hey. You still with me?"

"Very, very much."

Right answer. He rewards me for it with his mouth, the kiss not starting slow and ramping up, but skipping immediately to hot and heavy—where I am all too glad to meet him. Even with only our mouths connected, kissing Walker is a full-body experience. Each aggressive thrust of his tongue creates an echoing throb in my core. All my senses unite in a single plea for *more.*

It seems Walker is on the same page. He rolls us so we're on our sides facing each other, freeing up his hands to roam my

243

body. I shiver when he encounters an especially sensitive spot at my lower back.

He disconnects our mouths just enough that I can feel his crooked smirk as he whispers, "Cold?"

The smug jerk *knows* I'm not cold! Instead of feeding his ego with a response, I grab fistfuls of his shirt and tug him into me, silently demanding his mouth back on mine. His surprised chuckle tastes delicious, but even better is the moan he lets out when I run my palms over his abs.

Walker shoves one of his thighs between my legs, fitting us even closer together and lining our pelvises up perfectly. Frissons of pleasure spark through my nether regions, which are still sensitive from last night, and I rub myself against his hardness, seeking even more friction. He one-ups me by grabbing my butt with both hands and pulling me against him. Now it's my turn to moan; he does it again, tugging me down at the same time he thrusts upward, pushing his erection against my center.

Yes. That. More of that, please.

I inadvertently dig my nails into his sides, trying to get even closer, to make him do it again. It turns out Walker likes that *a lot*, given his resulting groan and the way he bucks into me harder than before (which *I* like *a lot*). His hands squeeze my flesh as he grinds against me. His palms are so large they nearly cover my entire backside, the long fingers curling down and ending just inches from where I'd really like them. He gives me another squeeze, grip rougher than before, the simultaneous punch of his hips making us gasp into each other's open mouths.

Walker breaks our kiss but doesn't go far, just takes a second to breathe raggedly with his forehead resting on mine. My breathing is equally harsh.

"Damn, Freckles. That's some kind of way to kiss a guy good morning."

"You started it," I pant.

He nips at my lower lip playfully.

"You know, I wasn't the greatest in school, but I think they call this chemistry, not biology."

How can Walker make me laugh when I'm this turned on? How does being with him like this feel so comfortable when I could barely speak to him without blushing a couple of weeks ago?

Also…he is not wrong.

"As much as I'd like to stay here all day, I have to get to work." I wonder if he realizes his hands are still on my butt, lightly kneading. It's incredibly distracting, but I decide not to mention it, because I don't want him to stop.

"When?"

He glances at the fancy wrought-iron clock on the wall. "Right after I shower. I guess you wouldn't want to join me?"

The newly sexified part of me wants to scream "Yes!" But stripping off clothes mid-make-out in the safety of a dark bedroom is one thing; full nudity in the well-lit bathroom is quite a bit more adventurous.

"Too fast," Walker concludes, watching my face.

"Yeah."

He plants a devastatingly sweet kiss on the tip of my nose. When he pulls away, his regret is obvious enough to quiet some of the insecurities trying to slip back into my brain in the fading heat of the moment.

"We are not done with this conversation, young lady," he declares with mock seriousness.

"Conversation?"

He lifts an eyebrow, and heat rises to my cheeks realizing he means we're going to revisit the hot and heavy make-out. (But also…*yay!*)

* * *

"Walker?" My enunciation is garbled by the elastic I'm holding between my teeth so I can use both hands to pull my hair into a bun.

We need to leave for our check-in meeting with Victoria, and we're in danger of being late if we don't go *right now*. My fault. I had a job interview and ran into traffic on the way back, but I just changed clothes in record time. Now if Walker would hurry up…

I still have my arms raised over my head when a hand shoots out of the bathroom, snagging my waist and dragging me through the open door. The hair tie flies from my mouth with my surprised yelp, sending it flying away. In the shock, I also let go of my hair, which comes tumbling down in a haphazard mess that leaves most of my face covered and a number of strands in my mouth.

Walker is lucky I recognize him by touch and scent—the rough but not careless way he manhandles me is also quite familiar—because otherwise, I'd be panicked, with my mind jumping to thoughts of serial killers right about now. Instead, I'm laughing breathlessly when the world finally stills and I find my back pressed against the now-closed bathroom door.

If I weren't already struggling to catch my breath after his sneak attack, it would have been stolen by the gentleness with which Walker begins to brush the hair carefully away from my face.

"What are you doing?"

He does the "planting his hands on either side of my head and looming over me" romance hero move he's quickly perfected.

"Figure I'd better kiss you real good before I have to keep my hands to myself for an hour."

"And this had to happen in the bathroom, *why*?"

"No mics in here. I want those sweet little moans of yours to be for my ears only."

I prepare to argue that I do not "moan," but he drags his teeth along the shell of my ear, pulling an irrepressible sound from my throat.

Huh. I've spent more than two decades in this body, but it seems Walker knows it better than I do after only a few days. The revelation should be concerning, but it's hard to be upset about that—or anything—when his mouth is still doing amazing things to my ear.

With a shiver, I make one last feeble attempt to advocate for responsibility. "We really need to leave if we're going to be on time."

"Another minute or two won't hurt."

I try to summon the willpower to retort that based on all available evidence to date, there is no such thing as "a minute or two" with us. It's been five days since the party—but who's counting, right?—five amazing days of kissing and orgasms and falling asleep spooning. And the more we make out, the more I *want* to, which defies all natural laws of consumption.

But then he dips his head again, and when Walker Garrison has you up against a wall, intermittently making love to your mouth and doing that thing with his tongue and teeth and stubble on your neck... Well, *you* try to do anything but close your eyes and give in. (Spoiler alert: it's impossible.)

We're *very* late to the meeting.

34. Best Friend Privileges

Walker

When the girl subletting Audrey's studio apartment reached out saying she wants to take over the rest of the year lease, I encouraged Audrey to go for it, because I know she hates that place. You'd think signing over a lease would be easy, but The Man's got Audrey jumping through all kinds of hoops, especially the utility company, who she's been in a game of phone tag with all week.

Understandable, then, why Audrey can't ignore the call back she's been waiting for, even though it comes right as she's starting a "BFF" video chat. What I *don't* understand is why *I* have to keep said BFF company while Audrey's on the phone. Callie's a big girl; she can entertain herself for a bit. (Or, here's a thought: she could call back later.)

But fuck, maybe all the making out has gotten my brain twisted up with horny chemicals, because I can't bring myself to say no when Audrey turns those big doe eyes on me.

Which is how I ended up alone in our bedroom with Callie on Audrey's computer screen. Out in the living room, I can faintly hear Audrey engaged in her—hopefully brief—conversation with the utility company minions.

At first glance, you might expect Audrey's best friend to be sweet and innocent. She's got a doll-like quality to her, or maybe a fairy princess who makes friends with woodland animals—round cheeks, pert little nose, giant chocolate-brown eyes, and black pixie cut hair.

Of course, I know better. I've heard stories from Audrey and crashed enough video calls to be well aware the girl is a feisty little thing who's not to be underestimated. Good thing too, because she wastes no time jumping into attack mode, coming right at me with the "new boyfriend" interrogation.

I try to be patient because I can appreciate her having Audrey's back, but as we all know, patience isn't my strong suit. After a few minutes of playing along, I try to wrangle this runaway conversation back into something I can tolerate.

"Listen, Callie, I know you've got best friend privileges or whatever—"

Only to be interrupted.

"I've got best friend *in another country* privileges, which is different." Yeah, no anecdote could have prepared me for the ferocious sprite putting me in my place from an ocean away. "Since I'm not there to watch you guys together and make sure you're good enough for my girl, you aren't allowed to do the big, manly, silent, broody thing with me over video. This is all we've got. So spill, lover boy."

"Due respect, Callie—"

"Meaning you're about to be disrespectful," she interrupts me *a-fucking-gain*.

Patience. I need to find some, and fast. Winning over Audrey's best friend is a level one priority. I cannot lose my temper, even though she's testing it more by the second.

"As I was saying… Straight up, Callie, you've got all my *legitimate due fucking respect*, because I know how important you are to Audrey, but if *our* girl thinks I'm good enough, isn't that all that matters?"

"Points for the corrected possessive pronoun," Callie says primly. "But here's the thing about *our* girl. She can be a bit standoffish and doesn't let many get close, but her natural state is softhearted. She looks for the best in people, and her tendency to give everyone the benefit of the doubt can work to her detriment. I don't know how you gained access to her life so quickly, but it's my job to make sure she hasn't missed any red flags."

"Where were you when Frat Boy Dickweasel was getting in there?" I can't help asking the question any more than I can hold back the accusatory tone.

"Valid. I deserve that." She earns another bit of my respect with her no-nonsense acceptance, not getting offended or trying to make excuses. "The Dickweasel—I'm stealing that gem, BTW—tricked me too, and I'll never forgive myself for not seeing through him. Which is all the more reason for me to take a close look at you, Mr. Six Pack Mountain Man, because even someone without a natural blind spot for people's faults might find themselves dazzled by that outer package."

"Are you flirting with me, Callie?"

"Are you hearing me, Walker?"

I'll give the girl this—Callie has a damn effective death glare, even delivered through a screen. Sucks that she's wasting this impressive display of best friend skill on the likes of me.

"I hear you. And I appreciate you looking out."

The fierce brown eyes on the screen are clearly not budging until I give her something. Damn, am I really about to get into this shit with a girl I've never actually met?

Appears so.

"Right. So, nothing you're saying is a surprise. I know Audrey's sensitive, and I know I can be a bulldozer sometimes. We're working on it. *I'm* working on it. All I can tell you is that I'm not out to use her like a rug to walk all over, and I'm not playing her. She knows exactly what the score is between us. And if your next bit is to tell me I don't deserve her, I know that too. She's silk and I'm sandpaper, but I'm going as gentle as I can, and we're doing this thing day by day."

"What did you just say?"

"We're doin' it day by day?"

"No, about the silk and the sandpaper."

Fuck, I can't believe that slipped out. "Forget it. That was stupid."

"I think it was beautiful and kind of sad."

Is this how Audrey feels every time I embarrass her and she blushes, uncomfortable and like she wants to run out of the room to somewhere far, far away? Damn, I owe her some Starbucks gift cards.

"Sorry, sorry, I'm here!" Audrey whirls into the bedroom. "What did I miss? Did you two play nice?"

"It's love. We're planning our elopement now," Callie quips.

Audrey throws herself onto the bed beside me, arms and head flopping dramatically as she pants, like she sprinted in here from the living room (all five feet). Her hair is everywhere, and before I can think it through, I'm reaching out to tuck away the largest bits that have fallen into her face. She smiles up at me and mouths "thanks," and if we weren't still on video with Callie, I'd kiss the hell out of her right about now.

"Sandpaper, my ass," Callie mutters from the computer.

"What?" Audrey turns confused eyes to the screen.

"Oh, nothing!"

After sitting through a few more minutes of their chat, I leave the room so they can talk alone. (Probably about me...awesome.)

When I kiss the top of Audrey's hair before getting off the bed, she tips her chin up and gives me a smile so soft and fond it hits me right in the motherfucking feels—something I didn't even know I *had* until recently.

So, like the big, tough man I am, I run away to the building gym as fast as possible.

Walker's Journal

Vickie—

Spill it; did you put Jenny up to asking about our sex life? Because that's what went down at therapy today. I've never seen Audrey's face so red. Okay, so it was kind of funny. But mostly, it was seriously uncool doing that to her. Remember, we're not all romance authors who sit around writing detailed blow job scenes on the daily, and Audrey's shyer about this stuff than most.

So, yeah, I shut that shit down.

I get that you've probably realized we're fooling around now, V, but if you want details on what we get up to off-mic, you should ask us directly. Strike that, just ask me. Gentlemen don't kiss and tell, but luckily, there are no gentlemen living in this condo... Not that I'd go into anything too deep with you, because Audrey's private and this is her business too.

I guess the point is, I'm drawing a line here. So you'd better get ready to fire up that imagination of yours when it comes to the sex scenes in your little book. And we both know that imagination is a hell of a lot dirtier than anyone would expect just from looking at you.

Walker

Comment added by Victoria Trulette: I assure you, Jenny asked that question of her own volition! Sex is a normal part of any healthy relationship and a far from unusual topic for couples to discuss in therapy.

Comment added by Victoria Trulette: If I didn't know better, I would think you had been reading my novels, Mr. Garrison...

Comment added by Victoria Trulette: Also, I wouldn't call writing oral sex scenes a *daily* occurrence for the average romance author. Perhaps weekly.

35. Don't Make Me Call Your Mother

NEW MESSAGE IN GROUP TEXT

VICTORIA: I have received word from building management that due to some complaints about pests, they need to fumigate certain condo units, including yours. Unfortunately, this means you will need to vacate the premises and find alternate housing arrangements for the next few days, starting tomorrow.

Walker

"What a load of bull."

"What do you mean?" Audrey asks.

I hold up my phone. "This shit. It's just Vickie messing with us."

Audrey's eyes widen, making her look like an innocent little doe. (Yet I still want to fuck her, which is all kinds of messed up.) It reminds me of those first few days (minus the preoccupation about fucking her, which is pretty new) back when I thought she was a naïve, spoiled princess.

"Victoria wouldn't *lie* to us!"

Nowadays, I'm down to just thinking she's naïve. (And dammit, why do I find that *cute*?)

"Whatever your rose-colored glasses tell you."

"What are your glasses, then? Grayscale?"

Shrugging, I concede the point. If she's trying to pick a fight, she's going to be disappointed. I'm too tired to argue today. Seems days of constant making out and epic orgasms can exhaust a guy.

Shit, but I want to kiss that little pout right off her mouth.

"So, where should we go?" Audrey asks.

See, this is how I know Victoria's playing mad scientist to our lab rats—if she weren't fucking with us, we'd already have a text from her or Matilda with info on the ritzy hotel she's setting us up in.

As if she's reading my thoughts, Audrey suggests, "A hotel?"

There are two big reasons why I'm a no for the hotel route. First, I'm trying to save every cent right now. I'm *this close* to quitting the auto shop, and shit is getting real.

Second? It's a bad idea for me to have Audrey all to myself in a hotel room, totally alone, without microphones or meddling bosses. That path leads to only one destination: both of us naked, with me balls deep inside her. As much as I want that—okay, I really want it, and my dick really, *really* wants it—I'm holding off.

At first, I didn't push it because I could tell she wasn't ready. But she's grown so much bolder and more comfortable over the past week and change (has it *only* been that long?), if I made a move to take things all the way now, I'm pretty sure she'd be willing.

Normally, that's all I'd need, but this is different. *She's* different. Sex is a line that can't be uncrossed. With a girl like

Audrey, who doesn't hook up casually, going there will *mean* something. It will come with unspoken promises that I'm not sure I'm ready or willing to keep. So, as hard as it is (pun fully intended), I'm keeping us safe at third base for the time being.

But come on, a hotel room? My willpower has limits.

"Nah. We'll go stay at my place in Everett, with Luke."

Nothing like using your own brother to cockblock yourself.

* * *

Audrey

What is Walker's house like? I can't wait for this glimpse into his "real" life, but I'm trying to keep my excitement on the down-low because he's being weird. More than once on the way there, I catch him sending me these odd looks. If he was anyone but Walker "gives no effs about anything" Garrison, I might say he's *nervous* about showing me his home.

After a surprisingly short drive across the Charles River, we park in the driveway of a two-story house. Walker jiggles his keys in his hand as he leads me inside the first floor unit he rents with his brother.

Starting with the ramp attached to the back door, the accessibility modifications are what immediately stand out about the house, which is otherwise pretty unremarkable. I confess I did a little bit of Google research last night, determined to avoid any repeat performances of my screw-up when first meeting Luke. So, when we enter the kitchen, I recognize that it's been almost completely redone with accessibility in mind, from the low height of the kitchen cabinets and appliances, to the gaps beneath the counters for a wheelchair.

Whoever did the renovations was unconcerned with aesthetics, making no effort to smooth the contrast between the

257

shiny new handrails and the chipped wood trim along the ceiling, or even to paint over the discoloration left behind by frames that were obviously removed to widen the doorways.

Is it beautiful? No. But a functional home where Luke can move around easily and be independent is far more important.

"Luke!" Walker hollers, threatening to deafen me in my right ear. "Come say hi to Audrey!"

A moment passes with no response. Walker says apologetically, "Don't take it personally, he doesn't come out of his room much."

Blatant surprise ripples over his face when we hear the distinct sound of a door opening and what I now recognize as rolling wheels.

Luke flicks us a single-handed greeting, showing off fingerless black gloves (which I know from my Googling protect his hands from getting cut up by his wheels). It's only a short jerk of his hand, yet somehow, he manages to make the motion sarcastic.

"Hey, Luke." (How does he make a wave look so casually cool while I'm over here doing a weird hand flapping thing?)

"Welcome to our castle. I see Walk went all out treating you to a luxury getaway."

I laugh while Walker rocks forward on a heel and lands a light punch to his brother's shoulder. "Shut up, asshole." But his lips are twitching.

"Well, this was fun, but I've got unimportant shit to do today."

Luke whips around on an expertly executed hairpin turn that sends my heart up into my throat. Then he calls out over his back, "Audrey, when you're ready for a real man, my room's on the other end of the hall."

Walker flicks off his brother's retreating form. As though he knows without even looking back, Luke holds his own middle finger over his head before disappearing through the doorway. Walker chuckles.

Seriously, I will never understand boys. How does giving each other the middle finger constitute a loving exchange, as Walker's face suggests?

"Come on, we'll put our stuff in my room."

Walker leads me into the same hallway but makes a right turn where his brother had gone left. I follow, trying to contain my excitement and curiosity.

"Sorry for whatever state it's in. I haven't really been home since we started this thing."

He flicks on the overhead light before tossing our bags into a corner of the room. (Good thing I didn't have anything breakable in mine…which he wouldn't let me carry myself.)

Much as I'd expected, Walker's bedroom is barren of what might be called "décor." His bed sports a simple navy-blue comforter. The nightstand, dresser, and shelf are all basic black and remind me of my own particle-board furniture, cheap and functional. The walls are bare, but I spy knickknacks and mementos on the shelves beside some books, as well as a framed photo on the top of the dresser that must be the Garrison twins as children—all of which I plan to examine closely when Walker isn't looking.

Unaware of my eyes darting back and forth, taking in as much as possible, Walker gestures to the opposite side of the room, where I glimpse some fifties-style peachy-pink tile through a partially open door.

"Best thing about the place is separate bathrooms. Mine's old and ugly as shit, but it works and it's clean. Well…give me twenty and it will be clean." He rubs at his neck, and again, I get the strange feeling that he's embarrassed.

I hold back the impulse to gush, to tell Walker I like him even more for dealing with a pink bathroom he no doubt hates because he prioritizes his brother's comfort over his own ego.

"Did you guys redo the kitchen for Luke?" I ask instead.

"Most of the mods were already here. A year or so back, I got lucky and heard about a guy who was having trouble renting out his parents' place because of all the retrofitting they'd done when his mom started needing a chair. His dad had just passed so the guy's mom moved in to an assisted living place, and he was stuck figuring out what to do with this unit from out of state."

"That *was* a lucky find. It's great." Since he seems somewhat open to talking, and I'm crazy curious, I ask, "Was that Luke's car in the driveway?"

"Yeah. Late 2000s Mustang," (As if that means anything to me!) "Bunch of guys at the shop pitched in to help me fix it up for Luke while he was in the hospital."

"How long ago was that?" I soften my voice, unsure if he'll respond and preparing myself in case he gets mad at me for pushing. Until now, Luke has been a blanket conversational no-go.

"About two years ago."

Later, I will soak in the knowledge that he has just handed me a tiny bit of trust. For now, I take a page out of the Walker Garrison handbook.

"So, this is where the magic happens?" I ask, dropping to sit on his bed.

"Not yet, but now that you're here, we'll have to see what we can do."

I laugh while he grins unabashedly, then let out an embarrassing shriek when he jumps on the bed, making me bounce.

"What? I thought that was a good one."

"It was, very good." My tone is teasingly patronizing, but I am impressed by the clever (if cheesy) dodge of mentioning any girls he's brought here. "Consider me seduced."

"Now I'm tempted to skip the studio." I don't think I'll ever get over seeing that heat in his eyes, directed at *me*.

"You have that big shipment to work on, right?"

"Yeah. Do you want to come with or stay here?"

"I'll tag along. I should get some more photos and videos for your social pages."

He smiles, brief but beautiful.

"First, lunch. You good with sandwiches? There's a place right around the corner we like. Don't worry, they've got vegetarian shit on the menu."

It can't be normal to get heart palpitations over the words "vegetarian shit," but my insides are all kinds of fluttering. Not that long ago, Walker was openly appalled that I'm vegetarian, and here he is, considering my dietary preferences without needing a reminder.

Who needs flowers to woo a girl, when you can offer her "vegetarian shit"?

If he were trying to woo me, which, of course, he's not.

I mean, we're just "enjoying" our time together, which does not require wooing.

* * *

Walker, Luke, and I eat dinner in the living room—lasagna, which I learn their mom dropped off while Walker and I were at his studio today. She even made a separate vegetarian one for me, which is so sweet it almost makes me cry.

Afterward, I watch while Walker and Luke play foosball and air hockey on the tables they have in their dining room in lieu of a table for actual dining. It's seriously intense; I can hardly keep up with how fast the puck flies back and forth across the simulated ice, much less follow the tiny soccer ball they maneuver with a series of dizzying handle twists. I turn down their invitation to take a turn playing; a girl could lose a finger with the way they compete!

Luke has remained quiet throughout the day, mostly staying in his room except for dinner, during which he didn't talk much. Now, as we hang out in the living room after their games are finished, Luke is more relaxed than I've ever seen him—perhaps thanks to his victory, or the beers he and Walker have been drinking. Maybe both.

"So, who's older?" I ask the twins. Walker groans; Luke smirks.

I giggle through Luke's brief account of their birth, made less so by Walker's frequent interruptions and commentary. Apparently, Luke came out nice and easy, but Walker was an obstinate rebel even then, putting their mother through forty-five minutes of hell before finally making his appearance.

"Had to make a dramatic entrance," Luke says.

"Excuse me for wanting some time all warm and comfy without your fat ass taking up all the room!"

They flip each other off, which apparently translates to "I love you" in the language of Garrison Twin.

A bit later, after the guys have gotten fresh beers and poured me more of the wine their mother brought with the food, Luke turns to me.

"You don't strike me as someone who'd quit a job without having something else lined up."

"I'm not," I admit.

"So, what happened?"

"All she's ever said is that her old boss was a jerk," Walker says to his brother.

"A jerk, how?" Luke asks.

Four gray eyes lock on to me, awaiting my answer. Far too late, I see the error of my seating choice; with a Garrison brother on either side, I'm surrounded by potent male energy.

Not wanting to look at either of them while I talk about this subject, I address my words to the novelty Patriots cup in my hand. (Are you really surprised Walker doesn't own wineglasses?)

"I was a personal assistant to an attorney—Mr. Simmons."

"She worked for the guy for a year and he didn't let her use his first name," Walker interrupts me to tell Luke. I glare at him for talking about me like I'm not here, then return to examining my cup, which lists the years of the Patriots' Super Bowl wins. (Wow, they win *a lot!*)

"He isn't the nicest person, and as a boss, he was demanding and critical. Honestly, he isn't a very *good* person either. I know that sounds catty, but it's true. For instance, he had both a wife *and* a mistress. This summer, they found out about each other and both broke up with him. He was particularly awful after that. One day, he took it too far, and I just…walked out."

In the silence that follows, I belatedly take note of the intensity pouring off the brothers.

"What did he do?" Walker growls, the sound downright animalistic.

"It wasn't a big deal." I try to backtrack.

"Right. It only made you walk out without notice or a backup plan," Luke scoffs.

"Do I need to find this dick and ask him directly?" Walker asks when I hesitate.

I can't tell whether he's serious. But I know for certain that Mr. Simmons would press charges for the slightest hint of assault, and it would really suck if I had to spend my paycheck from Victoria on bail.

"My last day, his wife had just served him divorce papers. He got drunk at the office and sort of…hit on me."

Oh boy. If I thought the energy was scary before, this is *scary.*

"What do you mean by '*hit on you*'?" Walker demands.

Damage control time. *Downplay, downplay, downplay.*

"Just, you know, made some comments that were rude and inappropriate, and on top of the way he treated me in general, I was just *done*."

I don't mention that one of those comments was a suggestion we update my job description to include "servicing" him on my knees beneath his desk. Or that he made it while trying to grab my butt.

Despite my understatement, the guys are wearing matching thunderous expressions. Without psychic powers, I can't tap into the silent conversation taking place over my head, but I have a feeling it involves pitchforks. (And possibly shovels.)

"It's okay. It's over. *Do not do anything stupid!*" I beseech Walker before turning to his brother, whose countenance is equally stormy. "That goes for both of you."

Their mutinous faces fill me with a rush of empathy for their poor mother. Which gives me an idea.

I turn to Walker. "If you run off to play badass, I *will* tell Victoria...*and* Jenny."

"You wouldn't."

His panic at the thought of me "telling on him" to our therapist would be hilarious, if I weren't legitimately concerned about the whole having-to-pay-bail thing.

"Who's Jenny?" Luke asks.

Deciding to let Walker handle that one later, I keep my focus on my fake boyfriend. *"I would."*

I'm sweating by the time Walker breaks our little staring contest, but at least I'm victorious, as he seems to have realized I'm being dead serious.

"Well, *I* don't care about this Jenny person," Luke mutters, forcing me to play my final card.

"Lucas Garrison, don't make me call your mother!"

Luke spews an impressive string of curses before also admitting defeat.

"Damn, Walk, your girl has some claws hidden under all that sweetness."

36. Exhale Relief. Inhale Annoyance.

Audrey

"Hey, where's that bracelet you usually wear?" Luke asks.

He's right; my wrist is bare.

"Dang! I must have left it in the bathroom." I'd been too focused on seeking out coffee in the kitchen, which is where I found Luke. (Walker is out running. Ugh, morning people!)

"What?" I ask, feeling self-conscious at the funny way Luke is looking at me.

"You're cute, that's all. *'Dang.'*" He shakes his head and chuckles. It's good to see him laugh, even if it is at my expense. I get the impression he doesn't do so often.

"I'm, um, just going to run and grab my wristband." Victoria wants us to wear them as much as possible while we're here since their house doesn't have mics set up like our condo.

"Don't. Your arm is pretty enough without it."

Is Luke *flirting* with me? He's probably just teasing, but I still feel heat crawling up from my neck.

"So, I know about you and my brother."

His abrupt change in tone and topic sets me on edge.

"It's not exactly a secret that we're dating." This time, my giggle is nervous and forced.

"*Pretending* to date," he corrects.

I freeze. I swear even my heart stops beating. Sweat prickles across my forehead.

"I know about Victoria, the contract, the money. Everything."

"How?"

"I got Walker to tell me." Luke is the picture of self-satisfaction, the cat that fooled the canary into breaking its nondisclosure agreement.

Whatever he sees on my face—sheer panic, most likely—makes him laugh again.

"Chill out, it's fine. I'm not gonna run to the press. Or tell our parents."

I exhale with relief.

My inhale is annoyed.

"Why didn't you start out by saying that?" I swat his shoulder with the back of my hand. I've never touched him before, and for a second, I panic that I've overstepped, but he gifts me yet another of his rare, quick grins.

"Sorry. Couldn't miss your expression. You should've seen Walker when I called him on it. I thought he was gonna piss himself."

I can only imagine. Poor Walker.

"Anyway, I knew we were good because you don't have the bracelet on."

Wow, Walker did tell him everything.

"How long have you known?"

When he tells me, I almost drop my mug. He's known for *weeks?* I can't believe Walker didn't say anything to me!

"Why are you telling me now?" I ask Luke. "Was it just to see my reaction?"

He shrugs. "Also thought it might be good for you to know someone else is in on it. In case you ever need to vent or talk it out or whatever."

Warm fuzzies fill me. I'm a little choked up at his kindness. If I knew for sure he wouldn't freak out or push me away, I would hug him this very instant.

Then, in typical Garrison boy fashion, Luke opens his mouth and ruins the moment.

"Walker doesn't know I'm talking to you. He actually asked me not to."

"Seriously? He's going to be so pissed!"

"Whoa there, now. That's some pretty strong language for you."

"What? '*Pissed*'?" I attempt an indignant glare, but it's hard to hold on to any genuine annoyance when he's being playful, gifting me with this glimpse of the man behind the grumpy façade.

"Yeah. Aren't you supposed to say 'ticked off' or some shit? I don't want to be held responsible if this is your gateway drug into real cursing. Next thing you know, you'll be dropping 'fucks' all over the place, and it will be my fault."

Helpless to do anything but laugh, I give in. Luke just watches with a smirk that strengthens his resemblance to Walker.

Huh. Here I am with an extremely handsome man—Luke's beard and unruly hair no longer detract from his appeal in my mind, merely lending an alluring wildness to all of the appealing features he shares with Walker. (Not to mention those muscles—Lord only knows what *his* abs look like!) Yet when I search within myself for any spark of interest, I find...nothing. Wouldn't it stand to reason that my off-the-charts attraction to Walker would transfer to his twin?

I spend a second in honest self-reflection, delving deep within myself to make sure the discrepancy has nothing to do with the wheelchair. It doesn't take long to brush that worry away. No, the *really* worrisome truth is that it has nothing to do with Luke at all, and everything to do with my feelings for Walker.

"You and Walker seem good," Luke comments. An innocuous enough observation, but I go on alert, recognizing his expression as one I've often seen on Walker when he's up to mischief.

"Yes, we're good," I reply slowly, waiting for the punch line.

"A lot better than when I saw you at my parents' house." *Where is he going with this?* "So, no more pillow wall, huh?"

O-M-G. Walker really told him *everything*.

I try to hide behind my coffee mug, cursing it for being too small to cover my entire face, which is definitely bright red. I hope there's a fire extinguisher somewhere in this building, because I may just burst into flames.

"Nope, pillow wall is gone," I manage.

Ugh. How did he know?

Wait. What if Luke overheard something? I think back to our last few days here. Walker and I have made out in his room, but we were quiet. Right? Then again, the world kind of disappears when Walker takes me *there*, so it's within the realm of possibility that I made some sound without realizing. Not to mention Walker's tendency to be vocal about his enjoyment when I use my mouth...

How *mortifying*.

Luke surprises me again. Rather than teasing me more, he simply nods and says, "Good. About time he got his head out of his ass."

I want him to say more, but Luke spins around to put another pod in the coffeemaker.

"You want a refill?"

Apparently, our little heart-to-heart is over.

"Uh, sure, thanks."

These boys are endlessly confusing. But I *think* Luke and I just became friends?

* * *

Walker

I finished my run a while ago, but I'm still lingering outside the door like a creep.

Just inside, Audrey and Luke are talking. Although I can't make out their words, the sound of Luke's voice was enough to stop me short. My brother doesn't talk much these days, and that goes double with people who aren't family. But I'm hearing his deeper tone as often as Audrey's lighter one, and he sounds...*happy*. He's even laughing, a rare fucking sound since the accident.

There it is again, slow and rumbly. Hearing my brother laugh strikes me somewhere deep within, the sensation a sort of achy joy that brings actual tears to my eyes. I blink them away fast, but the feeling in my chest remains.

Honestly, Luke has laughed more these past few days than in the last six months combined. He's even stuck around to hang out instead of closing himself off in his room, playing foosball and eating dinner in front of the TV with us. It's certainly not *my* presence drawing him out; he's never had a problem shutting me out in all the time we've lived together, and I doubt he misses me that much after a month and change of my absence.

It's Audrey.

Of all the people to finally draw Luke out, I have to say I wouldn't have bet on her. Then again, I also wouldn't have thought to pair myself with Audrey. But damn if she hasn't slipped under my skin over the weeks, until she's so deep it's kind of terrifying.

Perhaps it makes sense the same girl who's got me more twisted up than ever before would be the first person Luke's connected with since his accident.

Proof positive that I'm an even worse person and shittier brother than I thought, instead of being thrilled at this revelation, happy for Luke, I feel something more akin to dread. Here I should be making plans to ensure Audrey stays in my brother's life, perhaps even start plotting to set them up romantically after this job ends, but my instincts are screaming at me to throw her in my truck and drive off, to keep her to myself.

Christ, I'm a selfish asshole.

Not that it *means* anything. It's not as if I'm catching legit *feelings* for Audrey. We're hot for each other and just starting to get it out of our systems; of course I want to keep her to myself. And if thinking about her hooking up with Luke has me feeling a little extreme, like I want to break shit, that's because things always feel intense when they're shiny and new. Once the novelty fades, this intensity will too.

Yeah, we're going with that.

37. "Happy Bday Walker & Luke"

Walker

Today, we're headed north of the city for my twenty-fifth birthday party.

If you're thinking I don't seem like a person who gives a shit about birthday parties, you'd be correct. Unfortunately, according to Victoria, we "simply *have* to capitalize on the opportunity" for a socializing scene. So, she's throwing a birthday party for me—or I should say, for *us*, since Audrey insisted on including Luke (we are twins, after all).

Maybe I should have fought harder to save my brother from this circus, but I'd honestly expected him to beg out of it like he usually does with social stuff these days. I couldn't believe it when Audrey told me she got Luke to agree—until she mentioned she'd enlisted Ma to the cause. Between the two of them, the poor sucker never had a chance.

At least Victoria—or Matilda, or whoever actually planned this thing—chose a decent venue, a sports bar right off the highway in Woburn, smack dab in between Boston and Lowell. Nice place, not that I'd expect anything else with Vickie involved, but chill enough that I don't need to worry about my buddies getting that "fish out of water" feeling I always have at super fancy places, like the one where Jamie had her engagement party. Plus, there's plenty of parking and it's wheelchair accessible. Who knows, maybe Luke will even enjoy himself. (I seriously fucking hope so; that would make all of this nonsense worth it.)

Since anyone who's met me knows I'm not the "reserve a private room for my own birthday" kind of guy, we're telling people I won some radio contest. Personally, I think it sounds sketchy, but let's be real; my friends aren't likely to question anything too hard when it comes with free alcohol.

Figures my father would be the one person refusing to take the radio contest story at face value—though he's less suspicious about its plausibility than he is pissed about wasting money he'd rather have in his pockets.

"Couldn't they have just given you the cash?" Dad gripes, disdainfully eyeing the banner Audrey made that reads "*Happy Bday Walker & Luke.*" He and Ma just got here, but my mother was quick to dart off and socialize, leaving us alone. Ma hasn't been subtle about wanting my father and me to work out our latest "issues," aka Dad being an extra raging dick since he found out I'm planning to leave the shop. (Fat chance, Ma.)

I count to five before answering. Barely a minute in my father's presence and I'm already close to losing my shit. I wish I could say it's a record, but…

"That's not how it works, Dad."

"Did you even ask?"

I choose to ignore him rather than engaging with his saltiness. Without any conscious direction from me, my eyes seek out Audrey, finding her in a corner playing wallflower corner with Luke.

As though sensing my gaze on her, Audrey turns. A stunning smile breaks out on her face the instant we make eye contact. Directed at me, *because* of me, that smile is almost enough to steal my breath. I couldn't stop my mouth from curving into a responding smile even if I tried.

Memories from last night flash through my mind—the sexy as hell noises Audrey made when she came apart while I had my mouth on her, then later, how she damn near destroyed me with *her* mouth. (Something I've learned over the past two weeks: Audrey has no gag reflex. Seriously, is this woman my birthday present from the universe?) As if she can see the heat in my eyes and knows exactly what I'm thinking, she flushes. That pretty pink on her face creates an echoing warmth in my chest—fuck, but knowing I can make her blush from across a room makes me feel ten feet tall.

Distracted by Audrey, I've momentarily forgotten my dad's presence. A critical error.

"Audrey's a sweet girl."

I turn back to him and wipe my face blank, but it's too late; the damage has already been done. I've inadvertently handed him ammunition.

"She's too good for you," Dad says casually, like he's commenting on the weather. "You're fooling yourself if you think that devotion in her eyes is going to last."

Devotion? Is she really looking at me like that? I can't let the thought sink in, not when the rest of his words hit a little too close to my own worries.

Even though I refuse him the satisfaction of any outward reaction, Dad reads into my silence, leaning in to what he's interpreted (correctly, dammit) as a sore spot.

"Whatever delusions you've gotten in your head, living the high life down in Beacon Hill and throwing fancy parties, it's not reality. You're living on borrowed time with that girl. You think once she realizes you've got nothing to offer but your dick, she won't ditch you in a heartbeat for some rich city guy who can give her that life for real *and* nail her good?"

"You don't know what the fuck you're talking about."

Smug. The bastard is so fucking smug, having goaded me into a reaction we both know I didn't mean to give him. Rage has me damn near shaking, and it's a battle to keep my hands from clenching into fists. I shove them into my pockets and wrestle my face back into impassivity.

With his gaze pointedly directed over my shoulder, there's no fighting the instinct to peek over at Audrey where she's still hanging out with Luke. She looks like a candy-sweet dream today—exactly as classy and out of my league as Dad said—in a pink dress that subtly hugs her curves on top then flares into a skirt that swishes around her knees when she moves. The cardigan she's wearing over it, also pink, is strangely sexy, like it's beckoning me to come over there and rip it right off her.

"I give it two months, three tops, before you're crawling back to me begging for work because you've done what you always do and fucked up—with your little shirt business, or the girl. My bet is it'll be both."

"The business is taking off, actually. You'd know that if you'd ask about it, instead of bitching about not getting your way."

Anyone who looks over here would see a tender parental moment, a father smiling at his son, a loving hand on his shoulder. No one would ever guess there's pure rage glinting in Dad's eyes above that white-toothed smile or the bruising grip with which his fingers are digging into me.

"Watch yourself. I am still your father, and you will speak to me with fucking respect."

I want to shove Dad's hand off me and tell him exactly how little respect I have for him, release years of bitterness and swallowed words, but we're not alone. Now is not the time to make a scene. Not in front of nearly everyone I know. Not in front of Audrey.

With effort, I clench my jaw shut and step away, forcing him to drop his hand. He'll consider it a win—he's always needed to have the last word—but he's not worth ruining today. Especially since, *fuck*, I suddenly remember my wristband is recording this whole thing for Victoria.

Looks like today Dad isn't content with simply having the last word; he has to deliver a final crippling blow before making his exit.

"Deny it all you like, but I know what you're made of, boy. You're worth about half of your brother, even now."

This fucker is so lucky we're in public or he'd be on the floor for that implication that Luke is somehow *less* now—as if the use of his legs or a military career means shit. Luke is and always has been twice the man I'll ever be. About that, at least, Dad is correct.

"I wonder if she'll figure that out too?"

With that little mic drop, he walks off to do whatever— maybe work on growing his mustache so he can twirl it and complete his villain persona.

By now, the party is in full swing, the room full of people I should talk to, but after that inspirational chat with Daddy Dearest, I need a minute. Before I duck into the bathroom, I take a moment to observe Luke and Audrey. They're chatting, and my brother almost looks relaxed even in this crowded room, something I haven't seen since his accident.

Despite the stench of bullshit lingering in Dad's wake, I can't help wondering. Is the old man right? *Could* there be something more between Audrey and my brother?

As soon as I return from the bathroom, Tommy hustles up to me with an odd expression on his usually carefree face.

"Did you invite Suri?"

"The fuck? No, of course not." Why would I invite my ex-girlfriend?

"Well, she's here."

I peek in the direction he's looking, and sure enough, on the other side of the room stands the absolute last person I'd expected to see today. Quickly turning back around, I try to catch my bearings as I process this new development.

What the hell is she doing here?

While I got only a brief glimpse, it was enough to see Suri looked happy. Her wide smile is a stark contrast to the last time I saw her. All my final memories involve her crying, because like the fuckup Dad accused me of being, I broke her heart. Unintentionally, yes, but isn't that almost worse? She was in love with me, and I didn't even fucking notice.

One of those memories hits me, my mind shifting the image so instead of Suri, it is Audrey I see—*Audrey's* crying face, Audrey's anguished eyes spilling mascara-blackened tears, Audrey's pain inscribed on her cheeks with those dark streaks, like trails of blood left in my destructive wake. Nausea and regret churn within me; it feels like a premonition.

An appreciative whistle distracts me before I have to find the nearest trash can.

"Damn, Suri looks hot," Tommy says, eyeing my ex.

"Have at it, man."

Tommy's dark eyebrows shoot toward his hairline, but his surprise is no match for my own, as I realize with a jolt that I actually mean it. He's not lying about Suri's appeal—she's still a knockout, the embodiment of everything I usually want in a girl: curvy, sensual, and confident in her own skin—yet I feel no jealousy, not even a hint of discomfort thinking about Tommy hitting on her.

It's another girl, one with wild hair and a pink dress, I'm drawn to seek out.

"Uh-oh."

Tommy's meaning becomes clear a heartbeat later, when I find Audrey in the same corner with Luke—and now Suri.

Shit.

"The girlfriend and the ex," Tommy comments. "You want some backup—"

I don't hear the end of his sentence; I'm already booking it across the room, headed straight for the collision of my past and present.

38. Tricycle vs. Ferrari

Audrey

Funny how Walker failed to mention his ex looks like Princess freaking Jasmine. No—Kim Kardashian. The woman Luke just identified as Suri, Walker's only long-term girlfriend, is both Disney princess beautiful and sexy, with abundant curves and an aura of confidence.

The woman is impossibly intimidating.

She looks like a supermodel in her simple outfit of jeans and cropped tee, the world her catwalk as she swaggers through the room in booties with needle-thin five-inch heels. Suddenly, the pink dress that I felt so pretty in earlier seems juvenile, and I'm painfully aware that my hair, which Walker convinced me to wear down, has likely already reverted to its natural state of giant, messy frizz. *Suri's* hair is shampoo-commercial shiny and perfectly straight. If you put us side by side, we'd look like the "before" and "after" snapshots for a makeover…yours truly playing the pre-makeover disaster, obviously.

"You okay?" Luke asks.

Not even a little. I nod without tearing my eyes off Suri.

Don't stare, I scold myself, to no avail. The curiosity is too strong. What was it about this particular woman that captured and held Walker's interest for over a year?

Across the room, Suri and Walker's mother reunite with a joyful embrace. My stomach aches at the sight. She's done nothing to warrant my resentment—she has every right to her past with Walker, which obviously included a relationship with Laura Garrison—yet from somewhere deep within me, a possessive animal instinct rises up, urging me to go over there and claw Suri's eyes out.

I'm ashamed of myself. So much for all my self-righteous proselytizing about women building one another up instead of tainting the sisterhood with toxic competition! A few minutes in the same room as Walker's ex-girlfriend and I'm not only off my high horse, the animal has galloped away into parts unknown.

Am I jealous? Of course. How could I not be? Walker *chose* her of his own volition—no legal contract or manipulations from a romance author required. A strong thread of incredulity also runs through this resentment swelling within me, because Suri had everything I can barely let myself dream of, and she *threw it away*.

I've been in Walker's life less than two months, and I already know trying to trap him with a "move in or break up" ultimatum was the absolute *worst* move she could have made. He's like one of those wild mustangs, meant to run free, resistant to tethers of any kind. It's his nature to balk against restrictions—even unwritten ones, such as societal expectations like showing respect to authority figures.

Walker Garrison is simply not a man you can lock down, and I can't help thinking that if Suri truly loved him, she would never have even tried.

Why is she here? Was she invited? I'd gotten the impression Walker wasn't in touch with his ex. Then again, Luke is a living, breathing reminder this wouldn't be the first time Walker withheld information from me...

"Walk didn't invite her," Luke answers my unspoken question.

"Are you sure?"

"Yeah. They haven't talked in years." His utter certainty helps soothe the snarling, newly hatched green-eyed beast within me.

The next time I peek at Suri, she's looking at Walker. He is still talking to his father, as yet unaware of her presence.

"She still loves him," I realize aloud.

The realization hits me like a kick in the chest—perhaps delivered by that wayward horse I discarded in favor of pettiness.

While Walker and I are good at the moment—great, even—it's impossible not to fear his interest in me is a product of convenience. Two weeks of exploring this new phase of our relationship, and despite a copious amount of evidence proving it as fact, I still struggle to believe *he's* attracted to *me*.

How much of that attraction is because I'm simply *there*, a temporary madness that will vanish after the experiment?

Seeing the longing on Suri's face, I can't help imagining myself pitted against Suri in a contest for Walker's affections... No, it wouldn't even be a contest. The victor of that matchup is as self-evident as our respective positions in that "before" and "after" makeover visual. If you put a frizzy-haired tricycle and a sleek Ferrari on the racetrack, who would question the outcome?

"How do you know?" Luke asks, snapping me out of my mixed metaphors.

Is he joking? I wonder, but Luke's confusion appears genuine.

Perhaps I only recognize the enamored wistfulness in her expression because I've seen it in the mirror all too often lately.

"I just do."

"You've got nothing to worry about. That's ancient history."

The fact he's even making an effort to reassure me only worries me more.

"She's gorgeous."

Luke doesn't miss a beat. "So are you."

He ignores my glare. Of all people, I thought I could count on Luke not to patronize me (No, I am not being self-deprecating. Hello, reality… Tricycle and Ferrari, remember?)

Walker seemed to like tricycles just fine last night.

My memory serves up a visual not at all appropriate for public recollection. It does, however, boost my wilted feminine confidence.

Find your confidence in a way that doesn't involve thinking about Walker's penis in your mouth!

"Incoming. Don't look."

Like every person who's ever been told not to look at something, I immediately look—and find Suri headed straight toward us.

"You good?" Luke asks.

If I'm honest, the answer is *no*, but what would he do, throw me over his shoulder and wheel us away in a speedy blur using his superhero arm strength? Hmm, tempting…

Suri can really cover ground in those gravity defying heels. The sound of them clicking along the floor is now dangerously close. Even had I wanted to test out my "Luke to the rescue" theory, our window of opportunity has closed.

Manifesting bravery I don't feel, I turn to face the only woman who has ever come anywhere near to claiming Walker Garrison's heart. Up close, she's even more gorgeous— because *of course* she is.

Suri doesn't even notice me, her focus entirely on Luke. She stops way too close so she's looming over him, forcing Luke to crane his neck to look up at her. And she's staring at his chair—

more specifically, at his legs, which despite his loose jeans are visibly slimmer than the rest of his body from muscle atrophy.

"Oh my God, Luke!" Suri wails. Her eyes fill with tears as she covers her mouth Miss America style.

It's super awkward. By comparison, my disastrous first meeting with Luke seems like a slam dunk. I'm just standing here witnessing it and *I'm* miserable—I can only imagine how uncomfortable Luke is.

"I heard, but seeing it... I'm *so sorry* I didn't come and visit. You poor thing!"

There goes any molecule of sympathy I might have felt for her. Suri and Luke knew each other from high school, were likely friends even before she dated Walker, and she didn't even go see him after the accident? I could maybe understand not showing up at the hospital, to avoid Walker and post-breakup awkwardness, but she could have at least stopped by once Luke was home.

Suri dashes tears from her eyes. (And dang, she must be wearing waterproof mascara, because there's no smudging to undermine her beauty. Can I not even catch a tiny break?) I can't believe she's crying. She's acting like he *died*... He's *right freaking here!*

Luke remains stoic as ever, but when I note the tension in his jaw and his white knuckled grip on the arms of his chair, I can't stand by watching this any longer.

In a move so bold, I shock myself, I hop into Luke's lap. Thank goodness for his fast reflexes and insane upper body strength, because he manages not only to catch me, but right the chair when my momentum threatens to send us flying. (Apparently, the brake wasn't pulled... Oops!) He's so quick that if not for my momentary stomach flip from nearly falling, even I would be unaware the transition was anything but graceful.

Suri gapes at us.

"I'm Audrey, by the way." Somehow, I manage to sound casual even though my heart is racing. "And you don't have to worry about Luke. We're thinking about hiring a professional bodyguard to help hold back all the women. I mean, have you *seen* these guns?"

I reach for one of Luke's arms but struggle—wow, muscle must weigh a lot, because it is *way* heavier than I expected. Lips twitching beneath his beard, Luke plays along, lifting his arm and allowing me to manipulate it into a curled position to show off his massive biceps.

"Right, uh…" I've rendered Suri speechless with my ridiculous behavior, which I'm counting as a win. It's certainly an improvement over the waterworks.

Then, Walker shows up, joining our odd little tableau. My heart—stupid, masochistic little thing that it is—takes off at the sight of him, sending celebratory messages to all my extremities. Yep, his mere presence has me *tingling*.

Those flutters in my chest erupt into a full fireworks display when Walker lifts me out of Luke's lap in single, smooth motion that shows off his own considerable arm strength. While his brother may have muscles like the Hulk, Walker could still give Captain America a run for his money. He sets me on my feet at his side, steadying me with an arm around my waist. I note that he's not even out of breath after that. (I cannot say the same for myself.)

"What's going on?" he asks me with only the slightest quirk of an eyebrow. Only Walker could maintain a poker face after discovering his girlfriend on his brother's lap.

I smile up at him. "Just talking to Suri."

Rather than pushing for more details, Walker just nods, the tiny motion saying he trusts me enough to go with it and wait until later for an explanation.

Honestly, I think I might love him in this moment.

Oof… Now is seriously not the time to unpack *that*.

284

"Are you dating *both of them*?!" Suri gasps.

Oh, but I am tempted. Her eyes are already as wide as the cartoon princess I first likened her to, horrified and filled with disbelief. What would she do if I said yes?

Walker keeps me from walking off that ledge by answering for us both. (I wouldn't have *really* done it... I don't think.)

"Audrey's *my* girlfriend," he says.

"Not like Luke would have had time for me, even if I'd met him first," I can't help adding.

Walker's arm gives me a little squeeze, a subtle message that he expects me to explain all of this later. (And since when are we able to communicate through tiny, silent gestures?)

"Oh." Suri's big brown eyes, more espresso than my cappuccino, dart between us like she's watching a three-person tennis match—from Walker to Luke to me, back to Luke, then me again, before finally resting on Walker.

I'm not proud that my impulse is to hop back into Luke's lap to draw her focus away from Walker...or perhaps climb Walker right here and publicly claim him as *mine*.

Is he, though?

If I only knew that answer.

"Hey, Suri. Good to see you." Walker's tone is satisfyingly neutral.

"It's so good to see you too," Suri says, with significantly more emotion. "I hope it's okay that I'm here."

It's not. Leave! Hisses the possessive she-beast inside my primal brain.

Once again reading my vibe, Walker holds me a little tighter then murmurs against the top of my head, "Retract the claws, kitten." The warmth in his low voice suggests amused approval—despite his warning words, Walker appreciates my so-called claws.

I tip my head up and give him my most innocent expression, as if to say, "Who, me?"

With our faces so close, the current of electricity always seeming to hum between us sparks to life. At the sensual promise darkening Walker's eyes, my mouth falls open in anticipation while my nipples harden inside my bra.

A loud throat clearing, courtesy of Luke, ends the strangely intimate moment. Walker's brother seems to be biting back a smile, but Suri is staring at Walker and me in a manner I can only call crestfallen.

It seems I didn't need to jump Walker to stake my claim after all.

"Um, well... I'll just...go...say hi to some people." This Suri is not the confident vixen I first witnessed. "Good to see you. Happy birthday. Oh, and uh, it was nice to meet you, Audrey."

I don't even fault her for the insincerity. A brief flash of sympathy for Suri fills me, despite her cringeworthy behavior with Luke. It is far too easy to imagine myself in her shoes, how painful it would be to watch Walker with another girl, looking at her the way he just did me. The sensation is fleeting, gone as quickly as Suri.

"Okay, what the fuck just happened?" Walker asks Luke and me.

I think the tricycle just won.

[CONFIDENTIAL PROJECT RECORDS]
DAY 44

TEXT MESSAGE THREAD: VICTORIA AND WALKER

WALKER: I don't know how you pulled it off, but I KNOW you had something to do with my ex showing up today.

VICTORIA: I am sure I have no idea what you mean.

WALKER: Course you don't.

WALKER: Just to say, not cool at all. Even less cool than forced therapy.

WALKER: Btw, we're just heading back from the party now with Freddy, and Audrey is half asleep in the back seat. Don't expect a journal entry from her tonight.

WALKER: In fact, don't expect one from me either.

VICTORIA: At this juncture, I might remind you the journal entries are a requirement, as stated in your contract. Audrey's lapse, I'll accept, but this transgression is a tad blatant on your part, don't you think?

WALKER: I am sure I have no idea what you mean.

39. The Wrong Twin

Walker

WALKER: Hey Dad, thanks for coming to the party.

WALKER: Btw, I quit. Consider this my two weeks' notice.

DAD: Keep your two weeks, I don't want them.

WALKER: Fine.

DAD: Don't come crying to me when you tank and need a job.

WALKER: I won't.

* * *

It's well after midnight by the time we return to the condo. Audrey fell asleep on the way home. She rouses just long enough to throw on PJ's before crawling into bed, conking out the instant her head hits the pillow. I'm wiped too, with a bone-deep kind of weariness from the long day and its unexpected emotional land mines, but sleep doesn't come.

After downing a glass of whiskey, I lie in bed listening to the ambient sounds of the city and Audrey's rhythmic breathing. I'd usually drag her over here for cuddling, but tonight, I need the space. My thoughts barely fit in this room as it is.

Maybe if I close my eyes, I can trick my body into falling asleep. For a moment, I'm met with nothing but darkness behind my closed lids, but then images and sounds flood in.

My text exchange with Dad.

Keep your two weeks, I don't want them.

Audrey smiling at me, blushing from across the room.

"She's too good for you."

That pink dress.

"You're living on borrowed time with that girl."

Audrey's little claws showing as she stands up for Luke.

Suri's face when she saw me with Audrey.

"Once she realizes you've got nothing to offer but your dick..."

Audrey in Luke's lap, looking like she belongs there.

"You're worth about half of your brother, even now..."

Luke's laughter through the kitchen door.

Luke smiling as he talks to Audrey.

Luke seated across the fire-table, eyes free for once of any shadows but those cast by the night.

Those same gray eyes, haunted, full of invisible demons.

"You need to come to the hospital. Luke was in an accident. It doesn't look good..."

Chemical-tainted air scrapes at my senses, stark yet not quite strong enough to overpower the scents of blood and piss and despair, though perhaps that last one is coming from within me.

I don't know what time it is—it could be the middle of the night or high noon—but it doesn't matter. Nothing matters, not since I got the call about Luke's car accident. My whole world has narrowed to this hospital waiting room. To that door beyond which my brother's fate is being determined.

My coffee went cold long ago; I sip it anyway. Its stale bitter taste is almost sweet compared to my own acrid terror. The caffeine does nothing to touch my fatigue, but I'm in no danger of falling asleep.

Ma is a wreck, a shell of the indomitable woman who raised us. She intermittently weeps and prays in the chair next to mine. Dad is on her other side, the two of us flanking her like stone sentries—an offer of protection that's too little, too late; as futile against the damage already done as that lurking ahead.

Tommy is on my other side. He showed up a while ago—hours, days?—bringing the coffee I can barely swallow and a bag of sandwiches that remains untouched. Eating is as inconceivable as sleep; everything is on hold until that door opens. Until we know.

Is it a good sign, or a bad one, that it's been so long since anyone came to talk to us? Luke was already in surgery when we got here. The person who spoke to us then made no promises or attempts to hide how precarious his situation is.

None of us speaks. What words are there, when somewhere in this building my brother lies on the brink of death? I can barely breathe when I think that I might never see him alive again.

The not knowing *is unbearable. Everything seems muted around me, my outsides gone numb while, within, the vicious teeth of pain and fear are gnawing away at the very fabric of my being.*

It feels like I haven't taken a full breath in days. Anticipation has a tight grip on my lungs, while my stomach lingers in the perpetual sensation of that instant right before free fall. My fingers are bloodied and bruised from clinging so tightly to the edges of hope, all too aware that just below yawns the abyss of grief—so close I can feel its thick, cold tendrils reaching for me out of the darkness, swirling around my ankles.

Then the door opens. The message brings relief so powerful I am in tears. He's going to live.

Whatever blanket muted my surroundings these past hours vanishes, an overwhelming flood of sensory input rushing in. The fluorescent lights stab at my eyes as we're led down a hallway. The assorted sounds of the busy hospital assault me at an ear-bleeding volume—beeping machines and rolling wheels, chatting nurses and cries of pain from behind closed doors.

Then one of those doors is opening, and we're inside the room where my brother lies in a bed unconscious and nearly unrecognizable, battered and bandaged and hooked up to machines that make him look more like a sci-fi creature than the being I've known since we were mere clusters of cells.

I'd expected the hungry abyss to retreat once I hear he survived surgery, but it lingers. Will that chill ever leave now that I've faced grief up close, or did I somehow make irreversible contact during my hours of proximity with its dark waters? I sense it lurking in the room, poisoning my family's hope and happiness as we listen to warnings about potential brain damage, continued danger from internal injuries, the possibility of infection. I hear it in my mother's sobs at the words "spinal cord injury" and "paralysis," feel it in the devastated slump of my father's shoulders.

Waiting for Luke to wake up is a new kind of agony. Like me, my brother has always been active, forever in motion; it makes his current stillness that much more unnerving. I'm constantly looking at the numbers on the machines monitoring his condition, unable to interpret them except as tangible confirmation that he is alive.

My inner conflict is so stark I can almost hear myself ripping in two. Selfishly, I want Luke to wake up so I can see his eyes, hear his voice, reassure myself that he's still here with me. But I am also grateful for each minute he doesn't; another sixty seconds of reprieve from the pain and struggle that await him on this side of consciousness.

Later, Ma steps out of the room to take a phone call, leaving Dad and me seated on either side of Luke's bed. We don't talk. My father is back to his usual stoicism, any emotion he let slip earlier locked down, a paragon of the narrow definition of masculinity on which he raised us.

In Dad's eyes, I imagine when he looks at that bed, he's seeing his dreams lying there beside his son, as broken as the boy who was meant to live them to fruition. The prognosis from the doctor means there will be no West Point graduation, no decorated army career in Luke's—or Dad's—future.

When he speaks, my father's words—his first to me all day—are low but unmistakable.

"Shoulda been you."

Never one to linger once he's said his piece, Dad exits the room, leaving me more alone than I have ever been.

So, there's no one to hear my reply but the beeping machines and my brother's motionless form.

"Well, whadda'ya know, Dad. We finally agree on something."

Dear God, you got the wrong twin.

I wake with a racing heart to a gentle hand on my shoulder and a pair of worried cedar eyes peering down at me.

"Are you okay?" Audrey asks.

A long, controlled breath helps slow my pulse and clears some of the fuzziness from my head. Vestiges of the nightmare cling to me, so I focus on Audrey's freckles, counting the cluster on her left cheekbone to center myself. It's dark in here, but where vision fails, my mind fills in from memory. There are eleven. But I already knew that.

"Walker? Are you okay?" she repeats.

"Yeah. Sorry I woke you up."

"It's okay. A bad dream?"

"A memory," I murmur, not meaning to say it aloud.

Audrey lies back down facing me; I mirror her position, rolling onto my side.

"About Luke? You said his name."

When I drop my chin in assent, my four days' stubble makes a scraping sound against the pillow.

"Do you want to talk about it?"

"Another time."

Understanding eyes offer me grace I don't deserve, her nod of acceptance silent but for the whisper of petal soft skin brushing fabric.

That's us: hard and soft, rough and sweet.

I lose Audrey's eyes, only to get something even better. She snuggles into me, her head on my chest and her arm around my waist. I soak up the comfort, trying not to hold her too tightly in my desperation to devour it like desert soil does a drop of rain.

I hold her until she falls back to sleep, and for a while after that, then gently disentangle myself from her embrace and leave the bedroom. As tired as I am, I know there will be no more sleeping for me tonight.

Leaving the lights off, I navigate my way through the open living space by the glow of the not-so distant city and the sporadic traffic passing beneath the windows. After a quick stop in the kitchen, I take the whole bottle of whiskey to the couch.

Memories are a funny thing, you know? Most blur over time, the majority of my early childhood reduced by now to a series of pixelated thumbnails. Yet after more than two years, my memories of the days surrounding Luke's accident, which I'd actually prefer fade, haven't lost a single degree of resolution.

Tonight wasn't my first time reliving them in high-res in my sleep, and I doubt it'll be the last.

No words could describe the experience of seeing my twin suffer. The helplessness. If I could have shouldered Luke's pain for him, I would have, in a heartbeat. It would almost be a relief; at least I'd finally have a tangible way to fight in a battle otherwise beyond my reach. Instead, I've been stuck behind an impenetrable glass wall, relegated to the role of spectator as my brother combats an enemy that lives within his own brain and body. Forced to watch him fade away into that dark mental place where I can't follow.

Instead of the Jack Daniel's bottle in my hands, when I tilt my head down, I'm once again seeing Audrey draped across my brother's lap, Luke holding her with ease and sporting a confident smirk I haven't seen in well over two years.

"You're worth about half of your brother… I wonder if she'll figure that out too?"

All of the times Luke has needled me about Audrey, calling her hot, talking about making a move once the experiment is over… What if he wasn't just teasing?

The whiskey bottle crashes onto the coffee table, the sound a jarring violation of the dawn stillness. I hold my breath, but I detect no signs of stirring from the bedroom.

Could Luke have feelings for Audrey? Given how fast they connected, it's not a stretch to imagine there's potential for something more.

As for Audrey? Besides our unexpected chemistry (the kind you need to keep fire extinguishers close for), what is there to tie us together beyond the rapidly dwindling days of this experiment?

"It's only a matter of time before she realizes you don't have anything to offer her but your dick."

"Oh, fuck off with the Dad replays," I say out loud.

Talking to my own brain in the dead of night, sitting in the dark with a bottle of whiskey? I sure am a poster child for mental health right now.

The thing is, my father may be an asshole, but he's not a stupid one. Buried within his bullshit were two essential kernels of truth.

Audrey *is* too good for me.

And Luke is a better man than I am.

When I mix those facts with my mind's dogged recollection of Audrey draped over my brother's lap...

The more I think about it, the more the idea of Audrey and Luke together makes sense. Normally, Luke and I would never date each other's exes, but since he knows this relationship is fake, the normal bro code doesn't apply.

All right, so Audrey and I have been a hell of a lot *less* fake lately, but Luke doesn't know that. And if I step on the brakes now, he never needs to.

Maybe this is why I've held off from fucking her, no matter how much my body wants it—like some part of my brain has always known Audrey is not meant for me. If we stop fooling around now, there's no reason Audrey and Luke couldn't be together after our contract with Victoria ends. At the very least, removing myself from the equation means they could give it a real shot.

Sounds all kinds of rational in my head, but that logic is slower to filter down to the rest of my body, which feels sick at the thought of them together—of Audrey with *anyone.*

My stomach twists into painful knots. Deafening denial roars through my psyche, but I take deep breaths, pushing past the selfish impulse to keep Audrey for myself. Yes, I *want* her—but how long will that last? Even if it does, what could I give her? Audrey deserves everything. Not just companionship and passion, but commitment, softness, *romance.* Things I'm fundamentally incapable of—just ask Suri.

Fuck. Another swallow of liquor. This time, I'm more careful about setting the bottle on the table. The whiskey warms my throat but doesn't burn. That's my eyes (and maybe my heart).

How many times over the past two years have I thought I'd give anything, do *anything* to see Luke happy? Seems like the time has come to put my money where my mouth is.

I lived for almost twenty-five years without touching Audrey Mitchell.

I can survive two weeks if it means happiness for my brother.

[CONFIDENTIAL PROJECT RECORDS]
DAY 46

TEXT MESSAGE THREAD: VICTORIA AND MATILDA

11:00 AM

MATILDA: Something is wrong. W is totally shutting A out.

VICTORIA: How so?

MATILDA: I'm going through the recordings from this weekend, like I always do Monday first thing. On Saturday, W had a rough chat with his dad (I really do NOT like that guy), but otherwise, the party went well, even when his ex showed. A and W sounded as cozy as ever, totally on track toward their happily ever after. Then Sunday morning, it was like a switch had flipped. Steamy to frozen overnight.

MATILDA: WHAT HAPPENED SATURDAY NIGHT?

VICTORIA: Didn't you tell me typing in all capital letters is unnecessarily aggressive?

MATILDA: They're warranted. This is a crisis!

VICTORIA: Don't panic. I shall review your notes and the relevant sound clippings as soon as they are ready.

MATILDA: Sent!

VICTORIA: Thank you.

12:30 PM

VICTORIA: Hmm, yes. I see it too. Concerning, indeed.

MATILDA: Victoria, this can't happen. They HAVE to end up together! I've shipped them too hard for too long to have my hopes smashed now.

VICTORIA: You know how much I appreciate your dedication, my dear, but perhaps it is time for a break. When was the last time you took a vacation?

MATILDA: I see what you're doing, and you cannot kick me off the project! I'm seeing this through to the very end.

VICTORIA: I worry about how invested you've become.

MATILDA: Forget me. Worry about our protagonists. I need my HEA!

EMAIL FROM VICTORIA

From: Victoria Trulette

To: Audrey Mitchell, Walker Garrison

Subject: Faking in the Sun

Brava, my intrepid hero and heroine!

Thus far, you have overcome each hurdle and risen to every challenge, and your pretense of coupledom remains intact.

With only a short time left to us, our experiment enters the proverbial "home stretch." If you'll forgive the blatant mixed metaphor, it is time to take this show on the road!

Traveling together and meeting out-of-town family are both common elements in novels within our fake relationship trope, so it only makes sense that the two of you venture to Florida next weekend to see Audrey's mother.

Let Matilda know once your Florida plans are confirmed so she can arrange your travel and accommodation.

Sincerely yours,

Victoria

PS - Audrey, darling, I apologize for the short notice. My penchant for surprise sometimes works at odds with practicality. I hope you won't have trouble procuring your mother's agreement.

40. The Big Freeze

Audrey

Let's be real, my mom wouldn't care if I gave her three *minutes'* notice, as long as I'm coming home. Three days isn't a problem. That gives her more than enough time to clean my room to within an inch of its life and prepare the guest room for Walker—because while she was less than enthused to learn I'm bringing him, she would hear no talk of us staying elsewhere. How would she ensure we're in separate beds if we aren't under her roof?

A week ago, Walker would have pouted about that. Now, he's probably relieved. I suppose I am too, in a way; at least I get a few nights' reprieve from the new distant version of Walker I've been living with for the past week. Plus, if our hotel room had only one bed and Walker decided to build another pillow wall, I don't think my heart could handle it.

(Oh, yes—the pillow wall is back. It reappeared overnight without warning, fanfare, or explanation, much like the new Walker. At least Walker was already asleep when I walked into our bedroom and first saw the resurrected barrier, allowing me some semblance of privacy as I cried my eyes out.)

While three days may be plenty of notice for Mom, *I* usually require a week at minimum to mentally prepare for a visit to Florida. Add on that I'm bringing a boyfriend home for the first time ever—never mind that our relationship is fake, and he's currently treating me like zombie patient zero—and I'm a complete nervous wreck.

Far too soon, we're boarding the plane. My left leg begins a convincing impersonation of a Mexican jumping bean the moment we take our seats. Once we're in the air, the bouncing only increases, quickening with each minute that brings us closer to Florida.

Patience apparently used up, Walker plants a hand on top of my thigh. I stare, horrified and fascinated as it moves up and down with my leg that resolutely continues its bouncing. This is the first time he's touched me all day. One of the only times we've touched all week—and it's just because he wants me to stop fidgeting.

"What's going on?" he asks.

I shrug.

"Come on, talk to me."

I give him my fiercest glare. *Look who's talking!* For days, he blew off my attempts to discuss the Big Freeze—as I've privately dubbed it—deflecting with humor and feigning stubborn ignorance. As if I were *imagining things,* when he'd gone from acting like he couldn't keep his hands off me to demoting us to platonic roommates, without even the casual teasing flirtation he's been throwing out from the beginning.

When I finally pestered Walker into talking, all he'd say was that things had gotten "too intense." According to him, it's best if we "cool it" for these final two weeks to make sure we end this experiment as "friends" with "no hard feelings." All delivered with that blank, emotionless mask I hate so much.

Of course, I wasn't bold enough to tell him we are *long past* the point of walking away from this as "*friends*," or that my feelings over his freeze-out are anything but soft.

To think, I'd been close to gathering enough courage to finally ask that he abandon the (sweet, but oh-so-frustrating) respectful, "taking-it-slow" thing and have sex with me. In truth, I can't decide whether I'm more relieved I didn't, or devastated that now I'll never know what sex with Walker would have been like.

"You've visited before, right? You go home for holidays?" Walker presses.

"Yes."

"Why are you so nervous? Is it me? I promised to be good, and I meant it."

He did promise that. I even believe him. But I've never brought a boyfriend home before, and I'm not sure how my mom will react. There's also the little issue of Walker not always playing well with others. He's especially testy when anyone tries to assert authority over him, which my mom is highly likely to do.

"It's not you." *It's a little bit him.* "I just don't like going back."

"But this time, you've got me."

His cocky smirk is supposed to make me feel better. Instead, I want to cry.

"Yeah."

I don't, though. I thought I had you, but you took yourself away from me. And I don't even know why.

41. Florida. Fuck This Place.

Walker

Go to Florida, they said. *It's all sunshine and beaches and Disney World*, they said.

Yeah, well, those people can take their "happiest place on earth" bullshit and shove it. We've been here less than a day, and I'm already itching to get back to Boston, chilly fall temps and all.

Truthfully, I'd thought Audrey's level of anxiety about this trip was a bit over the top—annoying, even. I know I'm not exactly any parent's ideal boyfriend, but I promised her I'd be on my best behavior. Just shows what an egotistical ass I am, assuming her worry had anything to do with me in the first place.

Audrey's never said much about her relationship with her mom, besides mentioning she's "overprotective." Which doesn't seem all that bad. At least her mom gives a shit, you know?

Yeah, no.

Today, I've had a crash course in how toxic "overprotective" can be. Starting with our arrival at the Orlando airport, where Ms. Mitchell (that's "Miz," not "Miss" or "Missus," as she informed me right off the bat, no first name even mentioned) was waiting to pick us up, even though Audrey told her it wasn't necessary since we had a rental car reserved. Not five minutes later, Audrey was at the car rental desk canceling that reservation, having lost the brief argument with her mother— if you can call it an argument, since Mama Mitchell barely let Audrey get a word in. She didn't give her daughter much chance to talk in the car either. Although she peppered Audrey with a ton of questions on the thirty-minute drive, she rarely shut her mouth long enough to actually get answers.

While Ms. Mitchell is all about her daughter, I may as well be invisible for all the attention she's paid me. Whatever. I'm not about to cry in a corner over the woman ignoring me. But I do need her to acknowledge my existence while we're here, at least once, to give some verbal confirmation she believes we're really dating. Gotta keep Victoria happy, after all.

Here I'd been hoping to sneak away to the beach at least once while we're in the sunshine state, but it looks like those board shorts I packed are going to stay dry in my duffel. By forcing Audrey to cancel our rental car, Ms. Mitchell ensured we're reliant on her for transportation—the Orlando suburbs are not exactly walkable. (There's no hotel poolside relaxation in my future either, because although Victoria would have paid to put us up, we're staying at Chateau Mitchell.) Being shackled to the woman, essentially stranded, grates on my every nerve. I imagine it's a small taste of what Audrey's life was like growing up.

"My mom loves me. She can just be a bit much," Audrey told me once.

So fucking polite. She would never come right out and say, "My mom is so obsessive and controlling she almost smothered me, so I escaped to Boston."

Is it possible to micromanage someone to death? If anyone could do it, I'd put my bets on Audrey's mother. I don't think Audrey has made a single decision for herself since we got here—not what she's eaten or when or even what she's wearing. I overheard Ms. Mitchell dictating her outfit for dinner tonight earlier when I walked past Audrey's bedroom. (She was also unpacking her daughter's suitcase, folding everything neatly and hanging clothes in the closet despite Audrey's protests that we're only here for two days.)

Yes, *her* bedroom. Where Audrey will be sleeping alone. I've been relegated to a guest room—God forbid I have the opportunity to defile Mama Mitchell's baby girl! Man, but it would almost be worth the backlash just to see Ms. Mitchell's face when I told her that precious daughter of hers can deep-throat like no other, that she sucks me off so good I damn near pass out from coming so hard.

Shit. Not a helpful train of thought. When I say keeping my distance from Audrey this past week has been hard, you'd better believe I mean it in every possible way.

Tonight, we had dinner with Audrey's whole family—her aunt, uncle, and cousins came up from South Florida for the weekend. (They get to stay in a hotel. I hope the pool is closed for maintenance.) I've managed to escape out to the porch for a bit, though I should probably go back in soon so Audrey isn't alone with them for too long. But fuck, I needed a break, before I snapped and told them all off for the passive-aggressive guilt trip they've been laying on Audrey all night. (Kids grow up and move away from home. It is not criminal neglect. Jesus.) Not to mention a break from Audrey's cousin Frankie, who eye-fucked me across the table throughout dinner.

Speak of the she-devil...

I barely hold back my groan when the older of Audrey's two cousins, Francine aka "Frankie," joins me on the porch. She stands in front of the door, barring my escape. Her predatory stare is the same one she's been aiming at me all night.

Why, God? Why did it have to be Frankie?

Not that I'd be thrilled to find myself alone with anyone from Audrey's family. Her mom goes without saying. Then there's Aunt Chelsea, a ball-breaker who clearly hates me and doesn't seem to like her husband all that much either. Uncle Irvin is a twig of a man who either had his personality badgered out of him by his wife, or never had one at all. Their son, Audrey's younger cousin Philip, is equally bland—no wonder Audrey was awkward around guys when we met, growing up with those two as the only male figures in her life.

Still, I'd prefer to be out here with Philip over his harpy of a sister—at least he didn't hit on me, although he is gay, according to Audrey's detailed notes she forced me to study. Apparently, Philip's sexuality is the worst-kept secret in the family; basically, they all know and just don't mention it. (Which, sadly, doesn't even make the top ten list of fucked up things about this family I've observed so far.)

It's clear Audrey takes after her dad's side, because the rest of the women in her family are all short and curvy with straight dark hair. Frankie could be a pretty girl, but it's hard to tell underneath the blatant succubus persona. No lie, I'm pretty sure she ripped the already revealing neckline of her shirt before coming out here...like I've never seen big tits before. Her overall vibe is "Trying Too Hard" with undertones of screaming desperation.

Seems no one gave Cousin Frankie the memo that nothing's sexier than a woman who's confident in her own skin. Or they did, but she misread it as "aggressively pursue men who've shown you no interest and/or are currently dating your cousin."

"So, how much is she paying you to be here?"

All right Frankie, you've sure as shit got my attention now.

"Excuse me?" Thank fuck my poker face is epic. Is poker voice a thing? Somehow, I manage to keep mine flat, almost like I'm bored. Meanwhile, my mind is racing. Could she know about Victoria and the contract? How the hell did she find out?

"Oh, come on… Like *Audrey* would be able to snag *you* without some kind of bribery involved."

Okay, no. Fuck this chick. Rage immediately overpowers my relief that she doesn't have evidence of our relationship being fake. It's not the first time today a shitty comment from Audrey's family has made me see red. So far, I've kept my mouth shut, but my last thread of patience just fucking snapped.

"You wanna repeat that?"

Clearly, Frankie misses the warning in my voice, which strongly suggests she choose her next words carefully. Instead, girl's got jokes.

"You're a ten, and Audrey's… I don't know, how do you even rate a girl who barely speaks?"

She doesn't speak because no one in your family will let her get a word in edgewise, you snotty bitch. Audrey's been interrupted and talked over so many times since we got here it's unbelievable.

Finally realizing I'm pissed, Frankie's seductress act falters. She actually has the audacity to look confused.

I'm sorry, am I supposed to be *flattered* that she's dissing Audrey?

"I-I mean, look at you," Frankie sputters. "And look at her."

Oh, she is so fucking lucky she's a woman, because I'd never raise a hand to a female. (I swear, I never had so many violent impulses before Audrey came into my life. Maybe if she weren't surrounded by all these opportunistic fuckers begging to be taught a lesson, I wouldn't keep feeling the need to play teacher.)

"What I *think* you meant to ask is how much *I'm* paying *her* for the honor of sharing her goddamn air. How I got so fucking *lucky* a sweet, smart, sexy, classy girl like Audrey is giving me the time of day. Because I *know* you did not just insult my girlfriend right to my fucking face. Repeatedly."

Frankie's dark brown eyes are now the size of golf balls. I wonder if no one's ever put her in her place before, or maybe my cussing shocked her. (I've been good all day, per Audrey's request… Right, because her family can treat her like a doormat, but God help us all if I drop an f-bomb!) But Frankie's silence suits me just fine.

"Now, listen up. I won't be tolerating any more disrespect of Audrey. Nod so I know you're hearing me." She does. "Right. We're done here."

In her first smart move of the day, Frankie scurries back into the house.

I shake out my arms, but it does fuck all to dispel my unspent energy. I've been jonesing for a run all day. Having to sit still for hours on the plane was painful when I was already on edge, horny as hell after a week without touching Audrey, not to mention exhausted from the constant internal battle it took to stay away from her. Add this entire fucking day with her family, and the agitation in my veins is louder than a horde of angry bees.

Unfortunately, the run will have to wait; Audrey would have my neck if I ditched now and missed dessert. (She was pissed enough when it was my parents.) Plus, I should give her a heads-up in case that chat with Frankie backfires on me. I wouldn't put it past her cousin to run sniveling to the first real adult she sees, claiming I've "bullied" her.

I breathe deeply in an effort at calm, only to choke when the humidity tries to drown me. Forgot I was in Florida. Fuck this place.

Seriously, this trip cannot be over soon enough.

42. Gold, Baby. Gold.

Audrey

Being back in my old bedroom always makes me feel like I'm seventeen again—or sixteen, or fourteen, or ten... Helpless, trapped, desperate for a bigger life, but terrified of all that entailed.

At least I have no memories with Walker attached to this bed, and there's no pillow wall serving as a constant physical reminder of his rejection. In a new location, I should be able to sleep without any trouble, something that's proved elusive since the freeze-out began. (Pathetic, but after only two weeks, I'd grown so used to sleeping in Walker's arms my body has forgotten how to fall asleep alone.)

But, just my luck, it seems the bitter cold of Walker's dismissal followed me to the Sunshine State.

"Be careful, Audrey. Men like him only see women like us as a temporary amusement."

Remembering my mother's warning from earlier makes me wince.

"They're charming for as long as it takes to get what they want, then they get bored and walk away without another thought."

A protest had been right on the tip of my tongue. I wanted to tell Mom that she and I are not the same; just because my father left her doesn't mean Walker will do the same thing to me!

Except…hasn't he already?

Walker may be physically present, as compelled by our contract, but he's so walled off he might as well be gone. In private, anyway. In front of people, it almost seems as if he's gotten *more* affectionate. Which I can't help resenting, even though I should be glad he brought his fake boyfriend A game to Florida with us.

At this point, my body and heart can't differentiate between fiction and reality. Every bit of affection Walker shows me *feels* real, which makes it that much harder at the end of the day when I'm reminded it's fake. Tonight is a prime example. Pre-Big Freeze, Walker would definitely have snuck into my room by now.

I startle at the sound of my bedroom door unlatching. Then it slowly hinges open to reveal a familiar brown head of hair, followed swiftly by a set of broad shoulders and then the rest of the man they belong to. The door clicks shut, and just like that, Walker Garrison is standing in my childhood bedroom, looking even more aggressively masculine than usual amid all the soft purple and floral-heavy décor (my mom's choice).

I'd like to blame my pounding heart on that momentary fright, but who would I be kidding? These palpitations are one hundred percent Walker-induced.

"What are you doing here?"

Walker shrugs, casually strolling through the room like he belongs here.

"Wanted to see if your bed is more comfortable than mine."

With that same nonchalance, he hops onto my bed. Vaulting right over me, Walker settles himself behind me on the double bed that's barely big enough to fit him alone. I try to scoot closer to the edge, to put some space between us, but he just drags me in so I'm pressed right against him. He sighs loudly.

"Oh yeah, this is much better."

He's so ridiculous. So...so... *Mine,* my traitorous body whispers, seeming to heave out a sigh of its own as his warmth seeps into my bones. The urge to melt into him is nearly irrepressible.

A part of me—a big part, honestly—wants to simply give in, succumb to the comfort I can already feel dragging me toward peaceful slumber. To forget about the last week and swallow down all my questions about why he's here. Because he's *here.* And I missed him terribly, with the kind of desperation only possible when the object of your desire is right in front of you, yet out of reach.

There's even a part of me, one only recently awakened, thanks to Walker, that wants to roll over and grab him—tear that shirt off his body and replace it with my hands, kiss him until neither of us can breathe, unleash an entire week's worth of pent-up desire. *Make* him remember how good we are together, until he has no choice but to admit it.

Yet as much as I yearn for Walker, the voice of caution in my head is even louder, and it has been there far longer. Almost as long as the fatherless little girl who lives deep down in my soul, where she's spent almost twenty years nursing the never-closing wound of abandonment. Self-preservation instincts are strong when they're rooted to a lifetime of feeling unlovable—and now that I've let my guard slip and been burned again, they've returned to the forefront.

I pull away from Walker and sit up against the headboard, pulling my knees into my chest and wrapping my arms around them, making myself small to limit physical contact.

"What are you doing here?" I ask again.

"Told you, I'm mattress shopping."

The downside of my new position is that I have a clear view of that all-too-charming boyish grin. He's lounging on my bed like he owns the thing, making himself completely at home under the pale purple comforter and sheets. (This bed has never looked better.)

"What if my mom finds out?"

"You're a grown woman, Audrey. What's she gonna do?"

It's a good question. One I don't have an answer for.

"Do *you* want me to leave?" he asks.

He's dropped the flippant act, and I'm left looking into the eyes of *my* Walker, the man I'd started to fall for, whom I've only caught glimpses of over the last week.

"No," I admit.

Now, he's sitting up too. He's beautiful, and looking at him *hurts*, so I turn away.

"Hey," he says in the soft voice I only get in moments like this, when we're alone. Just a week ago, I loved that voice, but now it reminds me that he took it away with no explanation.

Anger heats my chest.

"What happened to *cooling it*?"

The bitterness in my voice shocks me a little. If it surprises Walker too, he doesn't show it. He just stares at me, tenderness softening his features, along with something I'm not foolish enough to hope is regret (although it sure looks like it). But he doesn't say anything.

I wish, for the umpteenth time, that I were stronger. Brave enough to tell him off for the way he's treating me, accuse him of toying with my emotions.

But I'm me.

"You—" I swallow hard. "You put the pillow wall back up."

To my horror, my eyes fill with tears. When one starts dripping down my cheek, Walker's face falls. In the next heartbeat, I'm pulled into his arms.

"Guess I could've handled that better, huh?" The self-deprecating question comes from just above my head.

"You think?"

For just a moment, I let myself cling to him, burying my face in his neck. How can I feel such immense relief and comfort from the same person who caused my pain in the first place?

"I wasn't trying to hurt you. That's the last thing I want. I'm sorry, Freckles."

Freckles. It's the first time he's called me that all week, and I'm so happy to hear it I think I might be in danger of crying again. It's funny, because if I'd heard that stupid nickname from anyone else at any other time in my life, I'd have despised being identified by a feature that's always made me self-conscious. But when Walker uses it, the name feels like a warm hug to my soul. The best endearment of all time. (Except, perhaps, "baby," which I also hate in theory—a fact I can never seem to remember when he busts it out.)

The hug lasts longer than it should, but not nearly as long as I'd like it to.

"We were just supposed to be having fun," Walker says when we're facing each other again. "And it was, a lot of fun, but it got intense really fast."

They're almost the same words he used the other day, as though he's repeated them often. *Why? Trying to convince himself?* I wonder.

"Then I felt it getting...*bigger* than that, and I figured I'd better step on the brakes before we hit the danger zone and someone gets hurt on day sixty."

Oh, it's way *too late for that.* If he's defining the danger zone as being so attached that saying goodbye will hurt, I've been there for weeks. I was there *before* we started our "fake dating with kissing benefits" thing. Seems it just took him a while to notice.

I don't realize I've averted my eyes until I feel his finger on my chin, forcing me to face him in that way he does.

313

"And it wasn't just you."

Is he...? Does he mean...? Did he just admit that he was getting close to having *feelings* for me?

"I should have done it differently, though," he admits.

"That's what hurt. Not that you did it—" Okay, not entirely true. Sue me. "But *how* you did it."

He sighs like a man who holds the weight of the world. His posture is slumped now, defeated almost, the antithesis of the cocky confidence he strode in here with.

"I fucked up. Again. In case you haven't noticed, fucking things up is kind of my specialty. That's not a good enough excuse for hurting you, but...it's what I've got." When he's being sincere like this, it's really, really hard to stay mad at him.

My body leans in closer as though of its own accord, wanting nothing more than to dive into his arms right this second.

But the only way to be stronger is to...*be stronger*.

"Why are you *really* here?" I hold my breath while I wait for his answer. If he makes a joke right now...

"I just needed to hold you tonight. Will you let me hold you?"

How am I supposed to say no to that?

(That's not a rhetorical question, Universe. Seriously, tell me HOW?)

One nod from me, and I'm in his arms again, being guided back down onto the bed where he stretches out on his back and pulls me so I'm half on top of him, my head on his chest. When he begins to stroke my hair, then down my back, I want to purr like a deeply satisfied feline.

"Hey, Freckles?" he says a few minutes later.

"Mmm?"

"Can I kiss you?"

He sees the yes in my eyes, and he's on me before I can form the actual word. I don't hesitate to kiss him back. It's openmouthed and deep but leisurely, a tender reacquainting where I might have expected hunger and urgency. (But then, when has Walker ever done what I expect him to?)

"You're so good at that," I breathe out, then cringe because *I can't believe I just said that out loud.* This man has a way of incapacitating my brain-to-mouth filter.

"*We're* good at that," he corrects. "So damn good, if kissing were an Olympic sport, we'd totally be on that podium."

"Oh yeah?"

Another soul-quivering kiss. Then he says, so close I can almost taste the words, "Gold, baby. Gold."

This time, *I* kiss *him.* The next time we surface for air, Walker breaks out in a mischievous smile.

"If you think about it, being this good at something comes with a certain level of responsibility. It would be wasteful for us to spend the next ten days together and *not* kiss. Almost criminal."

How does he always manage to make me smile? Even when I've spent days angry and hurt, he pulls me back in with frightening ease.

"So, our kissing is a humanitarian effort?"

"Think of the children, Audrey."

I giggle. It gets cut off by a huge yawn.

Walker's eyes scan my face. "I haven't been sleeping that great either. Come on."

Spooning. The most wonderful thing I never knew my life was missing.

"Hey, you okay?" he says into my hair. "After...today."

Since he can't see my face, I indulge in a private smile. It seems "*I need to hold you tonight,*" is Walker-speak for "I was worried about you and didn't want you to be alone," (with maybe a little subtext of "I want to make out." The man is multifaceted). I melt even deeper back against him.

"Yes, I'm okay."

"'Cause your family kinda sucks."

"They mean well," I defend halfheartedly.

Silence. I swear I can *feel* his raised eyebrow.

"They love me," I insist with more conviction.

"Baby, they treat you like shit. Talk right over you, like anything you have to say isn't worth *twice* the shit that comes out of their mouths. Like you aren't a smarter, better person than the lot of them put together. Not to mention cute as hell and sweet as all get-out, even when you're being fierce, busting out those little kitten claws."

That's...quite possibly the nicest thing anyone's ever said about me. I'm in danger of crying again, so I just squeeze his hand, hoping he knows how much his words mean to me.

"Please play nice, for me? I just want to get through this weekend with as little drama as possible, and then go home."

"Whatever you want," he agrees into my hair.

Snuggling with Walker is more effective than chamomile, the comfort seeping into my very soul as I drift off to sleep on a wave of contentment.

* * *

Walker

Leaving Audrey asleep in her bed isn't easy, when all I want to do is climb back under those purple sheets and burrow my face into her wild hair, then maybe wake her up with my mouth burrowed somewhere else. But even if I don't give a shit whether Ms. Mitchell catches me in here, I know it would upset

Audrey. Plus, if I don't run this morning, chances that I'll manage to keep my promise and play nice with her family are minuscule.

The house is utterly silent, so I try to step softly on my way to the kitchen, running shoes in one hand and empty water bottle dangling from the other. Even in socked feet, I feel like Godzilla crashing through a dollhouse, but that may have more to do with all the pinks and flowers Ms. Mitchell has chosen for the décor.

I'm so certain no one else is awake, I stop dead in my tracks with surprise at finding Mama Mitchell sitting at the kitchen counter in a flowery robe.

Dammit. Why didn't I just fill my water bottle in the bathroom? Well, too late for that now. Time to regroup.

"Morning. Mind if I grab some of that coffee?" Might as well get a bit of caffeine, now that stealth is out of the question.

Ms. Mitchell grants me permission with a nod so regal the woman should be wearing a crown.

I force my muscles to relax, sauntering into the kitchen and pouring myself a mug.

"Thanks."

After I caffeine is on its way to my bloodstream, I go about my business just as I would if she weren't here, filling my water bottle at the sink and putting on my shoes with deliberately casual movements. Like hell am I going to let this woman intimidate me into rushing, no matter how unnerving it is having that judgmental stare following my every move.

I keep waiting for her to drop some kind of word-bomb, but she's silent as I rinse out my coffee cup and wash it in the sink. The clean mug is on the drying rack and I'm starting to believe I'll actually get out of here without any drama, when Audrey's mother makes her move.

"You should leave my daughter be."

317

There it is. What I've been waiting for since she picked us up at the airport.

Props to Ms. Mitchell for the strategic use of anticipation, keeping me on edge so I would be off-balance when she finally launched her attack. It's a very effective tactic—but I grew up with John Garrison, who wrote the book on this shit. I've been training my entire life to stand here and lean casually against the counter with no tension evident in my face or body.

"How do you think Audrey would feel if she knew you were saying this to me?"

Pink spots appear high on Ms. Mitchell's cheeks, the color not at all charming, as it is on her daughter.

"If you care for her at all, you'll let her go now before you cause any permanent damage."

I hate that I actually agree with something this woman says. Not that I'm about to share that little fact with her.

"You keep this up, you're going to lose her," I tell her, before I think it through.

"Is that a threat?" Anger pinches her expression, and her voice has risen in both volume and pitch.

"No, it's a tip. One I'm giving you for free, not because I think you deserve it, but because Audrey loves you and what you're doing is hurting her."

She sputters, face fully red now. I keep going before she can find words.

"The more you try to control her into being who you want her to be, the more you lose the chance to get to know who she really is. And you're missing out, because that person is seriously worth knowing. Maybe think about that the next time you're tempted to treat her like some voiceless doll you can dress and manipulate."

Because there's really nothing else that needs to be said, I let that be my mic drop. Fast, but still not hurrying, I head out for a run in the humidity before Audrey's mom can pick her jaw up off the floor.

Sorry, Audrey. She started it!

[CONFIDENTIAL PROJECT RECORDS]
DAY 53

EMAIL FROM VICTORIA

From: Victoria Trulette
To: Audrey Mitchell, Walker Garrison
Subject: International (Fake) Relations

Dearest Audrey and Walker,

Welcome home! Can you believe our time together is already drawing to a close? How I shall miss you both; it's almost tempting to keep you all to myself for our final days. However, I have one more vacation planned for you, and it is so delicious I couldn't bear to keep you from it.

Therefore, relax and recuperate from your Florida visit but don't get too comfortable, as Thursday, you're back to traveling, this time internationally! A jet-set adventure seemed just the thing to round out our story on a high note.

Ask Matilda if you need some direction for proper packing, but be sure you're prepared to be away through the weekend. Please use these next few days to pack not only for your surprise getaway but also the rest of your belongings at the condo in preparation to move out upon your return.

Oh my, I miss you already! Worry not; I shall enjoy every minute of living this trip vicariously through you.

Sincerely,

Victoria

Audrey's Journal

(Written from PARIS! Ahhhh!)

Dear Victoria,

Thank you, thank you, thank you! I've always dreamed of visiting Paris. Which I suppose you already knew from our icebreaker questions… sneaky, sneaky!

Having the chance to come here at all is such an amazing gift, but then to get off the plane and find Callie and Patrick waiting for us?! I still can't believe this is real. I'm pretty sure Walker is at his wits' end with how many times I've asked him to pinch me (he refused, then got all growly when I pinched myself), but it feels like a beautiful dream. Or maybe that's the jet lag kicking in.

Being in Paris with my best friend is…everything. I can't even tell you how much it means to me. Okay, time to stop before I get all sentimental and start crying again. Walker really, really hates it when I cry.

I think today has been the best day of my life, and we haven't even done anything yet except check in to our hotel. We're meeting up with Callie and Patrick in a few minutes to go to the Eiffel Tower (!!!), but I wanted to write this entry now in case I forget later. Callie spotted the champagne bottle in our room before she and Patrick went to theirs, and she's insisting we bring it with us.

Truly, I can't thank you enough.

Sincerely,

Audrey

* * *

Walker's Journal

What did you do, book us the honeymoon suite? Subtle, Vick. Real subtle.

Well, go ahead and laugh it up. If you're expecting me to complain about the world's comfiest bed, the biggest bathtub I've ever seen, a kick-ass balcony, free booze, and a basket filled with fancy treats, you're going to be waiting awhile. You bet I'll be enjoying the perks of this trip while I can. (Don't read more into that last sentence, I didn't mean it like that. Probably.)

I admit when you had me apply for a passport back when you hired me, I'd been hoping for a wild weekend in Mexico or something, but Paris is a wicked cool alternative.

Callie being here, though… Okay, you got me with that one. Girl's a spitfire with more protective mama bear instincts than Audrey's actual mother. She'll be giving us a run for our money this weekend, that's for sure. Which I'm guessing is exactly what you were hoping for.

As much as I'd like to be pissed at you, I can't really commit to it when Audrey's so damn excited. She didn't say anything, because she's way too polite to risk sounding ungrateful, but I saw her face fall when we got to the airport in Boston and saw our destination wasn't Ireland. As psyched as she is about Paris, I think she's even more excited to be with Callie. So, I guess I can live with Callie's eagle eye and a few days of her giving me the third degree. (But for real, is there a fourth degree? A fifth?)

Seriously, I've never seen Audrey so happy. Thanks for doing this for her.

Walker

43. Of Course You Do

Audrey

"I can't believe we're here. I can't believe *you're* here!" I direct the latter statement to my best friend. I still haven't wrapped my head around her presence.

"I know!" Callie squeals.

"You're not going to start the screaming and bouncing thing again, are you? I swear that security guard at baggage claim was seconds from tasing us or throwing us into airport jail."

"Oh hush, you," I say, rolling my eyes at Walker. We *did* make a bit of a scene. But if my best friend and her boyfriend surprising us at the Paris airport doesn't warrant some scene-making, I don't know what does.

"What's that?" He sticks a finger in his ear and squints. "My hearing still hasn't fully recovered after the supersonic screeching."

"You and me both, mate," Patrick says. Callie scolds him with a swat to his midsection, but he intercepts her hand and defuses her (mostly feigned) irritation by lifting it to his lips. She melts, her expression turning dreamy—and okay, even I'm swooning a bit over that move.

"The ginger's smooth, I'll give him that," Walker mutters so only I can hear, then gives me a wink belying his grumpy front. I lean into him a bit, the long day of travel starting to catch up with me. I slept poorly on our overnight flight from

Boston, but as nice as a nap sounds right now, I don't want to waste a single minute of our time in Paris or with Callie.

"I'm *dying* to know who your boss is!" Callie gushes, not for the first time. "She must be the nicest person ever."

Walker and I exchange a look. Of course, I am beyond grateful to Victoria for arranging this surprise, paying for Callie and Patrick's flight here from Ireland as well as a room for them at the same hotel where Walker and I are staying. But Walker's sardonic eyebrow points out what we can't say aloud—Victoria has ulterior motives for this generous gesture. As final exams go, she's manufactured a brilliant one to test us as a fake couple. If there's anyone in the world who will be able to sniff out that we're faking—besides Luke, of course—it's my best friend.

"It literally took her assistant twenty minutes to convince me it wasn't some elaborate scam or trafficking scheme," Callie says, regaling us with her tale of the phone call from Matilda that set this plan in motion. "But what else was I supposed to think when I get a call out of nowhere saying my best friend's anonymous rich employer wants to fly us to Paris to surprise you and Walker?"

It's a fair question; lord knows she'd never guess the truth.

Callie and I insist that we *have* to go to the Eiffel Tower first thing, so the four of us take the Métro from our hotel to that part of the city. The boys trail us with matching looks of indulgent patience as Callie and I demonstrate zero chill, being complete tourists as we "ooh" and "ahh" at everything.

We stop at a grocery store to buy food for a picnic dinner to take with us to the lawn in front of the tower, very proud of ourselves for being so European as we put together our makeshift charcuterie board of sliced meats (for the carnivores in our group), cheeses, fruit, and a baguette, plus another bottle of wine.

Walker ducked out of the store while Callie and I were perusing cheeses, and he is still nowhere to be found when we're paying for our purchases. The total hurts—this little

324

boutique food shop is *expensive*—but I'm on an otherwise free trip to Paris, so the splurge feels justified. Just as I'm getting a bit concerned by his absence, Walker shows up holding a paper cup with a plastic lid whose contents I know even before he hands it to me.

He must have noticed my longing glance when we passed that coffee shop down the street and went back for me. God, how am I supposed to *not* fall for the man when he does thoughtful stuff like this?

I think I love you.

Luckily, I don't say that out loud. But I do throw myself into his arms.

"You wonderful, beautiful man!" I plant a kiss directly on his lips.

Oh, but a girl could get addicted to the way Walker is looking down at me, the indulgent little smirk accompanying his chuckle at my reaction transformed into something tender by the softening around his eyes meant only for me.

"Come on, lovebirds. I want to get some pictures while it's light out," Callie says.

"Thank you," I whisper to Walker before letting him go.

But before the hands at my hips release me, he presses his lips to my forehead, murmuring against my skin, "You're welcome, Freckles."

Callie mimes fanning herself with a hand, rolling her eyes back. I fully agree with her silent commentary on how hot Walker is, but she doesn't need to do it *right in front of him.* While his smirk turns cocky, I blush and hide my face behind my coffee cup (after a nice big sip... *Ahh, heaven.*))

At the Eiffel Tower, we take approximately three thousand photos and drink both bottles of wine with little help from the boys. Later, I'll be shocked Walker let me talk him into taking so many selfies with me and playing photographer while Callie and I pose with the Eiffel Tower behind us, but for now, I'm too caught up in the high of this whole day to give it any thought.

I'm in a state of near delirious giddiness, between the bubbly wine and my glee over being with Callie. She's right there with me. We're slap-happy, at the point where everything is hilarious, falling over each other giggling at our disastrous attempts to mimic the overhead speaker's pronunciation of the Métro stops on our way back. (Seriously… I am physically incapable of creating those vowel sounds for the French interpretation of "Franklin Roosevelt.")

At the hotel, Callie and I cling to each other, not ready to be separated. So instead of going to the room Matilda booked for her and Patrick, she comes to hang out in Walker's and mine. The guys leave to give us some girl time and venture out in search of "real food"—apparently our cute snack picnic was insufficient to fulfill their manly appetites.

Barely aware they're gone, Callie and I snuggle into the pillows on the bed and alternately chat about real things and giggle incoherently. The height of the intoxication from the wine has faded, but the happiness hasn't. Honestly, we could be this silly together without any alcohol.

"You and Walker are really cute together."

I bury my face in a pillow, far too pleased by Callie's words. I haven't even thought about faking all day, too caught up in the magic. It doesn't matter; at this point, there's no effort required to act like an infatuated girlfriend.

"I think I love him," I whisper.

Instead of screaming and doing a happy dance as I'd expected, Callie simply smiles. "Of course you do."

I stare at her, speechless, totally unnerved by her steady answer and utter lack of surprise, while I'm over here shaking from the significance of speaking that terrifying confession aloud.

"He feels the same."

"How do you know?" I'm whining, pleading with zero dignity, and I don't even care. My heart is racing. All I want is for her to keep talking, to tell me more, to say that the thing I've barely let myself hope for, much less believe, is true.

"You should see the way he looks at you."

"I have."

"No, Auds... I mean when he doesn't think anyone else is watching him. It's warm and kind of wistful, full of wonder, like he's awed that you exist."

"Now you're just being poetic for the sake of it."

"I am not! It isn't my fault that your boyfriend's heart eyes can be described while employing alliteration."

As much as I'd like to believe Callie's assertion that Walker has real feelings for me, he's never given the slightest indication of that. With his words, anyway. His actions seem to tell a different story—he's returned to full-time boyfriend mode since Florida—but without explicit confirmation, there's every chance I'm seeing what I want to see instead of what's there. When I'm with Walker, it's easier to brush off thoughts of the future and simply enjoy the present, but in his absence, I can't help worrying about what comes next for us.

"Why the sad face?" Callie asks.

For a few heartbeats, the urge to tell Callie everything, to unload all of these weeks of confusion and stress, is so intense it almost overpowers me.

But of course, I can't. Instead, I go for a piece of the truth.

"It's almost over—Walker's house-sitting job in Boston, I mean. You know the condo where we've been staying together? He'll go back to living with his brother, and I still need to find a new place..."

Since I signed over the rest of my old lease to the subletter, I've been looking at apartments, but there isn't much available at this time of year. So, when we get back to Boston, I'll be temporarily moving in to the guest room at Jamie's place—her fiancé's super-rich family bought him a two-bedroom condo, an unheard of luxury for people our age in a city as expensive as Boston. Jamie and Oliver said I can stay as long as I want, but I hate imposing on them, so that's been another stressor weighing heavily on my mind.

"You don't think you and Walker will stay together?" Callie asks. "You just said you *love* him, and he's obviously head over heels for you. I mean, he came to *Paris* with you!"

I suppose that *would* seem romantic—if you didn't know he's here as a job requirement.

"It's a weird situation." More than she'll ever know. "We've spent nearly our entire relationship living together. I'm just worried about things changing when we have our own places again."

"You do know that's how most relationships are, right?" Callie teases. "Billions of couples have successfully survived separate living situations, often for years."

"I know, I know."

Time to change the subject. I've brought us way too close to Reality Land, and I don't want to plant any doubts in Callie's head about Walker and me. There's a lot of money riding on her belief in us as a couple.

"Do you know what Walker said to me that day we were alone on Skype?" Callie asks out of nowhere.

"I *knew* you guys talked about me!"

Her lips slide to the side in a playful smirk, and I remember how she'd made some joke about them "running away together." But then she grows serious.

"He said that you're silk and he's sandpaper."

My eyes fill with tears, too physically and emotionally exhausted from this long day to hold back the reaction.

"I thought it was the most beautiful and heartbreaking thing I'd ever heard. I love that he knows you're precious, Auds, I can't even tell you how much. But it worries me that's how he sees himself."

"It's his dad, Callie. He's such a jerk. He thinks his way is the right way, and nothing else will ever be good enough."

"And I'm guessing his son being an artist isn't the 'right way'?"

"As Walker tells it, nothing but joining the army would have earned his approval, and that's just not how Walker's built."

"I can see that."

A familiar sense of frustration fills me at the thought of Walker's father. The man has two amazing sons, and his view of the world is so black-and-white he can't bring himself to love them the way they are. I feel sorry for him, but I also kind of hate the man.

"It will all work out," Callie says.

"I think I'm *in* love with him, Callie," I whisper, testing out the way the words feel tripping off my tongue, unnerved all over again by the taste of truth that lingers in their wake.

"Babe, I *know*."

Of course, this is the moment I finally remember my bracelet mic is still on.

[CONFIDENTIAL PROJECT RECORDS]
DAY 56

Transcript Excerpts: Audrey's Mic

Truncated and Annotated by Matilda

A = Audrey Mitchell, C = Callie Moreau (best friend)

11:00 PM (Paris Time)

C: "Wait…You haven't had sex yet?"

A: "Say it a little louder for the people in the back, would you?"

C: "I'm sorry, am I not supposed to react to that? How on earth have you been living with *that man* for two months without doing the deed?"

A: "It's…complicated."

C: "Not really. You insert part A into part B…"

A: "You're terrible!"

[giggling]

C: "Seriously. Uncomplicate it for me. What's going on? Has he treated you badly?"

A: "No, not at all! He knows I don't have a lot of experience with this stuff, and he's been so respectful. *Really* respectful."

C: "Too respectful?"

A: "Oh my gosh, *yes*. Way too freaking respectful! Ahh! It's driving me crazy!"

C: "You know what I'm going to say."

A: "Callie—"

C: "You've just got to jump him."

A: "I don't know if I can!"

C: "The way that man looks at you? I think even if you manage a tiny bunny hop, he'll catch you and take over the rest of the way. He's probably just waiting for a sign from you."

A: "I've been giving him signs for weeks!"

C: "Well, whatever you've been doing, he's not getting it. Boys can be really dense. You may need to spell it out for him."

A: [groans]

C: "You've done other stuff, though, right? I thought you said…"

A: "Yes. We've done…*all* the other things."

C: "*Nice*. And it's good?"

A: "*So* good. I can't even…"

C: "That's what I like to hear! Way to go, Six Pack Mountain Man!"

A: "You know calling him that just inflates his ego."

C: "Trust me, you're going to want that bad thing nice and *inflated* tonight."

A: "Trust *me*, he doesn't need any help there."

[laughter]

44. Stolen Treasure

Walker

Audrey and Callie are out cold when Patrick and I return to the hotel, curled up facing each other on top of the still-made bed, looking like they fell asleep mid-giggle. Seeing the slight smile on Audrey's face even in sleep, I feel this burning in my chest. Maybe something in the shawarma we grabbed down the road is getting to me.

"I think you're going to have a time of it getting your lass back to the US," Patrick remarks in a low voice.

"We're gonna need to double check the suitcases. Callie's small enough, she might try to stow away and come back with us."

We share a look. It's full of commiseration, the shared fond amusement of two guys whose women adore each other. I turn away as soon as the realization hits; I have no place slipping into the persona of a long-suffering boyfriend so easily.

Patrick walks over to the bed and picks Callie up. Her eyes blink open, but she doesn't startle. She just smiles at him and says, "Hi baby," before snuggling deeper into his arms, apparently falling back asleep.

I watch Patrick carry his girl the two doors down to their room. Callie's not a small girl—well, she's short, but curvy and not shy about showing it off—but despite his lean frame, Patrick handles her with ease, even managing to tuck her dress around her for modesty with an ease that speaks to practice. Damn that street food; the heartburn sensation intensifies watching the love and trust between them.

If I'd known this trip would be one long double date, I might have worried about all of us getting along, but it's been easy, even when Patrick and I stepped out to find food.

Or maybe it's simply hard to feel anything but content when Audrey is so happy. She was fucking adorable tonight, drunk on that wine the girls guzzled like apple juice.

It's weird, even though we spent most of the day together, I almost miss her, because she was so focused on Callie. I'm tempted to wake her up now, steal a little bit of her attention just for myself.

Probably for the best. With Audrey already asleep, this is one less night of struggling not to fuck her. I feel more than a small sting of regret when I note it's also one less night I have to enjoy doing everything *but* fuck her, when I have so few left.

I place my wristband mic on the nightstand beside Audrey's, making sure both are powered off before plugging them in to charge overnight.

"Hey, you," Audrey murmurs sleepily when I climb into the bed after gently maneuvering her under the covers. Barely opening her eyes, she tilts her head upward in a silent request for a kiss that has me smiling even as I press my mouth to hers. Then I curl my body around her as she wiggles backward, automatically slipping into the position we've found is optimal for sleep spooning.

Holy shit. I'm *that* guy, the one with an "optimal sleep spooning" position. The me of two months ago is laughing his ass off right now—and you know what? I feel sorry for that poor sucker. He doesn't know how goddamn good it feels to fall asleep curled around Audrey's body. How *right*.

333

But that must be the shawarma talking, too, because no good can come from indulging those kinds of sentimental thoughts.

"Did you and Patrick have a good time?" Audrey asks, sounding a bit more awake now.

"Yeah."

"You guys found food?"

"Yeah."

"Do you have condoms?"

Wait. *What?*

My muscles freeze, even as my insides begin to riot. I have to pull my hips back so Audrey won't feel my body's immediate response to her question poking her in the ass.

"Yes…" I answer carefully.

"Could you maybe get one?"

Her voice is so soft and timid, it takes me a moment to fully register what she's saying.

Is Audrey…asking me…to fuck her? In the world's most awkward but adorable way?

I reposition us so I can see her face in the faint glow of light seeping in through the partially open curtains. Her cheeks are stained pink, but when I scan the rest of her face, I can't find any uncertainty or sign that she's joking.

Well, damn. Awkward as her methods are, I know how much bravery this took her. I'm proud in the horniest of ways.

But I'm also me, so I can't help messing with her a little.

"Just one?"

She flushes a bit darker and her shoulders inch upward toward her ears in a tiny shrug, but she doesn't break eye contact.

"Maybe two?"

Holy hell. I almost choke on my tongue.

Then I'm up and making my way to my suitcase, moving slowly, giving her time to change her mind. She doesn't, just follows my progress with silent eyes as I retrieve two condoms from my stash.

(What kind of pig decides his brother should be with a girl and then packs a bunch of condoms for a trip with her? *Oink fucking oink.*)

Tossing the condoms on the end of the bed, I pounce, making her laugh when she's jostled by the impact of my weight hitting the mattress.

"Condoms, check. What now?"

"I was, um, hoping you could take it from here."

True story: I'm fully hard, and I haven't even touched her yet.

"Are you drunk?" I have to ask.

"No, Callie and I switched to water after you and Patrick left."

"You responsible little nerd." Then in case the teasing makes her feel insecure, I add, "Good thing I've developed a *thing* for cute nerds lately. Well, when that nerd is you."

We're making out, clothes coming off one layer at a time, when my conscience starts prickling along the back of my neck.

Yeah, I've given up even trying to stay away from her since Florida, but what's changed, really? We're having fun; I might even be falling for her a little. But the fact remains—this girl wasn't meant for me. She would still be far better off with Luke, and I'm no less certain that he is more deserving of that happiness.

Yet here I am anyway, selfish as ever, kissing her like my life depends on it. Using a little joke about the Olympics and humanitarian efforts to justify taking as much as she'll give me during the time we have left.

"I can't make you any promises," I say, a desperate last-ditch attempt to give her an out. If she calls a halt to this, I will back off in a heartbeat. But she has to be the one to do it, because I'm not strong enough to stop now.

"I'm not asking you to."

Hovering over her in a push-up position, my arms shaking more from how damn much I want her than the physical effort, I force myself to try one more time.

"All I have to give you is now."

I try to harden my voice, make it gruff, almost *wanting* her to pull the brakes on this thing, even as I ache with a desire greater than I've ever felt in my life. *Daring* her to push me away, to recognize that I'm not worthy of taking what she's about to give.

But Audrey just holds my eyes, sweeping me away into those intoxicating pools of sweetness, of cinnamon and cocoa, whiskey and honey, and says with a boldness she didn't possess weeks ago, "Yes, please."

And I. Am. *Done for.*

Unleashed, I take her mouth with shameless voracity, plundering it like the thief I am. Every kiss, every touch, every sigh and little sound I coax out of her—it is all so much stolen bounty, additions for the pile of ill-gotten gains I've already acquired these last weeks. A pile far bigger than it should be—more than enough, surely. But like any thief, I am greedy. Insatiable. Already strategizing how I can wring every precious drop of treasure out of *now*, how to take maximum advantage of this gift she's unwisely placed in my hands. Knowing none of it belongs to me, that I don't deserve a single sparkly gem, and planning to hoard them all the same, to pull back out later, when these memories in my lonely treasure vault are all I have left.

Then there's no room in my mind, in my universe, for anything but Audrey

45. Sexual Glow Up

Audrey

Perhaps I should heed the warning Walker is trying so hard to deliver. But where has playing it cautious gotten me? If I've learned anything, it's that you can hide away from life as much as you want, but hurt will still find ways to get to you; so why not reach out and grasp things like joy, and pleasure, when they're within your reach? Even if it hurts later, at this moment, I can't imagine feeling regret about grasping on to Walker Garrison.

So, I do, sliding both hands up from his shoulders to his head, savoring the softness of his hair between my fingers and tugging slightly, holding his face against mine even though he doesn't seem inclined to stop kissing me any time soon.

I can already feel that stirring inside, the pressure building in my lower abdomen. For so long, climaxing was frustrating and elusive and always a lengthy process. Now, it's as if after all the orgasms Walker has given me, he's conditioned me to physically respond to him. The merest kiss or touch is enough to trigger my arousal, like muscle memory, my body anticipating the forthcoming pleasure and remembering how to get there. So, instead of hiking to that peak from the ground, I'm starting somewhere halfway up the mountain.

If Walker is the bell, I have no qualms about being the dog in this metaphor. I can hardly imagine a more mouthwatering stimulus.

Speaking of which... I start sliding down his body, stripping off his pants on the way to my intended destination between his legs. I never thought I'd say this, but I've actually become quite fond of this particular piece of Walker's anatomy. Even when it's all angry-looking as it is now, rigid and veiny and big enough that I have to get creative with my mouth and hands.

Here's something I would never admit aloud, especially to Walker: I'm kind of *grateful* to Ethan, for all those months of guilt-tripping me into frequent blow jobs because I wasn't ready to have sex. Of course, afterward, I found out he was sleeping around on the side all along, his poor patient martyr act pure manipulation. But honestly, it was worth it, because all that practice means I know how to make Walker very, *very* happy. I don't know that I'm doing anything special, but Walker acts like I'm some kind of oral goddess, and that is an amazing feeling. There's this deep satisfaction, knowing *I* have that power, that *I* can make a man like him lose control and go mindless with pleasure.

I never once got turned on by going down on my ex, but a few minutes with my mouth on Walker and I'm squeezing my thighs together, thinking about those foil packets down at the end of the bed.

Did I really tell him to get *two*? Who *am* I?

I hardly recognize myself right now, though the new look is a definite improvement... Is this my sexual glow up?

I actually whine a little bit when Walker drags me up his body.

"Not tonight, baby. We've got other plans."

Still, he doesn't rush things, proving once again he's nothing like my ex. He kisses the daylights out of me, alternately exploiting the sensitive skin along my neck and working my tongue with his so skillfully I almost see stars. He knows exactly how to drive me crazy with his lips and teeth and facial hair, all the while I can feel that impressive erection between my legs, pressing against my clit. In my ear, he murmurs all the things he wants to do to me, how he's "getting me ready to take his cock" and going to "work my pussy so good."

If asked, in theory, I'd have said dirty talk was a turn-off for me. But the reality of Walker Garrison is a game changer, and *holy moly* do his filthy words make me hot!

When he shifts positions, I think it's time to use one of those condoms. But instead, he spends a couple of minutes giving attention to my breasts—a part of *my* anatomy he's especially fond of (a fact he shares with me often). Then his face is between my legs, and I can't even remember what the foil packet is for. Remember the whole Pavlovian conditioning thing? Oh yeah, my body knows *exactly* what's in store when Walker's mouth is in this zip code.

My breath falters when he shoves his face directly between my thighs, my hips shifting restlessly at the sensation of his hot breath through my panties. I shudder when he drags his nose down the center fold, pausing to provide pressure in just the right spots. I'm wet, and I squirm with both shyness and arousal when he inhales deeply with his face *right there*, then groans loudly to make sure I know how much he likes the scent of my body's desire for him.

I think he'll remove the last piece of clothing between us, but never one to do what's expected, Walker instead licks me through the fabric. The friction of the wet material dragging against my clit has little fireworks sparking off from those sensitive nerve endings. When he repeats the motion, tongue probing lower this time, I can't help threading my fingers through his hair, pulling him down even as my hips push upward.

He chuckles without moving from his position; the warmth and vibration of it directly over my sex makes my inner muscles spasm.

"Need something?" he asks, using his nose to trace back up then nudging at my clit with unerring accuracy. "Want me to take these off, maybe?"

"Yes. *Yes.*" I'd probably be horrified by how wanton I sound, if I weren't so far gone with lust—and if Walker didn't make it so safe for me to let go like this.

Then there's nothing between his mouth and my body, and it's all I can do to give myself over to the exquisite sensations. His warm tongue and skilled lips work my most intimate flesh, intermittently joined by his fingers, the scrape of his stubble against the sensitive skin along my inner thighs only heightening the pleasure. He might self-deprecate about not going to college, but I have no doubt Walker was an excellent student. He's certainly committed himself to the study of my body with impressive speed and thoroughness, figuring out all the things I like best—things I never *knew* I liked until he introduced me to them.

Walker seems to take great pleasure in keeping me guessing about what he's going to do next—like now, when he suddenly switches things up, removing the two fingers he'd worked into my channel and replacing them with his tongue, which he holds firm then pushes into me. The sensation is so new and different, almost shocking, and paired with the sudden, steady press of his thumb directly on top of my clit, it sends me rocketing straight to the top of that peak.

White lights, fireworks, curled toes, going boneless... All the ways the romance books describe ecstasy and more, that's what it feels like when Walker makes me come.

I hear a crinkling sound that I only identify as the condom wrapper once I've recovered and fully settled back into my body. I'm a bit disappointed that I didn't get to watch Walker roll the condom on, though I can't be too upset, because this means it's really, finally happening.

I'm going to have *sex* with Walker!

"Nervous?" Walker asks.

"A little," I admit, barely getting the two words out before Walker is pressing two fingers back inside me without warning, the penetration following so soon after my orgasm setting off delicious little aftershocks.

He grins at me, and if there were ever a smile that could be called wolfish, it's this one. "Have to make sure you're ready." Then he adds a third finger, and we both suck in breath at the tight fit. "I'm big, baby. You sure about this?"

I can *see* how hard he is, so the fact that he even asks? I fall for him just a tiny bit more. Which makes my affirmative answer one of the easiest of my life.

Walker tries to roll us so I'm on top, but I shake my head and return to my back. I've heard great things about that position, but I don't want to be in charge right now. I don't want to have to think or worry about what I'm doing. Luckily, it seems Callie was right; Walker once again takes my little bunny hop and has no problem leaping the rest of the way for both of us.

I've spent a not-inconsiderable amount of time with Walker's penis these last few weeks, so I know he's big, but when he nudges at my entrance then starts slowly pushing inside, that size takes on a whole new meaning. I didn't know I could feel this full, and he's not even halfway inside me yet!

I can tell from the faint tremors running through his arms that it's costing him to hold back. Even so, he asks, "You okay?"

He's such a good man, and he doesn't even realize it.

"Faster," I whisper, grabbing his butt and trying to pull him into me. The inch-by-inch method is giving me too much time to think.

I might as well have said "abracadabra" or pushed a "Go!" button. His careful restraint disappears. He pushes into me in one hard thrust, groaning and muttering expletives against my neck like he's in pain, except I know it's quite the opposite, because amid the unintelligible cursing, I make out, "So good... You feel so fucking good... So fucking tight, baby... Goddamn, amazing..."

It seems he loses all control of his potty mouth during sex. I should hate it, but I don't. I really, really don't.

"Relax," he whispers, kissing below my ear. "You've still got a little more of me to take."

There's...*more?!*

My mouth opens for him when he presses his thumb against my lips. I look straight into his eyes while I twirl my tongue around it, watching them darken as his pupils dilate until there's only a thin ring of gray iris visible. Down where we're connected, his hips jerk, pumping in and out with shallow motions, as though he's too turned on to hold back. I smile at the thought.

"Vixen," he rumbles right against my mouth before taking it. His tongue is slow and languid, dancing with mine like he's reenacting the way I sucked on his thumb—which I suddenly feel, because he's snuck his hand in between us and is now using that same digit I just licked to rub slow, tight circles over my clit. He begins thrusting in and out of me again, proving he was telling the truth, as he goes a little bit deeper each time.

On his next inward thrust, he presses down hard with his thumb while simultaneously wrapping his lips around one of my nipples. My inner muscles spasm at the surge of pleasure, and he slides impossibly deeper.

"That's it, baby. You're taking all of me now. That's my girl," he murmurs. His approval makes me preen in satisfaction, almost wishing there were even more of him I could take.

He pulls out nearly all the way and then slams back in with such force it would have sent me through the headboard if not for the firm hand holding my waist in place.

Groaning, he lets out another string of curses and nearly incoherent rambling, intermittently dropping quick kisses all along my chest and up my face. "Like your pussy was made for my cock. Fuckin' A, Freckles. If I'd known you'd feel this good, no way I'd'a been able to hold off so long."

Then he pushes my leg up until my knee is nearly touching my ear. On his next hard thrust, the new angle sends frissons of pleasure bursting throughout my body. I hear a sound that I only belatedly realize came from me.

"There it is," he murmurs.

I don't know what "it" is, but I've never felt anything like it. I want *more*. My hips cant upward as I wrap my other leg around his hips, trying to pull him into me, wanting to shove him deeper against that incredible spot. His hips buck a way that has me seeing stars and making that sound again. I'd be embarrassed if I weren't so focused on the incredible sensations he's creating—that *we're* creating—as he picks up the pace.

"Good call on the two condoms," he grunts out between labored breaths. "You feel too fucking good. This time isn't gonna last nearly as long as I'd like. Fuck, baby, *fuck*…"

His words, plus the way his thrusts are losing their rhythm, turning erratic, drag me closer to the edge. Feeling him lose control is such a turn-on, my inner muscles start to clench around him. Which only makes him move faster, his strokes hitting that magical spot every time.

Now I'm the one spouting incoherent words because *oh-my-freaking-God*, it feels incredible. I grab his butt so hard I'm probably leaving marks, but I don't even care. I just want more. I want him closer. I want him inside of me so deep he'll never leave.

"Don't wait for me," I say, feeling his muscles vibrate like he's struggling to hold back.

"Not gonna happen."

The thumb that's been alternately stroking and pushing on my clit leaves. Before I can voice a complaint, it returns with a friend and pinches, almost hard enough to hurt. At the same time, Walker lowers his head and wraps his lips around one of my nipples.

I explode.

For long moments, I am nothing but sensation and pleasure, faintly aware that I'm making some kind of sound but not fully able to register it and definitely not able to care.

When I finally come back to earth, I'm panting like I just ran a marathon, and he's slumped on top of me, breathing almost as hard.

"Did you come?" I ask him.

He laughs. The vibration travels down to where he's still inside me, making me contract around him. We both moan a little.

"Hell yeah, I came. I was fixing to blow anyway, but if I hadn't been, watching you go off like that would have sent me there. Hearing you scream? *Damn*, baby."

Scream? I'd be embarrassed, but it's impossible when he's looking at me like that, brushing the hair away from my sweaty face as his eyes caress my features like I'm something both beautiful and precious.

Dang, I refuse to be one of those people who cries after sex. (She says, as a tear rolls down her cheek.)

"So, you liked it?" I ask, hating the insecurities that drive me to ask.

Walker wipes the tear from my cheek, then gives me a long, slow kiss that's as sweet and tender as his blunt words are coarse (and I love both). "If your pussy hadn't just milked the hell out of me, I'd go another round with you right this second. But give me, like, fifteen minutes, then I'm going to fuck you for as long as it takes to make sure you'll never ask that question again."

And then, because he *knows* me, that a needy part of me can't quite believe it without direct words, he says, "Best sex ever, Freckles. Hands down."

Twelve minutes later, he's rolling on the second condom.

DIRECT MESSAGE THREAD: VICTORIA AND SIOBHAN

V = Victoria Trulette

S = Siobhan McMahon, fellow romance author and dear friend

S: So, how is the book going to end?

V: I am torn. The romantic in me wants to leave them be, to simply sign over their final checks and wish them well going into the future, hoping they will do so together. But I cannot lose sight of the larger objective—to discover whether two strangers, pushed together through unusual circumstances and forced to feign all the trappings of romance, can indeed fall in love in an abbreviated but intense matter of time.

S: And have they?

V: I believe so. All seems to be going well. However, there have been no declarations made, at least to my knowledge, nor indications of their intentions beyond the scope of their employment with me. I find I am not content to wave adieu at the conclusion of day sixty and send them off into the world, hoping the connection they've formed will be a lasting one.

S: No, you can't let the story end on an ambiguous note. You need drama. Something that will push them to shit or get off the pot.

V: A crude but apt aphorism for the circumstances. Every great romance must have a final hurdle, a climactic challenge that forces the couple to acknowledge and overtly declare their feelings as they would not under less extreme circumstances.

S: Yes, a test to prove love conquers all. Have you decided how you're going to do it?

V: Indeed, although I am loath to follow through. I have grown too fond of my protagonists and it pains me to cause them discomfort.

S: Think of it as doing them a favor. If you left them to their own devices, even if they chose to stay together after the experiment, who knows how long they might linger in this state of emotional limbo? From what you've told me, it seems likely those two would keep dancing around each other for months, feeding each other's doubts and insecurities in a ruinous, self-fulfilling cycle.

V: I agree. The thought does bring me some comfort.

S: So, you are going forward with the plan we discussed?

V: I am. After all, the true test of love is a willingness to sacrifice.

46. The Final Play

Walker

You know that phrase "calories don't count on vacation?"

No one *really* believes the calories don't exist, or that the food isn't going to affect their bodies—it's all about that shit not mattering until they get home. It's the suspension of reality, a temporary state of willful ignorance.

Humans are great at lying to ourselves, aren't we? Especially when it's in the pursuit of immediate gratification. We're greedy, self-serving creatures, eager to latch on to anything that can rationalize what we already want to do.

Okay, I'll drop the pretense of philosophizing about the greater human condition or whatever: I'm talking about myself here. Obviously. *I'm* the greedy, self-serving asshole in this scenario.

And oh man, did I let gluttony reign while vacationing in Paris.

For a few amazing days, I feasted like a king. (That metaphor's downright filthy in context—because, yes, I ate Audrey out plenty.) I did a damn good job of convincing myself that it didn't count, too. What happens in Paris stays in Paris, right? Whether it's calories or life-altering sex with the girl you can't have.

Problem is, no vacation can last forever. Reality is always waiting to rush in and bitch slap you the second you get home and step on that scale.

Or sometimes even before you get home, because you'd better believe I feel the weight of my decisions start piling onto my shoulders the second I step foot on our plane to Boston. I can't even distract myself from it by talking to Audrey, because she falls asleep on my shoulder not long after we take off and stays that way for most of the flight. I'm wide fucking awake, no matter how much I'd like to nap and get a reprieve from all the shit I don't want to think about. Plus, I got just as little sleep as Audrey these last few nights. (Which I cannot let myself think about in too much detail right now, because it would be super awkward to pop a boner when I'm sitting next to a family with young kids.)

Shit got real in Paris, way more real than I ever should have let it, and all those vacation decisions are feeling pretty damn heavy right about now. I can feel them crushing me more and more as every passing hour brings us closer to home. Normally, I'm restless on planes, itching to escape the confinement and forced inactivity as soon as possible. Today, seven hours feels too short. Because on the other end of this flight, consequences and impossible choices await me.

It's day sixty. Time for "enjoying the now" has officially run out.

When you think about it, it's a special kind of art form, the way we can delude ourselves while cleaning up at the buffet and all around carpe diem-ing the hell out of our vacation. How we manage to downplay exactly how shitty those consequences are going to be on the other end.

Yeah, yeah, I'm using the royal fucking "we" again… Give me a break, huh? I'm over here having an existential crisis while trapped in a giant tin can that's flying over the Atlantic Ocean, sitting between a couple with a hundred kids who look like they haven't slept in years and the girl my idiot self caught feelings for.

Oh, and I fucked her. Let's not forget that. (Like I could.) Which was seriously messed up, all things considered—and I can pretty it up with metaphors and shit all day, but when it comes down to it, I'm a grown-ass man, and I knew exactly what I was doing. Knew it was wrong, for a shit-ton of reasons, not the least of which was my decision to back off at the end of this job, so she and Luke could be together. And I still went on to fuck her as many times as I could fit into a three-day vacation. (Unfortunately, Audrey actually wanted to see Paris and hang out with Callie, so she didn't go for my suggestion of just camping out in our hotel room day and night.)

So, let's not pretend I don't deserve this hell—being stuck on a plane for seven hours, awake with no one to talk to, my thoughts making way too much of a racket to even let me escape into a movie, never mind sleep.

There's also the not-so-little matter of Vickie, who my gut says isn't quite done screwing with us. After all of this, I can't believe the woman doesn't have another card or two up that sleeve of hers. Now it's just a matter of *when* she'll bust it out.

I kept expecting it to happen in Paris. All while playing tourist and soaking up my time with Audrey, a low-key anxiety nagged at me, a warning that something was coming, thinking any minute, a message would arrive and throw a wrench or a curve ball... or whatever kind of object you can toss at people to mess up their lives and, in the process, make our little bubble of happiness and sex go *POP*.

That Vickie *didn't* send us any crazy assignments during our trip only puts me more on edge. We're at the finish line of this thing, which means whatever our devious employer has planned is going to happen *today*. Will it show up on our phones the second we turn them back on in Boston?

Answer: Nope. Victoria's last move doesn't arrive via our phones.

It *is* waiting for us when we return, once we're through customs and baggage claim, and it comes in a form I couldn't have expected.

Our old pal Freddy is waiting for us at the curb outside the arrivals terminal, gray mustache looking as fly as ever. After we exchange head nods and Audrey gives him a hug, I lift her suitcase into the back of his SUV. But when I start loading up my luggage too, Freddy stops me. He indicates the vehicle behind his, a black car that's identical to his except for the dark-haired woman behind the wheel, and informs me that will be *my* ride, per Victoria's instructions.

Separate cars.

There you have it. Card played. Shoe dropped. Curve ball released. Wrench flung. Bubble burst.

Anxiety squeezes my chest, a straitjacket stitched from pure, unadulterated panic.

I'm not ready.

We should have had another hour or two—or at the very least, the time it would take to drive through traffic from the airport to Beacon Hill.

I don't know if I can do this.

I have the crazy urge to grab Audrey and run off with her to the taxi stand, away from whatever these SUVs signify. To steal a bit more time with her, just the two of us, before reality comes crashing down and ruins everything.

"I'll talk to you later?" Audrey asks.

That's a question I can't answer, so instead, I kiss her.

As soon as our mouths meet, what should have been a quick parting peck spirals out of control, taking on a note of frantic urgency fueled by my desperation. It's a kiss far too intense for this public curbside, but I'm unable to hold back, not when I'm feeling damn near feral.

With one hand at the base of her skull, fingers grasping a fistful of hair just tight enough that she'll feel it without hurting her, I control the angle of her head so I can fuck her mouth with my tongue as deep and hard as possible. My other hand is on the small of her back, pressing our bodies together as I cant my hips to make sure she feels every inch of how badly I want her. I throw all my energy and my entire body into it, showing Audrey everything I can't say while giving her the only thing I have left to offer.

I'm devouring her moan when a rude blaring sound shocks us apart. A line of cars has built up now and quite a few of them are honking at us for loitering too long in the temporary lane (and probably because we're kind of making a scene).

Audrey's eyes are still a little glassy, but her cheeks are getting pink now that she's coming out of the lust daze and realizes where we are and that we've been holding up traffic with our PDA. I commit the look to memory, then lean in for one final kiss to her forehead.

"Bye, Freckles."

I throw myself into the waiting SUV before my resolve—which has never been so damn thin—crumbles.

Normally, I would be friendly and chat up my new driver, but I can't do anything but stare out the windshield like it's my job, locking on to the sight of Audrey's head in the back of Freddy's car as we trail behind them for a bit, all the way until we lose them when we're separated at the entrance to the tunnel.

As soon as we reemerge into the daylight, my phone rings. Seeing the identity of the caller, I answer with no small amount of wariness.

"Hey, Vickie."

"Welcome home, Walker." There's an unusual formality to her voice that immediately sets me on edge. My spine snaps straight from the slumped position I'd assumed after losing sight of Audrey and Freddy. "We have reached day sixty and, thus, the end of our experiment. However, before we part ways, I have one final challenge for you."

I fucking knew it!

352

"I will not drag this out unnecessarily. I am offering you a choice. You have two options, which are as follows. As per the original terms of your employment contract, you are due a final payment of ten thousand dollars at the conclusion of our project. However, I am prepared to give you fifteen thousand—"

Holy...

"—if you immediately cease all romantic relations with Audrey."

...Fuck.

My heart drops down to the soles of my boots, along with my stomach.

"I have a legal contract prepared, essentially a variation of a nondisclosure agreement, which you would need to sign in order to receive the additional five thousand dollars. That contract gives me grounds to pursue legal action against you for collecting funds under false pretenses should I become aware that you have continued your relationship with Audrey."

Did I call her devious? The woman is straight up *evil.*

"And the other option?" My voice is hoarse.

"You choose Audrey," she says, like it's that simple. "And your final payment will be ten thousand dollars, as originally promised. In just a moment, I shall present Audrey with these same terms."

I keep my mouth shut, because...what do you even *say* to that?

"So, there you have it. You have the remainder of your drive to decide. If you opt for the money, ask your driver to bring you to my house. If you choose Audrey, go to the condo. And, Walker? Choose wisely."

She hangs up, a dramatic exit for a bold fucking move.

"Choose Audrey." It couldn't be more obvious that's what Victoria wants. She's set this whole thing up to be some "grand

gesture," the final climactic moment of her book. Sacrificing for love and all that shit.

Love...

It's all so black and white to her. Maybe that's how things are in romance novels, but here in the real world, nothing's that simple. In my experience, life is a palette smeared with a whole hell of a lot of shades, but rarely anything as definite as black or white.

I know Audrey thinks she has feelings for me. Maybe they're even real. But that doesn't mean the guy she thinks she has those feelings for is real, or that what we had these last few days—these last few weeks—could survive outside the insulated fishbowl of Victoria's experiment.

It's only a matter of time before I disappoint Audrey and hurt her far worse than anything she might feel now. She deserves something with lasting power. Maybe she thinks I'm capable of that after our time in Paris, but anyone can be a good boyfriend for three days. Even doing it for a few weeks isn't too hard, especially when there's money on the line and microphones around to keep you in check. But long-term?

Audrey's had shit luck so far with the men in her life. Her ex, her boss, her dad... I don't want to be the next name on that list, just one more asshole who's permanently damaged her, but it's more than likely that's exactly what will happen if we keep going like this.

When my phone rings again, my immediate instinct is to throw the thing out the window, straight into midday traffic on Storrow Drive, thinking it's Victoria to drop more bombshells. I've settled for ignoring it when I glance at the screen and see the call is from Luke.

"Hey," I answer.

"You guys make it back to the US in one piece? Or do I need to call your secretary to ask, since you're a big international jet-setting hotshot now?"

I'm not sure how I keep my voice level enough to sound normal, but somehow I do it, because Luke doesn't seem to realize I'm damn near on the verge of tears during our two-minute conversation. But when we hang up, the breath I take is far from steady.

That. That call—how he sounded, what he said—the very fact he called in the first place…it's exactly why I need to stick to the decision I made weeks ago. Two months ago, that call never would have happened, and there's no denying I started to see this change in him after he met Audrey.

Hello, reality. Sure sucks to see you again.

You want some reality? Here you go: Audrey is a girl who deserves a happily ever after, like the endings of Victoria's books, and I am not that guy.

Luke is the one who can do the romantic shit. Take our senior prom, for example. He did something cutesy to ask his date to go with him, bought her a flower corsage, matched his tie to her dress. He took her to the dance in a limo with a group of their friends, and they were crowned prom king and queen.

I brought *my* prom date a half empty bottle of vodka I swiped from my dad. We drank it and fucked in the bed of my pickup instead of going to the dance. She ended up puking her guts out, and I had to call Luke to come get us because I was too wasted to drive home, ruining the end of his night.

See where I'm going with this?

I'm no one's Prince Charming. Never have been; never will be.

When we're stopped at a red light, the driver (whose name I still don't know… Add it to my asshole tab for the day) slides open the glass partition between us and asks me what our destination is. I know what I need to do, but when I open my mouth to give her my answer, the words dry up on my tongue.

I'm still hesitating when the light turns green, so she tells me to knock on the window when I decide, then goes back to driving. I wonder if she knows the significance of this decision, that wherever I tell her to go officially declares my response to Victoria's little ultimatum and seals my fate.

You know what knocks this mindfuck of a situation up another level into *seriously* fucked up? In a way, with her challenge, Victoria is making this *easier* on me. (And wouldn't that just kill her?) Honestly, these last few days, I've started wondering if I'd be able to do it at all, to go through with telling Audrey goodbye, stepping back and watching her and Luke fall in love.

My inner selfish asshole is almost…relieved. Because what Vickie's offering is essentially an easy out, one that doesn't require me to look Audrey in the face and find the words to cut the cord. Of course, "easy" here is still pretty fucking hard, but getting to walk away while Victoria delivers the news for me is as best-case scenario as this thing is going to get.

Does that make me a little pansy-ass coward? Fuck yes. I may be doing the selfless thing for once, but I'm under no delusions that I'm pulling it off with clean hands. (See note on all the Parisian sex.) So, sure, I'm not winning any hero points over here, but in the big scheme of things, what does it matter that I'm taking the cowardly way out? It's a means to an end, and what matters is that end is what's best for Audrey and Luke.

I don't believe in shit like this, but you've got to admit, Victoria's ultimatum almost feels like a cosmic message or something, confirming that this is the right thing to do. No matter how fucking hard it is.

What will Audrey choose?

Yes, I'm the worst kind of scum for even wondering— double that because I'm over here hoping she picks me, in spite of everything, in spite of knowing what I'm about to do.

Just another piece of evidence in the overwhelming pile proving that Audrey deserves better than me.

I physically ache as I tap on the glass and name Victoria's brownstone as our destination.

Victoria's going to hate me for this.

Audrey is going to hate me for this.

I hate me for this.

* * *

Audrey

Has Walker made his choice already? I wonder if he's struggling with it. The man I first met would have chosen the money without a blink, but the one I just spent four days with in Paris...I'd like to think he will at least pause.

Stop worrying about his choice. You still have to make your own! Except it's kind of impossible to separate the two.

A voice that sounds a lot like my mother is telling me to be sensible, how foolhardy it would be to throw away that kind of money on blind faith. Rationally, I know the money is the safer, smarter choice.

What are the chances Walker would actually choose me over five thousand dollars?

But...what if he does? After our time in Paris, I'm *sure* he loves me. He didn't say it, but I *felt* it.

And the way he kissed me before we had to get into our separate cars at the airport? It was soul-searing, heart-melting, earth-shattering, the kind of kiss you could never share with someone you didn't have a connection with.

If he chose me and I chose the money, I would regret it forever. Even the faint possibility is enough to have me tapping on the privacy glass and asking Freddy to drive me to the condo.

* * *

When my phone chimes with an incoming message, I have the ridiculous hope that it's from Walker.

It isn't.

MATILDA: I'm so sorry, Audrey, but Walker is here at the brownstone. Victoria doesn't know I'm contacting you, but I didn't want you to be over there waiting and wondering.

MATILDA: I know we don't know each other that well, but I'm here if you need to talk.

I don't even have the right to this feeling of betrayal. Walker never promised me anything. He actually went out of his way to tell me he *wasn't* promising anything. He never said a word about doing more than enjoying each other.

And yet...

After these last few days, I thought things had changed. I was *certain* they had.

But how could I possibly compete with thousands of dollars? Who would ever choose me when those were the options?

Stupid, stupid, *stupid.*

And I realize—that kiss at the airport wasn't a declaration of love.

It was goodbye.

47. Go Get Your Girl

TEXT MESSAGE THREAD: VICTORIA AND AUDREY

VICTORIA: Audrey, please call me back. I'm so worried about you, darling.

VICTORIA: This is not at all what I had in mind. You must know how sorry I am. If there's anything that I can do for you, just let me know.

TEXT MESSAGE THREAD: VICTORIA AND WALKER

VICTORIA: Walker, pick up your phone. We need to talk.

VICTORIA: This is not how things were supposed to go.

VICTORIA: Please talk to me. I believe there's still a chance to make this right.

Walker

Pain explodes along my jaw.

"What the fuck?"

I back away from my brother, glaring at him while rubbing the spot his fist just plowed into. Luke wasn't holding back either; this shit *hurts*. See what I do the next time he asks me to bring him something! (How rude of him to play helpless, then use the element of surprise to grab me by the shirt when I get close and slug me. I guess I'm just lucky he had a low angle or I'd be rocking a nice black eye tomorrow.)

"That was for being an idiot," Luke says.

"Can you be more specific?" I snark. I am not in the mood for this, whatever *this* is.

"For dumping Audrey, dumbass."

Hearing her name hurts even worse than my jaw.

"You've talked to her?"

He must have; he certainly didn't hear the news from me. I haven't exactly been chatty the last few days, too busy making myself scarce. Hiding out at my studio nursing the wounds I gave my own damn self and avoiding the brother I have no right to resent for it.

"She's a mess, Walk. Seriously, what the fuck were you thinking?"

"Were you with her last night?" I ask, ignoring his question. Remembering how I came home yesterday to the unusual sight of an empty driveway, how late it was before I heard him come in.

"Yeah."

"Well, you work fast." The bitterness slips out without my permission, and I immediately want to take it back. I have no right to it, not when this was the whole idea. But *three days*? They couldn't have at least waited a week?

"What are you talking about?"

"Nothing. It's good. I thought this might happen. I'm happy for you, man." I almost sound like I mean it.

"The fuck, Walk? You're not making any sense. How hard did I hit you?"

I sit down—a good distance from my twin and his cement fists. I can already feel my jaw swelling. Perfect, it'll go great with the pathetic unshowered, uncombed, sleepless zombie look I've got going on.

"You and Audrey," I say.

"What about me and Audrey?"

Oh, so he's going to play dumb?

"You were with her last night."

"Yeah. Jamie and Oliver had to go to some charity thing, so Jamie called me and asked me to come over because she didn't want to leave Audrey alone—you know, because my *shit for brains* brother broke her heart."

"She's staying with Jamie?" I shouldn't ask, but I can't help myself, desperate for any scrap of information about her.

He nods. "The girl is wrecked, Walk."

I grind my teeth. Clench my fists so tight my bones ache. Remind myself why I did this.

Still, my next words come out a hell of a lot more hostile than I meant.

"She'll get over it. She has you, right?"

"Okay, you need to drop this shitty attitude and tell me what you are talking about, or I'm going to really kick your ass."

I don't doubt he could do it. I move to a chair on the far, far side of the living room.

"We weren't right," I say, the words tasting wrong in my mouth even though I know they're true. "She deserves someone more like you."

He stares at me hard for a long, silent moment before comprehension ripples over his face.

"Bro, tell me you didn't do what I think you did."

"What?" I ask mulishly, not giving him anything. He's always been able to read me better than anyone, but...

361

"You said she deserves someone *like* me. Did you break up with her because you think she should be with *me*?"

Okay, so he reads me pretty damn well. I shrug, trying to look more unaffected than I am.

"You two seemed to hit it off."

"That's the stupidest fucking thing you've said in your entire life, and you've said a lot of stupid shit."

His voice is raised now, though I don't know what *he* has to be pissed off about.

"I'm not into her, you idiot!"

"But all that shit you said, when you talked about making a move…"

"I was fucking with you. Like we have our whole lives? Jesus, what's the matter with you?"

"You were fucking with me?"

"Name one girlfriend I ever had that you didn't pretend to flirt with to yank my chain."

I can't, and he knows it.

"But would you ever have moved on that?" he asks, pushing his point.

"You know I wouldn't. But this is different…"

"Do I have to take you to get your hearing checked? Listen up this time, little brother, because I'm not repeating myself again. *I am* not *into your girl*. Audrey and I are friends. Not that it would matter if I did want her—which again, you big moron, I *don't*—because for some reason, that girl is in love with *your* idiot self."

No.

He can't be serious.

He sure *sounds* serious, though, and the throbbing in my face is pretty damn serious, too.

"I see it's starting to sink in."

"Fuuuuuck."

"Yeah, that about covers it."

It's like someone just dropped a metric ton of rocks in the bottom of my gut.

At the same time, there's this tiny flicker of life a little higher up my chest, that spot between my lungs that's felt more like a dead hunk of coal than a working organ since I said goodbye to Audrey.

Because this means maybe…I *don't* have to give her up.

But right on the heels of that revelation comes one that has me groaning and damn near falling to my knees, because it also means that I've fucked up bigger than all my other fuckups combined, especially if that last thing he said…

"She's in love with me?" I sound like I'm being choked out, my throat is so goddamned tight as I push out the words.

"Yes, you chicken brain. Kinda like you're in love with her."

In love with her?

I… Shit, I think I am.

"He finally sees the light!" Luke hollers, as though to a studio audience or some shit.

I start letting everything else he's said trickle in from the place I'd stuffed it, determined to shut it all out and keep my resolve.

"She was crying?"

"Yeah."

"Fuck. Bad?"

"Yeah, bro. She cried a whole lot and got trashed on some Jack Daniel's. Girl's a lightweight, by the way. I think she made it through a third of the bottle before I had to take it away from her because she was so obliterated I figured more woulda put her in the ER."

"Thanks for that."

"Don't thank me yet. You're gonna thank me, don't worry, but first, you're gonna hear all about just how badly you fucked up, because if I had to listen to your girl bawling, you're gonna feel that pain too. So where was I... Oh yeah, so she cried and drank Jack and got shit-faced, and then she begged me—while crying her eyes out—to shave my beard so she could 'see *your* face,' and serious to shit, if she hadn't passed out about two minutes later, I might have given in, she was that wrecked."

His words are ripping out my insides piece by piece, but I know I deserve it.

Honestly? I hadn't let myself really think about it, what she might be going through. Any time those thoughts crept in, I told myself whatever pain I'd caused was temporary and she'd get over me quick, because she was really meant to be with Luke. I was so stuck on convincing myself what I was doing was right, I *had* to believe that's how it was.

Now, Luke's ripped the blinders right off my eyes. I fucking crumple, head to knees and hands shoved into my hair, because it hurts so bad, feeling the truth in Luke's words. I know how wrecked *I* am, and I did this to my own goddamn self. Audrey thinks I *rejected* her, dumped her in the most callous way possible. She's probably worked herself up thinking all kinds of bullshit about how she's not good enough. And *I* did that to her.

"Can I fix it?" I ask, without raising my head. My voice still sounds strangled, which tracks, as I'm struggling to swallow down the full extent of my own epic mistake.

Seeing that I'm losing it, Luke apparently decides he's through with the yelling and "tough love" part of this talk, and he switches to supportive mode.

"I think so."

Luke doesn't bullshit me; though, for once, I kind of wish he would.

"I wasn't trying to hurt her."

"I know."

"I thought I was doing the right thing. "

"I know."

"It hurt like hell to walk away from her."

"Walk—*I know.* The person who doesn't know this shit, the one you should be telling it to, is Audrey."

He lets me stew in silence for a while—five minutes, ten, who knows? Forcing myself to think about everything he's said. Then it's back to business, and he's all about making an action plan, because that's just Luke.

"You've got some groveling ahead of you. But there's a bright side."

"Yeah?"

"You have a couple of things working in your favor. One— she's in love with you."

Damn, but I like hearing that.

"And two?"

"Not to say you shouldn't put in the work—because you goddamn well better, or you'll have me to answer to—but your girl is the biggest pushover I've ever seen."

He *does* know her well.

"You're sure you're not in love with her?"

"Hearing aids, little bro. I'm getting you some for Christmas."

"Yeah, yeah. Okay."

I'm rearing to drive down to the Seaport and kick down Jamie's door right now, but Luke nixes that straight out.

After thinking for a minute, he says he knows just the right opportunity for me to make my move. "Audrey's going to a house party tomorrow night with Jamie. And heads-up, bro—Jamie is hell-bent on setting her up with someone."

That hits me like another kick in the gut.

"What, you're besties with Jamie now, too?"

He pins me with a dark look. "As of three days ago, I'm part of a group chat with her and Callie."

I start to laugh but can't quite manage it in my current state. Any amusement disappears entirely when he informs me drolly that the group is titled "Audrey's Emotional Support Humans."

"Seriously, those girls can talk. You owe me so fucking big, you have no idea."

I nod. I really, really do.

"Oh, and you better start getting Ma to light candles at church or saying some prayers that Callie stays on another continent for a while, because the girl is *not* handling this well. It is fucking killing her that she's not here for Audrey right now. I shit you not, she has already asked me no less than eight times to smother you in your sleep. And I don't think she was kidding."

Yeah, I can see that. The love between those two runs deep, and Callie is a fierce little thing. I really am lucky she's an ocean away.

"Thank you. I mean it. For being there for Audrey when I had my head up my ass."

"Yeah, you just go and get our girl, and then we'll talk payback. You think she's got any kinky twin fantasies?"

I glare at him. "Not funny."

"Too soon?"

The rumbling sound that comes out of me is barely human; Audrey would probably call it a "growl."

"We'll be eighty, and it will still be too soon."

He freezes, and I do too, as we both register the words that just came out of my mouth.

"So, it's like that?" Luke asks, not teasing anymore.

"It might be." I'm thinking it's more than *might*, but then, this is my twin, so he already knows that. Our shared look is weighty now, taking in the implications of my admission.

He nods. I don't need his approval, but having it feels damn good. Not because I want him to approve of Audrey—I already know he does—but because he approves of *me* for her. It chokes me up a little, no lie, because I respect the hell out of my brother, and his opinion means more to me than just about anyone's. Luke cares about Audrey, is protective enough of her to slug me, and yet here he is, *not* warning me off her, but encouraging me to win her back. It means a lot more than I could ever put words to.

"Hey, Walk—" There's something somber in his voice that's got my entire attention dialing into him. "You gotta know it means a lot. What you were willing to do, where you were coming from, even if it was boneheaded and completely fucking far off base..."

Did I say I was choked up a moment ago? That was nothing compared to this. I'm over here trying to find a way to respond without getting all weepy, but he goes ahead and fixes that dilemma.

"Though it is kind of messed up that you thought she should be with me and you still fucked her."

The fuck...? "How the hell do you know that?"

He gives me another dark, meaningful look. "She's a wicked talkative drunk. I now know shit I never wanted to have in my brain."

"What did she tell you?"

"Everything, bro. Absolutely fucking everything."

I groan.

"But, hey, congrats on the five-star oral skills and popping her non-self-administered O cherry."

"Luke, shut the fuck up. Or I'm gonna make you, even if I have to do it with my fists. I don't care about the damn chair."

It's drop-a-pin silent. He has the weirdest look on his face. When my pulse stops thudding so hard in my ears, I start to panic that I went too far.

"Luke, man…"

"Shut it. I've been waiting two years for that. Let me have a moment to enjoy before you ruin it, yeah?"

"Waiting for what?"

Then he looks me dead in the eye, something I'm only now realizing hasn't happened much in the past two years. Those grays, almost identical to mine, that I've seen mostly blank in that time are suddenly full of so much emotion I can barely breathe from drowning in it.

"For you to be totally normal with me."

I try to protest when he cuts me off.

"Nah, I'm not saying whatever shit you're thinking right now. You've done nothing wrong—it's been a whole lot of right from you, Walk, if nobody's told you. Shit's been messed up, for all of us, 'normal' gone straight to hell. But right then? I finally had my brother back, that little shit I grew up with who would tell it to me straight no matter what, especially when he was pissed."

"You're having a 'moment' because I threatened to punch out a guy in a wheelchair?"

"I'm having a 'moment,' you ape, because you just threatened to punch out your brother, *not* a guy in a wheelchair. You get me?"

I get him. I get him so much there's a tingling in my nose that says if we don't stop with this deep stuff right now, I'm going to ruin this moment by crying.

Because of that whole twin thing we've got going, it doesn't matter that I'm out of words for the moment. He knows—not only that I've picked up what he's putting down, but that I need a detour off Emotion Lane, stat.

He throws me a lifeline.

"Get out of here. Take a fucking shower, and get some sleep—you look like shit—then go get your girl. I think there's something in our lease that says only one broody fuck can live here at a time. It'd be a pity if you had to move.

48. Idiot with Good Intentions

Audrey

For the last few days, I've hidden out in Jamie and Oliver's guest room—much of that time spent under the covers—crying and nursing my broken heart. My friends have been amazing, bringing me ice cream (Jamie), whiskey (Luke), and listening to me go on about Walker for hours (Jamie, Callie via the phone, *and* Luke; poor guy had to deal with my drunken breakdown). But I can't expect them to coddle me and indulge my pity party forever. This kind of heartbreak isn't going away any time soon. I need to start learning how to deal with it on my own.

Which is why I agreed to come to a party tonight even though no part of me feels like socializing with anyone besides Ben, Jerry, and the various stars of my Netflix comfort shows. But Jamie has been so good to me, and she seemed so excited about this party that I couldn't bring myself to turn her down.

Now, I wish I'd told her no. For one, walking into a party as Jamie and Oliver's third wheel—a role I used to play regularly and with comfort—is an icepick-to-the-heart reminder of the short time when I *wasn't* a third wheel, because I had Walker.

Mostly, I'd rather be anywhere but here standing with Oliver's coworker Ricky, otherwise known as the six-foot-tall explanation for Jamie's enthusiasm over this party and the hours she spent beautifying my depressed, bedraggled butt earlier. No matter how many times I've told her rebounds are not my style, she insists getting *under* someone new is the only way for me to get *over* Walker. Apparently, she's providing me with a gift-wrapped solution to that problem in the form of Ricky—who is tall, dark, handsome, and zeroed in on the excessive amount of cleavage I'm showing in the corset-style top Jamie made me wear. And whom she's just left me alone with, winking. In other words, in classic Jamie fashion, with zero subtlety.

Objectively speaking, Ricky is hot. I should probably find the overt interest in his eyes flattering, but I feel absolutely nothing except a strong desire to be back in bed wearing comfy pajamas. I hope Jamie didn't sell him on the whole rebound idea too hard, because if he's expecting me to be a sure thing, he's going to be very disappointed.

As Ricky starts up some small talk peppered with low-key flirting, a remote part of my brain notes how I seem so cool and collected, when really I'm on autopilot, externally operating on a "polite" setting, while on the inside, I'm trying to figure out how long I need to stay at this party before leaving without seeming completely rude.

Callie and Jamie would give me a stern talking to if they knew I'd just had that thought. As far as they're concerned, Walker is public enemy numbers one through one thousand, and I should hate him. (Of course, they don't know the full details, but then, the truth is far worse than the version I told them.)

"Hey."

As though conjured by my thoughts, I hear Walker's voice. I whip my head around, half thinking it's a figment of my imagination, that the heartbreak has won and I've completely lost it.

But Walker is really here. Only a foot away, looking a bit rough, with bags under his eyes, unruly hair, and multiple days of untended stubble—yet he's still more beautiful than anyone has the right to be. His eyes are locked on my face, having spared my sexy shirt and heels only a tiny glance.

"You know this guy?" Ricky asks.

"Yes, I know him."

Walker completely ignores Ricky, even when my new acquaintance swaggers over to stand at my side, giving off a territorial air he's earned no right to.

"What did you do to your hair?" Walker asks with a small frown.

My quick burst of laughter peters out on a ragged note that sounds more like a sob. Over the last four days, I've cried more tears than I knew the human body possessed. I've thought of Walker constantly. Missed him so much it was hard to breathe at times. I could barely drag myself out of bed to come here. And *that's* the first thing he says to me?

"You don't like it?" I reach up and touch my hair, which has never been so sleek and shiny, the sensation of the strands Jamie spent hours straightening unfamiliar beneath my fingers.

"You look pretty. But you don't look like *you.*"

Only he would prefer my frizzy mane to this. The thought sends a bit of warmth to the Walker-sized space in my heart that's been cold and empty for days.

"Who *are* you?"

Oops, I guess Ricky is still here. I'm trying to figure out a way to nicely blow him off, when Walker (who, of course, has no such qualms) says, without even looking at him, "Go away. We're talking."

With a perfunctory, "I'll be over there if you need me," and a glare at Walker as though to save some face, Ricky stalks off.

"Nice date," Walker says in a way that suggests the exact opposite.

In my entire life, I have never truly contemplated violence, but for just an instant, a burst of anger hits me so hard and fast—how *dare* he comment on my life, like he has the right—I can actually *see* my hand reaching up and slapping his stupid, handsome face.

As quickly as they came, the rage, and the impulse, are gone, and I deflate. I've done nothing but nap and cry for days, but suddenly, I am exhausted. Walker has been here, what, five minutes? And in that span of time, I've gone through too many emotions for my body to even handle. I just want to crawl back in bed and stay there for another week or two.

"What are you doing here?" I finally ask.

"I'm here for you."

* * *

Walker

After four days of deprivation, the sight of Audrey is a breath of goddamn fresh air. Air, *period*; because the moment I laid eyes on her tonight was the first time I've been able to take a full breath in days, like there's been a weight crushing my lungs since the airport that's suddenly lifted.

Maybe love is recognizing your person from across a room even when she's disguised in unfamiliar hair, clothes, and makeup.

"I'm here for you."

Something I'd like to call hope flashes across Audrey's face. It's there and then gone in an instant, fast as lightning, before her features shut down once again.

Regret tastes sour as it coats my tongue, because the girl in front of me wasn't capable of such a cynical expression two months ago—another way I've done her wrong. Proof that I really *don't* deserve her, but I'm past the point of being able to walk away. Not again, not without putting up the fight of my life.

"Isn't there a legal document that says you *can't* be here?"

I should *not* be aroused right now, not when her voice and body language all scream of wariness. Her arms are crossed in front of her chest in a defensive stance she doesn't even realize lifts her tits halfway up her neck—it looks like they're fixing to bust right out of that push-up bra masquerading as a shirt.

It takes a serious effort to wrangle my attention back up to her scowling face. Imagine how pissed off she'd be if she knew how badly my inner caveman wants to cover her up with my hoodie then carry her out of this party and take her home, where I'd thoroughly mess up her hair before making her come over and over until she promised to never wear this outfit again unless it's for me, in private. (Jamie is officially on my shit list—for this outfit and that guy Audrey was just talking to, who I'm guessing is Mr. Potential Rebound Fuck.)

Focus. Audrey asked you about the contract.

"I tore it up this afternoon." *That* gets her attention. "Went to the brownstone and told Vickie the deal was off." I'd shown up prepared for a fight, but none was necessary. The woman couldn't agree fast enough.

"Oh." Audrey softens just a bit, my declaration seeming to steal some of the wind from her sails.

Recognizing an opening, I take a step closer, preparing to rip my chest open for her the same way I did that stupid document. Then I curse under my breath when a new song comes on and whatever idiot is playing DJ cranks up the volume.

"Come outside with me so we can talk?" I have to shout to be heard over the music.

After a moment of hesitation during which she eyes me so suspiciously you'd think I'm a stranger in a trench coat offering her shoddily packaged candy, she nods her assent.

Not wanting to lose sight of her even for a second, I trail just behind as Audrey finds Jamie in the other room. They have a hushed conversation, presumably about her leaving with me. Over Audrey's shoulder, the redhead shoots me a glare so scathing I'd swear I can make out the faint scent of scorched hair drifting up from the surface of my balls. The girls hug, then I follow Audrey to a back room where she retrieves her coat from a huge pile on the bed. I deserve a goddamn medal of sainthood for keeping my eyes off her cleavage when she slides her arms into the coat. (There's back arching involved... Yeah, start building the shrine.)

Finally, we're leaving, shutting the door behind us on the clamor of blaring music and increasingly drunk partygoers. The quiet is a relief, even though it's wicked cold outside, my lungs stinging on that first inhale of night air like it's full of little knives. At my side, Audrey shivers, huddling into the collar of her coat against the wind. I grit my teeth against the nearly overpowering urge to warm her up with my arms, knowing my touch is not welcome just now. My willpower is being all kinds of tested tonight.

In unspoken agreement, we put some distance between us and the party. Physical distance, anyway, because on the inside I already feel miles away from those twentysomethings focused on getting wasted and trying to get laid, utterly clueless that just down the street, my entire world hangs in the balance, teetering on the edge of disaster.

I'm suddenly nervous, even though I've spent the last twenty-four hours waiting for this moment. But before I can decide how to break the silence, Audrey beats me to it, gasping as we pass beneath a streetlight.

"What happened to your face?"

Her eyes are fixed on my jaw, which is slightly swollen and marred by a black and purple bruise, even though I iced it last night.

"Luke," I admit, wishing I'd thought to position myself on her other side.

"You guys got into a fight?"

"More like he sucker-punched me." She looks so shocked and worried, I feel the need to add, "I deserved it."

"Why?"

Big brown eyes peer up at me with concern, momentarily distracted from her hurt and anger. Damn, she's pretty—even if I'm itching to mess up her hair and wipe off all that makeup. (She looks gorgeous, don't get me wrong, but I'm resentful of anything hiding her from my view. No cosmetic can improve on perfection.)

I want to lean down and kiss that pink gloss right off her lips, then kiss her some more, because once won't be enough. With her, it's never enough.

"Walker? Why did Luke punch you?" she repeats, breaking me from my Audrey-daze just in time before I try to carry out that fantasy and ruin everything right off the bat.

"Well, see, I had a chance to be with this amazing girl. But I messed everything up and lost her."

"You didn't *lose* me," she spits out, eyes now blazing with fury. "You *threw me away*!"

"I didn't—"

"You chose money over me. I chose *you*, and you *left me*—" Her voice cracks under the force of her emotion, then fades to a pained whisper. "You didn't even say goodbye."

Just like her dad.

At the realization, all the air disappears from my lungs. *God-fucking-dammit.* Self-recrimination threatens to send me to my knees right here as—far, far too late—I appreciate the immensity of my error, just how deeply my actions have hurt her.

"I'm sorry." Those two words have never seemed so insufficient. "You don't know how fucking sorry."

A high-pitched chirp cuts into the night, the familiar sound of an incoming text message on Audrey's phone a jarring reminder that the rest of the world still exists beyond the two of us.

"I should check that. It might be Jamie. Excuse me."

Always so fucking polite.

I can't help watching as she unbuttons the top of her coat and reaches in. (If you're wondering where on earth a pocket could be hiding on that skimpy outfit, I'm right there with you—and the joke's on both of us. She pulls that phone out of her motherfucking *cleavage*. I damn near swallow my tongue.)

"It's from Luke," Audrey tells me.

Yeah, definitely didn't expect *that*.

"What did he say?"

She doesn't answer right away, just stares down at her phone for a long moment, her furrowed brows highlighted by the glow from the screen. I'm jumping out of my skin from the anticipation by the time she finally looks up.

"He said I should hear you out, but make you work for it."

I snort. Nice to know the asshole is at least partially on my side.

She jumps a bit when the phone, which is still in her hand, lights up with another notification.

"This one just says, 'He's an idiot, but he had good intentions.' What is he talking about?"

Well, here goes…everything.

"I *didn't* choose money over you. I, uh…" Fuck, where's a romance author when you need one to write the perfect dialogue for moments like this? "I chose to give you the chance to do better than me… I thought I was doing the right thing. Walking away from you killed me, you have to believe that."

I'm over here with my heart in my hands, desperation bleeding out my every pore, and what does she do? *Rolls her eyes* at me.

"I know you've been reading Victoria's books" —*Damn, here I thought I'd kept my "research" on the down-low*— "but *please* tell me you did not just try to feed me the 'I left you for your own good' line."

Well, shit. I guess that's not *completely* inaccurate.

"And you can't expect me to believe the five thousand dollars had nothing to do with it."

"No, it wasn't— I mean— I— I thought you should be with Luke!"

Dead silence. Guess I could have finessed that a little better, instead of getting frustrated and just blurting it out.

"I saw how you guys connected," I try to explain. "And I had this idea that, maybe, he was in love with you." Sounds pretty damn lame when I say it out loud.

"We're *just friends*," she basically shouts.

"Yeah, Luke cleared that up for me," I admit. "While he was helping me get my head out of my ass."

She walks away a few paces, then doubles back. Her heavy breaths create white clouds in the cold air.

"So, what? You thought you could just *give* me to your brother, like a toy?"

"Of course not—"

She's well and truly steamed up now, angrier than I've ever seen her.

"Did you think I'm so shallow I'd bounce from one brother to the next, just like that? No, I know. You think I'm *so stupid* that I wouldn't even realize there was a difference between you?"

"Jesus! No, I—"

She talks right over me, really on a roll.

"And what about Luke? You thought he somehow needs your charity, a hand-me-down girlfriend, like he's not fully capable of finding and attracting whatever woman he wants without having to settle for your castoffs?"

Fuck. I sound like the world's biggest ableist douchebag when she puts it like that.

"I wasn't trying to *give* you to him, for Christ's sake. And that charity thing is such a fucking insult, I'm going to pretend you didn't suggest I'd ever think that. I was wrong, okay? But I thought there was something there, and that the two of you deserved a chance. I didn't want you *not* to give it a shot because of me. So, I decided to take myself out of the equation."

"So you just made that decision *for* me? I didn't even get a say?"

"That's not—there was more to it. It wasn't just about Luke, okay?" I swallow. This shit's even harder to say than I thought. "You deserve better than me. I've known that since day one. No matter how badly I wanted to keep you for myself, how much it fucking *gutted* me to walk away—and it did, I need you to believe that—I knew I would only fuck things up, that it was just a matter of time before I ruined everything. I couldn't stand it if I hurt you, even more than I hated the thought of standing back and watching you maybe be with my brother."

"You *did* hurt me, though."

The words come out so soft they're barely audible, but I hear her loud and clear. I think I'd have registered her voice even at half this volume, that's how entirely my senses are focused on her.

Maybe love is the cells in your body tuning themselves not to the forces of gravity or the tides but to another person.

"I know, and I couldn't be more sorry. If it helps any, I hurt myself real damn bad, too."

How can one person look so sad and so angry and so beautiful, all at the same goddamn time? When did this girl become my everything, and why didn't I figure it out before I hurt her this badly?

379

"Why now?" she asks, just above a whisper. "Are you just here because Luke…?"

"Him telling me there wasn't more than friendly feelings between you knocked some sense into me, I won't lie. But, honestly? A few more days, and I would've broken and come after you, Luke or no Luke. It was always gonna come to this, me groveling with my heart in my hands, begging for your forgiveness and asking you to give me another shot. Which is what I'm doing right now, in case I haven't made that clear. Fuck… See? I can't even do *this* right. I'm in so far over my head, I've got no clue how to do this. I mean, I've never been in love before. I figure I'll be as bad at it as I am everything else, but I'm hoping you'll let me try anyway. I swear to you, I'll give it everything I've got and then some, because you're worth it. I think *we're* worth it. Am I making any sense?"

I'm breathing heavily, like I just ran a sprint. It took about that much effort to get all those words out—more than I've probably ever said all at once in my whole life—every single one dragged out from a soft place deep inside me that's usually locked up tight.

"Can we rewind a few seconds?" she asks, sounding inexplicably shy.

"I've gotta be honest, I don't even know what all just came out of my mouth, so I doubt I'll be able to do an instant replay for you, but I'll do my best."

"You said you've never been in love…*before*?" Her voice is soft and so very hesitant, as though she can barely bring herself to believe it.

New life goal—screw the T-shirts and the art and anything else; I'm going to spend the rest of my days making sure this girl never again has a second's doubt that she is beautiful and desirable and worthy of love. Worthy of a hell of a lot better than anything I'll be able to offer her, but that doesn't mean I'm not going to give it everything I've got to convince her to let me try anyway.

"So, here's the thing. I'm pretty sure I'm in love with you, Freckles. Guess I should have started with that."

I always thought saying those words to a girl would be terrifying, but nothing has ever felt more right. Especially when she melts, staring up at me with her whole big, beautiful heart shining out of her eyes.

"I miss you so fucking much," I whisper.

More tears slide down her cheeks, and I can't resist any longer; I reach up and brush them away with the tips of my fingers.

"So, what do you think? Want to give us another shot?"

Her hand—soft, pale, and so much smaller than mine— lands on my cheek, and the feel of it makes my entire body shudder with pleasure and relief. But then it's gone, and she's backing up, out of my reach.

"Thank you, for explaining. But—"

My chest squeezes with apprehension, her calm, steady tone scaring me far more than her anger from before.

"Do you know what it was like, taking that risk, *choosing you*, then sitting in the condo, waiting?"

Dread seeps through me, freezing my limbs and stalling my breath.

"You didn't choose me. Whatever your reasons were, when it came down to it, you left me to sit in that empty condo all alone."

"I'm so—"

She cuts off my attempt at another apology. Her smile is sad. "I know you're sorry. I believe you. A part of me wants to say yes right now, but I need some time."

No, no. I can feel her slipping through my fingers, can feel myself losing her. There's no thought involved, only instinct and need, as I reach out and take her in my arms, then lean down and kiss her before she has the chance to protest.

381

Rather than pushing me away, she surrenders, opening her mouth to my tongue without resistance and melting in my arms when I lick inside. I kiss her, slowly, deliberately, pouring all my emotion into it, declaring my love for her more eloquently than I could ever manage with words.

Then her lips are gone. Her hands are on my chest, pressing against it, and I'm letting her go, watching her put space between us even though it's the last thing I want to do.

"I need time to think," she repeats. "And I can't think when you're touching me. Please, give me some time and space to process all of this, to figure out if I can trust you again."

When she's looking at me like that, eyes glistening with unshed tears, pleading in that soft voice, how can I say no? I'd give her anything right now. I nod.

Maybe love is wanting her to have what she needs even if she decides that isn't me.

Shit, love is kind of the worst, huh?

* * *

WALKER: I'm going to need some kind of big move to win Audrey back, and I could use your help.

VICTORIA: I thought you'd never ask.

49. The "L" Word

Audrey

I don't know why Victoria asked me to meet her at the brownstone today, but I couldn't bring myself to say no, even though being back here *hurts*. Walker is everywhere I look in this house, each room filled with memories that haunt me and sharpen the ache in my chest from missing him.

It's been one week since the house party. One week since he told me he was *pretty sure he was in love with me*, and asked me to give "us" another chance. One week since I told him I needed time and space to think.

At first, Walker texted me every day following that night. I loved getting those messages from him. I also hated them. After a few days, I finally responded, asking him to stop. When he did, instead of feeling relieved, grateful he'd respected my wishes, I was irrationally devastated. Some needy, insecure voice inside my head whispered that he'd given up on me all over again, even as, logically, I knew he was waiting for me to make the next move.

So, why haven't I picked up the phone and contacted him? Why haven't I made a decision, one way or the other, to put us both out of our misery?

It's not like my feelings for Walker are in question. I love him. I loved him even before the soul-shattering, angels-singing, leave-your-body, more-positions-than-I-knew-existed, holy-multiple-orgasms, oops-we-dented-the-wall sex. The intimacy we shared in Paris only made me fall deeper.

I miss him every moment of every day.

But pain is a powerful deterrent. So is fear. My body and my heart may yearn for him, but my brain is in full-on protection mode, terrified of opening myself up to be hurt again.

So, here I am. In Victoria's office for the who-knows-how-many-ieth time, trying not to cry over a *chair* as I stare at the empty spot where Walker usually sits. Our small talk is stilted, my attempts at carrying on a conversation pathetic at best. Eventually, Victoria takes pity on my unhinged state and jumps to the reason she called me here—which is apparently a video I'm supposed to watch on the tablet she hands me before leaving me alone in the room.

What is she up to now? I eye the device in my hand suspiciously before pressing the button to wake up the screen. My breath catches at the image that fills it, unprepared to see Walker's face. I can't press play fast enough.

I recognize Walker's outfit; it's the same thing he was wearing on our plane from Paris, and I realize this must have been filmed the day we got home. The day he didn't choose me.

"All right, whatever this is, let's just get it over with," Walker says. He looks weary, his normally proud shoulders bent as though weighed down by a heavy burden.

Even knowing that at the very moment he was filming this, I was likely sitting in the condo waiting for him like a fool, I feel a pang of sympathy for him. He looks miserable; nothing about his demeanor suggests a man who just blithely cast aside his lover in exchange for a check. Seeing him struggle so blatantly, I feel a piece of my wounded soul stitching itself back together. For the first time, I start letting myself believe the things he told me last week.

"You've just spent sixty days as Audrey's fake boyfriend," Victoria's voice says. I'd swear he flinches the slightest bit, hearing my name. "As a final point of research, I want you to consider everything you've learned in that time and film a short video in which you give advice to Audrey's next boyfriend. How to be a good partner for her, what he needs to know about her, et cetera."

Walker's eyes narrow. "I know what you're doing, Vickie," he accuses. "And it's not gonna work. But fine, I'll play along."

"I shall step out and give you some privacy."

There's the sound of receding footsteps, then the door opening and shutting. Once he's alone, Walker leans forward, resting his bent arms on his knees and staring directly into the camera. I find myself leaning in closer to the screen as well.

"Well, New Guy, you're one lucky motherfucker. If the day comes that you wake up forgetting that, you'd better climb your ass back in bed and try again."

Geez, it's just begun, and I'm already on the verge of tears.

"So, advice about Audrey. Kinda seems like bullshit, because you should be putting in the work to find out yourself, but it's not like I have a choice about this. So, here goes."

He inhales, and I find myself breathing in along with him, my whole body buzzing with nerves.

"Get acquainted with vegetarian shit like yesterday, because the key to your peace and happiness is feeding her before she realizes she needs it."

Am I laughing or crying? I can't tell.

"Tell her she's beautiful and sexy every chance you get, even if it feels like too much, because chances are, she didn't let herself hear or believe you the first few times."

Okay, those are definitely tears I feel running down my cheeks.

"Never plan anything before ten in the morning unless you've got a cup of coffee ready to put in her hand the second she wakes up. She likes it sweet, the frillier the better. Like, if you're at the store trying to choose a creamer and you're looking at vanilla or *caramel cinnamon swirl explosion,* go for the one that makes you roll your eyes harder. Trust me, she wants it, even though she'll never ask for it and probably won't buy it for herself."

Why is *this* the thing that pushes me over the edge into straight up sobbing?

"In fact, any time she asks for something, go ahead and double it, because she's probably downplaying what she really wants. She's not high maintenance, won't demand all your time and attention and expect to be treated like a princess. But you'd better damn well do it anyway."

Walker turns his face away from the camera, and I see the muscles in his jaw working as he stares off to the side. He stays that way for so long I think maybe he's done. I start crying harder. At first, I thought I didn't want to watch at all, but now I'm desperate for it not to end. Somehow, it feels as if, when this video is over, I'll be saying goodbye to him all over again.

I'm inordinately relieved when he returns to speaking.

"If you get in a fight or do something shitty and Audrey seems fine afterward, she's not. She's holding that shit inside, and it's on you to man up and start making things better. Trust me on this one, because if you let it fester long enough, until she explodes, you're going to feel like a world-class douchebag. Though if you hurt her feelings in the first place, you probably already are.

"She may tell you about me—unlikely, but if she does, then you'll know I'm a huge fucking hypocrite for saying that. But then, you already know I'm the idiot who let her go, so it's best to learn from my mistakes.

"If you run into her ex, do me a favor and break a few bones. He damn well deserves it. If you don't know why yet, you will. And if she ever tells you what *really* happened with her old boss, feel free to reach out, because I've got a big-ass truck and some shovels, and I know a few places that would be good for hiding a body.

"Okay, well, I guess you'll have to figure the rest out for yourself. Just one last thing… I don't care who you are. If you fuck with her or hurt her, I have no problem using my truck and shovels and making sure it's *your* ass they never find."

The screen goes dark, leaving me brimming with so many emotions I feel liable to burst at any moment.

I need to go find Walker. Right now. After that video, I'm desperate to see him in person, to touch him. To tell him I still want him.

I'm out of my seat, intent on racing out of here to do just that, when the door swings open and Walker himself steps in.

I fall back into the chair, dissolving into tears anew, my emotions boiling over from the shock of his presence.

With a low curse, Walker shuts the door behind him and rushes over to me. Crouched in front of my chair so our faces are level, he takes in my tearstained cheeks with barely contained panic.

"Shh. Don't cry, Freckles." His hands hover just in front of my face, like he wants to touch me but isn't sure he's welcome to.

"How are you here?" I ask.

He grins, though it's smaller and less confident than usual. "Isn't it obvious? This is my big move to get you back." He scans my face, which is no doubt a red and puffy mess. "Are you okay? Was the video a terrible idea? This one was all Vickie."

The boy *really* hates it when I cry. It's kind of adorable.

"It was a good idea."

His sigh of relief is so exaggerated it's almost comical. Does he honestly not realize that entire video was him saying he loves me, just without using the "L" word?

"Yeah? Okay. Good."

He's so nervous. It's weird seeing him like this. At the same time, knowing I'm not alone in this soothes some of my insecurities.

"I'm sorry I didn't call," I say, feeling a little guilty now that I can see the toll this week took on him. "I was just...scared, I guess."

He moves into the empty chair, sliding it over so close to mine that our knees are touching. Even that small contact sends a zing of attraction coursing through me.

Almost whispering, I ask, "What if we do this, and it doesn't work out?"

"Well...it might not work out. I mean...I know you want me to promise you forever, but I don't want to lie to you. Life is weird, and shit happens. I'm not a psychic. I don't know who we're gonna be in a year or two or ten or...whatever. So, I can't tell you that, baby. What I *can* tell you, is that I had two months with you, and it was nowhere near enough. I can tell you that I spent the last eleven days thinking I'd never have you again, and they were some of the longest, worst days of my life. I can tell you that for twenty-four years, I was...well, you know, not a monk...and no one I've ever met makes me feel anything close to this. I'm so fucking in love with you, it's hard to imagine ever not wanting to be with you."

Walker rakes his eyes over me with a touch of panic, like he fears he's just messed up.

"That was a good answer." I bite back a smile. He's so worried about not promising me forever, I don't think he even realizes what he's said. A year? Two? *Ten?!* The fact that he's even thinking about us in those terms tells me how serious he is about this.

Not to mention how he's graduated from "I'm pretty sure I love you" to "I'm so fucking in love with you" over the last week. While his first declaration was an awkward mess I will always cherish, I'm a big fan of the new edition—expletive and all. I'm swooning so hard after that speech it's taking everything in me not to either burst into tears again or throw myself at him.

"Oh, and I, um, I talked to Jenny."

He...*what?* There's a possibility my jaw drops as I try to process that statement.

"Well, I talked to Vickie first and got permission to tell Jenny everything. So I did, and Jenny's agreed to keep seeing us. For real. I scheduled biweekly appointments starting next week. You know, just in case."

The man is literally squirming in his seat. I have never seen him so unsure of himself. That awkwardness, paired with the magnitude of this gesture? I'm too overwhelmed to speak.

"I just thought—I wasn't assuming anything. Hoping, of course. But I can cancel the appointments. Or maybe I'll go by myself. Or you can have them! Whatever, uh..." He clears his throat. "Whatever you want."

Obviously, he's misread my silence, and I've made him even more anxious. The reversal of our usual roles is somehow exactly what I need; any final lingering doubts melt away.

Walker Garrison is asking me to *go to therapy with him.*

"You really do love me."

A familiar smile replaces the uncharacteristic vulnerability on his face. That ever-present hint of cockiness returns; I love it just as much as his softness from a moment ago.

"You're just now getting that, huh?"

"I love you too, you know. I don't know if I've said that before."

He closes the remaining distance between us so fast I can't help but laugh at his eagerness, though the sound is quickly swallowed up when his mouth crashes onto mine.

Barely a minute later, his hands are on my thighs and he's lifting me off my chair and onto his lap. Straddling him like this, it's hard to miss the stiffness behind his zipper, but the kiss he gives me now is tender, the look in his eyes as he pulls back to gaze at me even more so. I wonder if he even realizes he's touching my hair, fingers threading through it on both sides of my head. I'll surely walk out of here with it looking a mess, but I don't care, because he *likes* it when it's a mess. He likes...*me.*

"Say it again," he whispers, staring at me with something like awe.

"You first."

Amusement sparkles in his eyes, but he doesn't hesitate. "I love you."

My turn. I thought it would be hard to say, that relinquishing this last piece of myself would be the height of vulnerability, but after everything he's done and said today, I feel nothing but safe.

"I love you too."

This kiss is harder and hungrier. Before long, he is snaking his hands up under my shirt and I'm rubbing myself on the growing bulge inside his jeans.

"Damn, I wish we weren't in Victoria's house."

"I wonder if the condo is still empty? Do you think our keys still work?"

"Look at you, Freckles. You sexy little deviant. I think I just fell in love all over again."

"We'll ask Victoria for permission first, of course."

He laughs, resting his forehead against mine. It feels like coming home.

"There's my girl," he whispers.

And...I am.

For real.

EPILOGUE

Audrey

Six months later...

"What chapter are you on now?" I ask Walker, leaning over the back of the couch where he's lounging wearing gray sweatpants and nothing else. (Just to complete the picture for you, he's also reading a paperback with a cutesy pink cover.)

At my question, Walker makes a face. "The same one as when you asked me twenty minutes ago. Jesus, woman. Not all of us are speed-reading nerds."

"I heard that," Luke calls out from the kitchen. He and I both finished reading our own copies of Victoria's book days ago, to Walker's disgruntlement.

Technically, *Go Fake Yourself* doesn't come out until the end of the month, so these advance copies were a gift from Victoria. Early reviews and the amount of buzz surrounding the book suggest it's going to be an even bigger hit than Victoria had hoped—in part due to the "inspired by true events" banner gracing the front cover.

"If you'd just tell me what chapter you're so desperate for me to read, I could skip to it right now and save us both a lot of hassle," Walker grumps.

I know I'm getting on his nerves by checking on his progress so often. I'm just *dying* for him to get to a certain chapter—one that's *not* based on true events, but which we are definitely going to reenact IRL. If he'd only get there already! But I'm not so impatient that I'd encourage skipping ahead.

Walker tries to lure me onto the couch with him, but I dodge his grabby hands, knowing what that will lead to (and it *won't* be reading). Not wanting to distract him from the story of Michelle Auden and Gear Waltham, whose fates become intertwined thanks to the machinations of romance author Trudy Violette, I dart away to our bedroom.

Yes, *our* bedroom. As of about four months ago, I officially live with Walker and Luke. If Walker had had his way, I would have moved in immediately after we got back together, but I held out for nearly two months on the grounds of "not wanting to move too fast." To his credit, Walker wasn't *too* smug when I finally agreed, only to realize all my stuff was already here and I couldn't remember the last time I'd slept at Jamie's place.

One of my conditions for moving in was being able to spruce up their house a bit, and it's amazing how much better it looks just from painting the walls and trim. Walker's bedroom underwent a full makeover—his idea, because he's secretly a big softy and wanted me to feel at home here. So, the bedding I'm sprawled across is brand new (I confess I chose the gray comforter because it reminded me of our bed at the condo), as is the bed itself, from the mattress to the dark wood headboard that matches the new dressers and nightstands. We each dipped into our money from Victoria to purchase it all, which felt justifiable since I'm once again gainfully employed and Walker's business is growing by the day.

Walker's success has only seemed to make things worse with his dad, but I think Walker has come to terms with their estrangement for the most part. While I know their issues are an ongoing source of tension, Walker's mom still comes over to our place for dinner about once a month, and she and I are in touch regularly. Building a relationship with Laura has been one of the unforeseen benefits of dating Walker. While my own mother has mellowed out a bit since our visit to Florida— Walker still won't tell me what exactly went down between them, though I know something happened—her narrow mindset will always be a barrier keeping us from true closeness. Getting to know Laura has been something of a revelation, giving me a glimpse of what a mother can be making the depth of the dysfunction in my dynamic with my mom clearer than ever before. But the ache of that knowledge is balanced out by having her step in as a warm surrogate maternal figure in my life. Unlike her husband, Laura is openly supportive of Walker's entrepreneurial pursuits, proudly telling everyone who goes through her checkout line about her talented son.

Speaking of Walker's business... I pull up his social media accounts on my phone, figuring I might as well get some work done while he reads. Seeing all the engagement on recent posts and the numerous client inquiries waiting in the DMs, I couldn't be prouder—mostly of Walker, but also of the work we've done together. He's now paying me a percentage of the monthly profits to continue managing his social media and consulting on his web presence "officially." There's not enough business for it to support us both full time (yet), but I enjoy being involved in this part of his life, and I've had no trouble managing it on top of my regular work so far.

After all my struggles to find the right position, the months of interviews in which I was told I was either too qualified or not qualified enough, it still feels a little surreal that I managed to land what is basically my dream job. Working at a start-up incubator, a program that consults with and coaches small businesses to set them up for success, is everything I'd hoped for back when I graduated with my communications degree— and it's all thanks to Walker. I was seriously underqualified for the original job posting, but he encouraged me to apply anyway, and my new bosses ended up being so impressed by my work with Walker's business, they decided to hire me anyway.

I'm so caught up in what I'm doing on my phone, I don't notice Walker coming into the room until he's right next to me, speaking into my ear.

"If you wanted to sit on my face then ride my cock reverse cowgirl style, you could've just asked, Freckles."

"Guess you figured out which chapter I was waiting for you to read." My voice comes out breathy. He hasn't even touched me yet, but I'm already worked up from his dirty words and low growl, especially knowing he's just read *that* scene.

"Damn straight. Now be a good girl and take your clothes off for me."

* * *

Much, much later, we're lying in a naked tangle of limbs, catching our breath. My head is on Walker's chest, ear right over his heart, listening as it gradually slows.

"I'm going to have to wash these sheets again," I say.

With my upper body draped over his chest, I both feel and hear the low, satisfied rumble of his voice.

"Worth it."

He is not wrong.

I'm especially glad we bought that second set of sheets, though, because I don't think I have the energy to do laundry right now. I'm not even sure I can trust my limbs to carry me to the linen closet after what we just did.

"Later." Reading my mind in that unnerving way of his, Walker pulls my thoughts away from laundry and back to the present. I snuggle in even closer to him, not caring that we're both sweaty or that I'm completely naked. It's hard to care about anything while he's stroking my back in a way that makes me want to arch into him and purr like a cat.

"You know," he says, when I've almost drifted off to sleep. "If this were one of Victoria's books, we'd get engaged right about now."

"*What*?!" I shoot up, lazy lethargy forgotten as panic sends adrenaline through me. I scoot back against the headboard, staring down at him as I fumble to cover myself with the sheet. "You can't be serious."

Slowly, so slowly, a smile curves across his face, followed by husky chuckling. I slap his arm.

"Walker Garrison, don't scare me like that!"

He catches my hand and brings it to his mouth so he can kiss my open palm.

"Should I be insulted?"

Now that the panic has ebbed, I realize that was a pretty terrible reaction. "No, I'm sorry, it wasn't... I love you so much, I'm just not ready..."

He drags me back down to lie beside him. "It's all good, Freckles. I was just messing with you. I know we're not ready for that shit."

"I'm sorry," I say again anyway.

Now he's recaptured my hand and is back to kissing it, making me squirm in something between ticklishness and arousal when he adds his tongue.

"I was really just saying that all those romance novels end with marriage and babies, you know? Even if they're our age and have only known each other two months. Kinda nuts."

I pull my hand free. I doubt either of us is physically capable of going another round, but if he keeps doing that thing with his tongue, I might end up jumping his bones anyway.

"Well, warn a girl the next time you're *not* proposing, will you?"

I'm joking, but Walker looks dead serious. "If we get there someday, baby, you're gonna know exactly what's happening, because I'd never half-ass something as important as asking you to be my wife."

And, well, after he has to go and say something like *that*... Yeah, I jump him

ACKNOWLEDGEMENTS

First of all, thank YOU for taking the time to read *Go Fake Yourself*. Publishing a book is a terrifying and vulnerable endeavor, but readers like you make it all worthwhile.

This book very nearly perished a whimpering death in my drafts folder. I wrote the first half of *Go Fake Yourself* in 2020 right at the start of the pandemic, before the chaos of the world and upheaval in my own life sent me into an anxiety-fueled case of writer's block that lasted nearly two years. It is not an exaggeration to say that this book wouldn't be available for you to read without the support of the people below, who have no idea they've been conscripted into what I've privately dubbed "Elle's Emotional Support Humans."

First of all, Shauna McDonnell / Mairead: If not for your instant enthusiasm and encouragement when I picked this project back up, I don't think I would have had the confidence to keep going. Thank you for being a friend and an all-around stellar human being, since ye olden days of Wattpad.

Jen Morris: My perfectionist soul sister! Bless you for consulting on this cover design. Thank you for your friendship, and for being one of the only people whose judgment I know I can trust even when I'm struggling to trust my own.

Melissa Grace: Thank you for being an ongoing voice of encouragement and positivity throughout this process!

Ana Elo-Harding: You were my rock through the home stretch of this process! Thank you for loving these characters so hard, for championing them and this book. I can't even quantify how grateful I am to you for reading and re-reading (and *re-reading*) chapter drafts and picking up continuity issues and typos like a boss, not to mention providing brilliant ideas and crucial insights about combining scenes and filling plot holes.

My beautiful beta readers! Andrea, Anna, Amber, Ana, Kayla, and Dose of Romance—thank you for your feedback and insights, especially on our frustrating yet endearing asshole, Walker.

Thank you to all of the ARC readers, bloggers, bookstagrammers and Booktokers who helped spread the word about *Go Fake Yourself*.

Finally, thank you to my local coffee shop—AKA my second home a—where the better part of this book came into being. I am not name dropping it because A: it's mine (yes, I'm channeling my inner possessive alpha over a café, deal with it) and B: I'm totes going to be famous someday, and don't want to make it too easy for the stalkers.

ABOUT THE AUTHOR

When she's not writing, Elle is a dog mom, artist, romance book binge-reader, and chai latte enthusiast. She is in a long-term (now, sadly, also long distance) love affair with the city of Boston, which she basically thinks of as a secondary character in her books.

Ella is also the author of *Us, Again*, a steamy angst-filled second chance romance with a dash of suspense.

Connect with Elle online

& VISIT ELLEMAXWELLBOOKS.COM

to subscribe for email updates about future books and access to bonus content!

Reviews are everything to indie authors, so if you loved Go Fake Yourself, please consider writing a couple of nice words on Amazon and/or Goodreads. It's an easy way to win the author's eternal love and some major karmic brownie points!

Made in the USA
Middletown, DE
27 October 2023

41437216R00239